Oh,
You
Dundalk
Girls,
Can't You
Dance
The Polka?

Oh, You Dundalk Girls, Can't You Dance The Polka?

Barbara Wernecke Durkin

William Morrow and Company, Inc.
New York 1984

Library of Congress Cataloging in Publication Data

Durkin, Barbara Wernecke.
Oh, you Dundalk girls, can't you dance the polka?

I. Title
PS3554.U687O35   1984   813'.54   83-19448
ISBN 0-688-01930-7

Printed in the United States of America

First Edition

1 2 3 4 5 6 7 8 9 10

BOOK DESIGN BY JAMES UDELL

For Ray and Della
and
For Tom and Dick

Prologue

Some nice ladies and I are sitting, sipping a before-lunch glass of white wine. We discuss, among other things, fashions and trends. One lady is speaking with a nostalgic lilt in her voice about hats. "I don't own a hat," she says. Then she turns to me and says, "Do you have a hat?"

The giggling begins.

"What's the joke?" she asks.

I say,. "Where I come from, in Dundalk, there's only one reason for asking that question. We used to yell, 'Hey, you! You got a hat? Yeah? Well, good. Go shit in it!' "

"Oh, dear," she says, and there is a damp little silence all around the table. "That must have been hard for you, trying to overcome all that."

"All what?" I say.

"The bad language, the—" And her voice trails off as she sees me redden.

The thing is, being a Dundalk girl isn't something I would have thought a person would have to overcome, really. For the first time, I am beginning to realize why I have always felt a kind of a distance, a separation, from these people. It is the result of my being, for all times and in all places, a Dundalk Girl.

Something familiar and perverse roils in me. I am, after all, only a Dundalk Girl. I must be forgiven if I laugh aloud in public and don't care all that much for white wine. "Gimme a Bud," I tell the waitress next time around. Something blossoms in my heart and spirit.

A black-eyed Susan. A tough, weedy flower with no sweet scent.

Chapter 1

It did not start in Baltimore. It began in another state, a place where green and yellow corn and golden wheat and oats outdid the gray and brown of Baltimore. In that other place, that Fox River paradise of Wisconsin, women did not spend their days vacuuming and dust-mopping and endlessly scrubbing and brushing the steel mill's grit and soot from row-home palaces. No, I was cheerfully (I am told) conceived in a place where people say hard r's and o's that sound like oo's.

Those absurd quirks in my pronunciation were counted high among the myriad things that later separated me from the Balmer kids. My mother and father and eleven-year-old Teddy carried with them a carsick, pudgy, cranky chunk of a baby, almost four, who had frolicked with lambs and piglets and cousins all her tiny days, and deposited her among the spindle-legged philistines of Dundalk (a part of the "spreading out" of Baldymore). These kids said eeoo for oo, ayo for o, and oddleno for I-don't-know. They laughed at me. I mocked them.

My name was Beatrice. Bebe, for short, and Beeb for shorter.

Worst of all, I was fat.

Nobody had let on before we moved to Dundalk that I was

fat. The kids I'd known in Wisconsin ("West Consin" to the Baltimorons) were as thick of leg and as hearty of appetite as I. What did we know about skinny? In the Great Midwest, vegetables were served creamed, gravy was eaten at every meal, whipped cream covered anything that sat in a crust or on a cake plate or lay jiggling in a pink Depression glass bowl. Thick hunks of roast beef and pork done side by side in the oven, cream-and butter-filled mashed potatoes. Ten million calories a day. Bread to sop up the leftover gravy. Rhubarb custard pie. Salad? Horrors. I never ate a salad in my life until I was fourteen, when Teddy took me out to dinner to celebrate his first decent job. Salad? Only dumb animals ate vegetables raw. Holy cry.

So I was the biggest kid on the block. Probably in the county, but who's counting? It so happened that my father, the Benign Intellectual, had begun early teaching me such things as: Any fool can fight, but a man will walk away. At nearly seven, I interpreted this sage advice as the better part of any valor I may have owned, but it had also set me up for daily humiliations those first three years among the savages.

Ah, DeeDee Waters, you skinny little witch. Even today I can see those black button eyes staring at me, willing my demise, their evil spell turning my chubby legs to oatmeal. DeeDee (short, I think, for Deirdre) never wore clothes in the summertime. Clad in cotton underpants, she and her baby sister (whom she carted behind her in a red coaster wagon, similarly undressed) were firmly locked out each morning just before the sun got blistery, about 10:00 A.M., and were not allowed back inside until Sidehill Groucher (more about him later) began his nightly prowl. By 3:00 P.M. both DeeDee and Sandra's pants were thoroughly soaked, and this unhappy circumstance gave DeeDee a bad case of the miserables. She would shake her strawlike hair from side to side. She would jump-jump forward and backward, side to side. It was a ritual of sorts, a jungle dance to signify, "I'm going to do something really horrible, oh, ye gods, so watch out." All the other kids had the sense to sneak off home. Sandra was usually whining, clutching at her starving tummy, and DeeDee was mumbling to her to shutupshutupshutup, and any ninny within a hundred yards would have known better than to hang around and be victim to DeeDee's lunatic outbursts.

But I always stuck around. In terrified fascination, I let her stalk me, let her threaten me with her singsong, "I'm gonna get you, I'm gonna get you." I had to. I had to be there to see if this were the time she would really do something unspeakable. Just as she lunged for me, I ran. At seven, my running much resembled that of a puppy's, Ted is fond of telling me. Galumphing in a kind of a sidewise lurch, I barrel-assed for home full steam. I knew what she'd do if she got me. She'd take bites out of me. Bloody bites. She was that kind of person.

Ted, thirteen and concerned in his amused manner, had urged me in a burst of brotherly affection not to let this jerky kid scare me, and to face up to her and give her a good one in what he referred to as "the breadbasket." But I couldn't. Pop had said that any fool could fight . . . and besides, if I hit her, I'd probably kill her. I outweighed her by about sixty pounds. Her stomach, pitifully unlike a breadbasket, was concave.

"Shit," Teddy said. "That kid would chew your heart out as soon as look at you."

"I'm telling Pop you said shit," I answered with a tennis ball in my throat, my bravado a cover-up for the terror that pierced my tender gizzard. He was right, of course. DeeDee was quite capable of removing a human heart with her teeth. I once saw her stoop down to a mud puddle after a hard June rain, a real soaker, and slurp up water out of which a worm had just crawled. A person like that could kill a fat kid without batting her narrowed eye. And there was nothing short of killing her back that would fix it. I suppose that's why I continued to let her chase me. And I was fast, despite my size. I always managed to beat her to my back door.

But then there was that terrible, terrible night when Teddy, disgusted at my cowardice, saw me coming and yelled out the door, "Fight! Fight that twerp! Don't let her chase you home. Fight!"

I figured we could discuss it later. My immediate objective was to fling open the door, pull it shut behind me, and leave DeeDee out in the backyard, panting, the saliva dribbling down her pointed chin, her wet pants filthy from the dirt and dust we played in.

Teddy locked the screen door just as I approached the back porch. I nearly broke my arm trying to yank it open, and when I saw him standing there, his face a study in righteousness, I could feel my heart being torn from my body . . . DeeDee's bare feet were slapping the pavement. She was catching me, catching me—

I went through the screen. At ninety-odd pounds, I was able to force my way through it with all my bulk, which knocked the wind out of the astonished Teddy and sent him sprawling, reeling backward into the parakeet cage, which then tipped crazily, forcing Petey the Keet to flutter and gurgle like a bird possessed. Seeds, hulls, and water all spilled onto the kitchen table, which caused Teddy to put out his hand to steady the birdcage, an action that eventually forced him to regain his own balance by madly grasping a one-pound block of summer-warm butter in his right hand and flinging it to the freshly mopped linoleum floor.

"You little turd," he roared at me. His face was mottled with fury. I don't know if he'd ever been mad at me like that before. "You little fat idiot."

My heart was still racing, my left forearm scratched and bleeding from the superficial scrapes the screen had made. But I would have offered DeeDee any organ in my body as a luncheon snack just to erase that look of hatred from my brother's face. Teddy and Pop, aside from walking on water, were my best companions, my reason for getting up in the mornings. If Teddy were going to hate me, then I would gladly die, and would not move from my spot on the buttery floor, where the blood from my arm had formed a neat cross-hatching. I lay facedown, then, and would not look up.

"What did I hear you say to your sister?" Pop said from the living room. He was getting up. His morris chair, brought from Grannie and Grampa's parlor in Wisconsin, creaked amiably whenever he got up. He was coming, and would see how Teddy hated me, and what a mess I'd made. I started to cry before he got to the scene.

Pop came to the kitchen doorway. I could hear his intake of breath, could smell the ripe scent of his seasoned pipe. He was wearing maroon felt bedroom slippers. He had carried the paper with him, out of habit. He read wherever and when-ever he could, and nearly always had a piece of the paper somewhere nearby.

"What did I hear you say to your sister?" he repeated to the guilty Ted.

"Nothing," Ted said. Boy, could he get sullen when he felt like it. Pop hated that.

"The hell," Pop said in quiet fury. "Are you gonna lie, now, too?"

Before Ted had the chance to frame yet another untruth, Pop deftly rolled up his newspaper into a neat little log and came down on Ted's head with it. Slap! Smack! Ouch.

I went for Pop's pantsleg. "No!" I bellowed. "Don't beat Teddy!" My tearstained face, my pose at his slippered feet, straight out of a Victorian melodrama, softened him. He de-sisted from this cruel and unusual punishment, and Ted seized the opportunity to scurry away on all fours like a cha-meleon, so embarrassed and so thoroughly unhurt that my father did a thing he could not help. He snickered.

Later that night, after the cleaning-up and the Merthiolate on the sore arm, and the admonition to Ted to "watch your mouth, kid," came The Lecture. We got a lot of these, not because we were so recalcitrant, or so unruly, or so often in hot water, but mostly because Pop loved to deliver them. It was a kind of a hobby for him, a man who'd longed to be a college professor, or a Maker of Speeches. Instead, he was a mild-mannered engineer by day, designing hulls for ships at the shipyard. By night, he became the Sage of Dundalk.

This night's lecture had to do with pride, dignity, false pride, all the stuff that goeth before a fall, ego, conscience, all sorts of other heady, marvelous trash. Ted was heartily praised for his desire to see me defend my dignity, but was simultaneously tongue-lashed for his foolishness in forcing the issue at an inopportune time. I was praised lavishly for my pacifism, and simultaneously berated for cowardice when confronted with no honorable escape. It was all a little confusing. The part I liked best was when Pop chewed out Teddy.

It all worked out all right. Ted liked me again before the evening was over. One of my father's favorite Wise Sayings was that it was a bad practice to go to bed angry with anyone. They might die during the night, and then how would we feel? Pretty damn bad, he assured us. Teddy, doubtless convinced that I might die from my wounds, gave me the mandatory hug and kiss on the cheek and said the best apology he could muster. He said, "You're not a turd. And you're not that fat, either."

It was enough for me. I hugged him back.

The next time DeeDee tried to chase me, I stiff-armed her and she flew off the sidewalk like a rag doll. Teddy, watching upside down from where he was hanging by his heels in a tree, put his little fingers to the corners of his wide mouth and whistled loud, long.

Pop, pleased with me and not quite wanting to say so, lit his pipe with hearty sucking noises as he pushed the Half and Half from the curious flat can into the bowl of his Kaywoodie and screwed up the left side of his face like a brunet Popeye. "Okay," he said, "so you got rid of her. Now leave her alone, and don't go looking for trouble just because you feel big and tough. Stay away from those people. They're funny people."

He knew whereof he spoke, if not how and why.

Mrs. Waters was indeed funny. I hadn't the vaguest idea what a mom would do all day locked up inside her house with the shades all drawn. But I used to hear the familiar radio sounds coming from the living room window, the humming of "Juanita" beneath the gorgeous baritone of the announcer's voice intoning, "And now, the *Romance of Helen Trent.*" That happened at just about noon. We always had our radio on, too, in 1950. *Wendy Warren and the News* (doo-doo-dit-doo-doo), *Helen Trent, Our Gal Sunday* (I envisioned the entrance to Black Swan Hall, black marble floors and long mirrors on either side), *Pepper Young's Family, One Man's Family,* Oxydol's own *Ma Perkins.* Best of all was *Stella Dallas.* That came on right near suppertime, when Ma was pulling the strings off celery stalks, letting the potatoes boil over, exclaiming in her Wisconsin voice, right through her nose, "Darn it all anyway! Holy cry!" I recall Stella's rough voice, thick with pain, lamenting some misdeed of her stinking, selfish, ungrateful wayward daughter. "Oh, Lolly. Oh, Lolly, baby . . ." Poor, noble Stella. And poor, dear Mary Noble, the Backstage Wife. By the time Lorenzo Jones and his wife, Belle, came romping in to the tune of "Finiculi-Finicu-whatever," Ma and I were pretty depressed.

Anyway, I did hear the soapy sounds of the radio come faintly through the drawn shades. I knew she was in there. Every so often I heard coughing, raspy coughing that came in fits and then subsided, and then nothing much again, no puttering in the kitchen, no humming of popular tunes, no vacuum cleaner. Something was decidedly funny in the Waters' house.

Mr. Waters was, Pop said, in the Merchant Marine and was almost never home. When he did come home once in a blue moon, the shades went up, the girls were dressed, and the doors were not, to my knowledge, locked during the day. I remember him, a giant in a blue uniform, hoisting DeeDee up onto his back for a piggy ride, holding small Sandra under one arm like a sack of potatoes, laughing. One of his side front teeth was missing. He swung the girls around by holding them under their arms. They shrieked and giggled and looked rosy and fine. DeeDee never chased anybody when her pop was home.

Then he'd go away again, and the shades would come down.

One night two police cars came and the cops broke into the place through the back-door window. Mrs. Webber, an oldish woman who lived on the far side of the Waters' house and who couldn't stand the sight of the two girls, had called the police when she'd noticed DeeDee and Sandra pounding on the door to get in long after the time when Sidehill Groucher would have begun his sinister journey through the neighborhood looking for little children to carry away in his sack. Mrs. Webber knew, she said, what was amiss.

"It don't take a college education," she said, "to see what's been goin' on over there. Cripes, that woman is nuts."

I didn't have the slightest idea what she meant, but I had to agree with her conclusions. The police looked doubtful, but knew better than to ask Mrs. Webber, who began complaining about her "very close veins" as soon as they mentioned her as a possible babysitter, to keep two little half-naked munchkins in her care all night until Mrs. Waters was sober enough to open her door. They reluctantly broke in, after a great ruckus of pounding, calling through the windows, and rapping sharply with their sticks.

A few minutes later an ambulance screeched up to the curb in front of the house and the attendants crept inside with their stretcher. What they brought out could have been a rolled-up carpet somebody had thrown out for the garbage men. It wasn't a person, because it was all rolled up, covered completely.

Mrs. Webber gasped and put her hand to her throat, covering her chickeny neck. "Holy shit," she said in awe. "I didn't know she was *dead*. Holy shit." She began to cry. I was appalled. Old people didn't cry. Only kids cried, and then only if mortally wounded. It was sissy to cry otherwise. But Mrs. Webber was crying openly, her sparse grayish teeth all showing in a grimace of horror, her tongue working in and out of her mouth in a hideous imitation of my Petey when he was thirsty.

I looked all around for my pop and my ma, but they were in the house, where they belonged, by God, peering out from behind the venetian blinds. I ran inside, my legs shaking, goose pimples covering my arms despite the humid heat of the evening. "Pop, what happened to DeeDee's mother?" I asked, my voice shrill with panic.

"She died," he said quietly.

I didn't know "died." I hardly knew, at nearly seven, "life."

Teddy knelt in front of them at the window, so still I thought he couldn't possibly be breathing.

"She was a drunk, wasn't she, Pop?" he whispered at last.

"We don't know that," Ma said. Ma was not given to idle yakking. She spoke like a telegram sometimes, eliminating all but the vital words needed to communicate her messages. Unlike Pop, who wove word tapestries around the simplest stories, Ma was famous for her one-worders. Move! Hush! Scram!

"We don't know anything much about it," Pop said. It sounded pious to Teddy and me, but we didn't exchange our usual looks of veiled disgust. Our parents weren't gossipers. They said gossip was as bitter as gall and would burn the tongue going in or out, so it was best to leave it to others. We said we understood, but, in truth, we thought they were acting like sisses. Being a sis in Dundalk was not quite as bad as being a fairy, but it came close.

"I could go over and ask," I offered, desperate for a task to do, something to accomplish in this awful stillness.

"You stay the hell in the house," Pop barked at me. It was one of the few times he'd ever spoken to me harshly. I did not know at nearly seven that people, upset over things they can't fix, that mystify them, sometimes lash out at their children, their spouses, their pets, or whoever stands next in line for blind devotion.

I took it personally. I cried.

Pop came to stand by my side. He picked up one of my caramel-colored braids, straightening the ribbon. "I'm sorry, Half-pint," he said. "I shouldn't take it out on you."

Take out what? What did it have to do with him? It wasn't his fault Mrs. Waters had disappeared, was it?

"What do you mean?" I asked. I couldn't resist. "It wasn't your fault."

"It was everybody's fault," he said flatly.

"It wasn't mine," Ma said. "I went over there once, and she threw me right out on my ear."

"That's just it," Pop said.

"What?" Ma said. "What's just it?"

"Once," Pop said. "You went *once.*" He looked at her meaningfully, and I could feel a Lecture coming on, although he was able to restrain the finger (index) that so desperately wanted to point and gesture. He was standing quietly, cushioned by his dignity.

"Remember," Pop said, looking past us all, to where his text for the evening was no doubt written on the evening clouds, "it was the lost sheep Christ went after, searching until he found it. Seventy times seven, that's how many times we're told to forgive our neighbor."

"I'm not Christ," Ma said, looking him in the eye. "I did the best I could, the best I knew how."

But Pop could not be talked out of his guilt. He went to the desk to look up pertinent passages in his well-studied Bible, and Teddy went up to his room to look out the window. He was fascinated with police procedure, and he watched avidly as they went over the Waters house in their lackadaisically thorough way. He loved that district attorney radio show, and all that junk about G-men and T-men in action, and

Dragnet. I walked in and kept him company for a time, but I could sense that I wasn't wanted by the way he kept shoving me around and elaborately walking around me to change windows now and then, so I went off to my own room and lay facedown on the bedspread, something that was strictly forbidden, and at which I always got caught due to the stripes it left on my cheeks.

From my open window, sounds came creeping in, the evening sounds we took for granted then but don't hear so often now: crickets, bugs zapping against the screens, indistinct chirpings of unidentified night insects, and crying. Crying. DeeDee's wild and screeching crying. It was darkening quickly now, and Mrs. Webber's kitchen light shone on the figure of DeeDee, sitting in her underpants on Mrs. Webber's wooden kitchen chair, her skinny shoulders working up and down. Mrs. Webber sat across from her, working embroidery or something—it was too far for me to see precisely. Sandra was nowhere in sight.

They were two people, separate and ugly, Mrs. Webber with her plaid housedress and her blue ankle socks and runover wedgies, DeeDee with her scraggly hair and her too-thin, bone-hard body. Mrs. Webber did not appear to be crying. DeeDee did not look as if she would ever stop.

I tried to pray for her before I went to sleep, but every good thought got stuck in my brain and eluded form. I was devastated. I was so sorry for DeeDee that I felt as if something inside me had ripped away from my rib cage. The warm tears dribbled into my ears, and my throat got sore from breathing so heavily through my mouth. What if they'd taken my ma away wrapped up like a worn-out old rug? I writhed in misery. Poor DeeDee.

I'm sorry, DeeDee. I wish I had the comfort of looking up sentences in the Bible that make everything all right. Maybe I'd feel better.

I know what my Pop means, though. I know quite well.

I didn't try hard enough. Once, a dozen, a hundred or thousand million times would not have been enough.

Seventy times seven.

I owe you some, DeeDee.

Chapter 2

Unlike most of the neighborhood six-year-olds, I took no pleasure in misbehaving, and tried hard to be good. I was so rotten at lying that it simply paid not to do bad things in the first place. Nevertheless, the road to hell is paved with just such crap, and I screwed up with a grim regularity that discouraged me.

Like the damn nail polish. Ma was a wonderful liar; she told us all manner of extraordinary things just to keep us in line, and these ghastly tales generally took root in our consciences, keeping us out of trouble. Her stories were so outlandish that they had to be true. Nobody would invent such strange stuff. On the strength of Ma's tales, I recall telling one of our grown-up neighbors that she really ought not to wear nail polish.

Her name was Estelle, and she spent seven months of the year cultivating a backyard suntan that made her look like a Masai maiden among a field of lilies. (The only black people we ever saw were the workmen who came and went daily around the neighborhood, the trash collectors; newly arrived from Wisconsin at four, the first time I saw these men, I screamed bloody havoc, convinced I'd seen the devil face to face; there were no black people in Wisconsin, as far as I knew.)

Estelle was a suspicious character, because she had no children and drank cocktails outside while sunning herself on a blanket. Her nails were long and red, and some were curved under like talons. She separated her long toes with small pieces of toothpick whose ends were wrapped with cotton. Fingers, toes, legs spread (to tan all the inner areas), she lay in the sun every day like a desert reptile, morning until dinnertime, listening to the radio she had on her dining room windowsill. Popular stuff. Les Paul and Mary Ford, Jo Stafford, Rosemary Clooney . . . the best of 1950.

The other women in the neighborhood detested her, found her vile and worthless, pitied her husband Melvin because he fixed not only his own lunch but also hers and brought it out to her (a delicate sandwich on a glass plate and a Coke with ice) on weekends. Such women were a blight upon the modesty and decency of the Dundalk housewives. Even if she did work part-time during the summer and fulltime in the winter at a downtown department store, she was worthless, lazy, an exhibitionist, and a dirty joke. Such was the consensus.

I feared her for her worthlessness. According to Pop, cleanliness was next to godliness (not necessarily in that order), and all honest work was honorable. Conversely, all laziness or unproductive activity was sin. Estelle never seemed to be doing any of the things my pop and ma considered productive, although she looked pretty clean if you weren't put off by all that baby oil and iodine she had slathered over her long, thin body. I feared that she might whisper things into my pink ear such as the serpent whispered to Eve, and I avoided Estelle whenever possible.

She always lay on her blanket, everything so ingeniously separated, and pretended not to mind being alone. I knew better, of course. I knew without a doubt that she would have preferred a little company, and I began to feel sorry for her one Saturday morning. There she lay, with no kids to do for, no reason to slave over a hot stove, no necessity for hurrying to do a batch of laundry (we had a Speed Queen wringer model that ran every day). When I approached Estelle, she pretended not to notice me.

"Well, hello," I said. When I talked to kids, I talked kid talk. To adults, I spoke in as adult a manner as I could muster. I saw no duplicity in this and had no ulterior motives. It merely seemed appropriate, proper, and natural.

"Yeah?" she said, not bothering to remove the little blue plastic cups she was wearing over her eyes (her eyelids, apparently, were tan enough). "What do you want, hon?"

In Baltimore, everybody, friend or foe, bosom buddy or total stranger, is "hon," short for "honey." My parents found this peculiarity of speech particularly distressing and flinched every time somebody used it.

"My name is Beatrice," I said. Miss Prim.

"Yeah, all right then, Beatrice. What do you want?"

"Nothing. Just thought I'd say hello."

"Hello," she said. The plastic cups still covered her eyes, but she knew who I was because of my funny midwestern accent.

"You know, you really shouldn't wear nail polish," I said.

"Why not?" she said, and this time she took off the eye coverings to look at her scary nails. "What's wrong with it?"

"Nail polish makes your fingernails turn black and fall off. See, your fingernails can't breathe right when they're all covered up with that thick glop, so they strangle, and then they turn black and fall right off."

"Oh, yeah?" she said. She had buck teeth, but they were kind of pretty. They made her mouth open a bit too wide when she smiled, and she was smiling now. "Who told you that?"

"My ma," I said. It was wonderful to be the carrier of vital information to the ignorant. I had a mission, a vocation.

"Well, I hate to tell you, hon, but your mother's a crock."

The term was not a Wisconsin word. I looked blank.

"A crock," she said. "You know. Full of it. Full of crap."

Crap was a word I knew. My ma was full of it?

"Nuh-uh," I said. It was a word all the kids said instead of "no." It was the opposite of "uh-huh," and not quite the same as "uh-uh."

"Uh-huh," she said. She replaced the blue plastic eye covers and lay down again. I noticed that her breasts absolutely disappeared when she did that, and I wanted to giggle out loud. Instead, I dropped to my knees with a thud and peered at them more closely, wondering where on earth they could have gone. I didn't see a sign of either of them. In our house, nobody ever said the word "breast." I think I called my nipples "toozies" until well after I was married. I was looking for Estelle's toozies when my mother called me into the house from the back porch.

"What in the world were you doing out there in Estelle's yard?" Ma demanded. Ma was deft with a wooden spoon, and she was holding one as we talked. She was rougher yet with her knuckles. She would hold you by the upper arm and give you a good one with the knuckle of her middle finger, right in the muscle. Jeeze. Now she merely set her blue-green eyes upon me and asked me point-blank what I was up to. An answer was required. I decided to let the skin go with the hide and tell the whole bloody truth.

"I was looking for Estelle's toozies."

"Mrs. Bobrich to you," Ma said sternly. It always confused me. Back home, children had always called neighbors by their last names—Mr. Adams, Mrs. Danielczyk. In this dumb place, adults wanted you to call them "Miss" or "Mr." and then their first names. It seemed absurd to us aliens, but I tried.

Ma had picked on my use of "Estelle," however, simply because she was so flabbergasted by what I'd said. I launched into a confused explanation, but she put out her hand, covered my mouth with it, and said, "Shush. Never mind. I don't want to see you over there again talking to her, you hear me? I don't like that woman. She might be dangerous."

Damn straight, she's dangerous, I thought.

"She said you were a liar," I said.

Ma let her mouth drop open. "Repeat that," she said.

I repeated it, and Ma sat down on one of our wooden-seated kitchen chairs with the bent chrome legs. "Come here, Beatrice," she said sweetly. "I want to hear you better." Hadn't I heard that line in "Little Red Riding Hood"?

Slowly I came to stand beside her. She slid her arm around my waist, a thing she did only when measuring me for the ridiculous shorts she made for me (they made me look as though I were straddling a hammock that someone had tied under my armpits). I squirmed and shifted.

"Stand still," she said. When her voice was that quiet, poisons were bubbling deep within her. I stood still. "Now just tell me what Mrs. Bobrich said."

"She said you were telling a lie when you said that nail polish makes your fingernails turn black and fall off."

Hmm. Ma's eyes opened a little wider. She gazed off into space for a while. "Did you tell her I said that?"

"Sure. You did say it."

"I know, but you don't need to go telling our business all over town."

"I didn't go all over town," I said. I could hear the whininess coming into my voice. It got on my nerves as much as it got on hers and Pop's. "I only told Mrs. Bobrich. I was trying to help her, and she said you were a crock."

"She doesn't need any help," Ma said. "She doesn't have a thing in the world to do, and she doesn't need you to help her not do it. You stay away from there, do you hear?"

"Okay, I hear, but—"

She was trying to pretend she didn't know what was coming. She was looking at a spot on the tablecloth, right between the ripe peach and the golden pineapple.

"Ma," I said. She looked up. "Ma, did you lie?"

"No," she said. "Fingernail polish isn't for little girls."

We stared each other down. Her lies were good lies, she supposed, and that removed them entirely from the "lie" category. My lies were always bad lies, but grown-ups' lies were okay. Somebody was always tugging the wool down over my eyes, even Teddy. I really hated that. He said that washing my belly button would cause some central mechanism in me to become unscrewed, and that my arms and legs would fall off. He told me about Sidehill Groucher, too, just as he'd been told, knowing better, and perpetrating the lie further anyhow, maybe to get back at a world that was out to deceive him, or maybe just for some kind of gleeful spite. The Tooth Fairy. Santa. The Easter Bunny. I fell for them all. Still do.

I went upstairs to ruminate.

From my bedroom window, I could see Ma stalking purposefully over to Estelle's blanket, blood in her eye. Estelle didn't hear her coming and jumped a mile when my mother said, unceremoniously, "Hey!"

"What do you want?" Estelle said. She sounded just like Teddy when he was trying to read and Pop called him to come and carry dishes off the dinner table.

"I'm here to tell you," Ma said in her "carrying" voice, "to keep your mouth shut about me in front of my daughter."

"Listen, I didn't—"

"Never mind," Ma said. She was straight. Straight legs, straight hair, straight neck, straight back. Now she towered above Estelle Bobrich, who looked suddenly very unglamorous all spread out on her blanket, like someone undergoing an exotic torture. Ma looked noble, commanding. Even I was impressed, although Ma was not in the habit of trying to impress people. She was not tall and had the idea that short women appear ridiculous when they attempt to take command. She was staring holes through Estelle, who started babbling.

"Look, the kid just came over here and started talking to me. I didn't even—"

"Never mind," Ma said again. "Just keep your mouth shut about her mother and father, do you understand? What we decide to tell her about right and wrong has nothing to do with you, do you get it?"

Estelle clearly did not get it. She shrugged her shoulders, said, "Sure," and turned onto her side, her round, tight rear now facing my mother. Then Ma did a thing that was frankly outrageous. She booted Estelle right in the behind. Not hard. Not cruelly. A medium-hard, neatly placed nudge in the fanny. Estelle turned to face her, alarm showing on her brown face. Without a word, she swiftly gathered up her blanket, baby oil, and magazine and rushed into her house. As my mother strode back home, a curious smile on her face, Estelle appeared at her dining room window and stuck out her head.

"Hey, woman! You're crazy, you know that?"

"I know it," Ma yelled back over her shoulder, still smiling. It was the first real indication I'd ever had that sometimes it is desirable to be a little crazy.

Up in my room, something in me rejoiced, although I could not have said just what it was. In the spirit of wanton joy, I removed the forbidden bottle of nail polish, "Claret" by name (I could read, but will get to that some other time), from its hiding place under my bed and ineptly attempted to sneak a bit of it onto just one thumbnail. Disaster. It blopped itself, instead, onto the precious chenille bedspread. Dark, indelible red.

That familiar sickening feeling of total dismay washed over me. Once again, I had gone and done it, and there seemed no way out. When younger, I had often walked away from such tragic circumstances humming a tune, convinced that if I got far enough away from disaster, it would eventually turn out that nothing had happened at all, or that if it had, someone else had done it. Now I knew what had to be done. Before anybody discovered the filthy deed, I had to repair the damage.

All I managed to do with my washcloth was to spread the sticky stuff a little more widely onto the bedspread and to make wine-colored stains on the washcloth. All right, God—come on, now.

Inspiration struck. (I do not mean to imply that it struck as a direct result of my prayers; that would be heresy in the light of what happened.) At any rate, it occurred to me just then that if my eye offended me, I was supposed to cut it out. Okay, then, out with the offending spot.

I sneaked into Ma's bedroom, pulled the sewing box out of her closet (I hated the bottom of that closet; she and Pop kept their shoes there, and it smelled like feet. The top of the closet smelled fine, like perfume, and Old Spice, and mothballs, but the bottom—yetch). I silently pulled Ma's shears from the box and tiptoed back to my room without arousing suspicion. In a few seconds, I had done it. The spot was safely in the bottom of my trashcan!

I smoothed the bedspread back onto the bed and saw for the first time what I'd actually done. Believe this or not, but the shock and pain of that realization sent me to my knees. I saw stars, heard the music of the universe, lost my vision for a few seconds. I thought I might die of sheer agony. That precious, blessed bedspread had been brought from Grannie's house in Wisconsin. Oh, my God.

I concocted one panicky lie after another. I was trying to cut out pictures and accidentally cut into the bedspread. But that was no good; it would still be my dumb fault, and I'd get punished. It just had to turn out that someone else had done it. I considered inviting my new friend Joanie over to play, maneuvering her into that area, and inducing her to cut the hole. . . .

I don't know how long I sat there pondering all the possibilities, but in the end, there was only one real course open to me. I could either commit suicide or disappear forever on earth. Somebody at Sunday School had said with positive assurance that suicides absolutely positively could never ever go to heaven, so I had no choice, really. Besides, I didn't have the foggiest notion of how to do a suicide.

Even at the tender age of seven I had a precocious knowledge of songs and could memorize the words at the drop of a hat. Now I sang softly to myself, and the tears slipped down my round cheeks as I whispered the words of "Bye-bye Blackbird." When I got to the part that said, "No one here can love and understand me . . ." I almost disintegrated, but something upheld me, some talk of Pop's about how important it was to do the noble thing.

We were people, Pop always said, to whom much had been given. Much, therefore, would be expected of us. But how much? And when? Nobody ever explained that to Teddy and me. We had the idea that only the ultimate was good enough in any performance of ours. It was a hard life sometimes, doing only those things that were Right, and doing them the best.

I wanted to leave, was almost ready, in fact, but something dragged me down onto the ruined bed and made me stay. I didn't know that I could feel so tired and so old, and so wrinkled inside. More tears fell, wetting the spread, fouling it with my inadequacy. The shame of what I'd done would never go away. This I knew. If God loved me, he'd let me die.

I heard voices. Ma and Pop, down in the kitchen, right beneath my room. The kitchen windows were open, and their voices, though not loud, drifted up and into my prison. I listened hard, because I lived and breathed on what I absorbed from the world, and memorized conversations as if my life depended upon it. This one fascinated me.

"So," Pop's voice said, rich with laughter, "that's your idea of kicking ass, huh? You really take things literally, don't you, Chickie?" He liked to call her "Chickie." Back home, out on the farm, she used to chase after the hens in the yard, yelling, "Chickie, chickie, chickie," with her dress whipping the backs of her sturdy legs and her apron flapping. Pop always sneaked up behind her and put his heavy arms around her middle and chirped, "Chickie-chickie-chickie," in an imitation of her calling; and then he'd squeeze her and turn her head around and kiss her out there in the yard, where any-body driving by could see, and then he'd laugh to see her face go scarlet in the pale sunshine. They didn't do that in Balti-more, but he still called her "Chickie."

"You said to kick ass, so I kicked ass," she said.

"You don't do anything else I tell you to do," Pop said, still laughing. I knew he was wiping tears from behind his glasses. When we laugh, we cry. It runs in the family. Ma, too.

"Everything else you tell me isn't so much fun," Ma said, and she broke into one of her rare laughs then, one of her chuckling, burbling giggles; and before long, I was snickering silently into my pillow, splashing around in the fun of it, wishing Teddy would have been there to see and hear what I'd seen and heard; and then the chuckling stopped down-stairs, and there was a little bit of shuffling around, and I heard my father's voice again, deeper now, and rich with the happiness he'd just felt.

"Chickie," he said, and the word melted in his throat. My mother did not answer him, and did not laugh.

I had hardly ever seen them kiss one another. Teddy said they probably did it, but we'd never see it. That was okay, though. We knew they did it, and that was enough. Now, on my chenille-covered bed, a warmth spread through me the way it did when Pop came home from work and lifted every pot cover on the stove and asked in his loud voice, "Where's that half-pint kid?"

It would be okay, I thought. I'd cry and say I was sorry, and they would forgive me.

Probably. And if they didn't, I could always run away later.

I fell asleep with my finger in the raggedy hole where there was a brief spot of claret-colored sin once upon a time.

Chapter 3

Because my birthday had come in January, I was not only the biggest kid in the first grade, but also the oldest at six and a half. I looked, in comparison to my diminutive classmates, like the sepia-toned photographs of Osa Johnson beside the pygmies in the zebra-bound *I Married Adventure,* my favorite book in 1950.

I thought I knew why Mrs. Holcombe hated me. It was because of the notes my father wrote to her. Ma would gladly have written them, but Pop wouldn't let her. He got too big a kick out of doing it himself in his own special way.

Pop always wrote with a fountain pen. Ballpoint pens weren't a big thing yet, and besides, he hated the one he'd tried out in the store because it blobbed and smeared, and he preferred the sensuous flow and stroke of his own personal pen. He said it had taken him years to break it in properly, and nobody else was allowed to use it. Not ever, not for anything. If anybody else used it, it would be wrecked.

In November, I caught cold, and this is the note Pop sent in to Mrs. Holcombe in explanation for my absence:

To Whom It May Concern:
    Beatrice was among those absent Thursday and
Friday last due to complications resulting from an

acute upper respiratory infection which incapacitated her and which doubtless would have contaminated others. Any inquiries regarding this matter should be brought to my attention. I remain, Yours Truly,

Herman J. Schmidt

Mrs. Holcombe had to read it two or three times before she got the gist of it. I think she caught me grinning and got the wrong idea. I was grinning because, even though I was only a kid, I knew that the note was a little much, as we used to say at home. She didn't get the joke. She glared at me.

"Did you have a cold?" she asked briskly. Was all that snapping really necessary? Her whole manner had never struck me right. She made me itch.

"Yes, ma'am," I said, regretting my grin.

"Fine," she said, and scrawled "Cold" across my father's beautifully penned note, followed by the code letters for legal absence. I just stood there.

"Sit down," Mrs. Holcombe said.

I thought she didn't like me, too, because I could already read when I got to her classroom. As a special gift (Pop said), I had been blessed very early with the ability to recognize entire words at a glance, as if they were symbols as easy to recognize as, say, "7-Up." Mrs. Holcombe hated that and grew aggravated when I sat yawning in my seat, wiggling and trying to stretch, while she laboriously drew Vs and Hs on the board, and urged the kids to repeat their sounds, and to think of words that began with those sounds. The adventures of Dick and Jane didn't move me much, either, except for one episode in which the moppets accidentally hit Daddy in the head with a toy airplane. A laff riot, I thought, since Daddy looked like such a simp and deserved to get his slicked-down hair ruffled up some.

Alice and Jerry weren't much better as subjects to read about. I guess my lack of enthusiasm must have showed too much, because Mrs. Holcombe used to say things like, "Are we boring, you, Miss Schmidt?" and the class would suddenly grow silent and tense, waiting for my response. All my responses were wrong, as it turned out, but I kept trying.

"Not really," I'd say. "I'll be all right."

"Well, we're all so relieved to hear that, aren't we, children?" she'd say, reaching inside her nylon blouse to pull at the many straps that were always falling off her shoulders. How many things was she wearing under her blouses? Her glasses made her bright eyes look small and sharp, like Jordan almonds. She was always watching me, snooping over my shoulder. Her favorite activity was having us cut out words from a paper—up, down, in, out—and then stick them with LePage's paste (not as tasty as the other brand, but cheaper, and it came with a dandy little wooden paddle that was yummy to suck on) onto a page with stick figures who were walking up- and downstairs or going in and out of doorways. Mrs. Holcombe would stand behind me while we did this fascinating exercise, and as soon as I'd got my last word stuck beneath my last stick man, she'd scribble, "SLOPPY!!!" across the whole shmear and make me start over (with a new ditto sheet).

I wish I could say that recess brought respite from my misery in first grade, but the unhappy truth is that the problems were compounded severely at noon hour after we'd eaten our brown-bagged lunches and put on our coats and caps and mittens. Out on the playground, it was every kid for herself, and being the biggest did not necessarily mean being the leader. Indeed, I was on my own out there, at the terrible mercy of the accursed Eugene, the Scourge of the Second Grade.

Eugene (pronounced "*Yoo*-jean" by the hooting, shrieking kids who galloped after him on the dusty playground) was a hellion of the first order. He forced kids to be in his gang by beating them up and making them pledge their loyalty to him. He smelled bad, he was dirty, had grut in his hair, didn't brush his teeth, and wore his pants too short and his socks down inside his shoes. The kids detested him.

I knew better than to venture too far away from the side of the brick building where the teachers hung out, blowing their noses and hopping from one foot to another in order to ward off the stiff cold wind that came whipping around the corner from the ball field. Sometimes I listened to their conversations, but it was hard to hear with all that wind screeching and whistling. Mostly I just stood around reading a book I'd brought from home. The teachers thought I was a precocious snob, and made no bones about it, either.

"Get out of here and play with the children," they'd yell to me, but I pretended that their voices had gotten lost in the wind and leaned up against the building, trying to draw warmth from the bricks, and went on reading. They lost interest in me.

Eugene didn't like me, though, and sought me out. No matter how inconspicuous I tried to be, I never turned into a brick, never blended into the side of the building, never became invisible. He found me nearly every day. I was on his Terror Route. There were several of us: James McCabe, the runny-nosed scarecrow who lived with his gramma above the dime store; Kate Thorogood, a kid who'd had polio and whose right leg was shorter than her left, and who wore a brace and a corrective shoe; Mickey Falkenhan, whose father was in jail for some unknown reason; Anna Mae LeBrun, who was not as fat or as tall as I, but who was clumsy and who wore glasses with a patch because her eyes were crossed. Eugene couldn't stand any of us, and his gang fell in with him, dutifully jeering and kicking sand and gravel onto the legs of us pariahs while yelling mortifying insults.

One day in December, a silver-gray afternoon damp with the promise of a sinister, short daylight and an early darkness, Eugene and his gang stopped in front of me just before the bell was set to go off signaling the end of recess.

"Hey, Fatso!" Eugene shouted into my face.

I didn't look up from my book. It was *Little Women,* and I

had just gotten to the part where the faithful black servant is rejoicing because dear little Beth's fever has broken at last. It wasn't the *time* to be futzing around with Eugene. I didn't look up, but turned a page. My reading infuriated Eugene, who, even the second time around in second grade and nearly nine years old, had not yet mastered the fine art of reading. "Put that damn book down," he snarled.

The kids gasped. Nobody cursed. Nobody. Not until you got to junior high. It was a law.

I did not acknowledge him, although my knees were shaking beneath the plaid dress I wore, and the hairs on my legs were perpendicular to the flesh. "Get out of here, you jerk," I said. Was that my voice? Was it I, tempting the devil? It sounded like Teddy, not Bebe.

"Shut up, Fatso," Eugene yelled, and hit the book out of my hands. Before I had the chance to react, he had planted his left foot in my stomach, sending me back against the bricks with a terrible "Ooff!" It was the first time I'd ever had the wind knocked out of me, and I didn't know that my breath would come back. I believed that he had killed me, and I fell over forward into a heap on the hard, stone-littered ground. The kids parted, their mouths gaping. This time Eugene had gone too far. This time he'd killed somebody. My eyes were closed. The roar of my breathlessness filled all my being, and I could not think, could not act. I just lay there, stunned.

Eugene backed away, surprised himself, a little scared. "Let's get out of here," he said, and started to run. Most of the kids followed him. A few of the guys and gals, the more lambish ones, still stood staring. Eventually my breathing returned to normal, but I still lay on the ground, shot to hell. I would have cried, except that Pop told us never, ever to cry outdoors. If you had to cry, then you had to come home to do so, because the world must not see that it has beaten you. Only at home is it all right to give in to the beating. Outdoors, one endures.

It was a long time until the final bell. That meant no tears until 2:45, when I would be safely inside my house. I staggered to my feet, picked up my book, and was dismayed to see that the page I'd been turning was half ripped out and hanging. Insult to injury. Maybe I could tape it together somehow.

My stomach was cramped where Eugene had kicked me. My peanut-butter-and-jelly sandwiches and banana were still in there, and were being squeezed out by the force of that untimely kick. It was such a short walk to my house, just across the playground and around a corner. I could go right on home and stay there, and nobody would miss me.

But I was too straight to walk out of school. We were supposed to be there until 2:30, and I didn't know how to break rules on purpose.

At my desk, I finally worked up the gall to raise my hand.

"What is it?" Mrs. Holcombe asked.

"My stomach hurts," I said softly. It was a kind of a secret.

"And what would you like for me to do about it?" she asked.

"I don't know," I answered. What was I supposed to say? I would have liked for her to swallow a fart, but we were carefully taught to respect all grown-ups, no matter how stupid, cruel, or insipid they were.

"Well, then, can we get on with our work?" she asked.

"I guess so," I said.

"Why, thank you," she replied. Blow away with the December wind, you old bat.

It happened, of course. Just as Mrs. Holcombe strode up my aisle to check some kid's seatwork, I urped all over my desk and the floor. Some of it hit her shoe, a high-heeled pump of red leather. I would cheerfully have expired on the spot if someone had been kind enough to shoot me. But all around me kids were gagging and retching themselves, carried away with the drama (and the odor) of the moment, while Mrs. Holcombe just stood and stared at her shoe, at the floor, and at me with soul-curdling distaste.

"Get to the lavatory and clean yourself up," she said at last, each word an effort.

I got up from my desk in a rush, almost upsetting it, and on the way to the girls' lavatory, I barfed again, this time in the hallway just outside the main office. The secretary jumped up and yelled for the principal, who yelled for the custodian, a black woman named Columbia Havilland, who shuffled through the corridors day after day with a bucket of sawdust and her push broom. Apparently there was a lot of regurgitating going on in those hallowed halls. Columbia came wandering into the lav where I was hanging over a toilet bowl, barfing my insides out.

"Lord, Lord, Lord," she said to my rear, which was more up than the rest of me at the time. "You sure makin' a mess, girl."

"I can't help it," I said. "A kid kicked me in the stomach." Columbia Havilland was the first black person I'd ever spoken to, or who had ever spoken directly to me. I couldn't decide how I felt about it—I wondered if it were a thing I ought to tell to Ma, Pop, and Teddy. It seemed important.

"Who?" she demanded. She knew by first name every kid in the school.

"Eugene, who else?" I said.

Columbia leveled with me. "Bust him up," she said. She poured some pine oil into a washbasin of warm water to overpower the smells I was creating, then yawned and made her way out again.

I thought about what she'd said. It made sense, but it wasn't our way of doing things. Any fool can fight. . . .

I returned to the classroom with a handful of paper towels against my chest, just in case. I did feel somewhat better, but Mrs. Holcombe's hatred was piercing my calm, poking at me. When would it ever be time to go home and cry? I looked at the big barefaced clock. One-thirty. A whole hour.

Mrs. H. was glaring at me.

"I couldn't help it," I blurted out. "Eugene kicked me in the stomach, and it made me sick."

"I hate a tattletale," she said, the disgust on her face an ugly mask. She loathed me.

"I'm sorry," I said.

"Never mind," she said, and went on with some Dick and Jane thing while I sat at my desk coloring a picture of a bell and writing capital and lower-case b's beneath it.

I didn't cry, after all, when I got home. The barf had washed out of my dress with cold water at school, so there was no need for explanations. I could have told Teddy. I could have asked him to beat the crap out of Eugene, but I didn't feel like it. I was twice Eugene's size anyway, and it seemed silly to ask somebody else to finish him off for me. I thought about it all night, and spent an anxious few moments looking for Eugene's footprint on my stomach, but it wasn't there. Maybe it hadn't happened. I would have believed that except for the aching in the muscles of my stomach, the aftermath of the violent and disastrous urping.

I feared Eugene more than I despised him, though, and that was making all the difference. I feared people who made fun of me. There seemed to be something separate about those characters who picked on people for fun, something evilly ethereal, as if one could beat them up and yet never touch them, really. If I beat Eugene up one time, I'd have to do it every single day for the rest of my life. He'd never get enough of tormenting me.

Maybe he'd die. Or disappear.

He didn't. The next day he was there on the playground, just as always, same shirt, same pants, same filthy, too-short socks. I was at my usual hangout up against the wall, my stomach quivering in anticipation of another session of humiliation. Kate Thorogood was standing a few feet away, also leaning, looking away from me, whistling a tuneless tune. Kate was always alone at school, too. She walked with a hop-skip-lurch that drove the little gremlins mad with glee when they had time to notice it. Most of the time, they were involved in other things and weren't paying attention to her. But when they turned their eyes on Kate, she went pink and started to twitch, which caused even more delight.

Today things were quiet as we stood side by side, but not by any means together. To tell the truth, Kate didn't impress me much. She didn't say funny things, didn't read books, didn't care about comics, and was too shy to laugh when droll things occurred, even as a spectator. I wondered if polio had done that to her, had robbed her of her sense of fun. It was weird.

I heard them before I saw them, and so did Kate. She ducked her head down, her chin almost on her chest. Her knitted cap covered her long reddish curls but didn't hide the truth the pinkness of her skin betrayed. I did something awful. I wished and hoped and prayed it was her they'd go after today. I wished them onto Kate.

Just as if they'd gotten a royal command, Eugene and his gang passed me by and descended on Kate, who was trying to flatten herself against the wall. Eugene halted just short of her and held his arms out to the side to keep his henchmen (and women) from colliding with the wall.

"Hey, Kate. Kate the Skate!" he cried.

"Kate the Skate. Kate the Skate," the idiots chanted after him.

"Hey, Kate! Why don't you run away?" Eugene taunted, his voice big, like a tuba. He did an imitation of Kate's walk which was inaccurate and inefficient, since he nearly fell on his ass, to the great amusement of his cohorts. "Is that how you do it, Kate?" he said, his face inches from hers.

Kate closed her eyes, and I was close enough to see the immense tears squeeze out from those tortured eyelids. "Get away from me," she said. Her voice was not crying.

"Make me," Eugene spat out at her. The others were

quiet. I wonder even now how much fun they had during these confrontations. They backed up a pace, not wanting to be inside the circle of animosity.

"You asked for it," Kate said, opening her eyes. They were cinnamon-colored, rusty, flashing now with hatred. She came at him with both fists, haymakers from right and left. The first punch caught him alongside the left ear, and his head swung to the right, only to get smashed by her left. Spit flew from his open mouth, and both his eyes shut as his head wagged back and forth, trying to get clear. She came at him directly then, stomping on both his feet at once, throwing him off balance, tipping him over backward. He fell onto his back in the gravel, and she hurled herself on top of him. His frantic kicks hit only her brace and were deflected. She pummeled him unmercifully about the head and shoulders, letting him have it in the gut too, with short, hard jabs. He expended most of his energy just trying to push her off and wasn't able to get in many punches of his own. The ones he landed were ineffectual. He was hitting her in the upper arm, or around the back with a curved hand. He was losing badly.

Kate was still crying as she creamed him, still sobbing as she abruptly pulled away and left him on his back in the gravel and dirt. She was still crying when she lurched and skipped and hopped away inside the building, strictly against the rules, to straighten herself out before school started again.

Eugene's friends dispersed. "Jeeze-oo," somebody said in awe. "Even a cripple can beat up Eugene."

Eugene picked himself up from the ground and didn't bother to dust off the grime. He rubbed his hand across his face, smearing a little blood from a cracked lip onto his sleeve. He looked dazed, washed up, like a soggy, popped balloon. For an instant, something in my heart went out to him. He was so dirty. Nobody washed his clothes. Nobody made him scrub his face or change his socks. He looked so skinny. . . .

"Get outta my way, Fatso," he said as he pushed by me.

"Shut up, you jerk," I said.

He made a rush for me, swinging like a maniac. I got out of the way and he smashed his fist into the wall. All the knuckles on his right hand were cut and bloody, and he put his mouth to his hand and looked dazed again.

"You better quit picking on people," I said. Why was I still afraid of him, perhaps more afraid than ever?

"Ah, shut up," he said. "Mind your own damn business."

Inside, I approached Kate Thorogood as she came down the aisle to the seat two chairs behind me.

"Good work," I said.

"Oh, shut up," she said, looking old, wise, and disgusted.

"What do you mean?" I asked. What was she mad at me for?

"You know what I mean," she said. She looked as if she might cry again, and I wondered if I was next on her list.

I just stood there in my favorite pose, looking really dumb.

"You're really dumb," she said.

"All I meant was that you did a good job on Eugene," I said.

"Yeah? Well, you should have been the one. You shoulda beat him up your own self," she said. Then she turned away.

Now I had two big bruises, two injuries. One from Eugene's foot, and one from Kate's words.

"The next time he says anything to me, I'll bust him up," I said. "I'll—"

"Just shut up," Kate said. That was all anybody was saying to me lately. Maybe I was talking too much.

I shut up. Then I sat down, and I endured two hours of Mrs. H.'s teaching. I felt tired enough to sleep right on my lilliputian desk, but I couldn't get comfortable. I looked sneakily out the window (Mrs. Holcombe went out of her mind if she caught you looking out the window) and watched a few white clouds poofing around among the gray. Soon it would be Christmas, and that would make everything all right. When the kids came back from the holidays, they wouldn't remember that the biggest kid in the first grade had let a crippled girl beat up the guy who'd been picking on everyone. They'd all have something else to think about, and this would be old, stale news.

I suffered more than Eugene did. He turned his attention thereafter to an older crowd and became the junior member of a bunch of sixth-grade rowdies closer to his temperament and abilities.

Christmas, as I'd predicted, came and went. Everybody forgot about my cowardice. The big deal after Christmas was kissing in the cloakroom, and my main objective in life was trying to keep the wet-nosed James McCabe from kissing me. Everybody had forgotten.

Everybody except me.

Nine years later, in high school, I got the nerve one day to mention the incident to Kate Thorogood, who was in my homeroom. She hadn't worn the brace for three years, and her right leg was very nearly the same size now as her left. Her long, wavy hair still hung in curls to her shoulders, and she was model-thin and graceful. When I mentioned Eugene Day to her, she looked at me blankly and then lit a cigarette (strictly forbidden in the lav, but Kate was never much for rules).

"What the hell are you talking about, Beeb?" she asked, sincerely puzzled. "I didn't even know we were in the same first grade."

"You don't remember Eugene, and his famous gang?"

"Who?" she asked. "No. Boy, you really take all this junk seriously, don't you? You remember everything, don't you?"

"I guess so," I said. "Somebody's got to."

Chapter 4

April of 1952 was gorgeous, full of blossoms—crabapple, cherry, dogwood. It was the first spring in my eight years I'd ever *noticed,* and I was in love with it, caught up in the essence of it for the very first time. Joanie and I sat in the crabapple tree and spied on people, making wild and improbable speculations as to where they were going and what they were about. (Estelle Bobrich had already been out, spreadeagled and baby-oiled, for two weekends running.) It was wonderful to be free, independent, not quite as worried about getting into the house before the first star came out so that Sidehill Groucher couldn't get us. Not *quite* as worried . . .

Teddy was about to be confirmed. What a fine and glorious thing that was, getting confirmed. Relatives from Wisconsin would come, bringing fabulous gifts of big money, a wristwatch, maybe, or luggage or a camera—the possibilities were dazzling. Confirmation for Missouri Synod Lutherans (we had learned early to identify ourselves properly as to denomination and type of Christian, perhaps in order to serve as reminder and reprimand to "looser" types) was and still is a big thing. Back then, confirmation was nearly always held just before Easter, which meant that the confirmands in Baltimore could be assured of perspiring beneath the rented white graduation-type gowns.

Teddy was to have a new suit—his first—and I was to accompany the family to Hamburger's, a good men's store downtown that Pop liked. I'd never been downtown that I could recall, but Ma told me she'd had me down there a time or two, and each time I'd gotten sick on the streetcar and had thrown up. I had the idea we were going downtown to buy Teddy a suit and to *eat* hamburgers, and was disappointed to see that the name of the store did not fairly indicate its contents. When we entered the store, a nicely suited gentleman came up to our gang and said, "May I help you, sir?" to Pop.

"You can help my son here," Pop said. You could see his buttons busting. Teddy was getting tall, almost as tall as Pop, though not nearly so wide.

"Certainly," the man said, and led Teddy off to look at sport coats. Teddy, fourteen and feeling it, was wearing saddle shoes that were scuffed and dirty-looking, a fad that curled Pop's toes. Pop always lined up his shoes in the kitchen every Saturday morning and shined them all, without fail. He paid a fortune for his shoes, choosing only the best brands in the most classic styles. They lasted him forever. Letting shoes get scuffed and dirty by deliberate design was criminal. He was embarrassed.

"Let's not look at sport coats," he told the man. "My boy needs a suit. He's getting confirmed."

"Catholic?" the man said. Nearly everybody in Baltimore was Catholic, it seemed to me.

"No," Pop said, a little miffed. "Lutheran. Missouri Synod."

The salesman was unimpressed. Pop could have said "Holy Roller" for all this character knew about differences in Protestant denominations. It was not going as swimmingly as Pop had hoped. And it was getting hot in the store. If the salesman knew what was good for him, he'd hustle this show on the road, I thought. Ma was fingering the ties, looking at belts, already aware of what she was in for. Pop was, in a word, finicky about clothes. It was liable to be a long haul.

"Why don't you and I go out and look around in the other stores?" she asked. It seemed like a good idea. I didn't mind, I said.

We ventured out into the too-bright day and inhaled the exhaust-filled city air. I wasn't used to it and was feeling just the slightest bit gaggy. "How far do we have to go?" I asked, my tone dangerously whiny.

"Don't start," Ma said, grabbing my hand and yanking me across the busy street.

We soon got where we—she—was headed, a store for large and tall women who were referred to as "gals" in the store's cutesy advertising. I thought "gals" meant it was a western store and was hoping for a cowgirl suit for my romps with the guys during the summer reruns of Hopalong Cassidy. Ma and I took an elevator up to the preteen girls' floor, and when we got off I suddenly realized that I'd been had. All over this floor were chunky little hunks of prepubescent flesh, their tummies sticking defiantly out in front of them, their faces sour and exhausted, their hair over-permanented due to their mothers' desperate efforts to glamorize them if it killed them all. Women and their daughters were arguing, groaning, slapping, bitching at each other. Cheeky salesladies were standing by with their thick salesbooks clutched against their skinny chests, chewing and snapping gum, offering well-meant and thoroughly inappropriate suggestions and comments.

"Awww," they chorused when some unfortunate lump of a kid emerged from a dressing room stuffed into a Chubette fashion (on my word, they were called "Chubettes") which gave her the general appearance of an egg roll with feet. They were high-priced, these dresses we hated, and made so that the sashes, cleverly sewn into the side seams of the dress, would pull out with a loud rrriiippp! if you sneezed too hard.

"I hate it," the balloon with freckles wailed.

"Awww," the salesladies murmured in unison, "that looks cute on you, hon. Honest ta Gawd."

"It does not," the kid hollered. "It looks *awful.*"

"Now, hon," said the saleslady in charge of this particular case of public humiliation," "let's come on out and let everybody else see."

"No!" the kid yelled, grabbing the dressing room curtain and hanging on like a bulldog. "Mommy, don't make me come out!"

"Get out here, you little heathen," the mommy said between clenched teeth. "Let me get a look at you."

"NO!"

"I'm gonna kill you, girl," Mommy said, going hellbent for leather for the dressing room. I started to gulp for breath in the hot store.

"I don't want anything," I said. "Let's go."

"You need something to wear for Teddy's confirmation, and for Easter. We only have to get that one little thing, and maybe some overalls, and some shorts and tops."

"I'm not wearing any old shorts," I said. The quaver had crept into my voice.

"You're going to have to, soon," Ma said reasonably, taking one of my braids in her hand. (A gesture of comfort, or a poorly veiled threat?) I pulled my head away.

"I'm not getting any dumb shorts," I said.

"Fine. Then I'll just make you some," Ma said, looking me in the eye.

Oh, God help me, those shorts. How in the world did she make simple pieces of cotton fabric look so strange? I can still feel the creeping shame of wearing those horrible shorts. As I walked, my awful shorts rode up and lodged themselves in the crack of my fanny, and the front stuck out like a full-bellied sail. My underpants never fit right, either. The waistband elastic was always stretched and saggy, the crotch was like a rope between my legs, the back rode up, and before I'd worn a new pair for five hours they hung at half-mast and came peeping out slyly from beneath those shorts. I had to yank frequently as the excess cloth stubbornly stuck up my rear, simultaneously splaying out my legs and hitching—sort of a one-two-three-four-five-six-seven-HITCH-KICK!—that sent Teddy into paroxysms of overt hysteria. Mortifying.

"I just want to get out of here," I said. I was tiptoeing on mighty thin ice. You didn't tell Ma what you wanted to do; you *asked* her what she wanted you to want to do. If you were smart. This wasn't one of my "smart" days.

"Quiet now," she said, all business. "Let's just look at a few of these things. Look at this. Isn't this cute?"

I wouldn't look. I couldn't believe I'd been bushwhacked this way. It was indecent. What if she made me take my clothes off? Oh, good God, help. A saleswoman was approaching, holding her tape measure out in front of her as she walked.

"What size you looking for, hon?" she said in clarion tones.

"I don't really know," Ma said. "She's grown a lot this year."

"They all do it, don't they?" the saleswoman said, winking as if she'd just written a joke for Milton Berle. "Well, just lemme measure her here, and then we'll—"

"NO!" I said, screaming maniacally. This was inhuman. They wouldn't dare measure a person right out in front of everybody.

"Come here," Ma said, clamping her farm girl's fingers around my forearm. She asked the lady for the tape and measured me herself, then wrote down the numbers on a little piece of paper and showed the lady. I'll give her that; she tried to be subtle. She was not totally to blame for what happened next.

"Let's see, now. That'd be about a size—"

"Shut up!" I yelled, my eyes squeezed tightly shut against the impending end of the earth. There was a roaring silence for a second, and I opened my eyes.

The woman looked at me as if I'd goosed her with a cattle prod. She stared at me, stared at Ma. She damn near lost her Dentyne.

Ma's hand and forearm came crashing across my face like a railroad tie. I went down to the floor on my knees, and my chin hit the wooden counter filled with cotton underpants. Crack.

"How dare you?" Ma hissed at me while the world watched in shocked wonder. "How dare you say such a thing to anybody?"

"Buh-buh-buh—" Nothing I wanted to say would or could come out of my mouth. I struck out at Ma's knees with both fists, pushed at her legs, wanting her to fall down the elevator shaft and never return. I lashed out sideways at the saleslady, who had pulled back behind the counter and was babbling, "Oh, Oh, jeeze—"

Ma grabbed my arm in her steel fingers and pulled me to my feet, but I was dead weight and fell down again. I wanted to go after Ma and the lady with both my teeth and feet. I wanted to spit on them, to tear them apart. We had attracted a crowd. I could see some of the other chubs watching with slitted eyes, willing me to take off after their own mothers, their own salesladies with tape measures. I flailed my arms and legs. I said, "SHIT!" out loud. Finally I got tired and just sat on my haunches while Ma pulled at me from my armpits, and then I stood up and put my forearm across my face and buried my head in Ma's bosom and sobbed. She stiffened, thinking, I suppose, that to comfort me would have been to condone my horrible misconduct. She pulled away, forced me to stand alone, turned me around to face the woman.

"Apologize," she said.

"I can't," I said.

"Right now," she said.

"I'm *not*," I said.

"Say you're sorry."

"No."

"Say it, damn you."

I stood silent. A firing squad could not have wrung the words from me. I was sorry for making Ma mad, sorry for kicking and hitting at her, sorry for saying shit out loud in the store—but for saying "shut up" to this skinny idiot with the mule face and the piano-key teeth, for this, I could not make myself apologize. I stood my ground, head down.

"Come on," Ma said. We got on the elevator, Ma daring anybody with her glittering eye to make a comment. Just as the doors slid shut, I heard somebody say, "Jeeee-*zissss*!"

Wordlessly, we walked back to Hamburger's. Pop and Teddy looked sweaty and harassed. The salesman had lost his chipper twinkle and seemed equally dishraggy. Teddy's suit was packaged and tagged for alterations, and was hanging on a hook. Ted was sullen, slouchy.

"What'd you get?" he asked me.

"Nothin'." I did not elaborate. "What'd *you* get?" I asked him, indicating his packaged suit with my head.

He glared at Pop. "Nothin'," he said meaningfully.

Pop's face flushed. "Shut up, you snotnose," he said. Pop turned to Ma. "I never saw such an ungrateful brat. You should have heard the stuff he was saying. He didn't like anything. Not one single thing we showed him."

"Oh, yeah?" Ma said. "What'd you get, then?"

"A perfectly good suit," Pop said. "Look." He picked up the paper wrapping and showed Ma and me what looked to us like a perfectly good suit, light blue, good for a kid with blue eyes like Teddy's.

"It's a piece of crap," Teddy said to me out of the side of his mouth.

Pop whirled around, ready to smash Teddy's smartass teeth down his smartass throat, but controlled himself admirably. "Get out to the car," he said. Teddy slouched out the door, both hands in his pockets. I was really feeling bad about the whole stinking day.

"How did you two do?" Pop asked. I wanted to faint, but simple desire was not sufficient to make it happen.

"Not so good," Ma said, staring straight into my eyes again. "We couldn't find a thing in that dumb Chubette shop.

Maybe I'll make her something for the confirmation. And maybe some shorts for the summer."

Bless you, Ma. Bless you, good old woman-of-few-words Ma.

For you, I'll spend another summer in those hammock pants.

Chapter 5

Teddy was duly confirmed with a maximum of pomp and a modicum of circumstance, and took his place among the adults of our congregation with a suavity and grace only occasionally ruffled by boyish frivolity. He and a kid named Garver were caught smoking in the Sunday School bus during a Walther League meeting and were hauled up in front of I don't know who-all in order to say something for themselves. I fell in love that night with my first Older Man. Clifford Garver, my hero, stood up in front of all those men and told them that he, and not Teddy, had instigated this foul plot, and that Teddy had been earnestly trying to talk him out of it when the two were apprehended by Darrell and Violet Brettschneider, the young couple who acted as youth leaders.

Teddy had stood (as he told it) sweating in his sweat sox and had not been able to let Garver take all the blame (although it *had* been Garver's idea, after all) and had offered to be equally reproved, no matter what the consequences. Honorable men, both of them. The church council was impressed. The two were let go with a reprimand and handshakes all around. Schmidt and Garver ran all the way home to our house, occasionally stopping to sling their arms around each other's shoulders and shriek a chorus of "Beer, Beer for Old Dundalk High" (sung, of course, to the tune of "Cheer, cheer for Old Notre Dame"). We heard them coming, and Pop watched out the window until he saw them in the distance.

"Shut up that hollering and get the hell in the house," he shouted through the open window. The late spring evening was thick with mammoth June bugs that zapped against the screens like bullets. Garver and Teddy got to the front stoop and collapsed onto the concrete, still whooping it up, but not as loudly as before.

Pop watched them from inside the doorway, and they talked through the screen at each other. I hung out the upstairs window and was told by somebody to shut the sliding screen or the June bugs would get me. I did as I was told.

"Aw, Pop, you shoulda seen Garver telling them all about how he was corrupting me."

Garver stood up and faced the street, the parked cars his audience. "Sirs," he said solemnly, "I come here tonight not to plead my own case, because I really am guilty. I really was smoking in the bus, and I know it's against the rules. But that's not why I'm here. I'm here to tell you that Schmidt had nothing to do with it. He was only out there with me trying to talk some sense into my thick head, and that's the truth."

Teddy leaped up and put his arm around Garver's shoulders. "That's not the whole truth, though," he said, his voice as solemn as Garver's. "Actually, I smoked a couple of puffs myself, just to show my friend Garver how stupid a habit it is, how dumb it looks, and how it makes you cough. That coughing is what brought Darrel and Violet out there, sirs. So it's as much my fault as it is Garver's, and we both apologize."

"Well said," Pop said. "Very impressive."

"Impressive!" Teddy croaked. "Pop, it was a goddamn *inspired* performance, right, Garver?"

"Well, gore, Mr. Schmidt, it *was* pretty good," Garver said modestly.

"Was it the truth?" Pop said.

"Well, yeah, basically," Garver said, pushing at his glasses at the bridge of his big nose.

"Teddy?"

"Oh, well, yeah, sure," Teddy said. The exhilaration was wearing off. He was winding down quickly

"All right, then," Pop said. "I guess it's okay if you two want to do a new version of *A Sale of Two Titties.*"

Garver and Ted ducked their heads down and snorted into their armpits. Pop walked away from the door; I could hear his slippers scuffing across the summer rug, could hear him approaching the stairway. I had just enough time to sneak back into bed and squinch my eyes shut. When he shut the bathroom door behind him, he began to chuckle. I could hear him in there rattling his newspaper and repeating, "Sale of Two Titties."

Outside, Teddy and Garver repeated Pop's joke two or three dozen times, giggling and chortling in the moonlight, gasping for breath. "Gore, Schmidt," Garver said at last, "your father's really a card."

"Yeah, I know it," Teddy said.

"You got a good family, you know it?"

"Yeah," Teddy said. They were sitting on the stoop now, speaking normally, the hooting forgotten and sloughed off like a childhood thing. Garver's voice was changing, and he sounded like Henry Aldrich from the radio.

"Even your little sister's smart, isn't she?"

"Who, Beeb? Yeah, she's okay. Yeah, I guess."

"My sister's a drip," Garver confided. "She's twelve, and already she's calling guys up on the phone, telling them she wants to kiss them."

"Cripes," Teddy said. "She's going to get banged like an old screen door one of these days."

"She better hadn't," Garver said. "My father would kill her."

"Jeeze, and she's only twelve," Teddy said, and then his voice and Garver's faded into the warm night, and I don't know what else was said.

When I woke up next morning, all I knew was that I was

in love with Clifford Garver. He had saved my brother's life in front of the church council; he thought I was smart; and his own family were a bunch of insensitive, promiscuous no-goods who didn't deserve him.

I followed him home from school, tagged along while he did his *Sunpapers* route, picked up his discarded gum wrappers and saved them in a wad in my bedroom. I listened in on every conversation I could when he was at our house to fool around with Teddy playing one-on-one basketball or chucking the lacrosse ball at me (nothing hurts more than being thwacked with a lacrosse ball, especially in the thigh, which was where I usually got it).

But soon enough I learned the pain of love unrequited. I hadn't given any thought to the freshman dance because we hadn't discussed it much around the supper table. And then one miserable night Teddy mentioned that Garver was going with Louise Hofstetter.

Louise Hofstetter. I'd seen her on the tennis courts. She was skinny as a stick, and had fuzzy hair and a band across her front teeth. Garver liked *her?* I couldn't believe it.

I ate two extra helpings of mashed potatoes and gravy as Teddy blathered on about the dance. It was going to be a record dance, and he was going to help buy and play the records, because he was on the dance committee. Patti Page. Joni James. Guy Mitchell. I knew who they were, but nothing mattered anymore, and I couldn't share in the enthusiasm. I would have sat there eating all night long if Ma hadn't finally taken the serving bowl and my plate away. "Get up from there and do your homework," she said.

I didn't have homework. The first grade didn't get home-work. Everybody knew that. I went upstairs to my room and lay on the chenille bedspread with the puckered-up spot where Ma had sewn up the hole. How could Garver have taken up with such a jerk as Louise Hofstetter?

Eventually I persuaded myself to cry very quietly and daintily into a flimsy hankie I carried in my see-through plastic church purse. The hankie had an embroidered ("embraw-dried") pansy at its corner, and I was careful not to let any goo desecrate the purple flower.

All of which left me ripe for the untoward advances of James McCabe. Even in June, his nose ran like the prover-bial leaky faucet, and his head was oversized and only precariously balanced atop his chicken-thin neck. No normal child could stand him, but most people were innately kind enough to let him be. That was because he had a weird and formidable family history that nobody wanted to get too close to.

James was from a Broken Home. There weren't very many of those in 1952, and it was quite a thing, especially when the kid's mother ran off to Philadelphia with a man that nobody believed she was married to. My mother and father did not discuss this sort of thing around Teddy and me, because they still had a moratorium on gossip; but I heard more than most kids did because I listened better, and because I hung around adults, standing idly at the fringes of their conversations until they noticed me and sent me packing.

So James was notorious because his mother and father were absent. Nobody knew where his father was. If James knew, he never said. James lived with his Gramma McCabe in a tiny apartment above the dime store where transients and single people and widows sometimes took residence in Dun-dalk. It was barely big enough for one person, but the two of them made do. Gramma McCabe had a job, old as she was. She was the lady who scrubbed and waxed the floors in the stores beneath the apartments. She got the apartment free for mopping the halls and cleaning the fingerprinted walls from time to time, and they paid her a little salary to supplement the welfare check; that mostly went for a little bit of food and lots and lots of booze, which she belted down like fresh spring water.

James made his own meals, all sandwiches (for lunch, peanut butter and jelly, every single day without fail, and a wrinkled apple), even sandwiches for supper. I found this fascinating. He was pale, thin, his clothes raggedy around the edges. There were a lot of kids who looked like that, but James also wore a hangdog expression that made him look like the old guys with the narrow black shoes who sat on the park benches and talked about the Great War, whatever that was.

James was, he told me, tired.

Gramma made him sit up half the night with her while she talked on and on about the way things were before, the way things ought to be now, the way nothing had ever worked out, the way people were no damn good, the way you couldn't trust nobody, the way poor people only got poorer, and them that's got keeps on getting.

The kid was tired.

He told me this on the hot and dusty June playground. The kids were wild with anticipation of the summer vacation. Everybody in Dundalk except me went to a place they called "The Ocean" (which I eventually discovered was Ocean City, Maryland, then a five-hour ride from Baltimore, and the farthest away most of them had ever been; those who did not go to The Ocean went to another mysterious spot known as Pensavania). Summer was really something then—so hot you couldn't breathe unless you went under one of the giant sycamore trees that lined most of the main streets and just *sat.* Then a sudden rain would come blowing up out of nowhere, with that mystic stillness as a warning, and we kids would walk slowly home, hoping to be splatted with the two-inch raindrops before we arrived. When the rain moved on, we'd come bursting from our houses and into the deep puddles. We'd squish our feet into the rain-drenched sod and look for worms. In the evenings, we sat out on the curbs and sang and sang and sang.

James McCabe was still trying to kiss me every day, and not only in the coatroom now but right out on the playground, where people could see and where I'd have to kiss him or paste him one in the nose in order to preserve my image.

"Cut it out," I said, pushing him.

"Aw, don't push me, Bebe," he said, his eyes watery blue. "I wasn't gonna do nothing bad."

"How come you're always trying to kiss me?" It would have been quite a feat had he done it. His forehead came to my armpit.

"I don't know," he said, bending down to tie his shoe. "Darn it," he cried in dismay. "Look. The shoestring broke. Gramma's gonna kill me."

"Why?"

"Oh, crapsake. Every time I wreck something she beats my tail. I gotta fix this before she sees it."

"You couldn't help it."

"Gramma don't care about that," he said, clumsily trying to repair the lace with trembling fingers stiff as popsicle sticks. "Aw, jeeze, I can't. I can't do it, Beeb."

"Here," I said, kneeling in the dust and gravel. "I can do this. I did it lots of times. Watch."

I showed him how to line up the laces so the knot would be just in the right place and wouldn't prevent the lace from going through the hole. He stood like a soldier, looking down at the top of my head, nodding and concentrating, trying hard to learn, just as he did when Mrs. Holcombe tried doggedly to drill the phonics into his head, and with about as much success. He seemed to have a hell of a time getting the hang of things.

"I'll never do it as good as you," he said. "You do everything good."

"I do not," I said. "I wreck a lot of stuff, too."

"Does your mom beat your tail?"

"Not usually. Only when I keep on doing the same thing three or four times. Then she says she's sick of me wrecking things and she gives me a good one on the arm."

"Does your father beat you?" he asked. He wasn't looking at me, seemed to be looking over the tops of the trees that lined the playground, seemed not to care, but was listening very closely, very carefully.

"No. Only one time, just once, when I gave him some mouth about wearing my Halloween costume before it was really the right night to wear it. He spanked me then. One smack on the rear. Then later on he came up to my room with two cookies and said we should be friends."

"Oh," James said. He pronounced it "ayo." "Just that once, huh?"

"Yeah. Once. Why?"

"I don't know," he said. "You got the shoe fixed?"

"Yup. Look. Just like new, except there's a little knot right there, and it's not as long as it used to be. But you can still tie it. Your gramma won't even see it."

"I know. She can't hardly see anyway."

A breeze blew up and lifted my skirt a little. Like a real lady, I put both my hands down at my sides to preserve my dignity, and in that unguarded moment, James seized my shoulders in his two hands and kissed me on the cheek.

"Hey, cut it out!" I said. "I don't like that." I was saving myself for Clifford Garver, but James didn't know that. Nobody knew it except God and me.

"Awright," he said. Then he grabbed my hand. I pulled it away so violently that he looked as if I'd smacked him. "I mean it," I said. "You better cut this crap out or I'm gonna bust you up."

Pop, in his inimitable way, had given me his Lecture on Men and Boys. Nobody was laying a finger on me. We were not really a demonstrative crew at our house, anyway. None of this public hanky-panky for us.

Poor James. He seemed to get skinnier as we stood there. "I'm sorry," he said. "I won't do it no more, okay, Beeb?"

"Yeah, James, okay," I said, the way you'd tell the dog

it could come out from under the sofa after it had wet on the rug.

Some kids were playing Greek dodge, hurling the ball at each other with such force that the thinnest of the girls were flying all over the place. It looked like fun, but I didn't like to leave James just standing there.

"Come on," I said. "Let's go over and get in the game."

"Nuh-uh," he said. "I'm staying right here. Them kids'll kill me if I get in the game."

"Not if you're with me," I said. "Come on, don't be a sis."

I gave him a shove and started to jog over to the game. The first time I looked over my shoulder he was just standing there like a fence post, but when I looked again, he was reluctantly trotting behind me, head down.

We stepped casually into the game, and people pretended for a moment to be gagging, and some held their noses, but we ignored them and soon enough the game went on, and James even threw the ball once in his anemic way. When the bell rang, James was just as sweaty and disheveled as anybody, by God, and his face was flushed with joy.

"I done it," he said to me as we lined up—boy line and girl line—in front of the big green doors. "I played, Beeb. They let me play just like anybody. Jeeze-oo. I got dirty, huh?"

"Yeah," Bobby Lucas said, giving him a shove from behind. "Now you look as dirty as you smell."

It was a real kick in the head for James, whose clothes were usually pretty stiff with crud and sweat. Apparently, Gramma washed clothes very seldom. Like Eugene, James was pretty much on his own when it came to keeping clean. I turned to Bobby Lucas.

"Leave off of him," I said. "He doesn't have a mother."

"So? He's got soap and water, doesn't he?" Luanne Somers said with her chin stuck out and her white curls blowing.

"Shut up, Luanne," I said. I was feeling sour all of a

sudden. Itchy to punch somebody's face off. Luanne always looked as if she were encased in plastic; nothing penetrated that sparkling aura of cleanliness that encapsulated her, and the boys went nuts over her, despite her mean spirit.

"My mom says that cleanliness is next to godliness," Luanne said. My Pop said that, too, but I wasn't going to agree with her. "My mom says that the two cheapest things in the world are soap and water, and that even poor people can still be clean. James isn't even *clean.* Eeoo." Luanne held her nose again in an elaborate gesture of distaste.

I grabbed a handful of those long white curls and pulled backward until I thought her eyes would pop out. "Leave off of James, you hear me, girl?" I said.

Luanne started to cry, and I let go. Luanne was a tattler, but for some inexplicable reason, her tattling didn't seem to evoke the same negative response in Mrs. Holcombe that tattling by a homely, dumb kid did. Luanne was petted, patted, stroked, praised like a sleek puppy for everything, even the pukey things she did to the rest of us. It was years, sixth or seventh grade, I think, until I could say a civil word to her. By that time her hair had gone dark blond and her pert little face had flattened out, and her legs just never developed curves, so she wasn't quite so Little-Miss-Precious. You could at least talk to her.

James had started crying out in the playground line, and I could have kicked him. Loud, snuffling noises accompanied our two lines into the building, and I knew without a doubt that I was going to the guillotine.

Sure enough, Luanne marched right up to her oak desk and reported to Madam Hatpin that Bebe the Hulking Oaf had pulled her cornsilk hair out by the bloody roots. Mrs. Holcombe's face was a study in contempt. She glared at me.

"Come up here, please," she said quietly. Mrs. Holcombe seldom yelled. Everything was low-key and deadly. I went up there. "What is the big idea of a great big girl like you picking on a small person like Luanne?" she asked.

"I wasn't really picking on her," I said. "I was only—"

"Did you pull her hair?"

"I guess I did, but—"

"Be quiet. You will apologize to Luanne in front of the class. Then you will stand in the corner for the rest of the afternoon."

The corner? In a pig's eye, I'd stand in a corner. The corner was for lowlifes like Eugene, or Bobby Kwiatkowski, who colored on other people's papers or put paste in people's sandwiches. Not for me. Not for a Schmidt. I wouldn't. Couldn't. And apologize to that little fart? Not in a million years. Not ever. Never.

Mrs. Holcombe was still waiting, looking hard at me. Her thick, square hands with their polished nails, encrusted with white chalk dust, were tapping softly on the desk. I had to go to the lav.

"May I go to the lavatory?" I asked politely.

Her voice was venom in a steel-tipped arrow. "You may not. You may apologize to Luanne in front of the class, and you may then stand in the corner." I thought wildly of a surreal game of "Captain, May I?" but in this game, we didn't take baby steps and umbrella twirls and giant steps. In this game Madam Captain gave you baby words and big betrayals.

"I can't," I said. I was so close to the ultimate dishonor —crying in public—that I thought I'd die of asphyxiation, trying to hold it all inside. Luanne stood beside Mrs. Holcombe, the two of them wishing me dead and buried. I didn't dare move or speak. I might betray my mortification. I stood like a statue.

"Do as you are told, please," Mrs. Holcombe said.

"I won't," I said. My last words hung in the air like a quivering chord. There was an audible, collective shudder from the rest of the class. Something unspeakable had happened. A kid had talked back to the teacher. A kid would now die.

"You're going to the office," Mrs. Holcombe said briskly, smiling in sudden, unaccountable glee.

The Office. The End of the Line

Our principal was seen only seldom, mainly at Christmas programs and at the occasional class party, to which we invited him every time. He always came (immaculate in a gray suit and red bow tie), ate a single cupcake, swallowed hard (those cupcakes always tasted the way I imagined an undamp sponge might taste), complimented everybody on his or her (he always said "his or her") good behavior, and discreetly retreated so that we could resume our rowdiness. While he was among us, we were made of cardboard. And now I was going to The Office.

His secretary greeted Mrs. Holcombe and me with annoyance. "What is it?" she barked. "Mr. Hallman is very busy."

Mrs. Holcombe's eyes sparkled. "Oh, but Mr. Hallman will want to see this child," she said. "This child has defied me in the classroom and has been very rude besides."

"Oh?" the secretary said. She sneered overtly at the ramrod with the glasses whose icy hand lay on my shoulder. "Having difficulties in the classroom, Mrs. Holcombe? Discipline problems?" she asked. Mrs. Holcombe's hand tightened on my shoulder, pinching a nerve. I nearly blacked out.

"Hardly," she said, still through that incredible smile. "I'd just like Mr. Hallman to have a little chat with Beatrice."

"But isn't this little Beatrice Schmidt, the reader?" the secretary asked. She was smiling at me, looking curiously bewildered, but I didn't dare smile back. And I really did have to go to the bathroom.

"This is little Miss Beatrice Schmidt, the smart aleck," Mrs. Holcombe said, enjoying her bit of wit, crackling it like chewing gum. "I'll just leave her here with you, and you can take care of it."

"Thanks a load," the secretary said. When Mrs. H. stalked out, I saw the young woman make a deliberate face at her. I could like this woman, I thought.

Sitting in the bench in the outer office, trying not to wriggle, I tried to count my pulse rate while I watched the second hand on the giant round clock face move me ever closer to my demise. Suddenly, in one swift motion, I was whisked into the Inner Office and deposited in a real chair just opposite the throne upon which Mr. Hallman sat in mortal judgment.

The place was eerie with artificial light, because the drapes were pulled shut even though it was hot, hot, hot. He had a fan going, and it swung from side to side like a great wagging head and caught me every fifteen seconds with a blast across the face. I sat like a lump, slumped, my shoulders hunched, legs straight out in front of me. He was doing some sort of paperwork and didn't look at me right away. I looked at him, though. He was completely bald on top. I hadn't noticed that from my usual perspective. I wondered if he knew I could see that he was bald. It embarrassed me, and I looked away. It seemed like a dirty trick, looking at a person's bald head while he was writing, unaware.

He looked up at last, blinked.

"What's the story?" he said.

As best I could, I told him what had happened. Pop had pounded it into our heads never to lie under pressure, because it just made things worse, into a bigger and stickier mess, so I stuck strictly to the truth and told it just the way I saw it. He sat back in his chair, which bent over backwards to an alarming degree. I talked as long as seemed necessary, then sat with my hands folded and waited for the inevitable decapitation.

"So," he said. He looked at the ceiling for a minute, then back at me. "So you were upset because this child Luanne was making fun of James McCabe, is that it?"

"Yes, sir."

"Ah-hah," he said, giving each syllable equal emphasis. "So the plot thickens. And what did Mrs. Holcombe say when you told her this?"

"She didn't let me tell her, sir." I added the "sir" in a sudden wave of inspiration. Teddy said "sir" to Pop when the situation warranted a certain amount of brownnosing.

"O-ho," he said, laying his hands flat on the desk. He was a man apparently given to dramatic words and gestures. He opened his eyes wide behind the glasses that made his eyes look like soft-boiled eggs, then squinted them shut, then looked at me again.

"Are you a smart girl?" he asked, point-blank.

"Yes, sir, I think I am, sir." Perhaps I was overdoing it.

"Good," he said. "Then this should be easy for you. I want you to go back to your classroom now and give the note I give to you to Mrs. Holcombe. I want you to apologize to her for not doing as she said, and then I want you to apologize to nobody else. Just sit down in your seat and resume your work as quietly as possible. Is that understood?"

"Yes, sir," I said. I was starting to feel better.

"Can you read handwriting?"

"I'm not sure, sir. I don't think so."

When he had finished writing the note, he handed it to me, folded, and made me repeat his instructions. As I got up to leave, he stood up and came around to the side of the desk.

"You're Herm Schmidt's girl, aren't you?"

"Yes, sir," I said proudly.

"I know your dad," he said. "He and I coached football together a few years ago for the YMCA when he first came to town. Ask him if he remembers Dutch Hallman."

Dutch? The name on his office door said, "Arnold J. Hallman." Dutch. It was a good name for a man, especially a man who didn't hold with brutalizing innocent kids for no good reason. I ventured a smile. "I'll do that, sir."

He grinned, showing lots of teeth. "Do you call your father 'sir'?"

"Yes, sir," I said. It was true. To a degree.

On the way back to the room, I opened the note and was thrilled to see that Mr. Hallman's handwriting was much like block printing, square and precise. I read it with ease.

Mrs. Holcombe,

In future, kindly take the time and trouble to find out all facts before sending a child to me for disciplining. It appears that this young lady was essentially in the right, and was defending an unfortunate child against the slings and arrows of the others' cruelty. A noble, though futile, effort, and one that ought to be rewarded, and not punished. *Listening* is at least half the job of an effective teacher, don't you agree?

He'd signed only his initials. That really made it look official.

The next scene was classic. I apologized, Mrs. Holcombe accepted, I sat down in my seat, and all over the room kids who'd been screwed by Mrs. Holcombe were smiling secret smiles of triumph. It was the day of the underdogs at last! Something had been won, some major point. Mrs. Holcombe was strangely subdued for the brief remainder of the year.

Considered something of a folk heroine after that, I was asked to lead up the games, to pick teams for dodge and tag, and to be at the head of the lavatory line at least once a week. One Friday afternoon as we all stood lined up in front of the door ready to bust out of there for the weekend, James McCabe put his grubby hand on my arm.

"Could you come home with me for a couple minutes? I got something for you. A present."

I was allowed to be a few minutes late. Ma knew that sometimes things on the playground were so absorbing after school that a kid couldn't go running straight home like a sis, so there was a little leeway allowed. I said I'd go. A living legend owes something, after all, to the little people who've put her where she is today. And besides, the prospect of getting a present of any kind was intriguing. James was ecstatic.

"Gramma won't even be home," he said. "This is the day she goes out to the country." Once a week Gramma made a trip out to the country on a Greyhound Bus, which she had to catch downtown. It was an all-day affair, and James wasn't sure where she went or why, but she always carried a package with her. (It was not until I was an adult that I discovered to my dismay that the euphemism "the country" meant Springfield, Spring Grove, or Crownsville, the mental hospitals closest to the city, among certain older residents who were too embarrassed to say such names out loud).

Fine. If Gramma wasn't going to be there, how bad could it be? We walked along through the park, a few hundred feet across, to the center of Dundalk and strolled through the dime store before going to the rear stairway. The dime store's wooden floor was worn smooth with years of heavy treading. People shopped leisurely there. It was a rambling place, full of treasures. There was always a record playing from the stack of 78s in the tiny music department at the front. The lunch counter was crowded with housewives having a Coke and a hot dog before beginning the walk home with two bags of groceries from the Acme market around the corner. The brown paper bags stood lined up behind them on the floor like soldiers.

We eyed the earrings and bracelets and pins at the jewelry counter. I found a pin shaped like a parrot, studded with rhinestones and red, blue, yellow, and green glass that really took my eye. "Maybe I could get that for you," James said, but when we turned it over to look at the price, I dropped it like a hunk of poison ivy.

"It's a buck twenty-nine," I said in awe. James shook his head, and we looked at the towels to embroider (embrawdry) and the baby yarn, and then decided after a cursory examination of the cap guns and the wax lips to go up to the apartment because it was getting late.

Gramma was quite a collector. Bits and pieces of rags and old food, newspapers, catalogues, magazines were stacked floor to ceiling everywhere. There were few pieces of furniture, and those pieces were piled high with junk and paper. Glasses and bottles were strewn everywhere, and the wood floor was bare. There was a stink of dirtiness, of spoiled food, rotted apples, wet dirt. I didn't want to come in any farther than the space just inside the door, but James pulled me by the arm. "It's in the kitchen. Come on, Bebe."

In the tiny kitchen the sink was full of filthy water with grease and scum floating on top. A jar of cheap peanut butter with oil at the top (not the good stuff we had at our house) stood open on the table, a knife sticking out of it. Cockroaches ran about freely, big fat ones and little bitty ones just hatched. I was in agony. I had to get out of there.

James opened the broom-closet door and extracted something from a large oilcloth shopping bag, the one his gramma carried over her arm as she went mumbling along the Dundalk streets. "Here," he said, thrusting it at me. It was a crumpled white paper sack of popcorn, partly eaten.

"Go ahead," he said. "It's real good."

He was the charmer and I was the snake. I took the bag he offered, put my hand into it, drew out a kernel, put it into my mouth, chewed, swallowed.

"Good, huh?" he said. "I had Gramma buy it for you at the movies the other night."

"Well, gee, thanks, James," I said. "I gotta go home now. Teddy's taking me to the public library, and I have to get moving."

"Just stay here a little while," James begged. "Gramma's not coming home till late. We could fix a samwich."

I looked at the knife, greasy and pocked with unidentifiable grut, sticking out of the peanut butter jar. I didn't know what to think about that half inch of oil at the top. Ours didn't have that. Ours was smooth, creamy, caramel-brown. I had to get home.

"Come on and eat some more of your popcorn," James said in desperation. His voice was getting high and squeaky.

His fingers were wiggling. I ate some more, putting the ker-
nels into my mouth one by one, finding them hard to swallow.
I held the bag out to him.

"No, I don't want none. It's all for you. I got it for you,
Beeb."

Just then the front door banged open and hit the wall
behind. Crash. Gramma was home, her navy blue hat of straw
wildly askew, her shopping bag bulging with bottles, her
stockings down around her ankles.

"What the hell you doin', James?" she asked. "Who the
hell is this?"

"This is, uh, a girl I know from school."

"Yeah? So?" Gramma said. I wasn't feeling welcome and
was inching toward the door. The dank and dreadful smell of
Gramma had already reached me. I had never smelled anything quite like it, body odor and dirt incompletely masked by
what I recognized as the dime store's "Blue Waltz" cologne.
It was smothering, overwhelming.

"Well, I invited her here and now she's going, ain't you,
Beeb?"

"Oh, yeah," I said. "I gotta get home now."

"Just a second, girl," Gramma said, grabbing my arm.
"What's that you got in your hand?"

"Nothin'!" James squeaked. "It ain't nothin'. It's just her
old lunch bag, Gramma, honest."

"You're a goddam liar, too, boy," she screamed at him.
"You know goddam good and well I got that there bag of
popcorn for the birds. You little heathen, gimme that popcorn," she yelled at me, lunging for my white bag. I gave it
up without a struggle, practically threw it at her, but she still
had hold of my arm and would not let go. I saw that she had
only a few teeth in the front of her mouth, and that scared me
so badly that I wanted to wet my pants.

"You see what he done?" she screamed into my face. "He
took and stoled the goddam bird food. I got that food at the
movies the other night from under the seats, and this little

heathen takes and gives it away to some goddam fat pig. What do you think of that?"

"I gotta go now," I said. "If you let go of me, I'll go right home this minute."

She let go of me and went after James. She caught him easily because there was no place for him to run. She hit him six or seven times across the face, then twisted his arm so hard he fell to his knees and screamed. She went for the butcher knife that lay on the rotting wooden counter top and held it in front of his face. "See this? See it? I'm gonna cut your heart out with this and feed it to them birds, you hear?"

James's face went blank and dreamy. The reeking witch dropped him and let him fall to the floor, and it was not until his teeth hit the linoleum that he let out a wail.

"Get the hell out of here," he said to me. "Get home. Don't never come back here. This aint' no good place. Get out of here and don't never come back."

"Shut up!" Gramma shrieked wetly and went for him again. I got out as fast as I could. My feet thumped on the wooden steps. At the rear of the dime store, just above the place where they kept the fish and the parakeets, the customers could hear dull whumps coming from the ceiling above them, but nobody raised an eye to look up there. I ran nearly all the way home, anxious to be near Ma, anxious to smell the pine oil and the bleach she used to clean our house, anxious to smell dinner in the oven.

James McCabe never looked me directly in the eye again, not then, not ever, as long as we went to school together.

Clifford Garver and my brother Teddy careened through an army career together, and spent two years helling around Germany and the other two challenging the virginity of every young thing in Fayetteville, North Carolina. Clifford eventually married a girl from there, and they lived happily ever after for two or three years before they got a divorce.

In 1964, James McCabe was killed in Vietnam. There was a tiny insert about it in the local news sheet saying that he had graduated with the class of 1962, so a few of my college buddies thought we ought to look him up in the yearbook.

"Here he is," Anne-Marie said, pointing to a picture of a rooster-faced boy with bad skin. "I don't think I ever saw him in school."

"I think I did," I said.

"Yeah," Sarah said. "Me, too. He was in Lewiston's algebra two class. He sat way in the back. He never said a word to anyone."

"I wonder if he was a hero," Anne-Marie said. "The article doesn't say."

"He was a hero," I said.

I didn't betray you, James. And because I did not then believe in heaven, I cried bitterly for you in the dark noise of the night.

Chapter 6

When we'd first moved to the townhouse apartments known as Freedom Gardens in 1948, they were the Eden of suburban Baltimore. We kids roamed and rambled among the back courtyards unmolested, slipping behind the greenery for hide-and-seek, running the longer expanses of grass for run-sheep-run and kick-the-can and red light-green light . . . roller-skating on the cement (*see*-ment, in Balmerese) sidewalks, skipping rope. Far into the dark summer nights we sang our songs (learned in Vacation Bible School and various day camps; Dundalk kids did not go to "away" camps) in sweet, high harmony, while our parents sat chatting out front in their wood-and-canvas chairs, listening to us with only half an ear, watching only casually because there was nothing whatsoever to fear, and Sidehill Groucher was a creature invented only to fool the little ones, the innocents, into coming home to bed.

By the time I was nine, and we had lived there long enough for me to feel possessive, a squatter, the rats had begun to take over. We attributed this to the existence of the "garbage garage," a cinder-block building some fifty yards from our tidy brick apartments in which the collected trash was held until trucks came to take it away. The rats thrived there. We used to watch them in the summer twilight, frolicking on the brownish grass, their hairy bellies full, their gall alarming.

One day in bright, hot August, the black workmen came marching through our courtyard armed with bars and clubs, swathed head to foot in heavy canvas wrappings, faces covered with netting, hands thickly gloved. They hurled open the door to the garbage garage and just as quickly let it roll back down again as they rushed inside. We kids stood in a huddle, inching closer as their hollering and clubbing grew more furious, more feverish. At last the door was flung open, and the men pitched the bludgeoned rats outside onto a giant pile. Guts. Sticky maroon blood. Curled paws.

I gagged and recoiled, unable to bear it. But the others were delighted, and stood hopping and cheering as the men lamented that they hadn't been able to get all the filthy mothers. Paul Rosling dashed home to get his Baby Brownie camera.

I was the biggest kid in the neighborhood, a roughhouser whose reputation by now for toughness would precede me into the fourth grade. To maintain the image, I stood sweating but erect, the ends of both my braids in my mouth, as Paul recorded the event on black and white film.

That evening Roberta, Joanie, Randy the Sis, and I sat playing Authors on the warm cement of the back stoop. From the corner of my eye I saw a milk-bottle-long gray rat emerge from beneath a sticker bush. The others all ran, scattering Shakespeare and Thackeray everywhere, but I sat rooted, unable to move. I, whom the kids now called Moose, despite my mother's vocal objections.

The rat stared insolently at me, edged toward me in the bold and lazy way a snake undulates toward the blind and deaf rabbit it will devour.

Within an inch of my shoe, the rat deliberately veered to the left and returned to its haven among the bushes. I felt the gush of boiling urine soak my shorts. I sat humiliated, knowing without a flicker of doubt that we have dominance over the rats only for as long as they let us. I saw again the empty, casual glance of contempt the rat had shot at me as he sauntered back to his bush.

More than two decades later, I am still frightened to think of that evening.

I remain a victim of that knowledge.

Chapter 7

Joanie Sheeley and I were pals. We played DyDee dolls together, sewed doll clothes, agonized over the Tonette permanents our mothers relentlessly administered every four months to our too-short bangs, fell in love with Audie Murphy, and went every single Saturday to the Strand Theater to watch (twice) every movie (A, B, or C) made between 1952 and 1954.

(I may be the only living human being to have seen more than once such winners as *The Green Glove* and *The Lusty Men*. The stars of the movies I watched in utter fascination were Corinne Calvet, Faith Domergue, Kurt Kasznar, Frank Lovejoy, Gloria Grahame.)

Our favorite movies, of course, were the gorgeous color musicals—*Three Little Words, The Great Caruso*—I'd have walked a mile across burning coals to see Howard Keel and Kathryn Grayson. Those long afternoons at the Strand pumped me full of my devotion to the American silver screen. Even today, whenever I sit in a darkening theater, my heart thumps with the anticipation and joy most people save for their wedding days. I don't ever recall walking out of a movie. Well, once, out of a movie called, I think, *Sylvia* (but maybe it was the *second* showing). I generally stick around until the last credit, because I believe fiercely that something I see on that screen is going to justify the bucks I've spent. I am often disappointed (more often now than in 1954), but still I go. Not to go at all would be so much worse.

I saw *The Greatest Show on Earth* twice every single day it played at the Strand. I wrote to Betty Hutton and got an autographed picture and a letter, and I hugged it to my heaving breast and lay down on the couch and *swooned* to think that Betty Hutton had sent me best regards always. Joanie Sheeley and I saw the vintage *King Kong* together, and for months we marveled, wondering how on earth they could possibly have photographed all those prehistoric monsters without being killed or maimed.

Altogether, it cost forty cents to go to the Strand. A quarter to get in. A dime for popcorn (mandatory). Nickel for a drink from the machine. You could get cola, lemon-lime, root beer, cherry, or orange. We got them all at once by turning the handle rapidly back and forth until the cup was filled. The cadaverous manager, an accomplished skulker and master snoop, was everywhere. "You girls cut that out," he said, his skinny finger pointing at us threateningly. "I'll put you outta here." We always said, "Yes, sir," with a great deal of dignity and then dashed into the ladies' room, giggling into our angora mittens.

The ladies' room at the Strand listed on its walls the names of all the girls in Dundalk. The word "shit" was scribbled everywhere. We always spent at least half our time inside its maroon-and-chrome splendor instead of in the prickly theater seats. Here was where the high school girls stood with one hip stuck out sideways and yakked. It was where Joanie and I listened and learned nearly everything we knew about anything.

I loved Joanie. She laughed at my jokes, hardly ever said I was fat, seldom remarked about how big my hands and feet were or how tall I was or how much I ate. She was petite, dainty (Tinker Bell, her father called her when he was feeling decent and not staring moodily out the dinette window; she never once referred to him as a nut, although that was what the world seemed to think of him; I thought that was admirable of her).

Joanie and I walked everywhere. Everybody did, then. For one thing, lots of people didn't have cars in Dundalk, and even those who did had only one, and not two or three. It was easy to walk anywhere you had to go. No more than a few minutes. And aside from the usual dangers like riding with strangers who offered candy, there was no reason not to go gallivanting around at will. Joanie and I hung out together, snooped in the dime store together, giggled, got jealous, fell in love with Eddie Fisher, played Authors, giggled, spied on boys, shared comic books, giggled. She was better than the sister I'd always yearned for, because I didn't have to love her.

In 1954, in the brilliant, brisk, orange-gold of an October afternoon, we walked home from a movie we'd seen twice. I hated to hurry, but Saturday night's menu of beans and hot dogs would be waiting for me, and Ma would have minced onions for the hot dogs, and probably there would be vegetable soup, maybe even potato chips. I didn't want to hurry, but it seemed urgent to get to those scents, that warmth from the steaming wienies. Joanie was sluggish, though, and draggy.

"Come on, Joanie," I said. "I gotta get home." She was never as anxious as I was to get home, but that was probably because at her house they ate things like creamed chipped beef on crackers for supper. Or eggs and bacon. Breakfast foods. For *supper.* I never could figure that out. They were upside-down people—like Joanie's mother going out to work and her father sitting home playing solitaire ("Solitary," he called it) and crushing out those stinky Camels into a chipped glass ashtray. People said the war had done something to him, but I never saw any holes in his body, or any braces or crutches. Anyway, they seemed upside down to me, or backwards. Joanie seldom mentioned them.

"Come *on,"* I said, pulling her arm.

"I don't feel like it," she said. A tear slipped out of her

right eye, another from her left. Ah, jeeze, another one of her "spells." She had them every so often, especially, it seemed, when we were on our way home and I wanted to hurry. She wiped the tears with the back of her mittens, and tiny, wispy hunks of white angora stuck to her face. She didn't want me to see the tears, though, so I didn't.

"You better hurry up, pokey," I said. "Else I'm going to leave you."

"Go ahead," she said. "I don't care."

I hated it when people said they didn't care. It was such a stupid thing to say. How could any person not care about everything? To me, everything was important—everything made an impression and was worth saving, noticing, judging, evaluating, discussing, absorbing, and storing. Joanie was poopy like that sometimes, though. Still, I hated to get mad at her. I gave in, slackened my pace a bit, let her try to catch up as the daylight dimmed.

I didn't see the man standing in the doorway until we were upon him. He was tall, thick, dark, dressed in work clothes with heavy-duty zippers and heavy, scuffed boots of dark leather. He came slowly, stiff-legged, his two hands out before him, eyes wild and wide open. All of his clothing was undone, unbuttoned, unzipped. The front of his chest was matted with black hair that covered his stomach in a thinning line and then thickened again at the crotch. He wore no underwear. His was the first penis I had ever seen. It poked out from between the dangling ends of his wide belt, bobbing as he walked.

No thoughts occurred to me, nothing about warnings or strategies or escaping. I simply stood, heavy and solid, and let him come to me. His mouth was open, wet, the teeth uneven yellow-brown edged with black, huge as horse's teeth. He was speaking, but the words were foreign to me, meaningless noises spewing from the dark hole of his mouth, and still I stood and let him come.

I recognized, knew him somehow.

"You don't understand," he slobbered, waving his right

hand feebly back and forth. "You don't know what you're seeing. You don't see. You don't understand."

His gaunt face crumpled and the cheeks seemed to collapse. His face was wet with saliva and tears and mucus from his nose. He said more words, but I couldn't hear him because somebody was screaming and screaming, and the man put his hand out again and tried to clamp it over my mouth. In seconds, as I twisted my head back and forth and thrashed against him, his pants were wet, strands of wetness hanging from his bobbling organ. One hand wet, too. Slick. Glazed.

My throat ached. My pulse pounded inside my neck and ears. Home. Pop.

My feet hit the bare dirt of the playground. I ran around the climbing castle and then skidded on the long grass of the playing fields. Home.

The living room light was already on. I could see it as soon as I rounded the corner. Pop sat reading in his chair. My body flung itself against the front door, my hand turned the knob, my scream ripped my throat open as I tumbled into the room.

"Paahhp!" I wailed. "Oh, Pop, help me!"

He was out of the chair before I could blink, catching me, scooping me up as if I were feathers in his hands. He checked my clothes to see if I had been torn apart, exposed, sensing the violation before I could tell him, realizing the terrible intrusion.

Ma came running in from the kitchen holding an onion and an absurdly large knife, a knife much too big for cutting onions, I thought. Her eyes were huge, scared. She was looking for blood, for bruises, for broken bones. She stood still, apart from Pop and me.

"There was a man—at the school—he came after me. He—"

Pop's hand came up to cover his face for a second. His voice was raw with bitter fury. "Did he touch you? Did he—"

"I got away," I said. "He tried to put his hand on my mouth, but I got away. He—"

Pop wouldn't let me tell. He pulled my head to his chest

78

and put his hand on my cheek forcing my mouth shut. "Shush, hush, now," he said, still kneeling beside me. "You don't have to tell. You don't have to talk."

"But, Pop," I cried, pulling away, "I know the man. I do. But I can't remember who he is. I just know that I know him."

Pop looked at my face, wiped tears with his folded handkerchief. "You're all upset," he said. "You're scared to death."

"But, Pop, I do know him. I swear I do."

"It's okay, Pint-size," he said. "It's all right now, Half-pint. I'll go outside. I'll look for him."

The realization hit me first at the back of the neck and then in the gut. "Joanie!" I screamed. "I left Joanie! She's all alone. He's gonna get Joanie!"

Pop leaped up from the floor and thrashed his way out the front door before I was finished. I got up and raced to the window, then to the doorway, straining to see him in the waning daylight, watching him run on his short legs across the school field, hearing him call for Joanie. "Joanie! It's Mr. Schmidt. Don't be afraid. Where are you, Joanie?"

A faint reply, Joanie's voice, thank God, thank you, God, from around the corner somewhere. I began to cry in relief and fright, and Ma sat down on the couch behind me, her arms awkwardly around me, her hands folded across my stomach. Her head was resting on the middle of my back, and she kept patting my tummy.

Pop came through the door holding Joanie by the hand. "Joanie!" I cried. "That man! Did you see him?"

She looked away from me, put her head in Pop's chest, where mine had just been. "I didn't see anybody. I'm tired. I want to go home. I don't feel good."

Mom dropped her hands, stood up, went to Joanie. "Are you sure you didn't see anybody?" she said.

"I didn't see anybody. I want to go home."

Pop looked at Ma over Joanie's head. "I found her sitting on the steps by the water fountain with her head on her knees." My mother hugged Joanie, gathering her up as if she were a bundle of dry twigs, a small package to be tied and mailed. A rush of resentment, unbidden and chilly, washed over me as I watched them, bewildered.

"She did so see that man," I said. "She's lying."

"Beatrice, hush," Ma said sharply.

"But I was hollering," I insisted. "She must have heard it."

"She says she didn't see anything," Ma said. "Leave it alone now. You're all right, aren't you?"

"I guess," I said. I was not all right, but I gave Ma the answer she wanted. Ma came and sat down on the couch and pulled me down beside her. She smoothed the fine hair up and away from my temples, hugged me close. "Did the man touch you?" she asked carefully, delicately, the unaccustomed softness of her voice alarming me. I didn't know how to answer.

"No," I admitted grudgingly. I was tempted to say he had, because it seemed suddenly as if the whole rotten experience didn't *count*, somehow, unless I'd been harmed—had a bruise to show, or a place where he'd cut or bitten me—but I knew in my weary way that lying would be useless and humiliating in the long run. I didn't know what kind of story to make up about it, so I told the lackluster truth.

"What did he do, exactly?" Ma asked. "Did he—"

"Never mind," I said, jumping up and pulling away from her, too, as I'd pulled away from Pop. "He didn't do anything. I didn't see hardly anything. Never mind."

Ma turned her head sideways and looked at Joanie. I knew the look. She was looking, listening, feeling for the truth. Joanie looked away from Ma, and went quickly to Pop and asked him again to take her home. Ma watched them go, watched until Joanie was safely inside her door. Pop walked quickly back home to our bright, warm kitchen where the steam from the hot dogs and soup was making me breathe deeply and heavily.

"Did you say anything to Ada Faye?" Ma asked him.

"Nah. She wasn't home from work yet."

"Did you tell Al?"

Pop looked her in the face. "What's the use of that? The guy's a zombie. Just sits and looks at you like you just crawled out of the goddam woodwork."

"I know," Ma said. "Ada Faye's got a cross to bear over there."

"Poor little tyke," Pop said, referring to Joanie. Why was it making me so mad, this sudden affection of theirs for Joanie? I felt awful.

All I wanted to do was to eat my hot dogs and then watch Jackie Gleason after my bath. I sat at the table next to Ma (Teddy hadn't come home yet and would get his tail kicked for being late) and ate hot dogs until I wanted to barf. Then I ate some more.

We all watched Jackie Gleason at 8:00 after having paid half-attention to Ken Murray for a while, but Pop's heart didn't seem to be in it. He didn't gulp and roar and cough with hysterical laughter the way he usually did, not even when Reggie Van Gleason looked the society lady in the eye and said, "Mmmmboy, are you *fat!*" I had to go to bed before Sid Caesar came on, but I could hear Pop chuckling his way through it despite his uneasiness. Nothing could keep him from cracking up over Sid Caesar on Saturday nights.

I went to bed restless, itchy. I kicked my feet and pulled at my braids. Finally, I found a sharpened pencil to take to bed with me. It would poke the eyes out of any would-be attackers. I drifted off to sleep, and later on heard the noise Teddy and Pop were making downstairs as if they were shouting through a heavy curtain. I would not dream of the man. No matter how hard he tried to sidle into my dreams, I forced him out. I shoved him away and turned my back on his dark presence.

Sunday School. How I detested going there. We all sat in a circle on wooden folding chairs that sliced into my thick thighs. We read paragraphs from the printed lesson sheets in turn and then went again around the circle reading a paragraph each from the Bible story. Finally, we answered all the questions from the study sheet. Then we sang songs all together in the common meeting room, led by the Sunday School leader.

Brian Mahler was pulling at my braids. Sissy Blue was giggling. When I got into my seat at last and Bobby Buchler had hissed, "Hey—what're you doing out of drydock, Queen Mary?" as I'd stuck my ample rear into his face, I glanced up and saw standing behind the podium the man who had accosted me on the playground.

He was looking all around the room, hitching his shoulders up and down nervously, pulling at his coat sleeves to show he wasn't comfortable in a suit, smiling, frowning, smiling again as if he couldn't make up his mind. Now he was calling for order, holding up his hand. That hand. Dry now.

I ducked my head and stared at my lesson paper. Oh, God up in heaven, is this really the man? No wonder I couldn't place him; it was too incongruous. I didn't even know him by name. He was just The Leader, and he had come a few months ago, and nobody in our class paid much attention to him, and I only knew his face vaguely. I stole a look up at him as he put his left hand to his left temple and rubbed it, and squeezed the skin over the bridge of his thick nose.

"Let's have it quiet, now, people," he said. He announced the closing hymn and began to sing it in an unenthusiastic baritone as soon as the pianist had finished the introduction.

> Abide, oh, dearest Jesus
> Among us with thy grace;
> That Satan may not harm us
> Nor we to sin give place.

He was not looking at me, had not yet seen me. My legs shook. My bowels felt chilly, loose. I was afraid to stand up, afraid the bottom would drop out of me in a whooshing, foul stream. The song was over. Kids punched at each other, shoved their way out of the seats, overturned a folding chair in their race for the door. The man was preoccupied with some of the bigger boys, and I slipped by him and out into the sunlight. Pop was waiting in the car, reading behind the wheel. Ma was chitchatting in her stolid way with some ladies who looked old enough to be her mother but who were, Pop said, her own age. She caught sight of me, waved her white-gloved hand, called in several directions for Teddy, who did not appear, then said, "The heck with him. He can walk home." I got into the backseat and we pulled out of the gravel lot.

I was not given to whispering, but the sound didn't want to come out no matter how hard I swallowed and tried to force it. "Pop," I said at last. "Pop. I know who the man was. On the playground."

He partially inclined his head toward the backseat. "You do? Who?"

"The Sunday School leader. That man." I pointed to the man, who was walking straight for a light green Chevy with his keys in his hand, shielding his eyes from the bright daylight with his free hand. Those hands. I knew those hands.

"You're kidding," Pop said.

"It's him," I said. My voice was returning to its usual pitch and volume.

Pop looked at the man. "It's not him," he said shortly, and then we pulled out of the lot and onto the road. I was stunned. Ma touched Pop's arm, and he gave her a sideways look. "Herm," she began, but he cut her off.

"It's not him, I'm telling you," he said. "Once and for all, it's not him."

Ma looked at me over her shoulder, wondering, pondering.

I didn't say another word. There was nothing to say.

Teddy got home in time for Sunday dinner at 3:00. He said he'd walked Eleanor Talarczyk home after early church and then had gone back to get a ride home with us and we'd already gone. He was wearing his wronged, righteous look and was trying to act pissed off, as if it were our fault for leaving him behind to fend for himself, but Pop just said, "Sit down and eat," so he did. He looked at me across the table.

"What's the matter with you, Bratface?"

"Nothing," I said. If he'd really cared, dammit, he'd have been there when it all happened, helping to prove it was real. It was too late now for him to be of any help. I was so mad at him.

"She had a bad scare yesterday," Pop said. "Nothing she can't handle. A man scared her in the schoolyard. But nothing happened. She's all right. Nothing to worry about."

Teddy put his hand across the table and squeezed my chubby arm. "Tell me about it, Bratface," he said. "What did the son of a bitch look like?"

"Watch your mouth," Pop snapped.

"He was—he was—" I tried, but I didn't know how to make it sound real. My mouth opened into a crooked O, and I bawled openly, wantonly, for the first time since the man had seized me in his wet hands. Teddy struggled up from his cramped position behind our crowded table and put himself next to me. "Poor little fart," he crooned, hugging me hard. "Tell Teddy."

The baby talk did it. Sympathy finished me off. The floodgates opened, and I was swept away with the misery of it. "It was the Sunday School guy," I wailed into his white Sunday shirt. "You know, the guy who leads the songs."

"Who, Mitchell?" Teddy asked, his disbelief making a harsh and hollow noise.

"Yeah, him," I said loudly, to make it true. "It was really him. He was there today, too, but he didn't see me. I can't go back there, Teddy. What if he sees me? He'll come after me. He'll know where I live. He'll come and get me, and he'll—" It was too terrible to say out loud.

"Why didn't you tell Pop?" Teddy asked.

"I did," I sobbed. "He didn't even care. He didn't even believe me."

"Pop?" Teddy said. I couldn't see, but I could hear Pop

sucking air in through his pipe, trying to light it. He said nothing. "Pop?" Teddy asked again, his voice rising.

"I think she made a mistake," Pop said quietly.

"The hell she did," Teddy said. "If she says this is the guy, then this is the goddam guy."

"Don't swear," Ma said sharply.

"Why the hell didn't you tear his ass apart?" Teddy demanded, letting go of me. "Why didn't you coldcock the son of a bitch?" At sixteen, it must have seemed the logical move.

"Teddy!" Ma cried.

"Sit down, Ma," Teddy ordered.

"Who the hell do you think you're talking to, you snot-nosed brat?" Pop said. His face was blotched with rage, pale around the mouth.

"I'm talking to you, *sir!*" Teddy spat, jutting out his jaw, tensing the muscles in his arms.

"Then use a civil tone," Pop said. "And sit down. Listen for a change, and stop flapping your lips long enough to—"

"I can't stand it anymore!" Teddy yelled. "You treat us like we were cretins. How retarded do you think we are?"

Teddy looked desperate, as if he'd run a long way and was still lost. He flexed and unflexed his fists. He was sweating, breathing hard. He flung himself suddenly from the room, leaving it emptier than it had ever been before. He left me sitting there with Ma and Pop, who were so silent that they could have been stuffed moose heads. I ate my dinner virtually alone. Ma sat staring at her lap. Pop looked out the window and blinked like an owl. I ate three slabs of roast beef, a mound of carrots, a boatload of mashed potatoes and gravy, orange slices dipped in sugar, three rolls, two glasses of milk, cherry pie, another roll to take outside with me . . . they sat there and let me do it. I'm not sure they even saw me.

It would still be light for an hour or so yet. As I pulled on my jacket, Ma shot me a hard look. "Why'd you have to go crying to Teddy?" she asked. "Don't you think your pop

85

knows how to take care of these things? You should have kept quiet. Now look what you've done."

I felt like a moldy, smelly rag. I scuffed my new shoes—red penny loafers, the Poll Parrot kind—on the concrete as I wandered outside to see what was up. I wished she'd have smacked me a smart one, or pinched my arm instead.

The courtyard was desolate, barren, and when a brisk wind blew into the roots of my hair, I pulled my jacket tightly around me. I looked over my shoulder every few seconds for the man, certain I'd find him lurking next to the brick wall, or behind the sticker bushes, ready to come staggering like Frankenstein, legs stiff, eyes staring. But the courtyard was still empty. Someone on another block was burning leaves, and a dog was barking. I strolled home, kicking leaves around and thinking.

Teddy was on the back stoop bouncing his basketball on the pavement. He watched me walk home, as he'd done so many, many times for as long as I could remember. But today he looked so tall, so much taller than Pop, really, with the long, stringy muscles of my mother's people, of my grampa Kessler, a rawboned giant with shoulder blades like concealed wings that made his flannel shirts hang as if they'd stayed on their hangers.

"Hey, Fartface," he called to me. "Come here." I came.

"You want me to get that guy for you?" he said. "I will if you want me to."

"I guess not," I said. "Pop would get mad."

"Pop," Teddy snorted. "Wonderful Pop. Yeah, he'd get mad, all right."

"So don't," I said. "Okay?"

"I won't," he said.

I sat down on the stoop and looked up to watch the leaves hurrying down from the sycamore trees, in a race to hit the cooling ground. Joanie's face flickered whitely at her bedroom window, then was gone. She did not see me wave.

"Joanie lied," I said to Teddy. "She lied about the man. She said she didn't see him."

"Oh, yeah?" Teddy said, still dribbling the ball on the sidewalk. "Why?"

"I don't know," I said.

For a terrible instant, I thought perhaps I had been the liar.

Teddy went thumping off to the basketball court looking for a game with the guys who always drifted over there late in the afternoon. Dundalk winters were so devoid of snow that the guys could play all year round, if they were willing to inhale the damp, cold air that gave the croupy coughs. I sat on the stoop with my chunky legs stuck out in front of me, pulling idly at the hairs on them, wondering how old I'd have to be before Ma would let me shave off all that crap. I did not believe her when she told me that body hair, once shaved, grew back stubbly and dark. She was the one who'd told me that nail polish made the fingernails turn black and fall off.

How much of what I'd seen and heard was true? Something was hurting my chest, and I diagnosed it as a frightful hunger pang that could doubtless be soothed with a massive triangle of cherry pie, all the better because it was leftover, and therefore thicker and soggier than it had been at dinnertime.

But I didn't want to move. In an hour it would be dark, and then I would have to go to bed right after Ed Sullivan's *Toast of the Town,* and I knew I couldn't spend my entire life battling the man to keep him out of my dreams. Sooner or later he would come creeping in, like the horror comic creature thick with pond slime, and I wouldn't be able to fight him off anymore.

I prayed one of my peculiar prayers. "God the Father in Heaven," I said, convinced that the formal approach would be most likely to open His great heart to me, "if this really is the guy, and if it all really did happen, then please just make him go away. You don't have to make him die, or anything, but just please make him go away."

A month or so later, the man was gone.

Nobody ever mentioned Mr. Mitchell to us at Sunday School. One rain-gray Sunday morning after the lessons, old Hazel Schmuldt just hoisted her immense and unwieldy carcass up onto the little stage in the meeting room, lifted up the podium as if it were a toothpick, and boomed to the rowdy hooligans of our Sunday School, "Let's have some quiet in here, people, and I mean *quiet*! Now point to the eyes, people. The *eyes*, Richard McCulloch, not the ears! I said *eyes*, you little heathens. Now *sing*!"

Holy shit. I'd have sung the Russian national anthem if she'd ordered me to. Talk about an authority figure.

Mitchell never came back. And nobody ever understood why I alone loved Mrs. Hazel Schmuldt, the corpulent harridan who single-handedly hauled the accursed Leonard Talarczyk, scourge of the Sunday School, out of his folding chair and into the churchyard and carried him, kicking, swearing, and screaming, into Pastor's study, where the diminutive fellow was giving his sermon a last-minute skim.

The astonished pastor was speechless.

"Pastor," Hazel panted in her heavy-duty bray. "Do something with this hellion!"

"I can't punish him," Pastor stammered, appalled.

"Well, then, for God's sake, *bless* him!" Hazel thundered, and clumped out of the study. She was my kind of Sunday School leader, old Hazel Schmuldt. Seeing her up there like Mount Sinai gave me courage and helped me to forget Mr. Mitchell.

But Joanie had lied, and God knew it, and she didn't want to come along as my Sunday School guest anymore. She said it was because she was scared of Mrs. Schmuldt.

Another lie.

Chapter 8

I f you know anything about East McKeesport, Pennsylvania, or Gary, Indiana, or any other steel town in the USA, you've got an idea of what Dundalk was like in the winter. In February.

Words like dismal, dreary, forlorn—they can approximate the drab and dowdy way the sun tries to shine, but they can't quite touch the bleakness of those watery, blue-gray afternoons.

It doesn't snow often in Baldymore, and when it does, the flakes diddle desultorily down as if they were on their way somewhere else and hadn't meant to drop by at all, but since they were in the neighborhood, well . . .

If the snow decides to "lay," the schoolkids rush to the windows as one to exclaim, "Hey! It's layin'! Hey! Are we gettin' out?" And the teachers say silent prayers that we are, indeed, gettin' out, because everyone will be impossible until we do. A half inch of "the white stuff" (that's what the newscasters always call it) is enough to pitch the city into a full-scale panic. Having dashed home from school, kids drag sleds atop the pathetically inadequate accumulation, convinced that they're sledding, unaware that there are places in this land where people wade hip-deep through freezing drifts that grow higher by the hour.

In Dundalk, the occasional snow lies for perhaps seven-teen minutes in pristine loveliness. Then the Sparrows Point steel mill grime settles down onto it, and the mothers yell out the windows for the kids not to eat the snow—it's dirty. Dogs pee yellow holes into it. Cars splash mud and slush into it, pocking its prettiness with traffic acne. In a few short hours, its charm turns to pain in the rear. Everyone is sick of it.

That's how it was in February of 1955. A few pissy little snowflakes fell almost unnoticed and the dampness crawled into the houses, into the minds and spirits of the warm-blooded people who lived for summer, for boating and crab-bing and the Oriole games (in the upper deck, where one is closest to God, one step from heaven we cheered for Gus Triandos, Willie Miranda, and the wonderful George Kell), for slow-pitch softball and weekends at Ocean City. Restless men stomped out of their brick row homes and headed for bars that overlooked Bear Creek to grunt at each other and to stare into their ten-cent glasses of National. Brooders and bitchers started arguments about who had the loudest-mouthed aunts and uncles in Highlandtown, and who ought to go and live in "the Heights" (O'Donnell Heights, once known as Hillbilly Heights because of the West Virginians and other "foreign" immigrants there) if she can't keep house no better than that. On other days, in other, better, seasons, the Highlandtown folks were highly praised, and relatives were visited after church on Sunday mornings, and the glad conversation was punctuated by the uncapping of short, squat bottles of the local brew, National or Gunther's, or Arrow, or American.

But that February, it was too cold to drink plain beer, and the discontented tossed down boilermakers, the steel-workers' cocktail, and the wives picked on the kids, and it was too wet to play basketball out on the school courts. Pop and Teddy and Ma and I were sick of watching *Meet the Press,* and the only other things on TV worth watching were an old Hoot Gibson movie and *Super Circus.* Teddy made a huge production of ogling Mary Hartline and crawling up to the TV on his hands and knees, pretending to try to look up her skirt, that short little skating skirt she wore while she cavorted in her white midcalf boots in front of her band, waving a little baton. Ma yelled at him for acting like a horse's rear end, and he said, "Why don't you just say 'horse's ass' like everybody else?" Even I, the kid who got bilious from heat and who couldn't bear direct sunlight, prayed for the warmth of April, May, and June. Pop rattled his paper (a signal for us all to shut up); Ma searched for a word in her crossword dictionary; I sighed and recrossed my ankles (already my legs were too thick to cross at the knee), and stared dully at the toothy ringmaster, while Teddy went to the Fibber McGee closet and started rummaging.

"What are you hauling out?" Ma asked. When did her voice get so strident?

"Furble," Teddy said. He must have had his tongue entangled in the net of his lacrosse stick.

"Speak up, dammit," Pop said, and banged his pipe furiously on the side of his glass ashtray.

"Watch out with that," Ma said, glaring at him. "You'll break that ashtray first thing you know."

"I will not," Pop said, staring at her in unmasked defiance.

Something crashed in the closet.

"What the hell was that?" Pop said, jumping up.

"Goddam punch bowl set," Teddy said, backing out of the Black Hole of Calcutta (his own name for the catchall closet) with his football.

"Your language is a sin," Ma said.

"Lay off, will you?" Teddy said.

"Leave him alone," I said.

"Mind your own business," Pop said to me.

"Leave her alone," Teddy said to Pop.

"Everybody shut up," Ma bellowed.

Teddy opened his mouth, shut it again, zipped up his black corduroy jacket with the zebra panel across the shoulders and his name in script diagonally emblazoned across the back, yanked a knitted cap down over his ears, tucked the football under his arm, and said directly to *me,* "I'm going over Garver's house awhile. See ya later."

Pop couldn't resist making a final dig. *"Over* Garver's house? What—on a broomstick? You mean over *to* Garver's house, don't you, son?"

Teddy looked into my face. "I'm going over Garver's, like I said."

I basked in it. "Right, Ted," I said, glad to be an accomplice to his rebellion, taking vicarious pride in his ability to walk out on this fiasco.

"Watch that TV or turn it off," Pop growled at me, reseating himself in his new orange chair, a piece that sat on blond wood legs and inclined slightly backward. He and Ma had blown many bucks that fall just before Christmas, buying themselves the first new furniture they'd ever owned. Everything else had come from one relative or another over the years, and they'd figured it was time, after all, to toss out the dated oak and dark walnut junk for this great new blond stuff with the wrought-iron accents and the metallic threads woven into the fabrics.

Pop called out to Smokey, the tall, elderly workman, one Saturday morning, and asked if he wanted to bring his truck around and pick up some nice furniture to take home or to give to his relations. "Sho thing, Mr. Herm," Smokey had said, showing his big gold teeth in a grateful grin, nodding his giant head in cheerful anticipation. That made Pop's day, doing a kindly act for the colored folks. "They work hard for such a little living," he always said, "and they deserve some rewards, too." So he gave to them (from his goodness, and with every ounce of his integrity and sincerity intact) his best leftovers in a spirit of benign generosity that nobody could have mistaken for malicious condescension. He would have been cruelly shocked and profoundly hurt if he had known how thoroughly his offerings had been resented and despised by those he'd meant to honor.

The New Furniture (it was referred to as the New Furniture for at least six years thereafter) arrived and was celebrated by friends, neighbors, and acquaintances, who gawked as each carton entered the house, and who peeked unashamedly through our front windows as each piece was solemnly uncovered and put into place.

"Great gawd awmighty," Paul Rosling's father cried in jubilation. "They even got new ashtrays, Lena! Lookit." And sure enough, Pop had picked out a handsome stand ashtray that stood on four wrought-iron legs and a gorgeous square black one for the glass-topped coffee table, also blond. The neighbors had taken the hint from us, Pop exulted at the dinner table a few days later, and before long cartons were arriving at many of the apartments in our section. We kids glommed onto those cartons and used them for rolling each other around. You weren't having any fun unless you got sick and staggered around like a sot, gagging. That was a pretty good fall, all things considered.

So Pop was banging his pipe on the glass ashtray in his new stand, and Ma was glaring at him, at me, and at her puzzle, affectionately known as The Puz, that February day. "Turn that TV down," she said to me. "You'll go deaf the first thing you know."

"I will not," I said, not moving.

"Do what your mother says!" Pop roared. I moved. Rebellion was one thing; out and out idiocy another.

Ma got up and started puttering around in the teeny kitchen making supper. On Sundays we just threw something together at about six or seven in the evening, because dinner was so late and nobody ever felt like eating much. A couple of sandwiches and a little Campbell's alphabet soup and five or six cookies were usually all I could stuff down, and the grown-ups ate cheese and crackers, maybe a little herring in wine sauce on saltines, nothing big. Best of all was leftover beef or pork sliced thin and put on thick slices of Ma's bread spread with butter. I used to say profuse prayers of thanks over those sandwiches.

Crabbiness had disintegrated into a rather harmless and quiet boredom. Ma shuffled around in the kitchen and Pop shuffled into it to see what Ma was up to, and I shuffled out to join them in my beat-up red loafers, my flannel-lined dungarees rolled up around the knees, sniffing the air to see if I could smell beef and butter. We all were just sort of standing around out there when we first heard stirrings of commotion, muffled sounds through the window glass signaling something amiss in the approaching darkness.

"What the hell?" Pop said, and made for the back door.

The trouble was at Joanie's. There was a policeman there, a young guy in a navy blue uniform standing with his legs apart on Joanie's back stoop, swinging his nightstick in his left hand and slapping it against the palm of his right. Pop stood solid, blocking the doorway so I couldn't see, so I hustled upstairs and cranked open my bedroom window to hear better. I was looking down now, at a slant, and I saw Joanie without her coat, Joanie shivering in front of her mother, standing in her own doorway in the cold and damp of February, wearing something silly and white while the policeman talked heatedly to Mrs. Sheeley, who stood like a rock and told the officer without shouting that he was mistaken and that there was no trouble.

"It's you makin' the mistake, ma'am," the officer said doggedly, slapping his stick forcefully into his open palm. "I know what the girl told me, and I'm not leavin' until I hear some truth outta you people."

"She's just made a mistake," Joanie's mother said in her slow, even way, the same way she always told Joanie, "Go outside now, or I'll beat you, girl," without the slightest element of threat behind it.

"Sorry, ma'am," the officer said. "I know what I heard."

He reached for Joanie, who had been simply standing and staring and looking at nobody. She went to him obediently,

94

and he knelt down and looked into her face. "Ain't you cold, darlin'?" he said, his voice so loving, so concerned. I wondered if he could possibly be her uncle, her brother or cousin, else how could he speak so tenderly to her, a child he didn't know? "Let's get a coat on you," he said, and stood up and said loudly to Joanie's mother, as if she were hard of hearing, or feebleminded, "Let's at least get a coat on her, huh?"

He tried to get inside the house, but Joanie's mother just stood there and wouldn't let him pass. "You can't come in here," she said. "We're gonna eat supper now."

Exasperated, the officer got loud. "I'm gonna have to call in on this, now," he threatened. "I got to, now."

Dumbly, Joanie and her mother stood, and the shaking did not stop. I could see her shaking from all that distance away.

My father, in his smooth and graceful way, appeared at Joanie's stoop and spoke to the officer, his voice soothing, dark and sweet like hot molasses on pancakes. "Is there some problem here, officer?" he asked in his Sunday voice. "Maybe I can be of some help. I'm Herman Schmidt, Mrs. Sheeley's friend and neighbor. This young lady and my daughter are best friends."

The young officer looked uncomfortable, scratched the back of his neck, took off his cap, smoothed his shiny hair gleaming in the light from Joanie's kitchen, put his cap back on, looked down at the ground, then spoke to Pop without really looking at him directly.

"Thanks, Mr., ah, Schmidt, but, ah, this is a matter I'd like to settle with the Sheeleys in private, please."

Mrs. Sheeley sprang suddenly to life, moving faster than I'd ever seen her move, coming close to Pop's side, grabbing his arm in her two reddened hands, clinging for dear life.

"No!" she cried. "Let Herman stay. Herman can help me, can't you, Herm?"

Pop was enlarged by the implied flattery. He stood taller. "Of course, Ada Faye," he said generously, delighted to have been called upon to assist. "Now, what can I do for you?"

"Well, it's a little touchy, Mr. Schmidt," the officer said. "See, me and my partner—he's out in the car—come across Joanie here about a half hour ago, walkin' without her coat on, and no dress, out in the park, see? Half frozen, ya know? We ask her where she lives, and she points this way, and we ask her the number and she can't talk. She just keeps chatterin' like she's got the chills and fever, ya know? So me and Hurlbut, we figure we'll walk her around here a minute till she finds her door, thinkin', ya know, she might be mental, or whatever, and she brings us here."

The air was so still that I could hear them all breathing, it seemed, from across the courtyard.

"What happened, Joanie?" Pop whispered. "Did something happen? Why were you out without your coat on?"

Joanie did not speak. She moved closer to the policeman, farther away from her mother, whose eyes never left Joanie for an instant.

"It ain't nothin' unusual in that," Ada Faye Sheeley said, still looking right at Joanie. "Any kid'll go out half undressed if you ain't watchin' every minute. And I was at work. I just got home."

"Not our Joanie," Pop said warmly. "She's got sense, don't you, Joanie?"

The officer was getting impatient. "Look, sir," he said, his voice taking on a tougher tone, "I think there's something you oughta know. This child isn't wearin' no underwear, you get it? This child is out in the cold weather wearin' no coat, no dress, no underwear. You understand?"

Pop did not understand. It was not in his realm of experience, a perception of that magnitude. Children ate, slept, did their homework, said amusing things, got spanked for acting up, gave hugs and kisses, learned multiplication tables, took baths, went to Sunday School, and wore their underwear. Running out into the night without suitable clothing and minus underwear simply did not register with him. He was at a loss, diminished. I saw him falter, look quickly at Mrs. Shee-ley, clear his throat.

"To be frank with ya, Mr. Schmidt, we think the girl's been, ah, molested."

Pop looked as if he'd been shot. He looked away from Joanie, unable to be that close to such a thing, and shuddered. I could see his body trying to shake off the ugliness with a violent spasm. Then he faced the officer once more.

"What makes you think that?" he asked. I started to quiver, terrified that I wouldn't hear, terrified that I would.

"Look," the officer said, and drew Joanie into the light. She let herself be handled, examined without protest, as the two men fingered her cotton slip, looked at a stain there, at a dark spot on her skin, knelt down in front of her to look her in the face. "Joanie?" Pop said, so softly I could barely hear him. "What happened, Angel-pie?"

"He got me," Joanie said simply. "This time he got me."

"Who?" Pop said too loudly. "That guy? That guy from the playground? Who, Joanie?"

Joanie licked her lips, looked up at her mother, whose face was dissolving into a cloudburst of agony, looked back at Pop.

"Nobody," she said. "I don't know."

"You can tell us, doll baby," the policeman said. "We'll catch him for you, sweetheart."

Joanie twisted her fingers, put one in her mouth the way she'd done when she was four, when I'd first known her a thousand years ago.

"You must tell us," Pop said. The shock was wearing off, and even from my distance, I could see he had blood in his eye. "You must tell us so that we can catch him and see to it that he can't hurt any other little girls, right, sweetie pie?"

By this time, some other inhabitants of the Freedom Gardens Apartments were gathering, having noticed the police car parked out on the front street, nosy as Pinocchio. They were edging closer, listening with all their ears. Joanie didn't see them.

"Who?" Pop demanded urgently, loudly.

Joanie looked up, stared dreamily for the first time at the gathering crowd, and pointed. "Him," she said clearly. "It's him."

She was pointing to Teddy.

Everybody turned to gape at him, the newly arrived, gawky, leggy, football-carrying character with his knitted cap pulled down nearly to his eyes. Teddy looked puzzled, wondering what all the hoopla was about.

"It's *him*!" Joanie yelled now, her tone rising to a screech, a banshee's spleen-splitting wail. "He did it to me! He did it to me!"

Pop rose from his crouch and surveyed the crowd. When his eye fell on the startled Teddy, my father's face went blank, bewildered.

"What the hell's going on here?" Teddy asked as the crowd parted on all sides, each person determined not to be contaminated by his accidental touch. In just a few seconds, Teddy had become a pariah, and he didn't know why.

"Son?" Pop asked softly.

"What?" Teddy demanded. "I just got here. I don't even know what's going on."

"This young lady says you, ah, put your hands on her, sir," the officer said politely. "She says, ah, that you, ah, molested her. Is this true?"

Teddy's answer was a panicky half-sob. "Me? Hurt Joanie? You're nuts. Never. Not in a million years. She's just like a kid sister to me."

"Where were you earlier this evening, son?" the officer, not much older than Teddy, asked in a new tone, a patronizing drawl he must have learned from one of the senior officers.

"At Clifford Garver's house. Honest. You can ask his mother."

"We will," the cop said, getting tougher every second

"And I just left. Just now!" Teddy sounded frantic.

"Right," the policeman said. "So then let's just go on down to the station and get this thing straightened out. Coming, sir?" he asked Pop, who rapidly came to attention. "Coming?" he asked Teddy, who wiped his hands on his pantsleg and said nothing.

"NO!" I shrieked from my window. *"NONONONO!"*

I galloped down the stairs and raced out the back door in a flash. My body collided with Teddy's and nearly knocked him down. "She's lying," I sobbed. "She lies all the time. She lied about that man on the playground, remember, Pop? She lies, she lies, she *lies*!" Teddy was holding me tight against him, squeezing me with all his might, his long fingers digging into my shoulders. I felt crushed and breathless. The officer was looking first at Joanie, then at Teddy, then at Pop, and then at the thrashing, weeping moose of a girl who was spoiling his neat collar. Joanie just stood there shaking. I couldn't stand the sight of her. I went for her.

"Liar!" I screamed into her face. "Dirty, stinkin *liar*!" I hit her so hard that my fingers felt the shock up to the elbow.

Ada Faye Sheeley stepped forward and yanked Joanie out of my way. I advanced on the both of them while Pop pulled ineffectually at the back of my flannel shirt. "You don't know how much she lies," I hurled at Ada Faye, whose face was bloodless and gaunt.

I was running out of accusations. Somebody would have to step in soon and stop all this, I thought in a whirl, because there was nowhere else for us all to go. I stood with my fists clenched, ready for action, ready to tear apart with my bare hands anybody who said another word against my brother, who was strangely silent.

The upstairs window above us opened wide, and Mr. Sheeley, Albert, stood with the light at his back. I hadn't known he was so skinny, so bony. He was wearing pants and a belt, but no shirt, and his body seemed to have no color, no blood or bone. He looked like a spirit.

"Have mercy upon me," he roared into the darkness.

"God have mercy upon my soul," he roared again. Then he threw back his shaggy head and howled like a mad thing, and then the howl was a keening and a throbbing groan, and then he held a gun up to his face and was deadly quiet for a second.

Then he blew his face away.

The force of the shot threw him backward into the closet behind him, and his body splintered the thin wooden door as it crashed into the shoe boxes and the clothing on the hangers.

Mr. and Mrs. Rosling were the first to react. "Oh, my Gawd," Mrs. Rosling said, sagging against her husband. "Oh, my great good Gawd in heaven, he's killed hisself."

"Albert?" Mrs. Sheeley called quietly, looking at the place where Mr. Sheeley had been standing just seconds before. "Albert? Are you all right?"

Pop stepped close beside her and caught her as her knees buckled and she fell straight down, sitting on the toes of Pop's shoes. Joanie stood still, her eyes and mouth wide open, and I stood facing her. The light from her kitchen made a halo around her fair head, and she stood straight, no longer shaking. I looked away, waiting for somebody to turn off this program, to change the channel. Teddy took my arm.

The young officer started yelling. "Hurlbut! Hey, Hurlbut! Get out in the back here. Come on, man. Hurry it up!" He opened Joanie's back door and strode inside, looking scared and pale. "Somebody call a ambulance," he said. Even I knew we didn't need one.

"It was him," Joanie's mother cried into Pop's shoulder, because he'd picked her up like a rag doll and was holding up her sagging body with his thick arms. "He done it to her. I know he done it. He tried before a couple times, but this time he really done it. He didn't want to do it, Herm, but he couldn't help hisself. He was sick, from the war, you know, sick in his head, and he done it. God help us."

Hers was like no crying I'd ever heard, a rasping, "Aahhhh my God, my God," that hurt my ears so badly that I thought

I'd come to pieces. From nowhere, Ma came and stood by me, and it was better with her on one side and Teddy on the other.

Joanie stood like a carved figure, light as balsa wood, ready to be blown over by the night wind, which was picking up. I had both my arms around Teddy's slim body now, my head facing her, not wanting to look at her, but having to. "I'm sorry, Joanie," I said over and over.

But Joanie was not listening to me. She was dreaming, it seemed, on a cloud of white fluff far away from us. A half-smile turned her small mouth up at the corners, and her gaze into the darkness was steady. Pop was busy with Mrs. Sheeley, hanging onto her, calling for Ma to help him. Teddy started to tremble and to babble to me all of a sudden about how scared he'd been and how awful this was. The Roslings held onto each other and said, "My Gawd," again and again, and Hurlbut the cop galloped into the kitchen after his partner, barking orders at everyone.

"Holy shit," we heard him croak from the open window. "Jesus. We gotta get the medical examiner over here. Christ Amighty, what a holy mess."

It was the worst night of my life. The worst, the longest, the scariest. We brought Joanie home to stay at our house while Pop, who kept pulling out his handkerchief to mop his sweaty face and to wipe his wet eyes, stayed with Ada Faye. They couldn't come to any decisions about whether to have a funeral, or whether Joanie should see a doctor. Mrs. Sheeley kept up a steady stream of thin-voiced chatter, asking countless questions, looking up at the ceiling or down into her open palms. She was as skinny as he had been, I thought. She needed some food. She needed something to fill her up.

Joanie slept. She fell asleep on the way across the grass to our place, and she stayed asleep all that night. I did not talk to her at all.

In the end they decided to have a private funeral for the family only. We could come if we wanted to. I wanted to, but Ma and Pop said no, it wasn't appropriate. I didn't know what that meant. I only wanted to be there to make sure Joanie was all right. But they said no, and Teddy said not to argue. So on that Tuesday I went to school for the second straight day without Joanie to walk with.

Something awful had happened to Joanie Sheeley, something so horrible that her father had shot his head off to be forgiven for it. He had done it to her more than once, it seemed, maybe lots times. My perception of the crime was vague, but filled with loathing and misery.

Mr. and Mrs. Rosling, bless them, did not tell Paul; and Ted did not tell Garver; and I, being the only character in the whole bloody scene who did not understand the script, wandered alone in the murky forest of unexplained events, of obscure motivations, and pondered all of it in my heart, and wished for some sort of enlightenment that would explain why Joanie Sheeley never came back from wherever it was they'd sent her.

Mrs. Sheeley stayed for a while, but Joanie went away to be with some relatives somewhere, Ma told me gently when I kept asking for her, month after month.

But I knew why Joanie stayed away.

I had called her a liar. I'd slapped her and blamed her right out in front of everybody, even the police. Whatever had happened, it wasn't her fault, but I had struck out at her in front of the world. No wonder she didn't ever want to talk to me or see me again.

There was no undoing it. She would never be back.

Chapter 9

I sang songs from *My Fair Lady* out loud as I walked down the street where he lived. Jack Price. Jack's street. March 1956.

I was in real love at long last. He sat across from me in our group of six, three facing three, in Mr. Paxton's classroom, and as I watched him work so diligently at his spelling, his social studies (The Counties of Maryland), and his arithmetic with his sweet pointed tongue between his two prominent front teeth, I knew I was in love.

He was short. Shorter, of course, than I, because in the sixth grade I was still a head taller than everyone, fifty pounds heavier, and had grown little buds of breasts despite all my efforts to suppress them. I was the only kid in the whole sixth grade, all five classes, who needed to wear a bra, but this unhappy fact so mortified me that I insisted upon wearing an undershirt over it in the vain and erroneous belief that nobody would notice.

Ha. Everywhere I went, prying little eyes would see the bra through my tight dresses (I was still wearing those hideous Chubette creations that pulled tightly across the front and had sashes sewn into the side seams), and picky little fingers, male and female, would snap it. The boys called me "Boobs" loud enough behind my back so that I'd be sure to hear them, but never loud enough so that I could identify the heckler and make sawdust of him (I was still called "Moose" to my face).

It was The Year of the Movie. All the girls carried home carefully concealed permission slips to see The Movie. The mothers had to sign and give permission for their daughters to witness the miracle of menstruation (*You're a Young Lady Now*) and conception (the cartoonist's conception of conception, that is), minus all that disgusting gutter corruption that was sure to infect us if we didn't hurry and see this interesting, wholesome, and informative film designed for the preadolescent mentality.

Cripes, what a joke. We'd known for years just from hanging out in the ladies' room at the Strand what was up, so to speak. And the girls from the YMCA's senior swim team talked so loudly in the showers and locker room that you couldn't help learning a thing or two. I will admit that certain things puzzled me, like why you could stand up or sit to do some things but had to lie down to accomplish certain other calisthenic acts of love. The film didn't help too much with problems of that nature. Still, it was entertaining. The best part of it was when Mr. Paxton told us it was perfectly all right (in fact, he *encouraged* us *sincerely*) to ask any questions we might have. And to protect us from embarrassment, we could write them down and put them into the question box after the film.

The opportunity was irresistible. I wrote my question—no, I *printed* it so that he couldn't identify the handwriting, and I noticed that everyone else was printing, too—and deposited it in the box. Everybody looked so expectant, so eager, that Mr. Paxton and Mrs. Womble, another sixth-grade teacher who was "sharing" our movie time, fairly oozed satisfaction.

Mrs. Womble opened the first folded paper, read it to herself, then flushed, handed it to Mr. Paxton, and sat down, leaving him standing there center stage in front of approximately forty preteen girls who hung on his every word.

"Ah, this is a tough one," he said, his face looking suddenly puffy and pink. "Let's see—ah—I may as well just read it off the paper the way it's written. And it's, ah, actually a very *good* question, really, and one that can be easily answered with no trouble at all, and, ah, I'll just read it to you here off the paper—"

The tittering had begun even before he got to finish this lame introduction. I couldn't help myself. I snickered out loud and gave a little snort, a characteristic of my laugh that I tried desperately to modify, without success. Snortsnort. Everybody burst into giggles, and Mr. Paxton got flustered.

"I thought we'd agreed, young ladies, that there would be absolutely no giggling today. I thought we said we were going to act like adults so that we could discuss adult topics in an adult manner."

The chittering hubbub subsided as we all smoothed our crinolines down and wiggled our feet inside our ballet slippers and tried not to look at each other.

"Now, can we get on with the questions, please?" he said to Mrs. Womble. "Next question, please."

"Hey, Mr. Paxton, you never answered the first one yet," Darlene Brewster complained. You could always count on Darlene Brewster's nasal whining to set Paxton off. He spoke to her through his teeth. "Hay is for horses, Darlene," he said.

"Yeah, but what about that question?" Darlene persisted. I never knew anybody who could act as stubbornly dumb as Darlene. The truth was, she was as sharp as her nose and her elbows and her knees, mentally. She stared Paxton down.

"Oh, well, of course. I just forgot about it. I'll get right to it just as soon as we do this one Mrs. Womble is holding in her hand here."

"Aw, come on, come on," we all began to yell. You could do that to him. He got rattled when all the girls ganged up on him at once. He didn't know how to handle girls. I don't think he was married.

He spread open the paper, held it in both hands, reread

it, took a deep breath, and said, "The question, as written here, asks, 'How long is the average penis?'"

We all stared, waiting, waiting. He looked at the ceiling high above him, pondered it, then said, "Oh, probably six inches, wouldn't you say, Mrs. Womble?"

Mrs. Womble studied the gradebook on her lap as if it were the Rosetta stone. "That sounds all right to me, Mr. Paxton," she said quietly. Very quietly.

Then Brewster stood up and held out the index fingers of both hands, about sixteen inches apart. "Like this, Mr. Paxton?" she whined.

"Uh, no, Darlene, probably more like, ah, this." Paxton was stuttering, holding his two fingers perhaps six inches apart.

"Doesn't look like much to me," Brewster said, kind of sad and disappointed.

"Well, maybe not," Mr. Paxton said, his voice small. Mrs. Womble's shoulders started to shake. She put her teeth over her bottom lip and looked hard at the book in her lap.

"Maybe," she said, squeaking rather badly, still not looking up, "we ought to get to another question."

Paxton declared that a capital idea and drew again. I had folded my question into a triangle, and he had zeroed in on it as I'd thought he would. He read it, handed it to Mrs. Womble, got it back from her. Mrs. Womble wasn't herself at all. Usually she was on the loud side, wise to all our moves, anticipating our plots, crafty. Today she seemed helpless, glued to the chair, her squeaks and snickers not only audible but infectious. I had never liked her more; before, she'd been only another class's teacher, a woman who sometimes watched over us with her hawklike vision when Mr. Paxton had to go to the nurse's office with a migraine or out to the store for some Anacin. Today I seemed to be seeing her for the first time—a woman, an ally, somebody to help us girls get the best of Paxton. I shifted and wriggled in my metal folding chair (narrower than my rear) as Paxton again held the question in his trembling hands.

"So," he said at last. "A young lady wants to know if having sex makes you, ah, bowlegged. Well, then, Mrs. Womble, do you have any thoughts on that?"

"Eeek," Mrs. Womble said, putting her legs together as tightly as she could. "Aak," she said. She reached down for her purse, opened it, pulled out a tissue and stuffed it into her eyes, nose, and mouth. Her whole body shook.

"Mrs. Stryker's bowlegged as sin," Brewster said through her long, pointed nose. Mrs. Womble opened up her mouth and roared, "Hawhawhaw," then restuffed the aperture with the wadded tissues. Mrs. Stryker was our vice-principal, a mustached chunk of a woman with comically bowed legs that nevertheless carried her far and fast when mischief was afoot. "Oh—oh, my God," Mrs. Womble wheezed through the tissues.

"Mrs. Womble, *please,*" Mr. Paxton said in a tight, low voice. "Darlene, your smart-alecky comments are not appreciated."

"That wasn't no comment," Brewster commented. "I was just sayin' that Mrs. Stryker's bowlegged. It's a fact, ya know?"

"Never mind," Paxton said. "The answer to the question is, ah, well, that it has never been shown that having sexual intercourse causes bowleggedness in females. To my knowledge, that is."

Mrs. Womble stumbled out of her chair, staggered blindly to the end of the stage, took the steps down two at a time, and headed for the women's faculty lounge, whooping and snorting. Mr. Paxton looked disgusted.

"It's a darn shame we don't have time for all the questions, young ladies," he said, looking at his watch. "It would be nice if we could answer each one individually, but since Mrs. Womble got sick and had to leave, I'm afraid we'll just have to call it a day, okay?"

We all glared at him in silence. Then Brewster spoke up.

"We got another fifteen minutes," she said, pointing to the large clock in the back of the auditorium.

"That's not working properly," Paxton lied, sweating now.

"Six inches," Patty McBride said just loud enough for our row to hear. Teeheeheehee. Mr. Paxton looked as if he'd been shot.

"What?" he asked sharply. "What was that?"

"Nothing," somebody said.

"Nothin' much, anyway," Brewster said, and another wave of giggling overtook us, undulating through the crowd like a wheatfield in the wind. Within seconds, fifty girls were repeating, "Six inches," and putting their index fingers up to indicate various lengths from two inches to two feet, hooting and screeching as if Red Buttons himself had come to entertain. Mr. Paxton yelled for us to shape up if we wanted recess tomorrow, then banged his hands together for our attention, stomped both his feet for a few seconds, and then finally said, "Dammit!" That brought the house down.

We were near enough to Dutch Hallman's office for him to hear the commotion, and within seconds he was among us, standing, actually, behind us and facing the panicky Paxton with his thickly muscled arms folded across his football coach's barrely chest.

Paxton's face went white, and we knew better than to continue the orgy in front of Hallman, so after a moment there was relative silence.

"Is there a problem here?" Hallman asked.

"Uh, no, sir," Paxton said hurriedly, making a great to-do out of rewinding the film and gathering together his notes. "We were, uh, just telling each other some little jokes to pass the time, and, uh—"

"Where's Mrs. Womble?" Hallman cut in. "Isn't she supposed to be assisting you today?"

"She went to the—that is, she had to leave the room for a minute."

"I see," Hallman said darkly. Then he left. His presence among us was enough to extinguish the spirit of fiendish glee. For a second or two I almost felt sorry for the wasp-waisted Paxton. His tie was awry, part of it flung over his shoulder. One of his socks was wishy-washy around the top and had piddled down over his brown shoe. He often wore his socks at half-mast, and I recall thinking it was too bad he didn't have a wife to do something about his clothes.

Brewster said, "I gotta pee," and that finished us off. A roar went up among us, and although Brewster got on my nerves and strained my patience much of the time, I had to give it to her—her timing was perfection. She knew exactly when to deliver a line. In the seventh grade she transferred to a school on the other side of town and I reclaimed some of the reputation I'd once won as class smartass, but Darlene had one great advantage over me: Nothing was sacred. Nothing. She'd say anything to anyone, just to get her laugh. I was somewhat more reticent, willing to wait for an opening, to temper my jokes with kindness. Darlene was ruthless, broad, a Roman. My own comedy ran more along "drawing room" lines.

I thought about the movie on the way home. For over a year I'd had my nifty equipment ready—the gauzy napkins, the belt, the sanitary panties, the deodorant powder, the Midol. Actually, that term "sanitary napkins" always amused me. I had the urge to deposit a dime in the dispenser in the girls' lav and tie one around my neck, pretending not to know that they didn't really mean "napkin." But I thought better of it. I had the idea I'd get caught, and it wasn't the kind of joke that adults would appreciate. Something told me that its crassness would outweigh its funniness. Still, I'd save it as a sure ace in the hole in case Darlene gained too much ground on me.

When would it start, this dreaded Period? I figured it would be in some crowded place on a day when I was wearing my pale yellow cotton gathered skirt, when I didn't have any money with me to buy a napkin, and I'd have to ask some stranger, some man, probably, for a dime. And what if Pop found out? Or Teddy? To have them know anything as secret and personal as *that* would be unbearable. How did Ma keep Pop from finding out about hers? How could you hide it? If Ma told Pop about me, I'd run away. It was not the kind of thing that men or boys should ever be allowed to know.

I wondered if Jack Price knew I was almost a woman. He couldn't help but know about the boobs. They were right *there* and wouldn't stay smashed down no matter what I did to them. But did he know about secret blood? What would he think if he knew that any day now I was going to start my Period? The very thought of Jackie's discovering anything so terrible about me made my stomach churn. I pulled a Tasty-Kake out of my pocket and carefully unwrapped it. My favorite. Butterscotch Krimpets, three in the package. I stuffed one into my mouth whole and waited for it to dissolve. The other two I would bite, chew, and swallow normally, but when there were three in the package, it was fun to stuff one and savor the others. You could have it both ways, then.

Jackie Price came out of his house that minute with Joey Santino, a kid we called Tex because he'd been out west with his father when his parents had separated. Incredible. A whole year out west. His mother eventually gained custody of him in court, and now he was back. All he seemed to like about Dundalk was that we called him Tex instead of Joey.

Santino (we were into last names that year) was taller than Price, but both were pretty skinny (Ma always used to say, "Aren't there any *strong* kids in that school?"). Price had no father at home either, and that was still a sort of a novelty among us, so the two of them hung out together as a natural result of their situations.

I liked the way Santino looked, but Price was still my

man. There was something about him—his smallness, maybe—that made me think he needed bolstering and affection, a girl who could liven up his days a little. All he did for fun, it seemed, was kick a football and practice the trombone. And he liked me, too. I know he did, because he told me I could kick the stuffing out of a football, and I know for a fact that he hardly ever complimented anybody on anything because he was too shy.

Santino had called me a smartass one time, and I didn't talk to him much. I could probably have wiped up the playground with him, but I was beyond wanting to. The real source of his animosity toward me, I think, was that I was the best reader and speller in the school. His abilities were average, and he couldn't seem to bear being less than king of the hill, not after having lived on a ranch where his daddy was a bona fide cowboy. I would just as soon have been his friend, but Santino didn't appreciate my jokes; and since he couldn't think of any better ones, he stayed away from me and I from him.

Price and Santino were talking so earnestly that they didn't see me, so I started to sing "Muskrat Ramble" (the McGuire Sisters' version, of course) rather overenthusiastically as I walked. I had already put the other TastyKakes back into my pocket because I didn't like people to see me eating and always took great satisfaction in hearing people say, "I can't understand why you're so heavy. You never eat anything." I walked up to where Santino and Price were standing, waiting to cross the street to the school field with the heavy afternoon traffic of The Point's (Sparrows Point's) seven-to-three and three-to-eleven shifts whizzing by on Liberty Parkway on their way to and from the steel mill and shipyard.

"Whatcha doin'?" I said. Always the brilliant conversationalist.

"Nothin'." Price was hardly looking at me.

"You gonna play some football?" I asked cheerfully. "I can come along and kick a few. I got an hour before suppertime."

"Naa," Price said, looking at the dirt and stones around the base of the lightpost. "Me and Santino are gonna go meet somebody else on the other side of the playground."

I looked at Price in disbelief. He'd always been glad enough of my company before Santino came back.

"We're just gonna chuck it around a little bit," he said lamely.

"I got time to chuck a few," I said, unwilling to take the hint.

"Forget it," Santino said. "Me and Price are playing with some guys."

"What guys?" I said. I knew I was making it hard for Price, but suddenly I wanted it to be hard for him.

"What's it to ya?" Santino said, wiping his nose on the sleeve of his sweat-shirt jacket. He emphasized the "to" in the phrase, as any Dundalk kid would have done. Some effin' cowboy, I thought.

Price intervened. "Come on, Beeb," he pleaded. "Go on home. Me and Santino got to go now. Honest."

"You're acting like a creep, Price," I said evenly.

"Go to hell," Price said, mad at me now. But I ignored Santino's grin and snicker, and as I looked a hole through Price, I saw the silent pleading in his round gray-green eyes. "Go on, now, Beeb," he said, less loudly now, less harshly. "We gotta hit the trail."

Santino lounged against the lightpost at a smartass angle. I could have kicked his feet out from under him and beat the living crap out of him in a matter of seconds, and he knew it; but I'd grown tired of thinking as a child, speaking as a child, understanding as a child, and was ready to look through a different glass now. I didn't want to be Moose anymore. I shrugged my shoulders and turned away.

"Getcha later," I said, giving it as a gift to Price, despite the chalky lump in my throat, the burning bricks on my chest. He didn't know any better and was doing the best he could.

"Not if we can help it, Two-ton," Santino said.

I hesitated for a second, waiting for Price to tell him to shut his stupid trap, but Price said nothing. Without turning to give Santino the satisfaction of watching me redden, I sauntered away down to my own corner and did not look back. It was the first time I'd lost one man to another. In a long and spotty career as friend, woman, and lover, it would not be the last.

I toyed for a delicious moment with the idea of having Teddy kick Santino's ass up Liberty Parkway to Dundalk Avenue but decided against it. Any fool can fight, after all, but a woman (well, *almost*) will wait for the next fish to come leaping up out of the water. Hell with 'em, I thought, as I walked home. It all sucked, this business of wanting people to be close and then losing them, and of loving people who deserted you so easily, and with so little conscience. Price had not defended me. That was the worst.

Best have a little sandwich before supper. Some milk, too. And those other two TastyKakes.

Chapter 10

Twelve years old and tender-breasted, I officially became a Young Lady that spring and was properly harnessed into more heavy-duty bras, nylon stockings with garter belt, and Kotex or Modess (because . . .) once a dreary month. There was no way out of it, and that galled me until my teeth grated together. It seemed one should have a *choice*—to curve and to harness oneself and to bleed, or not to, according to one's preferences. My mother laughed when I said that. "You don't have anything to do with it," she said, holding her hand over her mouth in real amusement.

"I don't like all this crap on me," I said. "It rubs my skin and it itches and it makes me sweat. It smells, too," I added, thinking that it might help. It didn't.

"Then use deodorant," Ma said. I couldn't believe it. Patty McBride's mother wouldn't let her use deodorant. Patty's mother said that if a girl kept herself well showered and talcum-powdered, she didn't need deodorant. I sat next to Patty in school, and I could have told her mother a thing or two about young girls. We smelled suddenly like *women*. I didn't like that, either.

We spent hours discussing sexual matters. Most of us weren't too gung-ho about finding out about these things in person, though. It all seemed kind of complicated and sticky.

Literally. The swim team girls let a few unsavory facts slip in the shower room that curled our sixth-grade toes . . . like about tongues that poked into mouths and breasts being squeezed (mine were still very tender, and the thought of having them squeezed made me feel faint), and of hands that were made to perform unspeakable acts upon the male organ. The male organ. No, thank you. I'd rather sit that out. The whole thing held little more than clinical interest for me. I'd be satisfied to marry a man who would be understanding, and who would demand no more than hugging and kissing and handholding, all of which seemed just dandy to me.

It didn't matter, though. Nobody was interested in any of us anyway. The boys our age were trading baseball cards and playing with yo-yos. The older boys were chasing after the girls in their own classes, who were ignoring them and chasing after older boys who weren't looking at them. It all seemed safe for a while.

Soon another year came to an end, and I knew I'd never head out across the field to Dundalk Elementary School again, and I felt so awfully old, as if I'd come a long, hard way. Six years of my life, I thought one hot afternoon as I scuffed across the playground to our house. Six years. Half my life I'd spent in that school. Next year it would be the bus to North Point at the Annex down in Sparrows Point. There were so many of us kids that they hadn't built the schools big enough or fast enough to accommodate us all. We were stuffed into every nook and cranny they could find. We'd pile onto buses and go across Bear Creek to Sparrows Point, in the middle of the thickest soot and grime in town, and spend three years getting ready to be high school kids. I was so alarmed at the thought of leaving elementary school that I wanted to spend the summer hanging around the house, looking at the school from my window, sighing.

But instead, we went on our yearly vacation, and my feelings were put away with the winter clothes.

Not being real Baltimoreans, we didn't take the traditional

Balmer vacations: The Ayshin (Ocean City), Wahlwood (Wildwood, New Jersey), or the Paykenaos (the Poconos). Not the Schmidts. We were different, embarking on noble forays each summer into Pioneer Land—back to Wisconsin (West Consin). Every year without fail we packed up the car and headed for home. The very word "home" choked up my Pop so badly that he always made a hurried trip to the bathroom so that we couldn't see him mist over like the bathroom mirror when Teddy took one of his long showers. My father, an ardent fan of Edgar Guest and Joyce Kilmer, wrote long letters home every two weeks and sat in a pipe-smoke haze dreaming of the lilac bushes in his mother's garden; of the tiger lilies in the beds he'd dug for her himself; of the painting and the pruning he'd do for his parents, regarding the sweat and the muscle aches as his reward for the grueling two-day drive.

The earliest trips we took there were in the days before the turnpikes were constructed, when our ancient, block-long Packard labored under the most adverse conditions imaginable to carry us home. (Originally it was wartime black, until Pop couldn't resist an Earl Scheib special for twenty-nine ninety-five, and allowed some Philistines to paint our yacht on wheels dayglow aqua—people stood aghast on street corners as we passed, too stunned to point; the neighbors guffawed openly; but Pop was pleased with it, he said).

Pop's endurance was sorely tried on those endless car trips. In the earliest years, I suffered from carsickness, and before we'd get beyond the City of Baltimore, I would have barfed once or twice already. The remainder of the trip for Ma was spent alternately holding me out the window and mopping me up. Each time I barfed, Pop would retch, too, his bleary eyes tearing so badly that he'd have to stop and wipe his glasses. Ma kept stuffing saltines down my gullet, and Teddy kept trying feebly (he was never feeling any too chipper himself) to crawl away from me. "She *reeks*!" he'd holler, hitting at me, and Ma would lean over the seat brandishing a wire mesh flyswatter, bashing at whoever was easier to reach, while Pop sat like a zombie behind the wheel and invented exotic curses. My personal favorite was, "Dirty rotten filthy stinking son-of-a-bitching bastardly shit-eating *farts*!" Teddy literally fell off the seat when Pop let that one fly, which was a mistake when there were nine more horrible hours to go and we'd had our second flat tire. Ma always said something appropriately helpful like, "Would anybody like to eat a little baloney and cheese while we're waiting?" and I could see Pop's grip tightening on the wheel as he measured out each syllable. "Not—right—now—thanks."

Somehow we always got there. We'd spend our nights in tourist rooms somewhere in the middle of Ohio. Teddy and I were invariably scared of the landladies, different ones each year but all remarkably alike. Teddy and I made ourselves willing to sleep in the same bed together, and while we were scrupulous in our efforts not to touch each other and to establish a blanket-roll barrier down the center of the sagging double beds we were always shooed into, we would sometimes secretly reach across the blanket roll to touch each other's hands. Pop would pitch and roll all night long, swearing in his sleep, while Ma snored softly and lay like a gunnysack full of stones. We used to kid her and tell her she might as well get dressed at night because she never moved a muscle in her sleep. It was phenomenal—her nighties were never even wrinkled.

I generally developed diarrhea within moments of our arrival in Wisconsin (which might account for my lifelong nickname of S.P.—ShitPot—among the aunts and uncles), and Pop would disappear for two weeks, reappearing only at mealtimes to wolf down all that Wisconsin beef, gravy, summer sausage, bratwurst, cheese, and the inevitable whipped cream on jello. Then he'd be far afield again, calling the cows home. They generally came home only for Grampa, and only in response to his single call of "Cooommme!" and then lumbered to the milkhouse, single file, a new lead cow and a new path each year. They were gorgeous Jerseys with huge, liquid eyes and pretty, dark faces, and reliable Guernseys, plain but solid, the salt of the earth. Grampa said he had them instead of the Holsteins, who produced more milk, because the milk of the Guernseys and Jerseys was richer, and he liked their looks. Pop and Grampa would attach milking machines to the udders, and I'd sit on a three-legged stool watching the milk through the glass bubble atop the lid of the milk can. The barn cats would mewl and yell for a squirt of warm milk when the men removed the milking machines.

Pop and Irmgard, Grampa's basset hound, walked out early every morning to the narrow but dense stand of woods at the far perimeter of Grampa's eighty acres. Pop would take his gun and shoot nothing.

In the summer of 1956 Teddy did not come with us for the first time. He was nineteen, finished at last with his first tough year at college, and he'd managed to wangle a job at The Point, a hot, dirty job that wore him out, took precedence over family obligations, and allowed him to fend for himself at long, long last. He was anxious to be rid of us; that was easy to perceive. He'd grown impatient with TV and his records, and snapped at me when I put his jockstrap on my head and pretended it was a bathing cap. "Get the hell out of my *life*!" he yelled at me in his hoarse voice. I almost fainted. He was sorry and he apologized, but to tell the truth, I was almost glad to leave him behind; he had become impossible to live with.

"College is tough on a fellow," Pop confided to me. Pop said the word "college" as if he were pronouncing the hundred billion holy names of God. Pop had learned his own brand of engineering from mail-order courses during the Depression, and in libraries, and on the job. He'd scrounged and scratched for every bit of education he'd been able to get, and now he wanted Teddy and me to bask in our opportunities to be thoroughly and brilliantly educated. He wanted us to become a part of the world of books and music and great literature and high culture, to become patricians with pieces of sheepskin mounted and framed, worded in Latin, those pieces of official paper that would give us privileges and rights he wanted for us. It sounded magnificent when he told it. Teddy would be, of course, an engineer. I, a competent pianist for my age, would become a professional musician, a concert pianist, probably, or a teacher of music. Teddy would play football. I would play concerts. Teddy would flesh out. I would thin out. Every time Pop talked about it, I trembled with anticipation. Teddy just looked at the wall and said nothing.

Now Teddy had completed his first grueling year at Johns Hopkins and had told me in his offhand way that everybody took pretty much the same stuff the first two years no matter what program he was enrolled in. I had the feeling he was trying to tell me something more, but I eased out of the conversation, not wanting, for the first time, to be a part of a secret he was harboring. He was so *itchy* all that year. I hardly knew him. He was reading novels I'd never heard of, ones that Book-of-the-Month Club never sent to Pop (all Pop's books had plates pasted in them reading "Ex Libris: Herman J. Schmidt"). He argued one Sunday morning about not wanting to go to church with the family, insisting it was his inalienable right to practice his own kind of religion in whatever way he wanted.

"What?" Pop roared. "Laying in bed is a *religion* now? And who's your supreme being—the Great God Narcolepsis?"

"Lying," Teddy said.

"What?"

"*Lying* in bed. Not 'laying.' You ought to know better."

"Holy shit, he's telling me how to talk. You know damn well I know more about the English language than you'll ever be able to learn in a lifetime. Don't push me, kid."

"For Christ's sake, quit calling me 'kid.' I'm nineteen years old, Pop."

"Who the hell gave you permission to swear in this house?" Pop said.

Teddy rolled his eyes toward heaven and threw up his hands. "God help us!" he said.

"You can do your praying in church with the rest of us," Pop said, hauling the lightweight Ted up from the breakfast table and hustling him up the stairs. I wondered if Pop noticed, as I always did, that Teddy always kept his fists clenched during these exchanges. If he saw, he did not say so.

Pop decided to concentrate on me while we were in Wisconsin that summer. He figured he and I should spend a few pleasant hours together fishing out at Cobb's Lake, one of the hundreds of little lakes thereabouts. His Uncle Gustav's cousin, a bachelor named Willard Frankfurter, had left an open invitation. The old guy loved visitors, loved kids, and wanted to spend his twilight years making himself available to the world so that he wouldn't turn into a vegetable out there all alone in the boondocks.

I loved Willard Frankfurter (Teddy and I always called him "Billy Hot Dog"). He'd been, by virtue of his bachelorhood, a hired man all his life and therefore had no farm to run alone in his old age. He just piddled around his little place like a leprechaun in the cool Wisconsin woods, waiting for people to come and visit, to talk and fish, and eat a little thick bread with cheese for lunch. He kept a jar of rock candy right out on the kitchen table, and he lived in a perpetual state of wretched disorder, which I found marvelous and fascinating.

He did not, for instance, do laundry. When his clothes got too filthy and/or worn out to be wearable, he simply burned them and bought new. "Two or t'ree times a year," he'd chuckle. "Wedder I need 'em or not. Heh, heh, heh." He was a chuckler, that Willard Frankfurter.

Pop was miserably uncomfortable in Willard's kitchen. I could almost see his toes curling inside his brown, rubber-soled, canvas casuals (thirteen ninety-nine, from Hamburger's). He would not sit down on Willard's rickety chairs, would not put his elbows on Willard's littered table. A disreputable-looking cat, her fur wild and filled with mysterious

clumps of sticky stuff, wandered among Willard's nearly un-
recognizable food supplies, and Pop eyed her with a mixture
of fear and loathing that made goose pimples pop out on his
short, bare arms despite the midday heat. He believed that
dirtiness and disorder symbolized Man's Fall from Grace, and
he shuddered. Seeing him suffer made me ill at ease, too, so
we quickly begged off Willard's invitation to eat and made our
way to the small, still lakelet fifty yards from Willard's weedy,
seedy backyard.

"Ahh," Pop said, breathing in the country air (like those
people in the Salem cigarettes TV commercials), turning his
head this way and that, and inadvertently sucking in a few
mosquitoes and gnats. "Aak," he said. "Ptui. Stinkin' little
bastards. Aak."

We picked our way carefully through Willard Frankfurter's amazing assortment of lawn trash. Over the years
he'd managed to accumulate an acre or two of old cars,
wringer-type washers, the odd engine, empty paint cans, re-
frigerators with their doors carefully removed (in case any
two-year-olds might come wandering the nine miles from
town to crawl into one of them), stacks and bales of old
newspapers and *National Geographic*s that had overflowed
from his parlor, wooden crates, buckets with their bottoms
rusted out, oak chairs with no seats, picture frames, broken
crockery, bricks broken in half, old shoes with no discernible
mates in the area, ice skates with no blades, blades with no
ice skates, tires and inner tubes, coils of frayed rope, five
hundred thousand tin cans, a felt hat with half its brim eaten
away, a potholder from Hinkle's Hardware, pieces of asbes-
tos shingle, tarpaper, rolled-up chicken wire, barbed wire, a
posthole digger with only one wooden handle, various
lengths of worn leather harness, a singletree, a rat-chewed
collection of horse collars, warped planks he'd doubtless
acquired years ago to shore up his sagging back porch,
empty Purina sacks, odd pieces of canvas, the shell of an
oak-and-leather couch with one leg missing, and a box of

assorted porcelain knobs. There was more out front, but Pop wouldn't let me rummage there.

"Look at all this shit," Pop lamented, shaking his head in perplexed sadness. "How can a man live like this?"

"I guess he likes it," I said, shrugging it off.

"It's offensive to all civilized mankind," Pop said, making one of his Sacred Pronouncements. "It's wrong, dammit. It's ungodly."

There was Right, and there was Wrong. This was Wrong. It hurt Pop personally to see a man let his home and things, gifts entrusted to him by a gracious God, go to hell on roller skates. He saw it as a parable for today, a lesson for life. He expounded on it as we picked our way through the junk and made for the lake. I let him do it without offering any arguments. He had a point, after all. But Teddy would have worn an expression of intense exasperation, as he always did, and would have half shouted, "For God's sake, Pop, let the old fart alone. He's happy. What business is it of yours?" And Pop's face would have turned to thunder and lightning, and he would have lashed out at Teddy, "It *is* my business, dammit. I am my brother's goddamn keeper. This man is polluting the earth with his filthiness." And Teddy would have said, "If you don't like it, go somewhere else and fish. Leave Willard alone," et cetera, et cetera, until one or the other of them would give up and walk away in high dudgeon. I would have stood by, distressed, wanting them to stop but helpless to stop them. It was just as well, I thought, that Teddy was home in Dundalk, better for us all. It was certainly better for this fishing trip.

Pop put his arm around my shoulders. "Look at this, Half-pint," he said, the Wisconsin creeping back into his voice a little more each day, the hard r's and the nasal o's. I liked it. It was natural to him and bound him to these people whose names were so foreign-sounding to me now: Groelle, Buerstatte, Waack, Blaufuss, Reich, Schnell, Maurer, Rodewald. He belonged there among them, and was happiest and most comfortable amid the farmlands, the rich, black Fox River Valley fields that beckoned him from the soot and grime and wet heat of Baltimore's shipyards. The sun hit him directly on the top of his head now, and he put on his favorite hat, a pith helmet bought for him as a joke by his crew of draftsmen at the shipyards two Christmases before. He couldn't stand the direct sunlight on his head any better than I could. I was wearing a Chinese coolie hat I'd won at the county fair the previous summer. The two of us looked like pugnosed circus clowns in our wide-legged shorts and funny hats. I could hear Willard chuckling to his scruffy cat as we walked away from his kitchen and down to the water.

My pole was bamboo, perfectly adequate, Pop said, for the kind of fishing we did on Cobb's Lake. Pop's was a standard rod, not too long, with standard reel and line. We used worms we'd dug that morning and put into a paper cup of dirt. They already smelled like compost to me, and I wasn't nuts about the idea of putting them on my hook, but I did it. I had to. Pop wasn't going to do it for me, he said.

For the first half hour, we got nothing but bismaroons—the tough little sunfish that battled like big game fish and then turned out to be four inches long. Pop got aggravated. "Hell with this," he said. "Let's eat our lunch."

Fried chicken in a shoe box, slices of garlicky summer sausage, homemade dill pickles, sharp cheddar cheese on Ritz crackers, chocolate chip cookies made yesterday and still chewy, Kool-Aid from a Thermos bottle. Heaven. Paradise. The two of us sat on an old army blanket that picked at the backs of our legs and chowed it all down, every last crumb, in the still noontime shade. Then we talked.

"Yup, this is the place," Pop told me. "This is the place where I'm going to retire. This is really God's country."

"Why did you ever leave if you loved it so much?"

"Had to. There's no work here for a man who isn't a farmer."

"Why didn't you want to be a farmer, like Grampa?"

"I don't know. I guess I just didn't have it in me. I like to design things. No—I like to see things get built that I've designed. Like the hull section of that oil tanker I took you and Ma to see, that Japanese one, remember?"

I nodded. "Yeah, but all you ever talk about is coming back here. You like to work on the farm. Look how you're always out on the haywagon pitching hay, right alongside Uncle Delvin and Grampa. You look like you like it more than anything."

"That's different," he said. "It's more like a sport, or a hobby." He stopped and considered it again. "Yup. That's it. A hobby. It's not my life."

"What is your life, then?"

"It's looking at problems and straightening everything out, and designing just exactly the right thing that will solve the problem. That's what it's all about, this life of mine. Building, you know? Designing, figuring, measuring, creating something out of nothing. That's what I keep trying to get your brother to see. But I never in my life saw a kid so stubborn."

I was duty-bound to defend Teddy. "He's all right," I said.

"I don't know," Pop said, looking distinctly doubtful. "He's got some problems. He's not *neat.* He's not organized. He's got his books and papers strewn all over the place. He doesn't always keep his fingernails clean, doesn't hang up his clothes, reads two-three books at a time. I don't know. If he'd do what I tell him, he'd be okay, but if he keeps on bucking me . . ."

Pop looked worried. He put the lunch things back into the hamper and picked up the fishing rod. The conversation was over. Suddenly he came to life. "Holy shit!" he said. Something was pulling his rod nearly out of his hands. "Look at the son of a bitch pull!" he said joyously to me. He probably had a black bass on the line; the weight of it was alarming. I saw the sweat bead up on Pop's face. He played around with his fish, swore at it, exulted in his impending victory, then looked bewildered as he found to his astonishment that his fish had gotten away at the last possible second. "The bastard got away," he said, stomping his foot like a toddler denied an ice cream cone. "Shit."

He sat down on the blanket and looked crabby.

"Aw, Pop," I said. "You yanked him too hard. He was a big fish—you should have played with him more; you know, coaxed him in, like you always tell me to do."

"Never mind," he said, looking away into the trees.

I kept quiet and started puttering around cleaning up the lunch junk. If we didn't leave soon, I'd have to make a visit to Willard Frankfurter's Famous Outhouse, and the prospect of sitting inside that black torture chamber chilled me to my quaking innards. There were big gray spiders in there; the webs were stranglers that stuck to bare arms and scared faces and invaded nostril and mouth. There was a knothole, of course, where a broad piece of sunlight came streaming in, but it had never cheered me. It only made the horror inside more visible. Teddy used to tease me about snakes. He said that they could easily slither inside the outhouse on their trips across the coarse brown grass, those slick little green snakes, those little garter snakes that could dart across your feet before you had a chance to scream. If you were trapped inside Willard's Outhouse, it seemed uselessly absurd to scream, anyway. What good would it do? And you couldn't run.

I wished Pop would get up and make some progress toward getting out of there, but I looked at him again, and I could see that he was slipping into one of his Netherworld Lapses, one of his ruminative moods. We could be there awhile if he got far enough into it.

Percipient even at twelve, I sidled over to him, harboring happy thoughts, willing myself to give him a handhold out of his self-dug pit. Sometimes it was easily done, and sometimes not. I had to go to the bathroom badly enough to want to make this effort count.

"Hey, Pop," I said, giving our small tablecloth-turned-picnic-blanket a snap to dislodge our crumbs. "Hey, Pop, remember when Ma used to go bowling on Wednesday nights and you had to babysit us?"

"Yeah," he said. "What about it?"

"Do you remember the time when Teddy was up in his room doing his homework and I was playing and you were reading the paper, and all of a sudden you looked up and offered to color a picture in my coloring book?"

"I don't know," he said, looking at the slow lap of lake on sandy ground. "Maybe, I don't know."

"You remember," I said, the memory of it really starting to tickle me. "You and I colored two pictures side by side in the book. You were coloring a pig wearing overalls, and you made little wingtip shoes for him and put birds up in the sky, and drew a tree and a bush in the picture. Then you signed your name to it, just like I always did, and the date."

"Yeah, maybe," he said, taking a little more interest. "Why?"

"Because the best part was when you started reading the paper again, and you fell asleep. I was putting my doll's hair up in those little pink rubber curlers. And I asked if I could just comb your hair, and you weren't really awake and you kind of grunted, so I got a bigger comb and parted your hair and wound it onto those little pink curlers, and then I went to bed."

"Oh, cripes, I remember that now," he said, the grin starting at his eyes and then pulling his mouth up at the corners. "Then Ma came home with those women she bowled with. She invited them in for a glass of wine, and there I sat, asleep in the chair, with those damn sissy little pink curlers in my hair. God, how those women howled over that one." The memory made him happy, made me glow in remembered

126

glee, made our day, saved him from his descent into introspective gloom. We laughed together that summer afternoon. We were a team. It was us against those pesky, wily fish. Pop's rod dipped.

"There he is again," Pop said, the excitement in his voice pulling me out of my cheerful reverie and into the task at hand. The pressure on my bladder was forcing me into a Saint Vitus's caper, but I had to stick around to cheer him on, so I stayed and hopped and grimaced.

"Don't let him get away this time," I cautioned inanely, and Pop hushed me, not wanting me to break his concentration. At the end of his line, the fish yanked and pulled while Pop reeled him in steadily, not jerking him around the way I always did, not wanting to lose this one, too, just trying to guide him. My job was to grab hold of the fish as Pop pulled him up and out so that he could remove the hook from his mouth and plop him into his bucket.

My father's fish came meekly home at last, and Pop lifted him out of the water. I grabbed for him but couldn't reach, and he dangled there, his beautiful scales flashing like sterling silver in the noon light, twirling at the end of the line, our prize, Pop's prize. Pop made a lunge for him, too, but suddenly the furious fish splayed out his fins and Pop's hand was slashed. He jerked the bloody hand up, released the fish inadvertently from the hook, and the fish quicksilvered and disappeared into the lake again. We didn't even see him swim away. Pop looked at the cut on his hand, a superficial slash that would close in minutes. "Shit," he said. "Just plain shit."

"Aw, Pop," I said, sorry and embarrassed for him.

"Never mind," he said. "He'll come back. These are the only fish in the county that bite all day long, come hell or high water. Just get your rear in gear next time, and don't let him get away from you again."

"Hey—" I started to protest, but checked it.

After five minutes or so, when the fish didn't return, Pop suddenly declared that he'd had enough. We packed up our stuff and didn't bother to say good-bye to the snoring, snuffling Willard, who sat on a busted-up rocker, his ratty-looking cat on his lap, amid the rubble of his treasures.

Back at the farm, Ma came out to meet us as the New Car, Pop's 1953 Plymouth Belvedere, a beige-and-brown marvel of efficiency I never quite liked as much as our outrageous Packard, pulled into the yard.

"How'd you do?" she asked.

"Great," Pop enthused. "We threw them all back, though. The fun's in the fishing, not in the keeping, right, Pint-size?"

"Right, Pop," I said.

I decided not to elaborate for Ma.

I looked around the neat, well-trimmed yard of Grannie and Grampa's farmhouse, a big house, white with green trim, and a huge front porch that spanned the width of the house. What if I came back someday and this place was like Willard's, sleazy with cast-off debris, rotten with rank overgrowth and peeling paint and sagging, soggy wood? What if Grannie and Grampa sat up on that porch in tattered old gray sweaters, idly petting cats, their swollen ankles crossed, their filthy slippers soleless, their fingernails yellow and ridged like Willard's? Suddenly I despised Willard and his hellhole of a house, lake or no lake. I would not go there again.

What if Pop stopped coming out here and making war against decay with his pruning shears and his paintbrushes and his hammer and nails? What if he couldn't come?

Who would do it, then?

Somebody had to.

Who?

That afternoon, as the late sun slanted over the milkhouse, I went with Grannie in my Oshkosh coveralls (Grampa's, cuffed eight inches at the bottom and tied around the waist with a rope) and scrubbed down the inside of the milkhouse with the boiling water and disinfectant they always used. I sweated and swore like a man, but under my breath so that Grannie, still a Methodist despite the Lutherans all about her, wouldn't wash out my mouth.

It felt good, at suppertime, to be honestly hungry.

I knew that this place would endure.

Chapter 11

I n November of 1956, Dr. Hamilton Bisky finally said it aloud. All my life, he'd been stringing me along, chucking me under my round little chin, patting my ample fanny and yanking at my dark blond braids, grinning around a set of oyster-white false teeth, the grin as fake as the teeth, which stank. "Baby fat," he'd always said, the way some people feel duty-bound to go slack-jawed and babble "googoo" to babies whose I.Q.s probably outweigh theirs by one hundred or so points.

When Petey the Keet got curmudgeonly in his dotage and bit me so hard on the finger that he chomped through cuticle and nail (I was trying to bathe him against his little birdie will) and gave me a horrible, smelly, roaring, pounding infection, the nincompoop Bisky grabbed the swollen finger, squeezed it hard, yelled, "That hurt?" into my face, and cackled as I went to my knees. "We're going to have to lance this, darlin'," he exclaimed with a juicy leer. I backed away.

"Ellen!" he shouted to his weary, bleary-eyed nurse. "Hey, Ellen! Come on in and get Miss Schmidt ready for a lancing, okay, hon?"

A lancing. He might just as well have said, "An amputation." I was feeling weak and nauseated from the squeezing I'd just endured, and Ellen's bewildered face didn't inspire much confidence. She was likable and cute in a freckly, Doris Day kind of a way, but always vaguely unkempt, like a doll you never quite dress up because you washed her hair once and it wouldn't comb out right, so what's the use? Ellen was a blinker, too—one of those people who blink so rapidly and in such quick succession that you always find yourself twitching and winking to keep up with them. There we stood—me, Bisky the Baboon, and Ellen the Nervous Ninny with the Needle. Cripes. I had to get out of there.

I took another firm step backward and heard a blood-curdling yowl from behind. I'd stepped squarely on the white-shoed foot of Ellen, who hadn't moved despite Bisky's entreaties that she give him some numbing spray stuff and the needle. Needle? No. No needles in my rear, thank you. Nono, they said. In your finger. My finger? *No!*

When I shifted my heft, Ellen got the full weight of me on her great toe, right foot, and then she sprang to life at last, nearly upending me.

"Jeeziss!" she hissed into my hair from behind. "How the hell much do you weigh, girl?"

"She's a lardass, isn't she?" Bisky hooted. "Always has been. Must go—what, Miss Beatrice?—about two hundred now, am I right?"

I stood so still and silent that my heart stopped pounding and my finger ceased its screaming. Stunned, I stared hard at the man who never missed an opportunity to tell me how small and dainty his own daughters were, and what baby dolls.

"No," Ellen said, openmouthed. "She can't. She's only a kid."

"Wanta bet?" Bisky snickered. "I say two hundred easy."

"Naa," Ellen countered. "One seventy, maybe. No more."

"Yeah, but she's solid as a rock. Feel her."

Ellen plucked at me with her cold fingers—rump, upper arm, midriff.

"I don't know," she said. "I still say one seventy. One eighty, tops."

"Come here," Bisky said suddenly. He grabbed my elbow and yanked me onto his office scale before I had a chance to call him a rude bastard. I wouldn't have anyway. I would have died before I'd have called a grown-up a name, even in private. He was, after all, a Healer, a Receptacle of Wisdom and Knowledge. Doctors studied all their lives to heal, to cure, and to ease pain. I wouldn't have cursed at him or spoken evil of him aloud. Bastard.

He fooled with the balances and hummed (I do not lie), "I don't want her, you can have her, she's too fat for me . . ." and I started to shake.

"Be still," Bisky snarled at me. The humming stopped. "Stand straight and stop moving." With a sickening clunk, the balances told the truth about Bebe Schmidt. Two hundred and two. Twelve years old. Two-oh-two. I hadn't known. We didn't even have a scale at our house—who needed to know how much anybody weighed? Nobody at our house gave a flying squirrel's patoot what anybody weighed. Why were these two making such a *deal* out of it?

Ellen didn't believe it. She came closer to look for herself. She checked the scale, looked at me for a second, then turned her head away so I wouldn't see the tears in her eyes. "Aw, hon," she said. "Aw, sweetheart. God love ya. I wouldn't have guessed in a hundred years."

She had the grace to be sorry for intruding into my pain and shame that way. She had the sense to turn her face away from me while I suffered so nakedly. But Birdbrain Bisky all but did a back flip, so pleased was he with his powers to estimate. He should have been in a freaking *carnival,* guessing weights and feeling butts and squeezing upper arms to his heart's content, the old rooster of a pervert. I got off his rocking scale and held my finger up in front of his face. It was the middle finger, right hand. I raised it with a vengeance, exulting in my first obscene hand gesture.

"What about my finger?" I said loudly.

"Yeah, yeah, we're going to get to that," Bisky chortled,

plopping his bones into the swivel chair behind the massive oak desk he hid behind. "First I want to give you something. You twelve yet, hon?"

"Yes," I said. "I was twelve last January. I'm nearly thirteen."

"Right, right," he said, beaming at Ellen and me. "Menstruating, right? Becoming a woman, right?" he said. Ellen looked away from this poignant vignette. The old windbag probably saw himself as something out of a Norman Rockwell magazine cover. If she realized, as I did just then, what a pathetic old crock Bisky was, she didn't say so. She just glided out of the office like a soft-soled spirit. Bisky was busy now, fiddling around in the crap that littered his desk drawer, and finally he whipped out a triple-folded piece of paper and showed it to me.

"WOMEN'S 1200 CALORIE PROGRAM," it said in boldface letters. "OBESITY DIET."

Obesity. What a filthy word, I thought. Obese. Like gas hissing out of a blubbery behind. Obese. Ohhh-*beeesss*! I felt sicker.

"Here ya go, girl," Bisky said, thrusting the paper at my face, enjoying every minute of it. "This'll do her for ya."

"Do what?"

"Melt that weight off you. That fat is not cute anymore, missy. It's not baby fat anymore. You ought to know that. You're getting up there in age now, and those boys are going to be looking at things they've never looked at before. You don't want to disappoint them, do you, now?"

I didn't answer.

"Of course you don't. So take a look here. I'll show you how it's done." He pointed one of his white, wrinkly fingers at the first page, and I barely could make out the letters of the words printed there through the tears I refused to shed in front of him. A stinking, lousy diet. And he'd called me a lardass. What an awful word. It was another "spitting" word, a word like "shit" or "piss," a harsh, ugly word that was only spat out to signal anger, disdain, contempt, disgust. People shouldn't be allowed to use words like that about people, I thought. They stung like yellow jackets. But what the hell, the other words for "fat," those soft, sissy ones—chubby, plump, roly-poly—were just as bad because they conjured up pictures of a gigantic beach ball going ba-wong, ba-wong on yellow sand. I hated them all. They all stank, the words that described me. I hated Bisky and his rattly teeth, and I was mad at Ellen for letting him abuse me this way. I wanted out of there.

"My finger," I repeated, all my defenses prickling. "What about my finger?"

"Right, right," Bisky said, oozing out of his comfy chair and hustling me into the room where he did his dirty work. "Let me see that," he ordered, and grabbed me by the hand. He futzed around spraying something and made a hard, quick motion, and suddenly—whoosh! Filthy, malodorous junk squirted out of my burst finger and across the little room onto the venetian blinds. "Damn!" Bisky said to nobody. "Damn it all." He squeezed again where he'd cut. I got dizzy, really dizzy, and sank to the floor while he held tightly to my arm. "Stand up, girl. Get up here where I can see." Why was he mad at me?

I started to gag. The smell alone would have made anybody sick, but mostly it was the pain. "Hey, Ellen!" he yelled. "I need you here."

Ellen returned and gasped to see me yanking at Bisky's pantslegs, trying to crawl up his legs and back into the reality of consciousness. "What's goin' on here?" she asked, all prim and proper. Apparently she'd never seen an adolescent girl climbing up a doctor before. "Why's she yellin' like that?"

"Ah, who knows?" Bisky said, fed up with me. "You gave her Novocain."

"I gave it to her? God, I thought *you* gave it to her."

They glared at each other while I found a chair and sat on it, trembling.

"You can go now," Bisky said gruffly to me as Ellen bandaged the evidence of her barbarian employer's latest atrocity. "And you get your tail back here in two weeks so I can check out that weight, you hear?"

I made a promise to Ellen that I'd come back in two weeks to check in on the scale. Dundalk G.P.s didn't make appointments. You just came, signed in, sat down, and waited. Two weeks. I wasn't crying anymore, and the nausea had subsided, although the finger still hurt like hell from the battering it had suffered. Ellen's silent treachery had dampened my cockiness, and I didn't go bouncing out of the office as I'd always done in the past. I hadn't known all these years how pathetic she found me.

Inside my head, some of Fats Domino's da-tata/da-tata/da-tata rhythm and lyrics pumped me down the sidewalk. I could hear that gravelly voice rich with world knowledge over the screeching noises of the good doctor's children wreaking havoc in the big house behind the office (which would have been a large side porch if Bisky hadn't been a doctor). Bisky's kids were the Village Idiots—scroungy-looking little dimwits with narrow heads and protruding teeth that would probably someday be as false as Dada's. I rejoiced in that for a wisp of a moment. Bisky's kids were not, I thought, among The Chosen, as we Schmidts were. Nobody would expect terribly much of them. If they chose to look like emaciated beavers with advanced cases of the mange, then let them.

Ma looked at my OBESITY DIET and frowned. "I never boiled a piece of good beef in my life," she said, sorrowing in advance for us all. "What's that gonna taste like? Soggy cardboard, I bet. It says no pork, no ham, no cake or cookies or ice cream, except for a quarter-cup of strawberry once a week. Holy cry. Who could live on this?"

I must have looked so rocky that she relented and hushed up her "meckering" (a Wisconsin word for "vocalized fretting") and said she'd give it a shot if Dr. Bisky thought it was best for me. She thought he was a real pro, a sweet talker who knew how to kid a woman into understanding that her aches and pains and problems were just part of the territorial curse of being born, unfortunately, female. She told Pop she thought Bisky was a card. A card. Right. The Ass of Spades. Pop didn't really know Bisky. Pop didn't go to doctors. "Doctors are for women and kids," he always said, and preferred to do his own singular brand of home doctoring when illness tried to lay him low.

"Dago red and Vicks'll fix me up," he always said when La Grippe struck. "Just let me work up a good sweat and lie down under the quilt for twenty-four hours with Vicks on my chest," he'd say. "I'll show you the fastest cure known to man." He believed so passionately in his own folklore that he was seldom off from work. The Chianti put him into a stupor and the Vicks kept his chest warm, and the sweat convinced him that poisons were seeping out of him and into the bath towels he'd put between himself and the mattress. One day later, he'd proclaim himself cured. That was, by God, *that, danke zehr.*

So Ma started boiling beef and skinning chicken, which all but broke her heart into pieces, throwing all that good chicken fat out before we were able to soak up its benefits. And we ate our vegetables without cream sauce and cheese just for the heck of it, to see if this OBESITY DIET knew its elbow from third base. Two weeks later, when I skulked into Bisky's office in the gray chill of a December afternoon, Ellen let out a whoop of delight as she balanced the scales.

"Eight pounds gone!" she hollered through the doctor's closed door.

"Huh?" he yelled back. "Open the door, woman."

Ellen flung open his door, despite the fact that a hairy, bare-chested man sat across from Bisky's desk with a worried look on his gray, jowly face, his white dress shirt held in his hands, a workman's hands, like a rosary.

"Beatrice Schmidt lost eight pounds in two weeks!" Ellen exulted, and even the strange gray man smiled at me. I stood at the doorway to the office looking Bisky in the eye. He grinned his clacking grin at me.

"How do you feel?" he asked, chuckling.

"Great," I replied, my sullenness lost on him. God, no wonder his kids were such apes. It was hard to get him to acknowledge the arrows of hatred you shot his way. No perception of irony.

"I knew it," he said, immensely satisfied with himself. "You know what you won yourself, baby doll? You won yourself a free office visit, that's what. Every time you come in here with a loss of four pounds or more for two weeks, you get your visit free. How's that, sweetheart?" I must have nodded and made a faint attempt at smiling. He always made me unsure, always made me lose my footing somehow. Bisky was patting himself on the back now, really thrilled with the job he was doing on this poor little fat girl. He probably figured we were partners, now that he'd been white enough to forgo the two-dollar fee his office calls usually cost. Ma would be beside herself when I came home with the money. She'd given me sixty-two dollars in all—sixty dollars for the rent, which I'd paid at the apartment office on my way to the doctor's, and two dollars for the doctor. Everything in me wanted to rathole the two bucks for a rainy day, but I knew I couldn't. Old, straight Schmidt. Anyway, Bisky was going on to the strange man about how I was his Pet Project, and the man looked at me again, smiling that same wan half-smile.

"I had a daughter your age," he said, and then caught himself with a gasp and a shudder. "I mean, I *got* a daughter your age," he said. Dr. Bisky motioned for me to close the door, and as I did his bidding, I heard the man's voice cry out, raw and ragged with the ultimate dismay, "Oh, my God. My God." I closed the door tightly and shivered.

Ellen looked at me. "He's very sick," she said.

"Is he going to die?" I asked, brave enough to say the word to an adult.

"We're all going to die," Ellen said. I thought her answer

wise and well spoken, and didn't ask any more questions.

As I hurried home, the misty drizzle that chilled my head and face couldn't erase the grin. I had done it. Jeeze-oo-eee. I had done it, after all. I conjured up an image of eight of those pound-sized cartons of Goetze's lard—aagghh. That fat that used to be on my body was gone. Just like you could melt lard, you could sloosh fat off your body. Hallelujah. I wanted to celebrate, to rejoice. When I got home and shared my news, we all hooted and capered for a bit, then spread peanut butter on saltines and had a minor binge in honor of the eight pounds that were no more.

By Christmas, I had to struggle to hold up my khaki skirt with the Ivy League belt in the back, bought especially for me when school started. My black cardigan, which I turned around backward and wore with the sleeves pushed up to my elbows, sagged down onto my hips and hung like a feedsack. Even my Elvis Presley tennis shoes got roomy. It felt good. I felt orderly inside, in control for the first time in my life. Drunk with success, I carried my best Christmas gifts, my Elvis Presley extended-play records, over to my girl friend Bernadette's house. We lay on the floor in her room with our feet up on her bed and listened to the songs over and over again, the tears streaming into our ears each time Elvis sang "Old Shep." To celebrate the blossoming of the new me, we took off our sweaters, stood shoulder to shoulder in our Maidenforms in the tiny bathroom of Bernadette's row home, and drenched our bangs with Nestle's Hair Rinse—Titian, I think —and waited to become irresistibly gorgeous.

Pinky-red was more like it. For Bernadette and me, excess was the word for the year. If the directions called for one capsule to a quart of warm water, we blithely dumped two capsules into a pint of extra-hot water. Our Tangee Natural lipstick was applied and reapplied with grim and heavy determination, hourly. Our single-minded dedication to these mutual beautification projects, however, didn't seem to improve our lot. The boys in our class down at the annex still didn't give a rat's rump what we did to ourselves one way or another, and the older guys in the ninth grade and the kids from the high school looked past or through us as we valiantly attempted to ingratiate ourselves with the crowd at Lillich's Pharmacy and The Arundel, a snack, coffee, and ice cream shop where everybody we admired "hung." (In Balmerese, you don't hang out, you just hang. When kids meet each other for the first time, their first words are likely to be, "Where do you hang?") Some kids, of course, hung at the bowling alley —but they were kids mostly from Sennalena (St. Helena, across the streetcar tracks). Lots of kids hung at Read's Drugstore, too, but for some reason, I didn't know them. Maybe they were kids who went to Catholic or Poly or City or Eastern or Western or St. Michael's or something. Thousands of kids hung at the YMCA—literally hung. There were sycamore trees at the entrance, and kids in dungarees were always hanging from them, hoping to be able to spot some bare flesh behind the open-just-a-crack windows to the locker rooms. It wasn't that hard. Just jump up onto the bike rack, leap for a low-hanging branch, and pretend to be witnessing some bareass in the building. Nobody ever saw squat diddly. At least, I never did.

Anyway, Bernadette and I hung at Lillich's Pharmacy and the Arundel, but we hung in a peculiar place—always at the periphery. We were just kiddies to these people. Still, we tried. We shaved our legs together one Sunday afternoon— a first time for the both of us. Holy Moses. I practically had to be hospitalized. Bernadette was more adept. We plucked our eyebrows the following week, just after the carnage with the Schick injector. I looked like Harriet Nelson before she met and married Ozzie, and Bernadette had to draw her eyebrows on with reddish-brown pencil for six weeks. "Bizarre," Teddy said when he saw us. "The Weird Sisters."

We stuffed our A-cup bras with tissues (because the tennis balls wouldn't fit and the oranges were too heavy and the load kept shifting), and we bought a pack of Salem (take a puff—

it's springtime) cigarettes, which we shared in the ladies' room of the Strand every Saturday for a month thereafter. Hack. Ark. Watery eyes and sore nostrils from French inhaling, which was Ultimate Cool among Dundalk girls. Then the breath mints, the walking in the wind to blow the stench out of our hair, the chewing gum, the talcum powder on the clothes which we damn near couldn't brush out again . . . and the guilt, the shame, the burden of deception.

On Christmas Day, then, we'd done just about everything within our realm and power to grow up, but we were still chubby, orange-haired little teens with baby fat on our chins and nobody to put on Revlon's Powder Pink lipstick for. We'd gone halfsies on it, vowing to share it equally, but Bernadette had custody of the tube because if my father had found out about it, or discovered it among my possessions, he'd have used it to write a personal missive to Martin Luther bemoaning the waywardness of his only daughter.

The cigarettes I kept. They were stashed at the back of my little 45s record case where no self-respecting adult would ever dare rummage. My father wouldn't have gone near a rock-and-roll record if his life had depended on it. He was heavily into Mario Lanza singing *The Student Prince* (which was fine; I liked *The Student Prince,* having seen the movie seven or eight times), but Pop liked only that kind of stuff and wouldn't even consider going eclectic in his tastes; so I had to play my records at Bernadette's on the weekends, or he'd go roaring about like a wounded elephant, bellowing his outrage.

Bernadette studied our pinkish topknots in the bathroom mirror. "Your father's not gonna like this," she said at last. "He's gonna have a conniption."

"I know," I said. "But it's Christmas Day. Maybe he won't lose his mind on Christmas Day."

"Don't count on it," Bernadette said glumly. My father referred to Bernadette Erdman as Erd the Turd. To say that he didn't have much use for her would be like saying that Hitler liked ham better than lox and bagels. I mean, Pop just didn't take to Bernadette. It wasn't that she and he ever argued openly, or that she did anything so drastically outrageous—he just didn't seem to like her face. "She looks like a bulldog wearing a wig," Pop said to Ma once, behind my back. I heard them, and it really steamed me. What a rotten hypocrite, to talk about a person's facial attractiveness when he's the one who'd told me all my life about judging books by their covers.

But I listened a little more, and eventually the truth came slithering out. It seems they were afraid that Bernadette, being Catholic and all, might lure me into the paths of popish tomfoolery. She was always bragging about being Catholic, as if she owned a piece of the Vatican or something. She used to wind a wool head scarf around her flyaway hair and announce to me as we tired of hanging at the Arundel that she was going to pop into St. Rita's and light a candle. What for? I wondered. Why would anybody go into a church and pay a dime to light a teeny little candle?

"To say prayers," she said solemnly.

"You gotta pay to pray if you're a Catholic?" I asked.

"No, stupe. You just gotta pay to light the candle."

"Then don't light the candle."

"Christ, you're dumb. If I don't light the candle, the prayer won't go up."

"Oh," I said, nodding to indicate my complete understanding. To this day, nobody has ever enlightened me on this practice of lighting candles and paying for prayers, but I stopped questioning it; and for most of that fall, I sneaked into St. Rita's beside Bernadette, disguised as a Catholic with a babushka around my guilty head, throwing dimes into the box and lighting those little red candles. It seemed a dangerous and forbidden thing to do then, but it uplifted me, and filled me with mystery and a vague sense of promise.

So anyway, Bernadette said, "Your father's going to blame this all on me again. He really hates me, don't he?"

"No," I lied. "Why should he hate you?"

"Because my father works for him, and he doesn't like my father, and he doesn't like me, and my father says he thinks he's hot shit," Bernadette spat at me in a spurt of illogical fire. For the first time, it occurred to me that maybe she didn't like me as much as I'd thought.

"Who, Pop?" I asked.

"No, King Farouk," Bernadette said, putting her hand on her hip and looking tougher than the drapes from North Point, those kids in the pink-and-black jackets who smoked without holding the cigarettes in their hands. Suddenly, she was scaring me.

"My pop thinks he's hot shit?"

"Yeah. My father says he's always bugging him about having clean fingernails at work. And he says he won't let anybody eat lunch at the drafting boards, either. He goes around making everybody pick up crumbs off the floor and crap like that, because he says bugs and rats might invade the place. What kind of shit is that? Who ever heard of a grown man acting like such a sis?"

"My pop's not a sis."

"Ah, he's queer," Bernadette said. "He makes me barf."

"Well, he's not so crazy about you, either," I blurted, wanting to stab her with something, even a word.

"No shit, Sherlock," she said. "Big hot flash. Call the *Sunpapers.*"

"Quit acting so smart," I said. I heard the sound of begging in my voice, and I hated it. Something was going wrong. Nothing should go wrong on Christmas Day. It was a rule, sacred and unbreakable.

"Grow up, little girl," Bernadette said. Her lip curled in contempt.

"I said to quit acting so smart," I said, simmering tears making a mask of my burning face, which I desperately willed to remain impassive.

"Oh, get fucked," Bernadette said.

Both our faces colored in a rushing blush. I could not

believe that she'd spoken the word aloud. It was a word for lavatory walls and chalk on brick, not a word that a friend says to a friend. I thought the sky must fall and put my hands up over my ears in a classic movie gesture of denial.

"Oh, what you said," I crooned. "Ohh, what you *said*, Bernadette."

"Shut up, queerface," she said, recovering. "Just shut up. I never said nothin'. What did I say?"

"Never mind," I said, looking around for my car coat and muffler and gray fuzzy earmuffs and angora mittens. "Never mind, girl." Rectitude and sanctimony breathed their heady strength into me, allowing me to move, talk, and walk as if I hadn't been decimated by that single, unspeakable word. If I stuck around any longer, though, I might come unglued. I left, ignoring the entreaties of the person who used to be my friend, who'd suddenly gotten into a cold sweat, sure I'd tell on her, sure her sin would be laid bare in front of my parents and, inevitably, hers.

She was wrong, of course. I wouldn't have told a thing like that. I was a sis, but I wasn't going to be queer about it. I would just drop her for a while, until she came to her senses and learned how to behave like a nice girl. The last thing I needed, according to my *American Girl* magazine, was to have my reputation tarnished so early in the game. What red-blooded American boy would want to date a girl who hung out with a trashmouth?

So school started up again in January, and I was without a companion at lunchtime in the pale green cafeteria with its wooden tables and benches. Alone in the battleship-gray lav, where the ninth-grade girls smoked and wrote things like "Phys. Ed. sucks" and "Marcie eats shit" and "Glenda and Dominick" and "Sparrows Point Blows." Alone on the orange school bus. True, I had a seatmate, one Rita Lee Zimmerer, but being with Rita Lee was a lot like being alone, only not so comfortable, because she never stopped her mouth for three seconds. And all of it, that whole endless stream of monotone drivel, was about her cats and her mother, in that order. What a royal, deadly *drag* Rita Lee was. I mean, how long can a person talk about a houseful of cats?

Everybody avoided Rita Lee, but she took a liking to me. She must have considered me a good and sympathetic listener, because she sought me out every morning and afternoon, and literally held on to the sleeve of my red car coat until the bus came. And she was never sick. That was because her mother made her wear an undershirt and snuggies all winter, right up until Easter. She was the laff riot of the Phys. Ed. class in those undershirts and snuggies.

It was awful.

Bernadette practically turned herself inside out avoiding me. We didn't speak at all, and she didn't look at me once. God, she was tough. She was having a ball, though, laughing her ass off over everything that happened in the tight little group she'd wormed into just to spite me. One of the girls in her new group was Carla Bisky, the good doctor's eldest daughter, whose age and I.Q. were pretty much in the same range. Ugly as cat pucky, too, despite the braces and the corrective shoes and the expensive haircuts (four-fifty, at Hochschild-Kohn's, downtown) her mother laid on her.

I heard them giggling like squealing piglets one afternoon as we waited for old thirty-seven, our bus back to Dundalk, to pull up in front of the school. Rita Lee was droning on about Lester, her newest kittycat, but my ears were pricked up to discover the subject of the giggling.

It was me. I. Whatever.

I heard bits and snatches of it, but what little I heard was enough to make my insides feel soupy. "Two-oh-two," Carla snickered. "Do you even believe that? My daddy calls her Two-ton Tessie! Isn't that a riot?"

There was more giggling, and one of the smaller girls, a kid named Barbara Foote, tried to imitate my voice and mannerisms. "You girls better cut it out, or Mr. Lambert will get mad."

They all hooted. It did sound kind of prissy and not the way I'd have thought I sounded, but the way they all were carrying on, I felt the sting of Barbara's accuracy. Foote, exhilarated with her success, kept it up. "And another thing. My poppy says that too much makeup makes a girl look *cheap*!" That brought the bloody house down.

The knot inside my chest made it hell to breathe, and Rita Lee's whine was rattling my shaky composure pretty badly. The wind sliced into my ears, and I struggled to find my earmuffs. But even with the earmuffs, I could hear the cackling behind me.

"Honest to God, Bernadette, how could you stand it so long? Two-oh-two. Crapsake. How could you hang with such a fat slob?"

"Ah, cut it out," Bernadette said, ending the hilarity with a wave of her hand. Everybody knew that Bernadette had been born up near The Heights, where the really tough kids lived, the kids who went to Patterson. Nobody gave her any crap. "Bebe's okay. You gotta get to know her. She's really smart. Smart kids can't help it if they gotta act queer sometimes. They think older, you know? Like adults."

Bernadette, like any good Dundockian, said "*add*-ult," but I forgave her. I forgave her, too, for saying my pop thought he was hot shit. The thing was, it was true. He did think he was hot shit. He even admitted it, in his own humble way. He was Chosen, and he had to be a cut above the rank and file in order to fulfill his sacred duties. He must have spread that personal philosophy around quite a bit, and maybe some people didn't like the way it sounded. I mean, we were used to it at home, and we could deal with Pop. But other people probably let it get to them, like Bernadette's father and, therefore, Bernadette. So it wasn't her fault, entirely. She probably felt for her father the way I did for mine, no matter how dumb he acted sometimes. Those were the rules. Neither of us could help it.

"Eeeooo," Rita Lee said in her best imitation of a myna

bird. "Those smart-alecky girls are making fun of you, Beatrice. Isn't that terrible? And Bernadette is right smack dab in the middle of them. Whell" [Rita Lee always said, "Whell!" to indicate indignation], "I'm not a bit surprised. My mother says that Bernadette Erdman is headed for hell on roller skates. My mother says that Bernadette's mother should be put in jail for letting her wear those French-heeled shoes to mass. She's only twelve years old, and my mother says—"

"Go pound sand up a pipe," I said. Rita Lee stopped mid-sentence and stared at me.

"What?"

"I said to go pound sand. Lay off of Bernadette."

"But she's—"

"She's all right," I said. Something joyful and triumphant was trumpeting in me, something full of burnished gladness.

"What's goin' on over here?" a voice behind me said, Bernadette's voice. She bumped me a little with her hip, which was higher than mine and which set me off balance.

"Nothing to write home about. You want to hear about Rita Lee's House of a Thousand Cats?"

"Rita Lee's Cathouse?" Bernadette said, elbowing me in the place where a normal kid would have had ribs. "God, I can't wait. Shoot, Rita."

Rita Lee stood looking at us sideways, uncertain. With Rita Lee, any gesture that was not overtly unfriendly or frankly obscene was unfamiliar and therefore suspect.

"We don't have to talk about cats," she said at last.

"Solid," Bernadette said, slapping her on the back the way Charlie Bratton the Loudmouth did on Jackie Gleason. "All right, Rita Lee. Let's not talk about cats."

Cheerfully, Rita Lee began to talk instead about her mother and her mother's hatred of winter. It seemed that Mrs. Zimmerer had the arthuritis, see, and a lot of trouble with bronichal assma. Lots of Baltimoreans suffered from identical maladies, often augmented by such ghastly complications as very close veins, the diarear, and chicken pops. Delighted to be the center of our attention, Rita Lee positively bubbled.

Bernadette and I adroitly avoided all talk of our disagreement and promptly resumed our sister act that very moment, to the astonishment of the Bisky Bunch. They couldn't figure out why anybody as basically cool as Bernadette would want to hang with a sis like Beatrice Schmidt, the former tomboy (football kicker, soccer ace, summer tentmaker). These girls hadn't been in our class last year. They just didn't know how fetchingly funny and regular I could act. (Bernadette eventually talked them into liking me, but it took nearly the whole year.) What a relief it was to have her back.

And there was a fringe benefit. I got even skinnier. Infuriated by Bernadette's rotten behavior, further alienated from the other kids by their cliquishness, and worn down by Rita Lee's catprattle, I dwindled daily. By February, I had lost twenty-six pounds and had grown a full half inch. No longer did Mrs. Masetti, our elderly neighbor across the court, refer to me as "Little Kate Smith." (She'd always meant, my father pointed out, to compliment my singing voice, but the nickname itched and I didn't want to wear it.) In fact, I really did start to look like Patti Page, but by that time, I didn't want to look like Patti Page, who was no longer a Big Star. I wanted to look like Debbie Reynolds. You can't have it all.

The diet got to be a habit, like the biweekly treks to Bisky's office for the weigh-in. I never let on that I knew he'd ridiculed me in front of his family. Any fool can fight . . . Still, it did my heart good to surprise the old crud with my steady success. It put me into a class he couldn't emulate. He knew it, too, I think, because his inane beaming eventually gave way to a grudging acceptance and respect, and by the time I'd lost another thirty pounds, he all but stopped taking credit for it and started calling me "Miss Schmidt" again, all business.

Victory. I was enough like the other kids to be, at last, "normal."

And that March I stopped growing, just as all the other munchkins seemed to sprout up overnight all around me.

Suddenly, nearly everybody was taller than I. It was like something out of *Alice in Wonderland.* Other people were gazing down upon me for the first time since I'd entered Holcombe's House of Horrors in 1950.

A Regular Person. I'd made it. I was not skinny, but I was no longer a lardass (a pox on you, Bisky, for putting that word into my vocabulary) either. And finally I was able to give hearty comeuppance to a world that had scourged me with rejection, ridicule, and misunderstanding for so long.

One yellow spring day Price was at my elbow in the cafeteria, asking me if he could buy me a Nutty Buddy or a Creamsicle. Santino sat smoldering across from us, making the occasional caustic comment and kicking at Price under the table. Then he sent Price to the ice cream line and leaned across the table so that his face was close to mine.

"Wanna go to the movies?" he said in a hurried whisper.

"Me?"

"Yeah, you," he said. "Cripes, who else? It's *Westward Ho the Wagons* Saturday at the Strand."

"God, I don't know," I murmured, all confused and panicky. I knew Pop would never let me go, and the idea of sneaking out without permission was so alien that it never consciously occurred to me.

"Come on, Bebe," Santino said, looking over his shoulder. "I'll pay."

"I can't," I said. "My father won't let me."

Santino looked as if I'd shot a hocker at him. He backed away and stared at the wall above and behind my head. "Would you go with Price?" he asked, oblivious to my sincerity. I didn't answer. Price was coming back, and I was feeling nervous and flustered. "Would you?" Santino pressed.

"No," I whispered. "I'm not allowed. I told you."

"Bitch," Santino said, and I reared back as if he'd slapped me.

"What's the deal?" Price said as he ambled back to us with two orange Creamsicles, one for him and one for Santino.

The ice creams were looking pretty impotent, kind of bent. Price peeled off the paper carefully, trying not to do any damage, and nobody spoke. "So what's the deal?" he said again, his face roundly innocent, waiting for the conversation to wind its way around him, too.

"No deal," Santino said shortly. "Let's shag, Price." He got up and pulled his duffel bag away from my arm. I looked down at the table, where "Kremer sucks cock" was carefully carved into the two hundred layers of pale green paint. I traced the legend with a fingernail. I felt hollow, as if a bell were tolling inside me, reverberating in my head and diaphragm.

"Hey, what—?" Price sputtered as Santino stalked away to another table. He looked at me, puzzled. "What crawled up his ass and died?" he asked. I kept quiet and shook my head. "Come on, Beeb," he urged me.

"He's mad because I won't go to the movies with him Saturday," I confessed.

"T.S. for him," Price said, grinning, which made him look remarkably like Howdy Doody.

"How come you're so happy?" I said. I really and truly didn't get it. Not at all. Not right then.

"Because now you can go with me," Price said, so sure I'd come leaping into his arms that he widened his grin and lowered his eyelashes in a coy and winning way.

"I can not," I said, wondering all of a sudden why I'd lain awake for two years dreaming and praying for the moment Price would fall in love with me at last. Fooey.

"Why not?" Price said, taken aback visibly and vocally, his voice ascending into a squeaking whine like the black cat's on *Smilin' Ed's Gang* (naaiice!).

I giggled.

"Beeb, why not?" Price demanded again, looking fierce.

Wearily, loftily, I answered the dreary question again.

"I'm not allowed."

Price blinked. "I thought you liked me."

"I used to, but you didn't like me."

"Yeah, but I do now."

"T.S. for you, then. You had your chance and you muffed it, Price."

I hadn't meant to do it and had never planned such a thing. But if anybody had ever told me that the flavor of vengeance was so rich, and its essence so nourishing, I'd have gone after it long before this. My head swam as if I'd drunk too deeply of new wine. I rose, Price's eyes still upon me as I glided away into the madding crowd of belching seventh graders trying like heck to get those last few penciled problems done before fifth-period math class. His eyes followed me all the way out to the hallway. Bernadette reported this later. She said he bunched up his trash, the second Creamsicle uneaten, and missed the can by a foot. He stumbled out into the hall and pulled open the lav door like a zombie, then disappeared inside.

"He'll get over it," Bernadette promised. She knew all about this stuff. She had an older sister named Carolanne who had lots of boyfriends, so I trusted her judgment.

We talked it all out that brisk March afternoon, Bernadette and I, over lemon phosphates (*false faces,* in Dundock-ese) at Lillich's. We had to stand outside to drink them on the noisy, crowded sidewalk, but it was good to have such a thing to talk over now that winter was past.

And that very day, in the process of doing an after-school errand for Ma, I met Vinnie Mancuso.

Oh, my God.

Vinnie Mancuso was not a lot taller than I was, but he was, as we said in the YMCA shower room, *built.* Shoulders this wide; thick, short arms; short legs with taut, heavy muscles at thigh and calf (his tight Wranglers showed every delicious ripple); and a timber of a neck upon which sat the head of a young god. Dark brown eyes fringed with heavy jet-black lashes, shiny lashes that caught the flickers of the sun; a wide

Italian mouth slightly upturned at the corners, adorably cupidlike at the bow; and Mediterranean skin, that yummy olive complexion that nobody in our family had ever even seen until we came east. Vinnie Mancuso could have come, I thought, right off the boat. That's how unspoiled he was.

I'd never met him before; I'd never even seen him before. But as I looked at my watch to see if I'd make it home in time for Ma to use the milk for the supper she was cooking (oyster stew, she'd said, and she'd gotten the oysters fresh in a little bucket and then had forgotten to buy extra milk), the A & P's little black panel delivery truck came shooting up the alley next to the store and from the back of it, flying out its doors like Superman, came Vinnie Mancuso.

The force of his body against mine threw me up against the wall, and I winced in real pain as my carton of milk caught me full in the face, sharp corner to nose. Vinnie's teeth grazed my chin, too, and I was shocked to see blood on his front teeth—mine. We stood like that for a few seconds, both of us scared and caught totally off guard, before Vinnie righted himself, turned on the high heel of his black leather motorcycle boot, and gave the finger to Carroll Matthias, Barbara Foote's cousin who was a senior at Poly. Carroll had never spoken to me—he barely spoke to Barbara even when he saw her, which he usually didn't, since his glasses were so thick (because he had to study so hard to pass the Poly A-Course, Foote said, which I personally thought was a crock and a half), and besides, he was royally stuck-up. He went with Margaret Mary Phelps, a girl at Catholic High who wore the plain green jumper and brown strap shoes and knee-highs that made us Dundalk girls who went to regular public school giggle. Anyway, it looked like Carroll Matthias had less than no use at all for Vinnie Mancuso, since he was obviously trying to kill him by taking off like that while Vinnie was still noisily attempting to shut the back doors of the truck.

"You okay?" Carroll shouted without even looking back.

"Get bent!" Mancuso yelled into the innards of the truck, which smelled like celery and yeast.

"Ah, grow up, will ya, wop?" Carroll said in his nasal way, like Henry Aldrich used to on the radio when I was a tiny girl. Mancuso rammed his hand into the crook of his elbow and gave Matthias the finger again, and then Carroll got out of the truck, came around to the back, his face pulsing at the back of the jaw, right near his ear, where the blood pounded when a guy got good and pissed. He shook his fist at Mancuso.

"Listen, twerp," he roared hoarsely. "I don't have time to mess around with clowns, you get it? Either you fly right or I'm tellin' Bellamy I can't work with you, and you're out on your ass, you get it? You get it?"

"Up your hole with a ten-foot pole," Mancuso said, looking at me out of the corner of his eye. "I don't need this fuckin' job."

"Well, I do," Carroll Matthias said, his face almost purple now, his fists clenching and unclenching. I started to shiver. What if they started hitting each other? I'd seen only one really bad fight up close, and that had been terrible, and I'd had nightmares. It had happened last year after school in the park, two guys getting off the bus amid yelling and shoving, and people egging them both on, pushing them into the middle of the park, shouting dares and insults at both of them, until, God help them, they had to fight or disappoint a crowd ready to rip them apart.

There was blood and noise, knuckles ripping into lips, joints popping and bodies slapping against bodies. I hated it. Soon the bigger guy—I didn't know him—held his huge hand over the other boy's face until the guy went limp and started to turn faintly blue. My God, I thought, he's going to die, and I started to pray. Then he let up his hand; the boy beneath him gasped long, shuddering gasps; and finally the big guy got up slowly and rubbed his hand on the front of his jeans, gathered up his jacket and books and walked away, tall in the afternoon shadows.

Now I was afraid again. Carroll really looked livid, and Mancuso was teasing him, playing with him.

"You moron," Carroll said at last, shaking his head, although there was no hair to fling to the rear of his skull. He'd gotten a crew cut (a whiffle, my pop called those haircuts), which made his scalp look pink through the reddish stubble. "Go play someplace, sonny boy. I don't have time for you anymore. Go on. Blow."

I watched Vinnie's face go tight again, the cocky smile vanishing. "I'll beat the livin' shit out of you, shitface," he snarled, advancing toward Carroll.

"Not today you won't punk," Carroll said, growling back at him. "I got these deliveries to make, and I'm gonna make them alone now, so you just go play."

Vinnie Mancuso let the taller boy get back into the driver's seat of the truck without further incident, but as the truck pulled away, Vinnie raised both hands to heaven and yelled, right in the middle of the late-afternoon crush of shoppers, the just-before-supper crowd, *"PRICK!"* at the top of his lungs, and then Carroll stuck his arm out the window and gave Vinnie the finger, too. When the truck was out of sight, I sighed in relief.

"You work here?" I asked in a small voice. I didn't want to go home and leave him there, leaning up against the brick of the building that way. It seemed cold and cruel.

"Shit, not now, I guess, right?" he said, trying to laugh an Elvis Presley laugh—a laugh that turned the corner of his mouth sideways. I laughed, too.

"Hey, don't make me laugh," he said, snorting the way I did. "I don't wanna laugh, babe. I just got fired, right?"

"Who fired you?"

"Matthias, the bald-headed prick. Son of a bitch hates me. And he's the head of the delivery crew, so what he says goes."

"Even if the boss likes you and wants you to stay?"

"Who, Bellamy? Fat chance of that," he said, digging into his back pocket for a wide blue comb that he used for smoothing his dark, wet-looking hair into a cunning D.A. The comb was not hygienically clean. I looked away from it and he put it back into his pocket. "That bastard said I looked like a bum the first day he laid eyes on me."

"How come he let you work, then?" I asked.

"Ah, Matthias said he needed the help, so Bellamy put me on. Big deal."

We stood there, wondering which direction to take, nobody wanting to be the first one to take the plunge. Finally Vinnie took the lead.

"You go to school?" he asked.

Uh-oh. I didn't want him to know how young I was, but there was no way to lie about it. "Yeah. I go to the Annex."

"Poor little girl," he said, turning on that smile again. "That's too bad, hon."

"How come?" I asked.

"Who'd wanna go down there with them queer Pointers?"

"I don't go to school with Pointers," I said, my back up suddenly. What a crummy thing to say. I'd die before I'd go to school with kids from Sparrows Point. They were Dundalk's arch rivals every year in the Steel Bowl football games. No Dundalk girl in her right mind would hang with Pointers. Cripes. He knew he'd insulted me, and he grinned again, putting his square right hand around the back of my neck and squeezing a little bit.

Holy God. No boy had ever touched me so intimately. It was more than a kiss, more than holding hands. I nearly fainted. He kept looking at me, right in the eyes. I leaned back into the wall in a near-swoon.

"I was just kiddin'," he said. "Forgive me, hon?"

"Yeah," I said. "Why not?"

"I go up Dundalk," he said. "Sometimes," he added, looking sly. "Most of the time, I hook out, ya know?"

Hooking out was a thing that most Dundalk boys did as a matter of course. The girls were more attentive to duty and generally went to school when they were supposed to, but the boys were famous for getting into somebody's car and taking off for Washington, where the drinking age was eighteen, and it was easy for them to get served. I was getting uneasy. Vinnie was a hookout. That was cause for concern.

"What grade are you in?" I asked.

"Tenth," he said. "Supposed to be in eleventh, but I flunked sixth grade."

Who on earth ever flunked sixth grade? I looked dubious.

"No shit," he said, taking out a cigarette from a rumpled pack of Pall Malls, offering me one. I shook my head. I still couldn't inhale without coughing and hacking, and I wanted a little more practice before I went public. Vinnie lit up, cupping his hands around the quickly lit match, protecting the flame from the little breeze that had come up while we talked. Then he reached into his back pocket and pulled out a blue farmer's handkerchief and dabbed at my chin. His touch was gentle, caring.

"What'd you do?" I asked. "How'd you flunk sixth grade?"

"Ah, the teacher was a sis," he said. "He hated me. He was always giving me shit, you know? Calling me names and making me do shit for him after school. I hated that man's guts. I wouldn't do nothing for him."

"Who was he?"

"Some jerk named, ah—jeeze, I forget."

"Paxton?" I offered, giggling at the picture of Paxton versus Mancuso, knowing how flustered Paxton must have gotten under the gaze of those root beer eyes, those Sal Mineo eyes. This boy wore denim and a black T-shirt with a pocket for his cigarettes and black leather boots and a belt studded with steel stuff, like James Dean. Paxton would have been no match for such a boy, not even if he were only twelve, and not tall.

"Yeah, Paxton. What a sis, huh?"

"Yeah, I guess," I said. Truthfully, though, I felt kind of bad about trashmouthing Paxton. He'd always been pretty nice to me, even if I did laugh at him and snicker when the boys called him "Prixton."

"Then I got Womble the next year, and she liked me. Passed me easy. She said I wasn't no dummy, either. I liked her better."

"What do you take now?" I asked.

"Regular crap. Shop. Gym. Fuckin' English." The word was so much a part of his out-of-school talk that it fell from him as easily as a leaf falls from a tree in autumn. He noticed my reaction immediately, however, and hit himself in the head in a gesture of self-abnegation. "Aw, I'm sorry, babe," he said. "I oughta know better than to talk like that around you."

"That's okay," I said quietly, meekly. He could talk any way he wanted, just so he kept on talking to me forever and ever and ever . . . .

"Naa," he said. "I gotta watch my language around you."

"Okay," I said. How long would it be before he discovered that I was only thirteen and not worth fiddling around with?

"What grade are you in?" he said.

"Going into eighth," I told him, and he backed off, laughing.

"Uh-oh," he said. "Jailbait."

I didn't know what that meant.

"What are you, fourteen?" he asked then.

"Nearly," I said, and that seemed to satisfy him.

"Ever been kissed?" he said, a dreamy look coming into his eyes, a faraway look I'd never seen up close like that in a boy.

"What's it to you?" I asked, flip now that the age thing had been settled, and he was looking at me as a woman and not as a dumb kid.

"This," he said, and pulled me to him, spreading my arms out sideways first and then pulling them around his body in a quick motion. He'd taken my crushed milk carton from me casually, moments ago, and had been pretending to straighten out the top of it, and all the while he'd been calculating, scheming, and plotting this move, I thought with awe and delight. He was in love with me.

The kiss was all it should have been, everything the books said it would be and more—much, much more than I'd ever dreamed a kiss could be. First urgent, then gentle, then the pressure increasing again, and the lips open just slightly; and then a little more, and the hint of Vinnie's pointed tongue just inside the place where my teeth were parted, just a hint of him and then a slow withdrawal, and some tiny kisses on my cheeks, on my face. I only wanted to stay there forever, against the A&P wall, kissing this person who loved me so dearly, so tenderly. He smelled like Bokar coffee, fresh-ground right in the store.

"Look, I gotta go," Vinnie said, pulling away from me. "I gotta go meet a guy, ya know?"

"Who?" I asked, as if it really were my business, because suddenly I felt entitled to know Vinnie's business, as if I'd rented him out for the season.

"Bunky Thrasher," he said.

The name was explanation enough. Bunky Thrasher was the Town Corrupter. That's what my pop called him—The Corrupter. Bunky Thrasher had been kicked out of Dundalk High (he'd been a year ahead of Teddy and Garver, and they always talked about him and his obnoxious exploits) a couple of years before, had then joined the army (his family hoped he'd come back a man), and had been kicked out of that before his time was up, and then had come back to Dundalk to futz away the rest of his worthless life. He lived in an apartment and from it he ran a few numbers, pimped a little bit for some black girls from Turner's Station (a very informal occupation—more of a hobby, actually), and made arrangements for Dundalk boys to get booze. He'd collect their money, make a list, go to the liquor store and buy it for them, then have them drop in at his apartment to pick it up. Naturally, he got a commission which helped to pay his piddly rent, so a kid ended up paying two bucks for a six-pack of National worth less than a buck, but the guys were so glad to get it that they paid willingly. So that's how Vinnie Mancuso spent his nights—paying dumb money to Bunky Thrasher.

"Don't hang with Bunky Thrasher," I said. "He's poison."

"What's it to you who I hang with?" Vinnie said, throwing his hair back into place, withdrawing from me suddenly, stiffly.

"You'll be sorry," I said. I felt like crying.

"It's none of your damn business," Vinnie said, and I turned away from him. "Aw, hon," he said, relenting finally, "I know how ya feel. But it's okay. I know how to handle Bunky. Me and Bunky are old buddies."

"I don't like you drinking," I said. I couldn't help it. DeeDee's mother . . .

"I'll be all right," he said. "Don't worry about me. Look, I'll see you, huh? Tomorrow, maybe. Right here, okay?"

"What time?"

"Three okay? Three-thirty?"

The sooner the better. "Three!" I said, more eagerly than I should have, according to Carolanne Erdman, but what the hey—I mean, it was a *date!*

He started to walk away, then slapped his head again, said a disgusted "Jeeze!" and turned to me again. "Hey—what's your name, babe?"

"Beatrice," I said. "Bebe. Bebe Schmidt."

"Bebe, huh? Like beebee gun?"

"Yeah," I said. It sounded dumb, like a kid's name. Why couldn't it be Celeste, or Adrienne, or something? Bebe.

"That's cute," he said. "I like that. Bebe. Phoebe B. Bebe." He pointed to his chest. "This is Vince. Vinnie. Mancuso. Don't forget it."

"I won't." Forget it? It was engraved on my soul.

"Okay, then, see ya, Bebe."

I floated home, swinging the damaged milk carton to and fro, unmindful of the cut on my chin that Vinnie's precious, gorgeous white tooth had made. Ma looked grim when I walked in.

"Where have you been?" she yelled, pointing to the clock that hung over the refrigerator, a cute little number, a kitty with eyes and tail that moved side to side with each tick and tock. It was after four. "And what happened to your chin? Did somebody hit you?"

"Not exactly," I said, unable to contain my electrifying news. I told her all about it, about the wonderful meeting, the chin, the near-fight between Matthias and Mancuso, and how brave Vinnie had been scaring Matthias off, willing to lose his job rather than take a load of crap from a smart aleck. I told it breathlessly, hurling all caution to the winds—well, some caution; I didn't say anything about the kiss, or the hand behind my neck. Ma wouldn't have liked that. Ma's mouth turned down when I told her he was sixteen and in the tenth grade. Pop would spit nickels if he found out, and we both knew it. I had put her in a bad spot.

"What am I supposed to tell your pop?" she asked sharply. It was always that way with Ma. If you didn't tell her things, she got hurt and resentful. If you did, then she got mad at you for putting her in a delicate position. She looked angry, as if I'd spoiled her day.

"What do we have to tell him for?" I asked. I knew the answer but wanted to force it from her in a perverse desire to make her itch a little.

"Because he's your father, and he has to know everything that goes on in this house."

"He doesn't have to know every single thing," I protested, knowing that he did, and would, or else.

"Yes, he does," Ma said tiredly, picking up her dish towel and hanging it on the little rack inside the cupboard door.

"Then let me tell him about it," I offered. "I know how to handle him."

Ma's eyes narrowed. Guileless herself, she regarded feminine wiliness with suspicion. "I don't like the way you said that. What do you mean, 'handle him'? It sounds sneaky."

"Aw, Ma," I grinned. "I'm no sneak. You know that, It's just that sometimes Pop lets me do things my way if I ask him right."

"Yeah, well, good luck," Ma said darkly. "You tell him tonight. I don't think he's going to let you see this boy again."

"Sure, he will," I said, smiling at her. "Just don't you tell him first, okay?"

"Okay," Ma said, relieved, I think, to be out of the discussion at last. She started paging through the section of her cookbook marked "SOUPS" for a tasty recipe for oyster stew. It was all nonsense—she'd read awhile, look in our teeny cabinets for ingredients, talk to herself, then put the cookbook away and go ahead and make the soup the way she always did and float those wonderful little oyster crackers on top of it.

When Pop came home from work carrying his briefcase, I felt a twinge of aggravation, knowing that he'd be less tractable if he had work piled up. Strategy was all-important with Pop. Soon after, Teddy came shambling in from Hopkins with his books and notebooks and slide rule and T-square and assorted junk, and he looked distracted. Ma's face was tense and sharp-looking as she ladled oyster stew into our bowls.

"Is this all we're having?" Pop asked, a dangerous note of complaint creeping into his voice.

"No," Ma said, all patience. "We're having ground-beef-and-tomato casserole, too. It's in the oven."

"Lucky for you," Teddy said. "Or you'd have been in big trouble, woman." Teddy said "woman" because that's what Pop called Ma when he was complimenting her on her cooking. "Good supper, woman," he'd say, burping into his cloth napkin (no paper napkins were allowed on *his* table, by God) and leaving her to bask in the warmth of his praise while she cleaned up the dishes, swept the crumbs, shook the tablecloth out the back door, carried out the garbage, and put all the dishes away. He sat in his chair reading the paper, calling out to her the most choice headlines, reading the stories aloud while she puttered and pranced, and she'd murmur "um-hmm" sixty or seventy times until he tired of reading to her, and still she wasn't done. I'd be doing my homework in my room, and Teddy would be swearing at his slide rule, or bitching about his thermodynamics professor, a guy who was Chinese and who'd not mastered the language sufficiently to make his material decipherable to English-speaking students. Pop was threatening Teddy, who was flunking, with death and dismemberment if he didn't pass the course. The only A's Teddy was getting were in English and history, and Pop was sorely disappointed in him. That year, the two of them couldn't talk without snarling at each other like rival tigers in adjoining cages.

I timed it perfectly, I thought, and waited till Ma was deep into the noisiest part of her puttering before I crept down-stairs and approached Pop where he sat in his chair, the paper covering his face.

"Pop," I said, touching his arm. He pretended he'd been wide awake, and came to consciousness with a start and a phony smile of comprehension.

"Who?" he said.

"Pop, I met a boy. He's nice. Real nice. He used to have Mr. Paxton in the sixth grade, too. He wanted to know if I could meet him tomorrow by the A&P and maybe he'd buy me a Coke or something, okay?"

"A date?" Pop said, blinking his eyes several times. "You know you don't go on dates till you're sixteen years old."

"This isn't a date, Pop, honest," I said, entreating him with such open earnestness that I felt shame creeping into my cheeks, pinkening them. "This boy—Vincent is his name—is having trouble with his schoolwork. He said he heard I was real smart, and he wanted to know if I could help with a few things. Then he said he'd buy me a Coke to pay me off. I know

I can help him, Pop. He's not dumb. Mrs. Womble even said so. I bet I could help him, Pop, and he's so sweet. Couldn't I, please? Pop, he *needs* me."

"And where does all this studying transpire?" Pop asked.

"The library would be the best place," I said, not wanting to lie, not lying, really. "Don't you think so, Pop?"

"I don't know," Pop said. "Let me think about it."

"But, Poppy, I have to know now. He'll be waiting for me there, and if I don't show up, he'll feel terrible."

"You already told him you would?" Pop said, ready to get mad.

"No. No, honest. I only said I'd have to ask my father, but that my father really believed in helping other people, and he wouldn't mind a bit. That's all I said, Pop. Honest."

"Shit," Pop said. He'd fallen into one of his own traps, and it disgruntled him. What choice did he have now? "All right, all right," he said at last. "Go ahead and help this boy. But no alone-together stuff, and no cars, and you'd better be in this house by four, understand?"

"Oh, yes, sir," I burbled. "You're so cool, Poppy!" I bent over and put my arms around his neck, breathing in the pipe smell of him and the Wildroot cream oil hair tonic he used, hugging him in true appreciation for being the kind of pop who would fall for such a crock full of holes, and who would care about me, and want to protect me by being a tough guy. I tramped up the stairs, glowing in triumph.

Teddy clopped downstairs in his brown loafers, a look of stony determination on his face, too. I hesitated at the top step, loath to walk away from what might turn out to be an important exchange. I couldn't separate myself from their confrontations. I always thought I had a stake in them.

Teddy pleaded his case calmly, reasonably.

"Pop, just *listen*. That's all I'm asking."

"When didn't I ever listen to you, son? When? Why are you always accusing me? Why are you so demanding and vindictive? Why—"

"Pop, you're not listening. You're talking."

"See how you are? A man can't talk in his own living room. Well, let me tell you something, you overgrown brat. When I was a boy all we did was listen. We were never allowed to venture our half-baked opinions in my father's house. I never had an opinion in my goddam *life* until I was a married man."

"Good, Pop, right," Teddy said. His voice was stiff with exaggerated patience. Without being able to see him, I could picture his tight, white fists, his shifting from one foot to the other, his looking at the ceiling, a gesture that made Pop's toes curl with fury.

"Am I boring you, Ted?" Pop asked, elaborately polite. "Because if I'm boring you, I can just—"

"No, Pop. Really. Just hear me out. I've got an idea."

"Another idea? You're full of bright ideas lately, aren't you?"

"Pop, just listen to it before you decide how dumb it is, okay?"

"Well, shoot, then. I'm always open to a good idea. You ought to know me that well by now. I—"

"This is it, then," Teddy said, plunging in as fast as he could before Pop could break in and steal his thunder. "See, it looks like my best subjects are all in the humanities area—you know, like literature, social studies, psychology, sociology, drama—all that stuff that engineers think is irrelevant. Stop looking at me like that, Pop. You're not listening to me. You've got to listen if you're going to understand me. See, the thing is, Pop, I could change my major. It's not too late. I've got enough credits to get a B.A. in English in another year, if I concentrate on the right courses and maybe take a few things in summer school. I've got it all figured out. I could drop thermo right now—just take an 'Incomplete' or something, and then I wouldn't have to worry about flunking it. I could concentrate on doing the best I could with the other engineering courses this semester. I'd want to do that much for you, Pop, since you've got so much invested here. But next year I could practically guarantee you all A's and B's—and it would be like getting a little more for your money, huh? And—"

"No," Pop said. His voice cut Teddy off mid-dream.

Silence.

Teddy began again. "If you'll just listen to the rest of it, Pop, I know you'll see it my way. See, I could—"

"No, dammit. I said no and I meant no. N-O. Is it penetrating your oafish skull? Schmidts don't quit things. No 'Incompletes' for my son, not while I'm paying tuition. You're not going to waste my hard-earned cash sitting around with some fairies discussing Byron and Shelley at a round table while your engineering degree—your one big chance at a real, honest-to-God job—goes flying out the window. No."

"Pop, I don't want to be an engineer."

He might have said, "Pop, I want to be a transvestite."

"What?"

"I don't want to be an engineer. I don't like math. I hate it. I'm not that great a student in my engineering courses. Surely you can see that."

"That's just plain jackassed spite. You're not the ignoramus you pretend to be. You think if you do badly enough, I'll be forced to go along with your harebrained ideas. Pretty sly, son, but it won't work."

"Pop, for God's sake. What do I have to do—commit suicide on the Hopkins Quadrangle before you believe me?"

"You'd do it, too, wouldn't you?" Pop said. "You'd do it to spite me once and for all. You're amazing, Teddy. You're a mystery to me. I've spent a lifetime trying to make things good for you—handed you an education on a platter made of gold, by God, and this is what I get? A skinny, crazy, lazy sissy of a smartass who doesn't have the heart to go on when the going gets a little bit tough? I'm telling you, boy, it makes me sick. It makes me want to lay down and bawl like a baby."

"Lie," Teddy said. "Lie down and bawl."

"Brat!" Pop shouted at Teddy. I could hear Ma dropping and clattering things around in the kitchen. She'd heard them, too, of course. It was hard for her to sort it all out. Pop had always been so right, and now here was this boy, this Teddy who seemed so bright, so self-assured . . .

"Yeah, I guess I'm a brat, all right," Teddy agreed, and I could hear the grinding contempt from my perch above them. "I'm incorrigible, aren't I, Pop? Worst son in the country. Hell, the *world,* probably. Well, I'm heartily sorry for all the humiliation and pain I've caused you. I'll just go quietly up to my room now and get my nose back on that grindstone, Father dear. I'll struggle and scratch to make you proud of me, sir. Yessirree. Old Herman Schmidt's going to make a man of me yet."

I scrambled into my room as Teddy fled Pop's glowering presence and made for the stairs. I could hear the rasping intake of his breath as the first of the sobs racked his slight body. Teddy crying. I couldn't believe it. He slammed shut the door to his room and I could hear him tossing things around, swearing, crying, yelling to nobody that he hated, hated, hated . . .

Downstairs, everything was quiet. Even Ma stopped banging things around in the kitchen. Pop didn't rattle his paper or turn on the TV for Douglas Edwards and the news. It was a ghastly evening, each of us locked up behind a door marked "Private." I did hear Ma break into Pop's silence once, just before I went in for my shower.

"Herm," she said. "He thinks you can't stand him."

"He's just acting up. He's being difficult. He knows I love him."

"Herm, he doesn't. He thinks you've shut the door on him. You've got to go and talk to him."

"The hell I do. He started this crap, now let him stew in his own juices for a while."

"You're as stubborn as your father," Ma said.

"What do you know about my father?" Pop said suddenly, like a spark that flares up into a leaping flame.

"Only what I saw and heard," Ma said, and let it drop.

"Leave my father out of this," Pop said. "My father was the personification of discipline, truth, and courage. Any boy would have been proud to be his son."

"And who loved you?"

"My mother. And Pa, too, of course. Of course." But Ma's point had been made. Grampa's love for Pa hadn't been his major contribution to the formation of his character, obviously. From father, discipline. From mother, love. It was pretty open-and-shut for Pop. He was doing his best.

I went to bed with my deception and its twanging, vibrant voice of danger singing me to sleep.

At the bus stop the next morning, I told Bernadette and Rita Lee all about Vinnie Mancuso.

"Vinnie Mancuso?" Bernadette gasped. "Vinnie? From Sennalena?"

"Yeah," I said. "Baltimore Avenue."

"Oh, jeeze," Bernadette sighed. "Do you know who he is?"

"No, who?"

"He got kicked outta Bettendorf's math class in the ninth grade for pulling a knife. He was suspended a week for that. Didn't you ever hear about it?"

A knife? Vinnie? "No," I said. "It probably isn't even true."

"Hell it isn't," Bernadette said. "Carolanne was right in the next room when it happened. She'll tell ya."

"Well, that was *then,*" I said inanely. "He's not like that now."

"Ooh, he's cute, though," Bernadette said, hugging her looseleaf to her chest. "I saw him at one of the teen center dances last summer, and he was so-oh-oh *neat.* He was dancing with Rose Del Vecchio. You know her?"

Yeah, I knew her. "Rink," the guys always called to her when she came around. "Rink" was a Dundalk word for "pig" and was pronounced like "oink," only dirtier. I knew all about Rose Del Vecchio. Even the girls on the senior swim team spoke of her in awed tones.

"He was probably desperate," I said, feigning a giggle. "He was just waiting for me to come along."

"He really kissed you?" Bernadette said. "On the mouth?"

I nodded. Rita Lee looked down at her penny loafers and pretended to wind a thread around a loose button on her navy blue boy coat. This wasn't the kind of talk she could relate to. I mean, what would her *mother* say?

"What else did he do?" Bernadette asked. "Did he ask you out?"

"Yeah," I said casually. Her mouth went loose. "This afternoon. He said to meet him at the A & P. Said he'd buy me a Coke up the Arundel."

"Holy shit," Bernadette breathed in the same voice that she saved for "Hail Mary." "You going?"

Is a pig's ass pork? "I guess," I said. "Nothin' else to do."

"Can I come?" Bernadette begged. "I want to meet him. Aw, please, Beeb. Just this little once. I swear I'll leave as soon as I meet him. I swear."

"Oh, all right," I said, giving in with a rush of happiness. It was the first time I'd ever been in a position to be envied, and I planned to milk it for all it was worth.

It was, of course, the talk of the classroom. Even the boys seemed impressed. Santino shook his head and looked disgusted. Price looked crushed. Bernadette told and retold my story to Bisky and Foote and the others, and they turned to look at me with new, wide eyes. It was some damn fine day.

Three o'clock came, and I went with Bernadette and stood up against the A & P wall and I waited for my man to come and kiss me, and it was wonderful there in the spring-warm sunshine, watching for him, waiting for him.

He didn't come.

Finally, Bernadette went home to start supper, disillusioned and disappointed.

Finally, I did, too. If Vinnie Mancuso was in love with me, he had a funny way of showing it. My heart iced over on that walk home. I slid in the door, said a perfunctory hi to Ma, and trotted upstairs as if I had urgent business in the bathroom, which I did. As soon as the door was closed behind me, the tears dribbled out and onto the front of my blouse and I put my forehead against the chilly tiles and just cried and cried until I felt limp and soggy. I also felt sick to my stomach. Hungry, I figured. The smell of pork chops baked with stuffing wafted up the stairway, and suddenly I knew that the gnawing pain could be assuaged at dinnertime, in the midst of people who loved and cared for me, sitting there at our family table where people were talked to and forgiven their trespasses and prayed with and fussed over. Everything would be okay as soon as dinner started.

I saw Vinnie again. He came running up to me as I walked through the park the following week. He'd forgotten all about promising to meet me that day and looked blank when I told him how rotten he'd made me feel. He kissed me, though, and somehow the pain drifted up and away from me, and then he kissed me again and again, and I found myself bending against him. He seemed so strong, so capable of supporting all my weight in his rugged arms. I wanted him to carry me away from the park, from Dundalk, from the Annex and the house on Liberty Parkway. I wanted to go far away from there, and I wanted him to take me.

But he had to leave early again. He had groceries to deliver (he'd gotten onto the other shift with a different guy), and besides, he never really went out with girls much. He had too many other things to do, and he liked to spend his evenings with Gary Cantalupo and Fritz Bender and a couple of other notorious hookouts sitting on overturned milk boxes in a corner of the park, just drinking National (gimme a BOH!), smoking Pall Malls, and talking dirty. I said I guessed it was okay. I wasn't allowed out at night anyway. Just so he'd keep meeting me in the park. Just so he'd keep kissing me like that.

A week later he came to the park where I sat reading, waiting for him. My *Modern Screen* was forgotten as soon as I spotted him hurrying toward me. He sat down heavily on the bench and stuck his short legs out in front of him, his hands jammed deep into the tight pockets of the Wranglers, his dark eyes closed.

"What's the matter?" I asked.

"Nothin'," he said. "Come here, babe."

I slid over. It was dangerous, meeting him out in the open this way. The neighborhood people walked through the park on their way home from shopping in Dundalk, and anybody could have seen me and reported me to Ma, but I didn't care. I felt reckless with Vinnie, invincible. Let people see. Let them tell.

Vinnie put his arms around me and pulled me close against his side. I felt like a pretzel, miserably uncomfortable, with my neck twisted and my legs bent awkwardly, but I sat there without protesting, not wanting to intrude upon his mood. He looked today more like Sal Mineo than ever, darkly sensual, sweetly tough. I loved him so much it broke my heart just to look at him sometimes. He was so beautiful.

"I got bad news, hon," he said at last, letting me sit up straight.

"What?"

"I got kicked out."

"Of school?"

"Yeah. And worse than that, too."

"What?"

"Kicked out of my house. My old man says to get my junk out of his house by tomorrow afternoon. He says if I'm home when he gets home from work he'll call the cops to come and get me. He says he's sick of the sight of me."

"He can't kick you out," I said, indignant. "He just can't."

"Hell he can't. He can do anything he wants."

"Oh, Vinnie," I said, tears thickening my voice. "Oh, poor Vinnie."

"Hey, can it, huh?" he said hotly, tossing his hair back. "I don't need your goddam pity, ya know? I got it made. I got it all planned out already. I'm joining the Marines. Soon as I can get out of this horseshit town, I'm going to Parris Island for basic."

"The Marines? But you're too young. Don't you have to be eighteen?"

"I am."

He'd lied to me. My face, wordless, accused him.

"So I lied," he said carelessly. "You never lied? Hell, I just didn't want you to know how many times I failed."

The tears that had been forming spilled now, and Vinnie's face softened. He grabbed me and started kissing me, all over my neck, my eyes, my ears, and he was whispering now, urging me to come with him someplace.

"Where?" I asked.

"You love me, babe?" he asked, looking so sad, so abandoned, so forlorn.

"Oh, yes, Vinnie, I really do. You know I do."

"Then come with me."

We walked together through the park in the sweet early spring sunlight toward the dime store. I seriously believed that he was going to buy me a last Coke, and the tears started once more.

"I can't stand it, Vinnie," I said, putting my hand over my eyes. "I don't know how I'm gonna live if you go away. You're the only boy I'll ever love as long as I live."

"Aw, you're only fourteen," he said gruffly. "There'll be a lot of guys."

"No!" I wailed. "Only you." People were looking. We walked faster.

He opened the door at the back of the dime store, but instead of going in, Vinnie put his hand in the middle of my back and guided me toward the stairs to the apartments above the store.

"Vinnie, where are we going?" I said. I was trembling now, remembering a day so long ago that I thought I'd forgotten it, the day with James, and coming down those wooden stairs with my braids out behind me.

I pulled away from the stairs. I didn't want to go up there.

"Go on up. It's okay. Honest. Bunky said."

Bunky? Oh, dear God. Where was I going?

"Go on up," Vinnie said, impatient with me now. He shoved me from behind again.

"I can't go up there," I said weakly.

"I thought you loved me."

"I do."

"Then get up those stairs."

God forgive me, I went. For love, I went.

Bunky sat on a lumpy couch in his hot-damp apartment watching a small-screen TV. A soap opera called *Young Doctor Malone.* My ma watched that at home. I thought of her there, sitting and mending something as she watched, potatoes boiling on the stove, smells from the oven warming the air. I was so scared I almost passed out. Bunky's legs were bare—he was wearing Bermuda shorts that had been cut off at the knee from khaki pants and left raggedy. He had on a dingy T-shirt that he kept pulling and stretching, and he scratched his pimply arms incessantly as he and Vinnie talked of nothing in particular. I scarcely heard their conversation until he addressed me directly.

"Sit down, hon," he said, patting a filthy cushion on the couch. A half-eaten bowl of chicken noodle soup sat next to him, and cracker crumbs littered his furniture, all three pieces of it. I wouldn't have sat anywhere, much less next to him.

"Never mind," Vinnie said. "We're going in here to talk awhile." He pulled me along a short, narrow hallway that led to the only bedroom, a ten-by-thirteen affair with a moldy-looking mattress on its floor. There were two ratty blankets, a greasy pillow at the head of the mattress, and various porno magazines flung around the room. Beer cans lay on their sides, wine bottles cluttered the corners, and burnt candles lay on the floor where they'd fallen out of the beer bottles they'd been stuck into.

"Sit down, babe," Vinnie said, pointing to the rank mattress. "We can talk here and nobody'll bother us."

The miasma of Essence of Bunky was choking me. I wouldn't sit.

"I've got to go home now, Vinnie," I said, breathing through my mouth so that my nostrils couldn't let in any of the stink.

In the other room, Bunky laughed out loud at one of the lines in the soap opera. Then he farted. Vinnie closed the bedroom door. "Don't pay no attention to Bunky," he said in a whisper. "He ain't even listening."

"Open the door, Vinnie," I said. I'd read enough *True Confessions* magazines to know that I was in for terrible trouble. "Vinnie, please."

"When are you going to quit acting like such a sis?" he said, holding me by the shoulders and looking into my eyes. "All I want to do is talk to you, baby blue eyes. What's the big bad deal? Sit down." He pushed me down onto the mattress.

"Ain't that better?" he said, settling in beside me. "Don't it feel good, just us being here like this, with nobody to bother us?"

"Uh, yeah, great," I said, afraid to talk above a whisper.

"See?" he said. "Nothing can hurt you now, babe. Vinnie's right here."

He began running his hands over my legs, over my belly, pulling me down onto the squishy mattress and putting half his body over mine. "Isn't it great?" he murmured over and over. "Isn't it great, baby? Ooh, you're gonna love it, baby. You're gonna love it."

And his hand was opening the thick snap at the waist of my jeans, and then the hand was inside, forcing the heavy zipper open, and I could feel the heat of his palm on my belly through the cotton underpants; and then something deep inside me caught fire and I gasped and I begged him to move his hand away, and he did, up to my little breasts, pushing the bra up toward my neck, not bothering to unhook it, putting his tongue on my nipples, one at a time, murmuring things I couldn't understand. He was making noises that weren't words at all, scaring me, taking little bites out of me, and I was so scared, so scared. My legs kicked hard at him, and he laughed deep in his throat and chest, and put his whole body over mine and said go ahead, go ahead, little girl. He kept biting me and putting his tongue inside my ear and my mouth while I turned back and forth, trying to bite him, bucking and kicking and swearing at him then, screaming and fighting.

Bunky banged open the door and roared something unintelligible and started yanking at Vinnie, pulling him up by his jeans. He threw Vinnie out into the hallway and hollered at him, the spit flying in all directions, telling him that I was jailbait, no more than a little kid, and what the hell was he trying to do, get him thrown in jail? Didn't he have no better sense that that? The Marines better knock some brains into that fat wop skull because the good Lord sure didn't give him none.

I was scrabbling around on the floor, trying to get my pants back together and my bra pulled down; and Vinnie was shouting and cussing at Bunky; and Bunky was shushing me and hustling me down the hallway, telling me to run along now and to keep my fat mouth shut and don't tell nobody or he'd have a contract out on me so fast.

Then the door slammed shut behind me, and once again I took off running down that smelly linoleum hallway, running for my life down the wooden stairs to where you could hear Kresge's parakeets raising hell in their cage. I smelled the fish food and the dried flies they fed the tiny turtles and the licorice-y smell of parakeet Treetfood. As I slowed down and walked through the store, panting, the girl at the record counter put on "I'm Stickin' with You," and I felt a little easier, less panicky, almost real again, almost back inside my own body again and ready to get the heck home where I belonged. I prayed all the way, saying glory to God in the highest, and thank you that Vinnie didn't Vinnie didn't Vinnie didn't.

A little later that month, I heard that Vinnie Mancuso had left for good and had gone to Parris Island. Two years later, I saw him at the teen center one Saturday night, and he didn't seem to recognize me. I'd gained weight, so maybe he just didn't know me. But I knew him. The dress uniform with its gorgeous white hat and gloves and that nice gold braid didn't fool me. He still had those bedroom eyes, and he still looked at girls in the same old way. And he still looked, at twenty, for girls young enough to be his baby sisters.

My first real love, my Vinnie.

Barbara Foote asked him to dance, and he held her so close that I watched her knees go weak, and she leaned deep into him, into that place where his pants were probably going stiff. I smiled inside to butter the pangs that were wounding me.

Vinnie Mancuso.

What a dip.

Just before Vinnie left for the Marines, a day or two after our tussle at Bunky's, Santino sidled up to me at the bus stop after school and said, "Hey, you still hangin' with that grease-ball Mancuso?"

"Shut up, Santino," I said. I didn't even want to talk to Bernadette about Vinnie, much less a simp like Santino.

"Make me," Santino said, a filthy grin showing his nice, even teeth.

I always carried my junk in my left arm, like a baby on the hip, so with my free right hand I let him have it right in the left cheek—so hard that his head nearly snapped off his neck and it sounded as if I'd loosened most of his pearly Texas teeth. He shook his head, blinked his eyes, which had begun to tear, and backed away, then opened and closed his mouth a few times to check if his jaw was broken.

It was my last formal act of childhood.

Chapter 12

The first time I called my mother "Mother" she looked startled, did a little double take, then went right on kneading the immense wad of bread dough she was working. Ma didn't knead dough, as such; she manhandled it. I've watched other women baking bread, and it always makes me giggle. They look so neat when they do it. My mother and I worked dough like lady wrestlers, going at it with fist and forearm and elbow, leaning into the work with gusto.

"Hairnets!" my father would yell from the living room, lowering his paper and craning his neck trying to peer around the corner, checking to see if we were complying with his number-one rule: No Hair in the Food. He was a gagger. He couldn't help it. Even as a tiny kid, my grandmother told us, he couldn't abide an "off" food smell or a hair anywhere near his plate. So we had a set of balled-up hairnets, encrusted with flour, in our supplies drawer. Hideous.

"Yes, *hairnets*," Ma—Mother—hollered back to mollify him. Then she muttered a little "Dammit" under her breath. I was shocked.

"Mother," I whispered. That's when she did her double take. Just stopped for a piece of a second, and then went right on kneading, as if she hadn't heard me. "Mother," I repeated in my eighth-grade prep girl twang. "Really."

That "really," that one word, had become the word with which Bernadette and I placed our parents somewhere to the rear of the newts in intelligence and *savoir-faire.* "*Really,* Father," I'd said the previous week, looking over his shoulder as he addressed and sealed his weekly letter to his parents. "Your letter form is atrocious."

He looked up briefly, then looked back at his letter. His handwriting was beautiful, much like I supposed Charles Dickens's might have been, bold and yet embellished with a subtle curlicue or two to indicate the breeding and sensitivity of the writer. It wasn't Pop's—Father's—writing I objected to, really. It was his lack of finesse in matters of proper heading, return address, date—all the things that we were graded on —that upset me. I told him all about it. He let me finish, then leaned back in the chair, sighed, and said, "Listen, you terrible infant. You're talking about business letters. This is a personal letter. You don't do all that crap in a personal letter."

Personal? Not business? I was getting the tiniest bit confused. But when were you supposed to do all that "heading" stuff, and put the address in, and all that? It was getting hazy already, and we'd only had it in school four days ago. Pop snorted as he lit his pipe.

"You know, it doesn't do for a girl to be a fool of books," he said gently, smiling his Cheshire cat smile. I hadn't the slightest idea what he was getting at, but I'd heard him say something similar to Teddy, so I knew he didn't mean it kindly despite his tone.

"I'm not a fool," I blurted.

"Then quit acting like one and get upstairs and do your homework," he snapped. I went with dispatch. Sometimes I let him have his way in order to avoid an uncouth scene. I hadn't studied the word "expedient" on our vocabulary list for nothing.

Father snorted every time I referred to him as such. Mother was more subtle. She merely seemed to shrug it off

176

and went about her business as usual, bustling and bullying and bullwhipping our place into shape without too much fuss and feathers. She could adapt, it seemed. Father found it too hard to accept, though, and continued to snicker each time I said it.

"*Really*, Mother," Bernadette said to her mother when Mrs. Erdman insisted we stick around for a while after school one day just to yak it up a little before going out to hunt for boys.

"Ah, don't give me none a that 'Mother' crap, girl. What's this, some kind of a new phrase youse two are into?" she asked me, her orange hair plastered in waves across the top of her head like huge strands of rickrack.

"Phrase?" I said. Oh, jeeze, it was starting. Bernadette got up and sneaked into the kitchen to put water on to boil (we were going on fourteen and too old for afternoon milk and Oreos), leaving me—deliberately, purposely, leaving me—alone to deal with her mother, the Madam Malaprop of Dundalk.

"Yeah, new phrase. You know, some new act youse two are pullin'."

"No, ma'am," I said, fighting to keep the laughter inside its delicate cage.

"Ma'am? Hey, Bern! Shiz callin' me 'ma'am' like she did the first day she met me! I swear, if youse two ain't a riot and a half !" She laughed her big laugh and then started to cough, pulling in great wheezing lungfuls of air. Her lower lip sucked itself almost down her throat, because she wouldn't wear her bottom teeth (they hurt her and made ulsters on her gums, she said), and the racking coughs seemed about to crack open her narrow birdlike chest, to split her like a tough little old chicken. Soon she recovered, though, and lit another Chesterfield Regular, picking the tobacco bits from her top teeth and tongue with a polished nail, flicking them to the linoleum floor of the little dining room where we sat.

"How do you like my new sexual furniture?" she asked,

indicating the curved sectional sofa of aqua nubby fabric with its matching smaller loveseat.

From the kitchen Bernadette gave a sort of a "hoo-whip" as she first emitted a part of a guffaw and then sucked it quickly back inside.

"Best you can git, you know that? It just came yesterday. Nobody's sat in it yet, though. Not till Plastishield comes, right, Bern?"

"Right, Mother," Bernadette said, having regained her cool.

"Who's that?" I asked.

"Cripes. Plastishield. The slipcover guys. Jeeze-oo-whiz, girl, don't your mother keep her stuff covered?"

"I don't think so," I said. Bernadette came back in. Her mother shot her a glance that read: Clods—don't even keep their furniture covered.

"She ought to," Gert Erdman went on lavishly, blowing an immense cloud of smoke into the air. All the windows were shut, and it wasn't cold enough yet to be so insulated from the outside air. I nearly choked dead away in the smog from that Chesterfield. "Here, lemme give you their number. She can call 'em." Generously, without making me ask, she wrote out the name and number of the Plastishield people who came and took away your new furniture and sealed it in heavy, clear plastic slipcovers so that the fabric showed through but nothing could penetrate.

"See, that furniture can't never get old now," Gert explained patiently to the Farm Girl. "It's always gonna look that good."

"I see," I said. She must have felt the same way about her lampshades, because they were still wrapped in their store covering of cellophane, wound round and round like bandages.

"Daddy, he wanted Early American again, but I said hell no, this time it's the good stuff. This stuff's gotta last through

Bernie's graduation and wedding, ya know? Another four-five years yet, right?"

Bernadette and I nodded gravely. Apparently Bernadette had not yet confided to her family her ambitions to become a WAC. I hoped Mrs. Erdman wouldn't be too disappointed if Bernadette graduated and did not fall immediately into a marriage bed with some nice kid from Saint Rita's CYO.

Bernadette did not wait for the kettle's whistle to shriek. She ambled back into the teeny stand-up kitchen and poured almost-boiling water over a single Lipton's tea bag because it would easily be good for all three cups, and why waste anything ("Waste not, want not")? Into ours went milk and sugar; her mother's was black. "Hot and black—that's how I like my coffee, my tea, and my *men*!" Gert cackled. It was one of her favorite jokes, one she told damn near every time we drank anything over there. It drove Mr. Erdman wild when she said it. He had no use for such low-life jokes; she was lowering herself saying shit like that, he told her. Gert just kept cackling. She was forty-two years old, she said, and ought to know by now what she could get away with.

I never understood exchanges like that, and I always got unaccountably frightened.

"Ah, you're goozey," Mr. Erdman would say in disgust, leaving the house for a quick trot up to Dundalk to snoop around a little at Joe the Motorist's Friend, maybe catch one at the bar, pick up a *Saga* magazine, or maybe an *Enquirer* (that was our favorite, Bernadette's and mine, among his stockpile of magazines on the bedroom closet floor).

"Hey! Spread that there African out on the sofa if you're gonna sit there and drink, Hunky," Gert said to me, pointing to the crocheted afghan that lay across the sofa's low back. Gert's vocabulary was rich with superficial hatreds. Nigger, jigaboo, jungle bunny, Polack, Hebe, bohunk, spade, spick, mick, redneck, cracker.

In truth, she had never had any dealings much with any-

body outside her immediate friends and family since she'd
quit school at fourteen to marry her first husband, a German
kid from Highlandtown named, of all things, Emil Borgerding
(which she always pronounced "Borgadeen"), and had had
four children in quick succession. Borgadeen had died ripped
and tangled in a machine down at The Point during the rush
for steel in 1941, and she'd married within a year the reticent
Eddie Erdman, a tall man a little younger than she, she said.

She seemed to lord it over him with her slight advantage
in years, a thing that always amazed me, since it seemed something that a woman would want to keep to herself, being older
than her husband. But not Gert. She was always telling him,
"You don't know nothin'. You haven't lived enough yet to
know nothin'." He would stomp out of the room.

Gert's world was filled with her parents and brothers and
sisters and their various families—a vast number of people, it
seemed to me, each time I saw them assembled. I never saw
Bernadette's Aunt Mim (short for, no lie, "Mimosa") that she
wasn't holding some sort of oversized and obstreperous child
under one arm while it kicked and struggled to get away from
her. Apparently these people were truly dedicated to the concept of keeping the earth properly peopled.

("Catholics!" my father muttered blackly when I told him,
rattling his newspaper like a machine gun. "They're trying to
take over the goddam *earth.* That's their plan, see? They just
keep on cranking out these kids they can't afford to bring up
properly, then first thing you know, *Pow*! It's the Catholics
running the world, with the Pope as head of the government.")

A regular visitor at the Erdmans' was Viola, the Pegeen
Personal Products lady from across the street. Once every
few weeks she'd breeze in with her pink-and-purple plastic
satchel full of goodies. There were cunning little samples
for us all to try, huge poufy sprays of sweet, lingering cologne and room freshener, glossy folders full of makeup
tips. It was fun. Viola herself had nine teeth, tops, and

looked pretty much like the Phantom of the Opera at a drag ball, but Bernadette and I enjoyed the hell out of ourselves while Gert and old Vi just blew unfiltered smoke into thick, swirling clouds around us. Old Vi's daughter, Lucy Grabowski, was a new friend of ours from school, and sometimes she idled on over, too, once her homework was done (she always did hers first, even before dinner), and they were some pretty good days, all in all.

When I'd come home from afternoons at Bernadette's, my mother used to sniff my hair and pout out her bottom lip. "Dirty smoke," she'd say. "It doesn't smell anything like pipe smoke." To my mother, my father's pipe smoking was a suitably manly thing, a hobby that she found inoffensive. But a woman's smoking offended her more than words could say. The smell, the stains, the phlegmy cough, the brashness of the act all repelled her. She pushed me away when I reeked of cigarettes. "You smell like the bowling alley," she'd say, shoving me out of her way. I'd go upstairs and whirl around in a cloud of Pegeen Products spray cologne to mask the odor from Pop. He found the smell of bowling alley intolerable and noxious.

One November night I donned "full regalia," Ma's term for my dress-up clothes, complete with makeup and hairdo. Teddy was taking me to a movie. It wasn't that he couldn't get a girl to go with him. Ha. Half the girls in town would have paid money to go with him. He was taller than ever, arrow-straight and thin, with dark hair whose slight wave did not give way to outright curliness. His features were like those of Mother's people—straight, firm, somewhat elongated. They were like marathon runners, with long bones, stringy muscles, athletes who went for speed and endurance. They had strong hands, thin feet, large noses, intense eyes.

My father's people were stubby, tough, compactly built people of deceptive bulk and heft. They were thick and barrely, wide around chest and calf, square-handed.

Teddy had gotten all the best of everything, I thought. He

was my mother on stilts, while I looked like Father in a wig, standing in a hole. Ted wore his clothes easily, gracefully; they hung naturally from his wide shoulders and narrow waist. My clothes had to be yanked and coaxed to induce them to stay unrumpled while I was standing still. He must have looked like Robin Hood graciously accompanying an underprivileged munchkin that night as he paid for my ticket at an "art" theater in the city.

"Why didn't you ask some girl to go with you?" I wanted to know.

"I did," he said, grinning at me on the way up in his car, a 1949 Chevy some guy at school had sold him for forty dollars. "I asked you."

"No," I said, flushing with pleasure to have been so chosen. "You know what I mean. Some *girl*."

"To tell you the truth," he said, "I really and truly want to see this movie. If I took some girl, I wouldn't see half of it, right?"

"I get it," I said, shivering inside to realize that Teddy was probably Doing It with girls, and that it probably all started right here in his car, and in the movie theaters with kissing and hugging and leg feeling and all that jazz. Someday it would be me in the movies with some guy, trying to watch a movie while he was sticking his tongue into my ear, trying to get me all hot and bothered. Jeeze. I kind of felt sorry for Teddy.

"What is this thing we're going to see anyhow?" I asked.

"It's an Ingmar Bergman movie," he told me. He pronounced it "Bear-man," and not "Berg-man," like Ingrid Bergman.

"So?" I said. You don't find out anything if you don't ask.

"So, it's a Bergman film," he said. "Watch and see."

I kept quiet. The thing was, it was all in subtitles, and for the first few minutes I was tickled to pieces to be hearing whatever language it was singsonging over my head while the words stood harshly in front of me. Then the reading got to be second nature, and it was wonderful, and my imagination took wing, and I fancied for a moment or two that I was understanding the language, absorbing it into my consciousness somehow. I went quietly nuts on that fantasy.

The movie itself was pretty interesting. The way I perceived it then, a servant girl was pregnant, and the people she lived with weren't very nice to her. Their daughter went out to do something—I don't know, pick flowers or visit Gramma or something, it was hard to tell—and some of the grungiest guys I'd ever seen raped her and beat her up and robbed her while their little brother watched. She died. They ran away. Her father found her. He vowed revenge. The bad guys came to that very house for a handout, and the father gave it to them. He discovered (I forget how) that they were the culprits and killed them with his bare hands, even the little boy who hadn't done anything. Then a clear, bubbling spring appeared in the place where the daughter was murdered. A couple of people threw up right on camera. I forgot what happened to the servant girl.

"Wow," Teddy breathed as the houselights came up. "God." I could see he was impressed. He rubbed his eyes and just sat for a moment, and didn't leap up toward the aisle the way he usually did when a movie was over. Finally, he pulled himself up and we headed for the street. "God," he said again. "That was some beautiful work, wasn't it?"

"Yeah," I said, mimicking his reverent tone. He looked surprised.

"Yeah?" he said, looking pleased as all getout. "You mean you really liked it?"

"Sure," I said. I was so proud to be next to him, invited along to share in his pleasure, that he could have taken me to a turtle race and I'd have been ecstatic. "It was great."

"What did you like about it?"

"Let's see," I said, hoping to say something profound. "It was—I know. There wasn't any of that dumb music they always have in the background, right?"

"Hey, that's right. You're right. Good. You're learning, Half-pint."

I'd scored a point, and I was elated.

At home, Father was waiting up for us, his head flopped forward onto his chest atop a crumpled *Evening Sun.* His pipe had gone out.

"Pop," Teddy said, shaking him gently. "Time to go to bed, pal."

"Who?" Pop asked, bolting upright, dropping his pipe and knocking cinders and ashes all over the place.

"Bedtime, Pop," Teddy said again, smiling into Pop's face.

"Cripes, what time is it?" Pop asked, alarmed.

"Only a little after ten. Why?" Teddy said. "Something wrong?"

"You best believe something's wrong, hotshot," Pop said. "Since when does a thirteen-year-old kid stay out till all hours on a goddam school night?"

"Aw, come off it, Pop. It's only a little after ten. If she'd stayed home, she'd still be awake, for God's sake."

"That's true, Father," I said. "I never go to bed before ten-thirty."

"The hell you don't," Pop said, standing up shakily, still partly asleep.

"Well, let's don't fight about it, okay?" I said.

"Nobody's fighting," Father said loudly, belligerently.

"You are, Father," I said coldly. "Teddy and I were just about to go to bed, and you're keeping us awake."

"And what the hell is this phony-ass 'Father' crap anyhow?"

"Oh, *really,*" I said, turning on my heel and stomping up the stairs.

"Who's this, Princess Graceful of Monaco now?" Father called up the stairs after me. "You're too big for your damn britches is your problem," he yelled, really pissed.

"Father, *please,*" I said. I sounded like Tallulah Bankhead, and I knew it. I closed my bedroom door, while Father and Teddy had a few more heated rounds down in the living room. I could hear them going at it. But I didn't even bother to open my door. I was too tired, and I wanted to recall the images in the movie. Finally, though, the noise downstairs got too loud to ignore.

"No kid of mine needs to be out walking the goddam city streets of Baltimore like a sleazy tramp," Pop shouted.

"Get off it, Pop," Teddy said. "Bebe's getting too old for you to be breathing down her neck every second. Can't you just trust her, for God's sake? She can't be held down all her life."

Pop's voice was jagged, as if he were in pain. "Somebody's got to look out for her," he said. "Right? Right? Who the hell's going to look after her if I don't? You? *You?* Hardy har har. In a pig's eye."

Teddy said nothing. I heard his footsteps ascending the stairs.

"Well, *who?*" Pop bawled up the steps.

Teddy did not answer.

Christmas came and went. More Elvis records this year, and a plaid pleated skirt made of wool, and my first "laced" eggnog. Wahoo. Bernadette and I sloshed down about a gallon of the stuff out of little glass cups Christmas Day before we realized that it only looked and tasted like milk mixed with sugar and vanilla; we were oily-eyed and ankle-walking for an hour or so, and Bernadette finally had to head for our microscopic bathroom to do a little finger-in-the-throat before she could safely totter home on her four-inch heels with their somewhat pointed toes (you had to walk pigeon-toed in those shoes, with your knees bent; instant hammertoe). Wow. Later that week, we bragged to Lucy Grabowski about how gassed we'd been and how disgustingly sick we'd gotten. Wa-double-hoo.

January passed without major incident, but February, that month infamous for brittle nerves and flaring tempers, brought Pop and Teddy almost to the end of their road.

Teddy got Found Out at last.

His grade slips from Hopkins came in the mail the first week of February, and he didn't show them to Pop right away.

"Aren't you going to show them to him?" I asked cautiously. "Don't tell me you flunked something." Neither of us ever had, and wouldn't dare. It was unthinkable.

"Naa," Teddy said, running his fingers through his wavy hair as he contemplated the one wall where the paper was figured. "Nothing like that."

I looked over his shoulder as he sat holding the grade slips in his shaking hand. All A's and B's. Beautiful. "Pop will do a back flip!" I said, hugging Teddy.

"Damn straight, he will," Teddy said, looking so gloomy that he resembled Droopy, the cartoon dog we loved so much at the movies. Teddy pointed to his first "A." "He's gonna love this one," he said. I looked again.

"History of Dramatic Form?" I said, unbelieving. "And what's this one? Contemporary American Poets? What's all this? Where's the engineering stuff? Teddy, what did you do?"

"What does it look like?" he snapped, suddenly irritated, defensive, all elbows and chin. "I just took some courses I wanted to take for a goddam change. What's it to you?"

I shrank out of the living room, already anticipating the worst.

Nobody said anything that night, but Teddy wolfed down his meat loaf, mashed potatoes, carrots, and beans and then dashed out of the house and went to the movies with Garver. It wasn't until the next night that Father asked him pointblank if his grade slips ever came.

"Well?" Pop insisted, staring hard at Teddy.

"Yeah, they came," Teddy said. His mouth was full of cabbage.

"Well, where are they?" Pop demanded.

"I don't know. Around somewhere, I guess," Teddy said.

"So go get them," Pop said slowly, elaborately. Teddy

didn't budge. "Now!" Pop roared, and all of us jumped. He hadn't yelled in a while, and it was a surprise. My ham stuck in my throat and I could not swallow.

Teddy glared at Father, hurled his napkin down on the table, and pushed himself rudely away from his place. He thumped upstairs, made a lot of noise searching, then finally came down and gave the grade slips to Father, who read and reread them, and finally seemed to be trying to memorize them as we all sat with breath appropriately bated, even Mother, who didn't quite know what was going on. Then it all came rushing out in a welter of invective that would have put H. L. Mencken to shame.

"You pea-brained little nincompoop. You sniveling, snot-nosed little twerp of a turd. You lying, sneaking, two-faced little son of a bitch."

"Herman!" Mother said, appalled and shaken. "Don't you dare call him names like that."

Father ignored her completely. There was nothing on earth except him and his son, this serpent's tooth in his heart.

"Ah, for Christ's sake, Pop," Teddy said, his face crimson, his tight knuckles ash-white.

"Shut your dirty mouth," Pop said. I had never seen him nearer tears. His rage made the tiny veins near the surface of his face purplish. "You'll speak when I goddam *tell* you to speak, and not before."

Father held out the grade slips to Mother, who looked at them carefully. "Teddy, what's all this?" she asked him in a hushed voice. "What did you do, son?"

She never called him "son" like that unless he had a high fever. Mother looked, too, as if she were about to burst into tears, a thing she never did. This was big, this thing that Ted had done. The biggest thing ever. I started to shake inside, my teeth chattering out loud. I wanted nothing more than to get out, but there was no escaping. I'd be able to hear it all over the house, and I knew I wouldn't get permission to leave.

"You had no right," Pop said quietly, so quietly that I could scarcely hear him.

"I had every right," Ted replied, just as quietly.

"It's my money," Pop said.

"It's my life," Ted answered. He was not flinching, not floundering around as he usually did when he fought with Father.

"Get the hell upstairs," Pop said. He jerked his thumb upward as he used to when he preferred not to tell us again to go to bed.

"Gladly," Teddy said calmly. "I've got work to do anyway."

"What work?" Pop asked, sarcasm oozing from his voice. "Memorizing 'Trees' for tomorrow's class? Practicing ballet steps and basket weaving?"

"Cut it out now, Herm," Mother said. "Leave him alone. He must know what he's doing."

"Him? He doesn't know shit from Shinola," Father said. He looked down at his messy plate with its coagulating juices. "I said to get upstairs. Move."

"Yessir," Teddy said, saluting smartly. Mother winced. Ted climbed the stairs and shut his door.

"May I be excused?" I asked timidly. I wanted to be behind my door, too. They hadn't fooled me. I knew the tornado was still coming.

"Finish your dinner," Father said. He wasn't looking at me, either. I stayed.

"I can't handle this anymore," he said at last, letting his great head fall down onto his hand in a gesture of despair. "The kid is hopeless. He's nothing like I thought he would be. He's a liar and a cheat and a punk."

"He's a good kid, Herm. Let him be," Mother said, patting Father's hand.

"He's a shitty little sneak," Pop said. The steam was building again. Mother removed her hand from his.

"Come on, now," she said, moving dishes around on the

table, not giving in to his anger. "Relax. We'll get over this hump. We've gotten over all the others."

"I know what I'm going to do," Father said, slamming his wide hand down on the tabletop, making the cutlery jump in little jerks as his hand came down again and again to punctuate his words. "I'm going to call Pastor. He'll straighten out this kid for me." Father's eyes were alight with inspiration.

"Oh, don't call Pastor," Mother said. "He'll think somebody's dying or going to the hospital or something. And look—it's starting to snow, Herm. Herm, come on," she said, watching Father stride to the telephone like a man on a holy mission. She slammed her own hand down on the table then, mad, sputtering.

"You stubborn ox," she hissed at him. "Get away from that phone. Leave this whole thing be. You'll get over it, Herman. Herman!"

But Father had a duty to perform, and no nagging woman was going to change his mind, dammit. He told the operator in stentorian tones that he wanted Dundalk 3486 and waited for Pastor to pick up the phone. He said he'd appreciate it if Pastor would come by for a while to help straighten out a little problem we were having with Teddy. He outlined the situation, and I could hear Pastor on the other end, asking if we wouldn't rather work this out ourselves without involving an outsider. He sounded hopeful. But Pop was adamant. Pastor must come. This thing was beyond the layman. Of course, then, Pastor would come, and gladly.

Mother rushed to get the dishes done, and I hurried through my piano lesson, some scales and a Czerny exercise, a minuet and a rondo. In a half hour, Pastor's 1954 Plymouth Cranbrook pulled up to the curb, and the small, thin preacher got out and came slowly up the sidewalk. I beat it to my room before he even got inside the door. I saw Pastor twice a week at our rigorous confirmation classes, and that was enough. He was always checking to see if we'd been at both church and Sunday School, giving us check marks in his black book, asking us to repeat passages memorized exactly from *Luther's Small Catechism* (we should fear and love God that we may not curse, swear, use witchcraft, lie, or deceive by His name, but call upon it in every trouble, pray, praise, and give thanks), and telling us that when we were old, we wouldn't depart from our training. He was suspicious of all teenagers (with good reason, he always said, seeing as how it was we who were always meckering around to have dances and parties and hayrides and all that body-contact stuff), and seemed more comfortable among the Ladies' Aid members at their monthly meetings.

Pop asked Pastor to speak to Teddy in his room. He said it would be more private up there. Besides, he and Mother could watch the news downstairs, and that might calm him down. He had a broad smile in his voice as he spoke to Pastor. His faith in Pastor's ability to bring this prodigal kid to his senses was infusing him with a new enthusiasm for the project. He all but slapped Pastor on his bony back. I heard Pastor's slight footfalls coming up the stairs, heard him knocking on Teddy's door quietly, asking to be let in. There was a murmur of voices, a long pause or two. . . .

And within minutes, it was all over. Pastor's footsteps disappeared down the stairs, he spoke briefly to Pop in a monotone half-whisper, and then he put on his black hat and bundled his spare body into a thick black coat and left. Pop called for Teddy to come down, so I strolled down, too.

"What the hell did you say to him?" Pop asked.

"Nothing much," Ted answered. "I just said I wasn't going to change my mind to please you. I said it was my life, and my gifts were *my* gifts, not yours. My father has had his life, I told him, and now let me have mine."

"Oh, good grief," Mother said, shuddering. "What did he say after you went through that whole rigmarole?"

"He said it was fine," Teddy smiled. "He said good. He said it was reasonable for a guy my age to choose what he wants to do for his life's work. He said Pop and I should talk some more to straighten it all out. He said he had had to stand up tall to his own father a long time ago over the same kind of conflict. He said to stick to my guns in a spirit of love and honor. All in all, it was a pretty impressive speech. Thanks, Pop."

"That's all?" Pop said, incredulous. "That's all the skinny little weasel could think of to say? I don't believe it. I don't believe it. Holy shit, what are we paying this guy to do? Knit and crochet 'Love Thy Neighbor' place mats with the goddam Ladies' Aid, for God's sake?"

"Herman, stop it," Mother said, mad as hell now. "Stop making fun of him and pay attention to what he told Teddy. All he wants is for you two to work this thing out on your own. He knows better than to try to make Teddy give up his dreams."

"Dreams?" Pop said with a mock guffaw. "Dreams? Well, let's whatever we do never, ever, on pain of death, stomp on little Teddy's precious *dreams*. Let's do whatever it takes on earth to see to it that little Teddy gets his *dreams*, by God, and never the hell mind who the hell else suffers."

"You're not even trying," Mother said.

"The hell I'm not," Father said. "I'm trying like hell to figure out this whole shebang. What a stinking mess."

"Pop, I only want to do what's best for me," Teddy said, his own sarcasm giving way to a look of desperation. "Pop, please just listen to me for once. Just give me a fighting chance."

"Bullshit," Pop said over his shoulder as he rummaged in the closet. "I'm getting the hell out of here. I can't talk to you. Your skull is like cast iron. Impenetrable. Dreams, shit. I never got a dream. I never had time for a goddam dream. Ah, what the hell. You've got your head full of fairy tales and there's no talking to you. Get out of my way, goddammit. I just want to get out of this nuthouse."

"Poppy, don't go out!" I begged him, daring to speak for the first time since this whole dumb scene had begun. "Please

191

don't. Look at the snow coming down. You'll get buried."

"Good," Pop said sourly. "Then you'll all be rid of me. You can glop lipstick on your mouth three inches thick, and you can cuddle baby Teddy under your great big beautiful wing," he yelled at Mother, who was livid now. "And you—" he said to Teddy who looked about ready to tear out his sexy hair—"you can go upstairs and play medieval tunes on the goddam *lute* for all I care, you little creep of a goddam quitter."

He stuffed his arms into his overcoat and pulled on his rubber galoshes, stumbling in his haste to be away from us. He lurched out the front door and set off across the school field to the place where he knew the Dundalk guys would be boozing it up at the stag bar. He was making silly tracks in the deepening snow, having pulled his galoshes onto the wrong feet. From where I stood looking out the front window at his footprints, it appeared as if he were trying somehow to walk away from himself. In moments he had blended into the blizzard, and I was scared.

"Teddy, go get him," I said. "Don't let him go."

"Ah, let him go," Teddy said, disgusted and tired. "There's no use trying to stop him when he gets like this. He's the stubbornest man I've ever known."

"He's all upset," Mother said, unwilling to let Teddy badmouth Pop in her presence. "You've got him all confused and tied into a pretzel. He's not used to being bucked."

"Well, maybe he ought to get used to it," Teddy said darkly. "It's time somebody told him what's what. He thinks he's Julius Caesar or something. Caligula."

"I don't even know what you're talking about," Mother said, her back up now. "You don't need to get superior, sonny."

"Never mind," Teddy said. "Everybody leave me alone for a while. I'm going up to study now. Let's just forget about it, okay? If he wants to act like a prize jackass, let him."

"Go on up, then," Mother said, shrugging. "I guess he'll be all right."

She switched the TV on to watch Perry Como, and I flopped down into a chair where I could look for Pop out the window.

He didn't come. I peered out into the storm every few minutes, but I couldn't see across the street. I was getting prickly in the scalp, each hair perpendicular to my head. I was praying in little, quiet mumbles, under my breath so that nobody would know how scared I was. I walked upstairs in a trance, knocked at Teddy's closed door, and opened it a crack.

"Teddy, please go and find Pop," I said. "It's getting so late. I can't see him anywhere." A sob escaped, despite my best efforts to be adult. That sob was all it took to move Teddy. He got up and went downstairs. He put on his heavy jacket, his leather gloves, earmuffs, muffler, galoshes.

"Don't worry, Half-pint," he said, smiling like a preoccupied old man. "Just stay calm. I'll find Pop."

"You better," Ma said without inflection, without moving her eyes away from the TV picture.

Ignoring her program, I watched out the window, straining my eyes for the sight I most wanted to see: Teddy and Pop walking side by side, heads down in the wind. I saw nothing. Only drifts piling up higher in the howling wind as the snow swept across the playground.

"Teddy!" I yelled, seeing him staggering across the snowy street alone. "Teddy!"

Ted burst in the front door like a mountain man, his face and body covered with snow. "I found him," he gasped. "But I gotta get help. I can't move him, Ma. He's dead weight. We gotta go get Art Keefer and maybe Milt Rosling. Quick, Ma. Give me something hot to drink."

Ma put leftover coffee into a saucepan and heated it while I scrounged among the Fibber McGee for our old army blankets. Teddy made his way across the courtyard to pound on the doors of the Keefers and the Roslings. He was frantic. When the Roslings finally came to their back door, they looked alarmed, but Milt was out in twenty seconds flat, ready to help. He and Teddy roused Art Keefer, and soon the three of them were lumbering across the dark playground with the blankets, searching for Pop among the shoulder-high drifts.

My heart was beating painfully in my chest. Pop had been gone so long. "God, let him be all in one piece," I prayed. "Don't let him be frozen." I envisioned his frozen fingers, toes, nose, and ears snapping off, and the tears streamed forth.

Finally my vigil was rewarded. (They came into view, and I whooped with new hope.) "Ma!" I yelled. "They're coming. Come quick. Look."

Art Keefer and Milt Rosling and Teddy carried Pop as if he were on a stretcher, but he wasn't. He was so stiff that he might have been on a board, a long plank that they'd laid him on. They stumbled in the drifts, the three rescuers, and had trouble finding their way. Teddy's flashlight bobbed up and down as he staggered beneath Pop's weight. I held my breath until they were safely inside, where Mr. Rosling's glasses fogged up at once.

"Holy shit, he's nearly froze to death," Milt Rosling said, ripping off the useless glasses, his teeth chattering. "We got to get some good circulation going real fast. He's about to freeze solid."

Pop's eyes were closed, his skin dangerously gray-blue. He's dead already, I thought. We can do whatever we want to melt him down, but he's dead.

"Holy gee, call a doctor," Mother said, her voice rising in panic.

"No doctor's coming out tonight," Art Keefer said gruffly. "Too dangerous. Cripes, we nearly cashed in just going out to look for Herm. Nobody's driving, for God's sake."

194

They were unwinding Pop from his snow-sodden wrappings. Mother was chafing his skin, rubbing his hands and feet. I was ordered upstairs to the linen closet to find a hot-water bottle, blankets, quilts, a pillow. They had him on the sofa, stretched out rigidly. He's dead, I thought. We're rubbing the skin of a dead man. Who do they think they're kidding?

I came down with the junk and watched as Mother and Teddy and the two neighbors tried to pour brandy down Pop's throat. His eyelids fluttered. He moaned. Tears sprang to my eyes again. He was alive.

"What the hell's going on here?" Pop muttered through stiff lips. "What the hell are you doing?"

"It's gonna be okay, Herm," Milt Rosling said, grinning. "You're okay now, buddy. It's gonna be all right now, pal."

"What the hell?" Pop said, trying to sit up, falling back again.

"You damn near froze to death out there," Keefer said, laughing out loud in embarrassed joy and relief. "You damn near cashed in, boy!"

"Who, me?" Pop said, amazed to be at the center of the hubbub.

"Teddy found you," I babbled. "Teddy saved your life," I said.

Pop looked around, eyed Teddy, blinked at him, then turned his face to the wall. "Thanks for nothing," he said. Teddy dropped the hand he was holding and rubbing. He looked at Ma, then at me. Without a word, he got up, backed away, then walked in measured steps up to his room. Keefer and Rosling stared at each other.

"Keep working on him," Mother said to the two men. "He's not out of the woods yet. Look how blue his fingertips are. Rub!" she urged, all business now. I was stunned by what Pop had said. I was shocked and furious.

"You're going to be sorry you said that to Teddy," I said loudly.

"Bebe, shut up," Mother said. "We don't have time for that now."

"You should be ashamed of yourself," I blurted. "How could you talk to him like that? He saved your life, damn it all. He saved your dumb *life,* and look how you act. Shame on you. Shame on you."

"Get to bed," Mother said harshly, giving me a shove in the middle of my back. "We don't need you down here aggravating everything. Shut your big mouth and get to bed."

"I won't," I hollered. "He can't talk to Teddy like that. He can't."

"Do what your mother tells you, Bebe," Art Keefer said, putting his hand on my shoulder. "You're all upset now. Just go on and do what she says."

I went halfway up the stairs, then turned and looked down onto Pop's still-rigid form lying on the couch. He looked ridiculous to me, absurdly pathetic, like a Victorian lady with the vapors. "I'm not going to do what you say, either," I yelled down. Something perverse, some imp on my shoulder, made me go on despite Mother's murderous look. "I'm not going to take any damn dumb A-Course at Eastern High School. And I'm not going to study music at Oberlin College, either. You can carry on like a maniac if you want to, but you can't make me go."

"Shut up!" Mother yelled at me. "Get to bed before I beat the stuffings out of you."

With a wanton raggedy sob, I flung open Teddy's door and hurled myself into his long arms. "I hate him, Teddy," I said, breathless with rage and pain. "He's so dumb. He's so goddam mean. He doesn't care about anybody but himself. He hates us. He just wants everybody to do what *he* wants to do. He doesn't care anything about anybody but himself."

Teddy let me boo-hoo until I was limp and spent. Then he stroked my pale hair that had come all undone, and he told me something that unwound me. "Naa," Teddy said, patting my back. "He loves us. He'd do anything for us. Never forget that. He wants only the best for us, and just because he doesn't know what the best really is doesn't make him a monster. He loves us. Never forget that."

Ma burst in upon us as we stood comforting each other, her face set into a bitter mask.

"You two ungrateful skunks. You're lucky your pop's alive. His head is flat from carrying this family, and look how you two treat him—like he was some kind of a tyrant, trying to ruin your stupid little lives. You ought to be down on your hands and knees thanking God he's alive, and look at you— crying on each other's shoulders about how cruel he is. Pigs. Take, take, take—that's all you know how to do. Shame on you both. Shame."

Her face crumpled up like burning paper as Teddy and I watched, astounded. Her tears gushed out in a torrent of anger and frustration, this quiet woman who had always showed her passion in her cooking and her baking and her washing and ironing and curtain hanging.

We went to her, putting our arms around her in an awkward embrace.

"We're sorry, Ma. We didn't mean it. We're sorry," we repeated in a liturgy of remorse. From downstairs, the sounds of Pop stirring made her pull away from us.

"Okay, then," she said roughly, willing to forgive, but grudging. "Okay, then, you just remember to stay sorry. You just remember."

Teddy dried my tears and sent me to bed. I could hear him pacing his room all evening as I smoked two Salems from my cache and flicked them down into the snow where I knew they'd dissolve before the Big Thaw. The icy, damp air crawled into all the corners and crannies of my room, and I shivered as I thought of Pop slipping and falling and scrabbling around out in the white drifts, panicky, then resigned, allowing himself to be swallowed up by the storm. It was eerie.

Pop drank some more brandy, satisfied himself that his fingers and toes were intact, then went to bed gratefully.

When he awoke the next morning he seemed to have forgotten Teddy's Great Transgression, and he made no allusion to my own terrible, defiant speech. He seemed diminished, though—smaller, shorter, less portly. He faded. He stood looking out the dining room window with his hands clasped behind his back, watching the relentless snow that still fell. "We're snowed in, all right," he said. "Just like when I was a boy in Wisconsin. Isn't that remarkable?"

We got out the cards and played for a week while the snow and ice and wind buried Dundalk and all of greater Baltimore. We watched all the old horror movies in the local stations' stock (I saw Spring Byington in *The Werewolf of London* seven times that week). We played shmear (the midwest version of pitch) and sheephead, an old Wisconsin card game. We bundled ourselves up at last in our full winter outdoor garb in order to sleep in an unheated house because the heating-oil trucks could not get through.

My father never recovered from his burial in the Blizzard of '58. He never grew large again. Silently, strangely, and almost unknown to me, I began to mourn his untimely passing while my mother watched us all through narrowed eyes, with a wisdom that was ancient and alien to me.

Chapter 13

In 1958, late March, I was confirmed on Palm Sunday along with about twenty other pubescent Lutherans with oily skin, a crush on Carole Lynley, and visions mystical and sublime. In my white three-inch heels and my white cocktail dress (necessary to wear, for some unknown reason, *under* a white robe and collar for the ceremony), and my tight permanent, I could have been a bride of thirty rather than the wobbly fourteen-year-old I was. In our group photo, a B&W glossy, we look like a bunch of stern new missionaries posed in front of the altar, the thin, smiling young pastor in our exact midst, presiding over all the proceedings like a benign but half-hearty angel.

It was a Big Huge Deal, this confirmation. Relatives came Down East, Aunt Krista and Uncle Del from Wisconsin, along with Grannie and Grampa Schmidt and my maiden aunt Caroline.

Aunt Caroline (pronounced caro-lyne) was not really a "maiden," having been married for a few disastrous months to a man named Oscar Welles. Welles was not a German Lutheran, or even a Methodist, but some bum of unknown persuasion who had turned out to be what Grannie called an "oily" character, and probably a fish-eating Catholic. Welles had disappeared one early fall evening in 1924 after he'd said he was going to take a little stroll downtown for a Coney Island hot dog.

Caroline had opted to have the whole mess legally declared null and void or something, and had reassumed her maiden name of Schmidt with a dispatch, dignity, and derring-do that had never sat well with anybody among her close relations. She'd also refused two subsequent offers of marriage because she said the men who had proposed them had borne a striking and dismaying resemblance to her first husband. As a result, she lived rather quietly and nicely (albeit frugally) in an apartment in town with a small dog (a rat terrier, she said it was) named Major Domo, taught school (thank God for the training at the Normal School) to grades three and four at the Lutheran Day School, and minded her own business. She arbitrarily switched her alliance to the Wisconsin Synod of the church, the evangelical branch, which (I thought) frowned upon nearly *everything*.

Still, I found Aunt Caroline a refreshing breeze in our midst. She sat tall and cool among our perspiring, overweight bunch of rowdies, never overeating or getting messily snockered, never making disgusting and uncouth digestive noises, never having to apologize for boorish behavior.

And she read. History, geography, sociology, political science, the novels of female southern writers, poetry by Emily Dickinson and Walt Whitman and T.S. Eliot.

Auntie Caroline wiped her lips with a dry hankie every few moments. I never knew why. It was just a habit, probably, but it made people feel uncomfortable, as if she were displeased with what they were doing or saying, although she never said so. Of us all, Teddy most resembled her, although in truth he did look much more like my mother's people. Still, only Teddy would sit as tall and straight as she, and neglect his food in order to hold forth about some political or literary opinion.

He and Auntie Caroline were pals, sharing looks with lifted eyebrows, making jokes and allusions I didn't get, and talking for hours about things like the aftermath of the McCarthy Era and the effects of the newfangled rock 'n' roll music on the musical tastes of America. They called it a flash in the pan, whatever that meant. I knew all about rock and roll, but my contributions to their animated conversations seemed puerile and ineffectual and intrusive, so I mostly stayed quiet.

But it was wonderful anyway, being in the limelight for seven whole days during the Great Conformation Week. I really milked the whole thing, grabbing the mail every day looking for checks from relatives who couldn't make it in person; acting "old" in front of the company; asking for (and generally not getting) wine or beer at mealtimes; strutting around in high, pointed shoes, demanding a trip to the hairdresser for the occasion.

The Sunday before confirmation, reverently known as Examination Sunday, was a winner, too. We examinees were all seated in front of the congregation and asked questions (which we answered smartly) concerning our knowledge of the faith by various elders and church council members to determine whether or not we were truly fit (after two solid years of Wednesday-after-school and Saturday-till-noon) to represent the church. At our Examination Sunday, I felt a little sorry for Loretta Fundakowski, though. She'd been staring glassy-eyed at the stained-glass depiction of Christ carrying his cross when one of the elders popped her a question. Not being all that swift to begin with, the poor kid started to stammer and asked that the question be repeated.

Sternly, solemnly, the balding elder folded his arms and repeated the question. "What is the prayer that our Lord Himself taught us to pray?"

Loretta gaped. Her mouth worked soundlessly.

Leonard Talarczyk snickered, and twenty hands shot up. Even dowads, people who had never in two long years volunteered a single answer, couldn't let this one get by. Myron Castle nearly wet his pants trying to get the elder's attention, flinging his arm and hand into the man's face. My chubby hand was flapping, too, and my Mum deodorant was failing fast.

Pastor was fidgeting about, yanking surreptitiously at his collar, shifting from foot to foot in the narrow, squeaky black shoes he wore on Sundays. His lips formed the words for her, but the flat-chested little dip didn't have the sense to look up at him. Her fair head was bent and drooping.

"L-lll-llllaa," he began to sing quietly. At last she stared up at him. "Love!" she blurted. "Love prayer!"

Pastor's face reddened. He strained piteously to make her see. "Lll-la, la, lo, lor-la, looor, la, lor-lor-da, duh."

"Lorda mercy!" Loretta squeaked. "Lorda hope. Lord help. Lord-helps-us-sinners prayer."

"Lor—lor—duh—" Pastor said, both hands extended to her, trying to shove the words into her frantic mouth.

"Lorda, lorda," Loretta repeated, caught up now in the liturgy.

"Lord!" Pastor exploded. "Lord! Lord!"

"Lord, Lord!" Loretta gasped.

"That's it! Lord's Prayer! She said 'Lord'!" Pastor shrieked in triumph as the congregation burst into an ovation of hysteria. I could hear my father's roar of merriment, hear Teddy's madman cackle. I was prickling with irritation. They were getting the wrong kind of pleasure out of my second-to-biggest day.

The elder, having been forced to notice Myron Castle (despite his efforts to ignore the little redheaded elf) directed the next question to him. As Myron beamed up at him, the elder put on his most serious, most Lutheran face.

"As a final question, Myron," he intoned, the Very Representative of Our Lord on Earth, "how can we, as confirmed and committed Christians, deal with those stiff-necked people who will not learn and accept the word of God?"

A real poser. I would have been hard put to reply. But Myron was equal to the challenge and did not falter. Without a blink of his azure eye, he was ready and willing to prove himself.

"Kill 'em!" he declared nobly, in clarion tones.

My father and Teddy left the pew practically on their hands and knees. Even Ma said later on that she didn't know how she stuck it out there for the rest of the service without wetting her pants. I didn't think it was so funny; Myron Castle was just probably showing off to impress the wilted Fundakowski girl, and I found him distinctly uncouth and singularly despicable for making fun of God and His Church that way.

I had become Transformed these past few weeks, lifted up into the thin vapor of religious mysticism where the young saints went to touch God. Pastor would have cringed if he'd heard me rhapsodizing about the saints, but I couldn't help listening to Bernadette going on and on about their deeds and sacrifices and adventures and persecutions. I loved those saints, the more persecuted the better.

Lucy and Bernadette told me of Isaac Jogues, of Stephen the Martyr, of little Bernadette at Lourdes. I loved the exotic names, the miracles associated with them. I wanted to be one. Desperately. I took the pillows from my bed and replaced them with a short stack of hardcover books, which nearly caused me to expire from vertebral subluxation after about fifteen minutes. I left the windows open so that the too-cool air would chill me. Joan had burned, and I would freeze.

Lucy Grabowski and I had a long and deep talk about sainthood on the Monday that marked the first day of Holy Week, the last week in Lent. She had worn ashes on Ash Wednesday, her forehead proclaiming her sinfulness, her public admission that we are all as dust, as ashes, and we mourn our worldliness. I had envied those ashes. We didn't get them at our church. I mean, we mourned our worldliness and all, but ashes might make us look too Catholic.

Now Lucy and I sat on my bed cross-legged, filing our nails and Being Serious. The radio was off. No Coasters or

Chantelles or Jerry Lee Lewis to distract us. And Lucy was the person to talk to about such things. The authority.

Lucy had almost become a nun.

It was true. She had been away at a convent in Pennsylvania for the whole seventh grade, in a school where the girls were preparing to become nuns. Now she was home for good. She had decided, she said, to become some other sort of servant for the Lord. Maybe a secretary for a bishop or a monsignor, if they had one.

I watched Lucy Grabowski as she talked. Her huge dark eyes were almond-shaped, with a long, sweeping fringe of black eyelashes that she hadn't yet seen fit to enhance with her mother's Pegeen Mascara. Lucy wore no makeup at all, saying she just wouldn't feel right about it. Everybody knew she'd been away at that school (Leonard Talarczyk always called her "sister," and sometimes it made her cry), and every time she tried to do "regular" things, like dance or smoke or say "crap" or go googoo over some boy, the kids looked at her as if she'd crawled out of a hole.

Great Things were expected of her, she'd been told, and she was incapable of becoming just one of the gang. Six years of parochial elementary school had made her uncomfortable in everyday school clothes; she still craved a uniform. That way you were always sure you were dressed right, she said. As it was, she always thought she looked out of it, and the truth was, she usually did. It was just a borderline case of out of it, but there it was.

"See, people expect me to be good," she said earnestly. "And I want to be good. I do. But it *is* teejus sometimes, you know?"

"Yeah, I know," I said. She didn't know yet that I smoked. Hardly anybody did. Bernadette and I had come upon the source of our difficulty with smoking—that ridiculous and painful choking—while reading a popular novel for older teenage girls in which the heroine's best girl friend, a floozie with money, tells her that you've got to keep on sucking in the old breath even after the smoke gets caught in your throat; breathe it in, all the way, and then out in a slow and steady stream. That lesson had turned us into Inhalers. We were hooked, I on menthol, she on Winston.

We didn't tell Lucy. She would have been crushed, we decided. Now I felt like having a Salem, but it was suddenly unthinkable. Would a saint smoke? Good Lord, no. There was going to have to be some serious overhauling of my sins and vices if I was going to become a saint. Lucy reinforced my feelings by reciting some of the things you had to do just to get to be a *nun.*

"They wouldn't even let us *have* makeup, much less wear it," she mourned. What a loss. She could have gotten all that nifty stuff from her mother's Pegeen business. "And you weren't allowed to talk about boys, not even old boyfriends who were just friends of yours in elementary school. And they censored your mail, too."

"Why?" I asked, openmouthed. That was one right that was *sacred,* I thought.

"Just to be sure no impure thoughts were being brought into our midst, I guess," Lucy said, shrugging. "I don't really know for sure. But you couldn't argue with them. They said it had to be that way, and you just had to keep your mouth shut and agree."

"The hell with that," I said. It just slid out. I clapped my hand over my offensive mouth. "I'm sorry, Luce. I shouldn't have said that. I gotta stop talking like that. All that cursing and swearing and all." What must God think? A would-be saint whose language shamed the squeaking of a gutter rat. My face burned with embarrassment.

"Forget it," Lucy said. "I don't care. It sounds good after a year of 'My goodness' and 'Golly Ned.'"

"Golly Ned?" I repeated, fascinated.

"Yeah," Lucy grinned, her round pieface broadening with laughter. "That's convent talk for 'holy shit.'"

I'd never heard her say such a thing before. My mouth fell

open, and I felt as if she'd poured a bucket of cold water on me. "Lucy!" I said.

"Sorry," she said automatically, resigned to my reaction.

"I mean, really," I said, to explain myself.

"I know," she said. "You don't expect to hear that kind of crap coming from me. I'm supposed to be above all that."

"Well, aren't you?" I said.

"Maybe. I don't know. I'll tell ya, though, it's hard, trying to be back with regular kids and not being allowed to be normal."

"But you're doing God's work," I protested, as if that fact would enable her to straddle the sacred and the secular without further trouble. "How come you want to be *normal*?"

"That's what I'm trying to figure out, Beeb," she said, and suddenly her pain and her struggle came to the surface, and it was no longer a silly little conversation we were having; it was not a talk about some absurd idea I was pursuing just for the hell of it. We were talking about a real, live *person* here, and I regretted my snotty implications that she ought to be perfect. I wanted to pull her into a hug, to tell her it was going to be okay just as soon as we told everybody to lay off her—

But Lucy's tears came gushing forth, and I was unprepared for unhappiness of that magnitude. "Oh, Bebe," she sobbed. "I feel so bad, so rotten. I practically got kicked out of the convent, did you know that? They wanted me out of there. They said I was a disturbing influence on the other girls. They said I didn't know how to stand up to discipline, and that I was more interested in my own personal selfish needs and wants than in serving the Lord. Oh, God, it was awful. My father told them where they could put their discipline. He said I was a damn fine kid, the best kid in the world, and then, do you know what they up and said to him?"

"What?"

"They said, yeah, right—the best kid in *the world*. But that *wasn't* the world, see, and there was no place there for a kid like me who couldn't seem to understand why she always had to take orders that didn't make sense. There was no place there for a—a—rebel."

Lucy Grabowski? A rebel? James Dean, Sal Mineo, Marlon Brando—those were rebels. But Lucy Grabowski? Having said it, she crumpled.

"They called me—a—*rebel!*" Lucy wailed, putting her hands up in front of her face, hiding it from me to mask the shame and degradation the good sisters had heaped upon her heart, soul, mind, and spirit. She cried so hard I thought she was going to be sick. Then, finally, the crying waned. The tears just rolled and did not splash, and at last she gave me a feeble smile.

"They didn't mean it, Luce," I said. "They were just saying that to get your father steamed."

"That's what he said, too," Lucy said. "But I don't know. Maybe they were right. Maybe I'll never be good enough to serve the Lord. I just can't figure it out."

"Jeeze," I said, the light having suddenly dawned. "If you had trouble, where does that put *me*?"

"God, right at the bottom of the barrel, I guess," Lucy said, half grinning, half grimacing. I, too, didn't know whether to laugh or cry.

"Well, what should I do in order to get straightened out?" I said. I had the half-crazy notion that she was going to say, mercifully, "Nothing, Beeb; you're fine as you are." She didn't. She looked around my room, scrutinizing my things, measuring me with her stout Catholic yardstick.

"First of all, you've got to watch that dirty mouth," she said. I knew that. "Then, you've got to quit your smoking."

"How did you know I smoke?" I asked, shocked.

"Anybody in a five-mile radius could smell it," she said, as if I'd asked her to prove that two plus two were four.

"What else, then?" I asked. I was starting to get itchy.

"Well, you'd better give up hanging with Bernadette," Lucy said. I couldn't tell if she was serious.

"Why?"

"Bad influence. Dirty mouth. Smoker. Reads her father's men's magazines and the *Enquirer*—all those stories about people killing people and eating them and all. Tells those dirty jokes and sings those horrible limericks."

Bernadette's father had Rusty Warren records, and we used to play them when he was at work and Ma Erdman was outside smoking and yakking with the lady next door or else pottering around with her two-plant garden, which she tended as if it were a truck farm. All she ever produced that I could see were a few inedible gourds and some infinitesimal pinkish roots she said were oxheart carrots. She held about a dozen of them in the palm of her hand. "Here's my hawr-vest," she said, laughing her phlegmy laugh. "Gonna go make some stew from 'em." You never knew with her; maybe she was kidding, maybe not.

I stared guiltily at Lucy. All Bernadette's sins were mine also. Lucy knew that, of course, but she was merciless. "I mean it, Beeb," she said. "You can't expect to give up your bad ways if you keep hanging with her."

"I guess not," I said at last. I felt as if I were trying to swallow a mouthful of sawdust.

"And look at this," Lucy said, picking up my copy (my precious, hidden, contraband copy) of *Peyton Place*. God, I was ashamed. Imagine Saint Teresa of Avila, or of the Roses, reading something like *Peyton Place*. Lucy held it at arm's length, touching it only with fingertips.

"Filth!" she said shrilly. "Garbage!" She dropped it into the waste basket, and something in me rebelled.

"Don't," I said weakly. Trash or no trash, filth or no filth, I loved books so much that I couldn't bear to see one mis-treated, not even this Terrible Influence.

"It's gotta be done, Beeb," Lucy said, her mouth set. "Face it, kid. It's for your own good."

She seized my stack of magazines, picked through them. All my *American Girl* magazines she saved. *True Confessions* and *Official Detective* went into the trash. I started to tremble inside.

She was efficient and matter-of-fact. It was weird. I was shaky.

"You know, I think I'm in love," she said suddenly, incongruously. She looked around to gauge my reaction. She got a kick out of it. I was stunned.

"Yeah, I am," she said. "With guess who?"

"Who?" I said in a whisper.

"Price."

I swallowed another dose of sawdust. "Well, you're welcome to him. I don't want him anymore. I'm through with boys."

"Great," she said enthusiastically. "I'm going to go after him, then. *You* play nun for a while."

"There are no Lutheran nuns," I said.

"Hurray for Martin Luther!" Lucy said, and suddenly she was giggling and rolling around on the floor. "Old Martin got *something* right, after all!" she went on, and before long, I was teeheeing, too, because the Cathedral of Notre Dame didn't have to fall on me to make me realize that Lucy had been kidding me, trying to make me see how ridiculous all this "shaping up" was. I wasn't going to be a saint, a nun, or a choirboy of some sort, was I? Hardly.

We laughed until I felt weak, and it was good to hear her laughter, to see her unwinding and acting like a normal nut.

"Let's call Bernadette," I said finally. "We could use a partner in crime over here."

Bernadette came over, and the three of us spent the rest of the afternoon playing 45s on my little square record player. We had to tape a penny to the needle arm because it would skip if we didn't. "Oh-whoa, I wonder, wonder who, ba-whoa-whoa-WHO? Who wrote the book of love?" Lucy sang in a mock baritone along with the record. "I know!" she shouted suddenly, and she dashed for my trashcan and retrieved my well-thumbed copy of *Peyton Place*. "This lady did," she said grandly, pointing to the back-cover photo of a heavy, pony-tailed, dungareed woman half scowling in front of a typewriter.

"Grace Metalious," Bernadette read. She stared at me. "She looks like you, Beeb."

"All right, okay, so I've gained some weight. Jeeze."

"No, I mean it. It's something in her face. Look, Luce. See what I mean?"

"Hey, yeah," Lucy said, looking back and forth from the book to me, tickled.

I looked, too. "Nuh-uh," I said, dismissing them, half aggravated, half pleased. "I'm not anything like her."

Lucy threw the book at me and it plopped onto the floor, disturbing a dust bunny that had been lurking under my bed and sending it floofing out into the open on the other side.

"Oh-oh-oh-Johnny B. Goode!" Chuck Berry hollered, and we forgot about me and the dour-faced woman on the back cover and just lay on our backs for a lazy hour and sang along. Then we did the Stroll sloppily back and forth and let the Coasters take us to paradise, and I forgot in an hour about the arduous road to my sainthood and decided to settle for being a Good Girl. That was probably more realistic in the long run, anyway.

Later, after supper, after TV and a real crack at social studies, I stood before the bathroom mirror and pulled my ash-blond hair (it got darker every year) severely back from my face and wound a rubber band around it to make a ponytail, stuck a Salem into my mouth, and stared at this wise, sullen, world-weary young woman who would chronicle and expose the grayish-white underbelly of her own phony little town. Yeah. I'd give it to 'em good. Mrs. Holcombe behind closed doors. Yeah.

But how the hell were you supposed to find out who was doing what to whom? Not sitting alone in your room like a *nun*.

"Beatrice, get to bed," Pop called up the stairs.

"Yes, Father," I said, detached from all his provincial nonsense intellectually, but too tired to put up a fuss. In bed, I let my hand warm my round belly, and when it wandered north on a reconnaissance mission, it and I were surprised to find how high the mountain range had become.

"Thirty-eight B, at least," I murmured to the roaming hand and went to sleep easily, rocked in the bosom of rock and roll and my good, good friends and the czars and the promise of a brand-new Maidenform.

Chapter 14

On the Fourth of July, 1958, Pop and Teddy got to drinking a few Nationals and fooling around out in the backyard. They were wrestling and heaving each other around with a great deal of grunting and oofing. Suddenly Pop was on the bottom and Teddy was holding him down, and Paul Rosling's father yelled across the court, "Hey! Herm! You gonna let that skinny kid keep ya down?"

Pop tried to grin, but his face was gray and then his mouth was moving and a little, weak sound came out of it, and there was a spasm, a small retching noise, and he said, "Uh. Uhhh."

Teddy was still laughing, kidding around, telling Pop to holler "Uncle," and Pop was twitching a little, and trying to roll to his side, and still trying to make those noises.

Then Teddy got off and knelt down beside Pop as Pop stretched his arm out onto the grass and laid the side of his face on it. Teddy put his hand on Pop's chest, on his heart, lungs, gut, back, saying, "Here, Pop? Is it here? Where's the pain, Pop?"

I came outside, and Mr. Rosling came walking over, not laughing anymore. He knelt down beside Pop and Teddy, and said something I did not quite hear. I could see Pop trying to wave them away, trying to rise, to lift his head, but instead his knees came up toward his chest and he stayed that way for a few more moments. Finally Teddy and Mr. Rosling kind of pulled him to his feet. Pop swayed a little, and took out his handkerchief and wiped the sweat off his forehead and cheeks and neck, and grinned a wobbly grin and said, "Kink. Right in the goddam gut. I couldn't even move for a minute there."

Teddy clapped him on the back and said, "Too much beer, old man," and Mr. Rosling invited them both over for a brew.

"In a minute, maybe," Pop said. He sent Teddy along with Milt Rosling while he came into the house and trudged up to the bathroom. I could hear him belching and running water in there.

Ma, unaware, sat out front on her aluminum lawn chair, reading yesterday's paper and watching the last of the Independence Day rioters dancing about on the school grounds. The sun had begun to set on our row home, where the bricks baked and the curtains bleached and the radios played outside so that nobody would miss what the O-ree-oles were doing at any given moment.

When Pop came back down the stairs he went out to join her, carrying a paper. He looked a little better, and not so ashy pale.

"Feel okay now?" I asked casually.

"Sure. Just gas. Damn hot dogs and sauerkraut and beer. Cripes, I ought to know better."

He sat down and rattled the tired old paper and looked at it without reading as the long shadows fell and the bricks cooled and the sycamore leaves rustled.

"Must be just gas, huh, Chickie?" he asked Ma, who nodded, her head thrown back, eyes closed. They sat awhile longer, then Ma folded up her chair and let a little night wind lift the back of her skirt and cool her hot legs before she came in for the night.

Chapter 15

"Bernadetch goddam anshrin shervish," the crackly voice roared at me on an October afternoon so vivid with the colors of autumn in Baltimore it could have been a movie and not real life at all. Bernadette's father always answered the phone that way, because he worked nights now and had to sleep at what I considered odd hours. We were always waking him up, Lucy and Rita Lee and I, and he was fit to be tied. Sometimes he said, "Oh, hell—I mean hello!" That made us giggle so uproariously that he usually hung up. He was the crabbiest, nastiest, meanest man in the world. We adored him, all of us.

Bernadette had started dating some poor kid who was the youngest brother of a family of boys and who didn't usually know his butt from third base. But he was cute, if you didn't look too closely into his eyes, which carried signs that read, "Nobody home, thanks."

Burton was no catch, but he was a boyfriend, and none of the rest of us had one, so who were we to snicker? All the brothers had names I regarded as bizarre, considering they were all from the same family. There was Ramon, the oldest, a guy who worked as a driver for Dundalk Cab, and who was fond of telling people he'd been born a twin, but that the other twin had been absorbed inside his body and was giving him cancer of the liver. There was Rafael, who was starting a rock 'n' roll band and who played the same three chords over and over, amplified to an alarming degree, while he sang "Love Me Tender" and "Jailhouse Rock" (alternately) through his pug nose. When it was raining, he put together model airplanes and obviously didn't do it in a room with the proper ventilation, because he was always slightly buggy afterward, giggling and doing things like putting polish on his nails for kicks. I was frankly afraid of Rafael and not too nuts about Ramon, either.

Harmon was the next guy, and I think he was a high school senior. He was always following girls around saying things like, "Hoo-hah! You got quite a swing on your back porch, baby!" Harmon reeked. Bernadette said it was probably something physical or chemical. Pa Erdman said it was good old-fashioned Dundalk dirt, soot, and sweat, and that a couple of sandblastings followed by a shower would probably cure the kid. I once saw Harmon Gerstmeier break open a Vicks inhaler, pop the stuff inside his mouth, and chew on it until he nearly fainted right at the bus stop.

Reynard was just a creep. He was a year younger than Harmon, but a little taller. He lurked. He was always standing around not seeming to be looking at anything in particular, but actually staring at people and peeking into windows and doors. They all scared me. All except Burton. Burton was just Not There. I couldn't believe Bernadette was wasting her time with such a nonentity.

"Youse are just snobs," Bernadette said when we tactfully asked her what she saw in Burton Gerstmeier.

Lucy was indignant. "We are not. We just wondered."

"Well, I don't know. He's cute, I guess. And . . ."

"And what?" Rita Lee asked, pressing her now, getting ready for an attack of the gigglies, because that's what those Gerstmeier boys produced in most girls—gigglies. You couldn't help it. You either giggled or gagged, and giggling was easier.

"Ah, cram it, Zimmerer," Bernadette said tiredly. "He's just a boy, ya know. It ain't anything to write home about, okay?"

"That's for damn sure," I said with a snort, and she was on me in a second, her face furious.

"Shut the hell up, you smartass! You don't know nothin' about it, so just shut up, okay? You're just so jealous you can't see straight." We all backed away in alarm, knowing Bernadette's penchant for physical violence if the occasion warranted it. Rita Lee's teeth were chattering. "All of youse!" Bernadette went on, holding us captive with her anger. "Nothin' but a bunch of jealous, nosy, bitchy sisses. You make me sick."

She'd spent it all on that one speech, and we were properly chastised and subdued. None of us wanted to be the first, but finally I broke down. "I'm sorry, Bern," I said quietly, my head bent forward, my toe tracing patterns in the gravel of her back alley while Rita Lee and Lucy recited Hail Marys in the background.

"Me, too," Rita Lee muttered.

"Me, too," Lucy echoed.

"Awright, then," Bernadette said graciously. "Forget it." She was generous, easy, when it came to forgiving. I should have remembered that. Unfortunately, we had been loud out there, and without warning Mr. Erdman's head popped out of an upstairs window. We had awakened him, and he was livid.

"What the hell's goin' on down there?" he bellowed. He would not wear his teeth, upper or lower. He, too, had "ulsters" in his mouth and teeth that did not fit. He ate foods you could easily mash up with a fork or spoon, and overcooked vegetables that would sort of dissolve in his mouth, like mushy broccoli and cauliflower and squash.

"Nothin', Pop. We were just leaving. Go to bed now."

"The hell I will. You're punished, girl. Get the hell in the housh. I wanna talk to you."

"Aw, Pop," Bernadette whined. "Come on. We're gonna go up Dundalk and get a Coke, okay?"

"I shaid no, dammit. Who the hell's this boy who keeps callin' up here every goddam five minutch?"

"Must be Burton Gerstmeier," she said, squinting up at him, her hand over her eyes.

"He's a goddam idiot," Pa Erdman roared. We were dangerously close to giggling.

"How come?"

"He's talkin' a blue shtreak to me. I don't even know the poor jerk, and he's givin' me his goddam life shtory here. Shomethin' about gettin' a harmonica."

"Oh, yeah. He's getting a harmonica so he can play in his brother's band."

"An electric harmonica? He said electric."

"Yeah. It's gotta be electric in a rock-and-roll band, Pop. Jeeze."

"Electric harmonica? Chrisht, tell him to plug it up hizh ash!" He can probably fart better muzhic than he can play!"

He slammed down the window as all four of us, Bernadette included, laid ourselves out and quite literally wept with laughter.

"That's it," Bernadette said, wiping her eyes and wheezing. "I quit. I give in. Youse all win. I'm givin' him up. Goodbye, Burton Gerstmeier. Go blow some chords on your harmonica, son!"

Five more minutes of loud, long laughing. If Burton was hurt, he didn't show it. He just disappeared into the bosom of his family and was not heard from again until his senior year in high school, when he was caught carrying a concealed weapon, a rather long, sharp knife, behind the Strand, where he had been threatening the people who came out the back exit onto the parking lot. Unfortunately for Burton, the Strand movie theater was situated about twenty feet from the Dundalk police station, so a few hair-raising screams brought almost instant help.

(I always wondered, though, if Ramon's twin brother, the galloping humunculus, ever finished him off. It would have been interesting to follow that story.)

So anyway, it was October 1958, and I was on the phone with Pa Erdman, and he was breathing heavily, which meant that he was as mad as cat pucky; and I felt like a fool asking for Bernadette because he always asked who was calling, and I had to tell him, and then he always yelled at me. "Bebe," I said timidly. "And don't get mad, okay?"

"Me? Mad? Why would I get mad jush because a bunch of shilly little girls keep wakin' me up every ten minutch?"

Bernadette jerked the phone out of her father's hand and dismissed him with polite thanks. I could hear him bouncing off the walls as he made his weary way back up to his third-floor bedroom. Bern's house was like lots of houses in the center of Dundalk, row homes of stucco in a sort of a weird European—or maybe even Elizabethan—design, narrow and high with attic rooms and winding stairs and tiny, stand-up kitchens. They had been built as temporary housing around 1915 for the men who had come to build ships, and the streets were called Shipway, and Eastship, and Flagship, and Northship. . . .

At Bernadette's house you never knew who was going to be in which bedroom. They moved furniture a lot over there and were always changing the sleeping arrangements. For a while when we were much younger Cara (our nickname for Bern's older sister) and Bernadette had shared the attic room, and it was there that I had first encountered falsies. Lying on Cara's bureau, they looked like something quite different. "Does your sister wear these for swimming?" I had asked naively. They looked to me like things you might put over your ears under a bathing cap to keep the water out. I wanted a pair.

"Jeeze, I hope not!" Bernadette had hooted, clapping her hand over her mouth and hopping around like a maniac.

"What's so funny?" I asked.

218

"Jeeze-oo-whiz, Beeb," Bern panted. "You don't know shit from Shinola, do you?"

Boy, I hated that. Why did people always have to treat you like an idiot just because you didn't know something?

"I'm sorry I asked," I said with dignity.

"Aw, never mind," she said, relenting. "These are falsies." (She pronounced it "fossies".)

"Fossies?" I said blankly. She picked them up and put one over each budding breast, on top of her blouse. I almost died.

"Falsies!" I said, and did not know whether to blush or roar, so I did both. "Give me them," I said, and when she did, I clapped one over each ear and said, "For swimming. Oh, God. I can't believe I even said that!"

Bernadette fell down on the floor. "I'm gonna die," she said between squeals. "I'm gonna wet myself."

Cara's cold voice cut through the laughter. "What the hell do you think you're doin', fatso?" she asked. I turned to face her, and the falsies fell off my ears. Tears were in her eyes, and she was sixteen, at least. "Give me those," she said hotly, coming for me across the small room. I clutched at them, but they'd fallen to the floor, and I bent over to retrieve them and bumped my head against Cara's, and we both staggered backward. "Get out of here, you little heathens," she said.

Bernadette was still laughing, but I knew better. Cara was ready to cry. Her chest was just like a washboard. Even Bernadette had more than she did. I know she used a cream to encourage them to grow. Pegeen's Bust Enhancer, it was called, and it stood demurely at the back of her bureau. Maybe she would have had better luck taking it internally. It sure wasn't doing much good just to rub it in.

Cara snatched the falsies away from me and stuffed them into her top drawer. Then she looked at me in her mirror, not even bothering to turn around. Her greenish eyes were slitted, her pageboy hairdo separated in the back into two equal parts, some hanging over each wide shoulder. "Listen to me, girl," she said. "You think you can just go snooping around other people's stuff. You're always into everybody else's business. Well, stay the hell out of mine, you get it? I'll kill you if I ever catch you in my stuff again, no shit."

"Ah, cut it out, Cara," Bernadette said. "She's sorry, aren't you, Bebe?"

"Yeah. I really am," I said, looking at Cara's face in the mirror, reading her embarrassment, her humiliation, her pain. "I shouldn't have been fooling around your bureau in the first place."

"All right," Cara said, relenting. "Get out of here now."

Cara had forgiven me long since, but I still recalled that day. Now Bern and I went down to the teeny-weeny bathroom and took out the Marchand's Golden Hair Wash. If blondes were having more fun, and if only Miss Clairol knew for sure, we were duty-bound to try anything legally available to us to enhance our attractiveness. This particular experiment was slightly more effective than the others; I mean, you could at least see that we'd done something. The results were still a little too subtle to suit us, but we were moving right along toward the realization of our hidden glamour. Our bangs were fluffed dry, then examined under the bald bathroom light.

"Kind of strawberry blond, don't you think?" I said.

"Maybe more like that Titian we tried that time," Bernadette said doubtfully, and I disagreed.

"Nuh-uh. That was really reddish. This is definitely blonder."

"You really think so?" she asked, sounding more cheerful.

A dark presence filled the doorway. We both turned slowly to find Pa Erdman glowering down at us, his jowls wobbling as his jaws worked. He was building up a real head of steam.

"What in the name of God are you two cookin' up now?" he asked. His voice was surprisingly calm, considering the way his fists were clenched.

"Just combin' our hair, Pop," Bernadette said brightly,

giving her bangs a little flip, winking at him. He was a sucker for cuteness.

"Well, comb it the hell out of your goddam *head* and make a bird nest out of it for all I care," he said, shaking his fist at us. "Just leave me alone. Just leave me, for once and for all, in *peace*!" (*"PEASH!"*)

It was a powerful speech. We ducked to walk under his arm, and he half closed the door as he took a leak. I remember thinking how in our house nobody would ever go to the bathroom without first locking the door and then turning on the water so that people who were listening couldn't hear what you were really doing in there. At Bernadette's, people walked around in their underwear and dashed almost naked from bedroom to bathroom without shame. It always unnerved me, being so close to bodies that might at any moment reveal themselves.

(I had once gone to a pajama party at Carla Bisky's and had to call home to have Pop come and pick me up early because Barbara Foote had whispered to us that Dear Old Doc Bisky usually slept in the raw, and that sometimes he got up in the night to go down the hall to the bathroom, and maybe we'd see him if we kept quiet. The thought of seeing Bisky fully clothed put me off; how was I supposed to deal with the possibility of seeing him *naked*? "Pop, come and get me," I said flatly. The fun had gone out of the party.)

Newly coiffed, we headed on up to Dundalk. Rita Lee was in the park walking one of her cats, a runt who, she said, needed the personal attention she could give her, as well as the exercise. When she saw us, she blinked. "What did you two brats do to your hair?" she asked incredulously. "Looks like you set fire to it, or something."

"Stuff it, Zimmerer," Bernadette said, pulling a cigarette out from her sweater sleeve. One of her mother's. No filter. She lit it expertly, cupping her hand over it to protect the match from the little wind in the park.

"You better stop acting so smart," Rita Lee said, hurt. "I

hate it when you start acting like hot stuff. I don't need it."

"You're a pain in the ass, you know that?" Bernadette said. She was so blunt. She'd just come out and say anything that popped into her head. Sometimes I envied her her candor; at other times, like now, I felt sorry for the person her arrows hit. Rita Lee bent down to pick up her cat, a skinny thing named Pinky who looked wary and stuck out her claws just in case, hooking them into Rita Lee's childish little sweater and clinging there with ears flattened. Bernadette blew smoke into the cat's face.

"Hey! Cut it out!" Rita Lee said, her voice quavering. "It's bad enough you get me all full of smoke, but you could at least have some consideration for Pinky."

"Rhymes with stinky," Bern said, grinning malevolently.

"You'd better cut it out," Rita said shakily.

"Or dinky," Bernadette said.

"Stop it."

"You made fun of my hair," Bernadette said, in explanation.

"Well, it does look funny, now that you mention it," Rita said, backing up a little. The kitty hissed.

"Take it back," Bernadette said.

"I won't," Rita said. A surge of pride coursed through me. I was happy to see her speaking up.

"I'm gonna wear you out," Bernadette said, advancing, advancing.

Scritch! The cat's paw came out like lightning and opened Bernadette's cheek, leaving three bright red lines from which the blood began to seep almost at once. Stunned, Bernadette put the hand holding the cigarette up to her face, and the wind blew an ash into her eye. She was simultaneously crying and yelling, warning Rita Lee to get out of there, saying she never wanted to see her again, and that if she did see her, or that goddam cat, she would tear either or both of them apart with her bare hands.

Rita Lee did not go at once. She stood her ground and

waited for the tantrum to cease. Then she spoke again, and although her voice was shaky and high-pitched, her words were brave and true.

"Bernadette Erdman, you are a disgrace to Saint Rita's church and school. You are a smart aleck and a pain in the rear. I'm sick of you showing off and acting smart all the time, bossing everybody around and acting like a tramp and talking like a piece of gutter trash. I'm not hanging with you anymore, and if you don't like it, you can just change your ways, girl, because I don't have to stand around and listen to your mouth anymore. I got better things to do."

"What, shovel up the cat shit?" Bernadette howled, so angry that her eyes glazed over, looking like the day-old doughnuts from the Strand Bakery with the little raisins in them.

"Yeah, I'd rather shovel cat poop than be with you when you're showing off," Rita Lee said. She was about five-one with her shoes on, and she was still wearing that pathetic undershirt to school. She'd only recently begun wearing stockings instead of the anklets her mother bought her, and her glasses always slid down her narrow nose and made her look schoolmarmy. Her elbows were bony, and she was long of foot and pigeoned of toe. She didn't look as if she were ever going to mature, but she stood her ground against Bernadette of the Bulging Bustline, and I was proud of her.

"You better wise up," Bernadette said.

"Yeah, well, you'd better *grow* up," Rita Lee said, and walked away.

Bernadette did not turn to look at me. She must have sensed my lack of sympathy. She started to walk up the path to Dundalk, assuming I'd come along sooner or later. I did.

My father was beside himself when he saw my hair. "This time you went too far!" he yelled at me at suppertime. "Now get upstairs and wash that crap right out of there. I don't want to see you again until you look like a young lady, and not some trollop off the street."

I always told him that the stuff washed out and not to worry. Little did he know that this was slightly different. I went upstairs and ran water and wet the bangs, but all they did was glop against my forehead. I went back downstairs and started to practice my piano lesson in hopes that he wouldn't notice that they were drying orange, but he did.

"What the hell have you done to yourself?" he moaned, as if I'd had myself tattooed or something. "What's the matter with you? Where is your brain?"

Teddy said calmly, grinning, "If she wants to look like Howdy Doody, who are we to complain?"

Pop wailed, "Look at her. She looks ridiculous. She can't go out looking like that!"

"It's her prerogative to look like the Creature from the Black Lagoon if she wants to," Teddy said, defending me with a snicker.

"It's *not* her prerogative, dammit!" Pop said. "Not while she's still a kid in my house. She's a goddam embarrassment to her mother and me. She's got no right to make us look like fools."

"Not yet, anyway," Teddy said in his snide voice, fueling the fire, and thanks a lot. "Not till she's my age, huh? Then she can do just like I do, huh?"

"Ah, never mind," Pop said. "It's no use in talking to you. It's your fault anyhow. You're the one who makes her think she's big stuff."

"All I do is take her to the movies and a concert once in a while. The ball game. Sometimes to the library. For this I'm getting reported to the House Un-American Activities Committee? Cripes, Pop."

"Hold it down, will you?" Pop said. "I got a headache."

Teddy left it alone then, and I was relieved. I didn't think I could stand to hear another word about my waywardness. I already felt bad about how dumb my hair looked.

* * *

In November all of Dundalk celebrated a Rite of Passing Autumn by going to the Steel Bowl rally. I went with Bernadette, Carla Bisky, Barbara Foote, some guys from Dundalk High, and some kids from the ninth grade at our school. It was a giant "Beat Pointers" rally. Since there was then no high school football in Baltimore County public schools, we put all our marbles into the YMCA teams and urged them to victory against the arch rival Pointers every Thanksgiving Day.

In Baltimore City, the two rival high schools, Poly and City, played at the stadium. It was the biggest amateur event of the year, with thousands of fans screaming and cheering. Not to be outdone in the county, the Dundalk and Sparrows Point YMCAs staged an equally exciting grudge match every year, and we stood with feet numb and freezing, glugging burning hot chocolate down our scalded gullets, keeping our eyes open for the twenty or thirty fights that were likely to break out. I do not ever recall watching more than four or five minutes of actual play. It was hard to get near the field for one thing, and for another thing, the crowd was infinitely more interesting than the game.

The rally on Thanksgiving Eve, though, was the best. A bonfire as tall as the elementary school across from our house was built and set aglow in the middle of the school grounds. There was a speaker's platform where the coaches and the teams were introduced, and cheerleaders came and drove us into a frenzy of loyalty and determination. (HOLD YOUR HEAD UP TO THE SKY! Hold your head up to the sky-eye! MIGHTY DUNDALK'S PASSING BY! Mighty Dundalk's passing by! HYDIE-HEY, HYDIE HO-OH! Hydie-hey, hydie ho-oh! SKIDDLY WIDDLY WADDLY WO! Skiddly widdly waddly wo . . .)

The older guys, the ones from Dundalk High, jumped into the snake dance and pulled us with them. Wonderful revelry, lots of shouting, breath clouds in the cold night air, and some minor acts of vandalism that gave me a thrill inside. Some cherry bombs in a few sewers. A few broomsticks on lawns, some doorbell ringing, and a little soaping of car windows. One of the older guys, Chuckie Barzac, hugged me after the snake dance, and I almost died of shocked delight. He was so adorable, with his flattop haircut and his khaki pants and his Ivy League shirt and V-neck sweater and brown loafers and sweat socks. He had those wonderful, squared teeth, the kind where the front ones go straight across, and then the eyeteeth form two corners, and the rest of the teeth go straight back. When he hugged me close to him, I fit right under his armpit, and he laughed and called me "Midget," and for weeks I went around trying to get people to call me that, dropping Chuckie Barzac's name in nearly every casual conversation. When I saw him at the teen center a few weeks later, though, he didn't seem to remember me. At least he didn't wave or say hi or anything. Maybe he'd hugged me by accident, thinking I was one of the other girls, one of the thinner ones like Carla or Barbara Foote.

I got home from the rally forty minutes late. No fool, I stood on our front steps and carefully adjusted my watch so that it showed around nine-thirty, maybe a little past. When I came inside, Pop was staring at his TV in a smoldering rage, and I had the sinking feeling that I'd blown it.

"You're forty minutes late," he said, not looking at me.

"Not really," I said, consulting my watch. "Really, I'm only about eight minutes late, Pop. It's only about nine-thirty—"

"How stupid do you think I am?" he asked. "You're late, and you know it. Your mother's in bed already. All that watch crap doesn't cut any ice around here. Get to bed. You're punished."

"I'm sorry, Pop. We were in the snake dance, see, and—"

"Get the hell to bed!" he said, and I got. Halfway up the stairs his voice stopped me again—cold.

"And don't make plans to go to the game tomorrow. You're not going anywhere."

"You're kidding, of course," I said, using a line I'd borrowed from Ricky Nelson. I was half smiling.

"The hell I'm kidding. You're punished, and that's that. Now get to bed."

"I won't!" I screamed. "You can't make me stay home! I have to go to that game. Everybody's going. Everybody!" (Chuckie Barzac would be there!)

"I don't care if Jesus H. Christ is putting in a guest appearance. You're staying here."

"Now, Herm," my mother said from upstairs, insinuating her steady voice between us.

"Quiet," he said, cutting her off. "I'm handling this."

"I just wanted to say—"

"Quiet," Pop said, and his tone was deadly grim.

I was crying now. "You can't make me stay here. I can go out and get a ride with someone. You can't hold me here, because I can get away. I can go anyhow."

His mouth went slack. I had never been so brazenly, brashly defiant. Only the time when he'd gotten frozen, and he didn't seem to remember that, and I never reminded him. Now he looked as if I'd come down with my head shaved bald. Stricken.

I held my breath and waited.

He got up from his chair and came to the stairway. I started yelling, babbling, thinking perhaps that words spoken loudly enough, hatefully enough, could ward off the blows.

"What am I, Rapunzel? You can't keep me locked up here. I have a right to go out wherever I want. You never let me do anything! I hate you!"

He put out his hand and grabbed me by my right arm and pulled me down the stairs and into the living room, onto his level. I was yanking and pulling away, wretched with impotent fury.

"Shut up!" he said.

"I won't!" I screamed. "I'm gonna keep on talking. Nobody else cares about me. I gotta talk for myself. You can't order me around. You can't keep on bossing me around!"

He raised his hand to strike me. I closed my eyes and half ducked, but the blow did not fall. I opened my eyes. His hand was stalled midair, his face a granite statue. Slowly, like a sunset, a long, dark shadow passed across his features, and then the hand came down and the eyelids closed over the bulging eyes. There was no breathing, no movement except for the falling hand, and then a single monotone noise. "Ohhh," he said. And, "Ohhh," again, and my mother, startled by the sudden quiet, came down and stood between us, her own eyes puzzled and wide.

"What's the trouble? Herm! What's wrong?"

He put his arm around her shoulder and leaned a little, a thing I had never seen him do. She held him there, absently pushing at me to get out of the way. His eyes were still closed as she led him to his chair. He sat gingerly, pulling his legs up close to his body. Spasms rippled over him, and he said, "Oh. Oohhh," again, and it was beginning to sound whispery and distant.

Then he opened his eyes and looked at me. He spoke.

"The hell with it. Go wherever you want. Do whatever the hell you want to do. I don't care. Get to bed."

I don't care. He knew how I hated that. How could he say such a rotten thing to me? How could he not care where I went and what I did? I really cried then.

"You have to care," I said, pursuing him with relentless anger. "You're not even acting like a father."

"You're not acting like a daughter," he countered, the shadow passing again through his voice. He had lost interest in the fight, had somehow passed the point of anger and had descended into a quiet bitterness. He went back to his TV show, dismissing me. He shifted in his chair slowly, carefully, as if he were sitting on pieces of broken glass, shards of our argument.

I went to bed. Not because he told me to, but because I wanted to. I opened my window a few inches and inhaled my

Salem, blowing the thin smoke out into the night, and the wind that blew into my hot face was damp. I flicked the cigarette out onto the courtyard, and the bitter smoke at the back of my tongue made me know how hatred tasted. I couldn't bear to live in the same house with my father anymore. At the first opportunity, I would leave this awful place where people didn't care about me. How could he say such a thing? He hated me.

At Christmastime, things were quiet. I was one month shy of fifteen now, so there were not as many surprises as there had been in the past, and no cookies left out on a plate for Santa, and no glass of milk to cheer him on his way. Instead, Teddy and I went out and picked up a tree, a smallish one because the living room was so crowded, and then Ted put it into its stand. It wasn't as much fun as when Pop did it, because he always got tangled up in the light strings and swore a blue streak at the tree (which, despite his careful choosing, generally had an S-shaped trunk or three flat sides). Teddy didn't swear at all; he whistled carols and popular tunes and kept his smile on at all times. We got silly when we put on the finishing touch—it was just too damn much trouble to put each of those little silver icicles on one at a time, so we got to throwing them on in little clumps from across the room. Mother came in, covered with flour, which stuck to her wool skirt and cotton shirt and made her look like the Abominable Snow Woman. She made us take all the icicles off and put them on the right way.

When Pop came home from work after the office Christmas party stone sober ("I had a little ginger ale," he told Mother, who was surprised to see him so cheerless), he looked at the tree, thanked us for our good work, and went upstairs to wash for supper. Teddy and I were both disappointed. The last time we'd done a tree alone, Pop had all but dismantled the entire effort in an hour-long criticism of our methods and follies.

On Christmas Day, as always, I strode over to Bernadette's in the damp, cold early afternoon, with the pale sun gleaming from so far away it might have been heaven. Bernadette and I escaped upstairs from her noisy family and locked ourselves in her bedroom and played some of the new records we'd gotten—"Sea Cruise," "Stagger Lee," and some others.

We both got desert boots, hers tan and mine red. We called them fruit boots for some inexplicable reason, and were just Too Cool for mere human words as we hotfooted it over to Lucy's down the street. Dressed alike in barracudas (tan raincoats with red plaid linings), plaid skirts, white blouses with Peter Pan collars, circle pins, crewneck cardigan sweaters, and our fruit boots, we went on parade down the streets of Dundalk.

We passed the Strand Theater and were not surprised to read the crayoned sign reading, "Closed Christmas Day." The Strand Five-and-Dime was closed, as was the Strand Bakery next door, but just for the heck of it, we peered inside because it was, without doubt, the most jam-packed, cram-packed treasure trove of pure unadulterated junk in all the universe. Gewgaws, knickknacks, flapdoodle and crapola, all heaped atop the wooden counters that were divided by wooden lath strips to hold an astounding assortment of plastic toys, wind-up things, artificial flowers, elastic, buttons, oilcloth; every conceivable variety of cheap candy manufactured anywhere on earth, some of it mottled with age; hard as rock, inedible, and delightful (licorice sticks that cracked when you bit them); caps and cap guns, caps for your head; Chinese parasols, kites so encrusted with dust that they could not fly from the weight, balsa wood chunks for carving, paper dolls, yo-yos (and every year on the playground the men came from the exotic land, those Filipinos, those guys with the bowed legs, canvas shoes, and shirts with palm trees on them, doing the yo-yo tricks, walking the dogs and making the cradles and luring us up to Dundalk to the dime stores to buy yo-yos). There were odd bits of hardware, baseball cards in packages with cardboardy gum, wallets with pictures already in them (Cornel Wilde and Ann Blythe and Lassie); figurines, crepe paper in rolls, already faded.

Kresge's, with its stainless steel and its linoleum and its bubbling fish tanks, was fascinating in its breezy way, but the Strand Five-and-Dime stood without competition for downright variety.

Now we Big Girls, too big, really, to go in there since we were far past the yo-yo and baseball-card stage, passed to the next doorway and peeked inside that one, too. The Strand Bakery. For as long as I could remember, the same ladies with gray hair had worked there, measuring out the dozens of doughnuts, the caramel sticky buns, the jelly rolls, the rye breads. White paper and so much string that I used to laugh out loud, certain they'd run out while the thin, fragile stuff kept spinning and spinning on its spool as they tied and retied the boxes they'd packed.

Next door was the police station, a small building with painted yellow bars to match the window frames. None of us had ever been inside, but when the door was opened on that Christmas Day, I had my first real glimpse. A tiny old lady who was coming down its three steps was taking a long time, long enough for us to gape inside looking for criminals. I didn't see anybody except a blue-uniformed guy behind a tallish desk. We prepared to move along to check out Read's Drugstore for guys, but just then the little old lady coughed and retched and spit an immense hocker onto the hem of my new barracuda.

I stopped dead in my tracks. Something about her total lack of concern for me, her thorough cruelty, made me physically unable to move or to utter a sound. The dread that settled down over me might have been a heavy canvas sack. I felt isolated, singled out for destruction. It was one of the worst things that had ever happened.

"Help!" I said, finally, as Lucy and Bernadette hooted and

gabbled and scrabbled in their leather purses for tissues. "Oh, dear God, help me." I was nearly sobbing. "Oh, my God, my God," I said, as if I had been spattered with the blood of the martyrs. I was paralyzed with some veiled terror, some dread unnamed and impossible to recognize.

"Get it off," I begged as they laughed and dabbed. "Clean me up. I can't stand it. I'll die. I'll die."

I know they thought I was kidding, laying it on thick so that the passersby would laugh, too, and go along with the ugly joke. And I had to let them think so, because I could not have explained my horror and dread. I still cannot.

But as I knew she would, the old woman turned to look at me. She turned her whole body around slowly, because her neck would not bend, and she clutched with bony fingers at her buttonless rag of a coat. She watched the girls on their haunches, cleaning away her own spit and phlegm from my stylish new coat; and she watched me shudder and gag in revulsion and fear; and she made some sign with her fingers, some sign she believed I would read; and then she smiled at me, and her few teeth were brown, the gums purplish and scummy. She laughed. She laughed and turned around and went on her way mumbling.

The girls announced that the dirty deed was done, the mess wiped away, and now there was only a damp spot where her filth had been. I looked at it once, and then would not look again. Bernadette and Lucy were in high spirits, two jingling Christmas bells ringing out songs of good cheer. They urged me to forget about the old bag and to come on now, and we'd go up the street and find some guys we knew, or at least walk down to Bisky's or something to see what she'd gotten from Daddy Dear—

But I said no, I couldn't. I just remembered we were having our dinner early, and I had to peel carrots and potatoes, so I had to go. Then Bernadette asked if we were having any of that eggnog like we had last year, and could she and Lucy come over and have some; and I said sure, after dinner, maybe, or even tomorrow, and they laughed and said good-bye and Merry Christmas, Beeb; and I hurried home so fast I might have been pursued by devils.

Teddy and Mother were out visiting friends who had invited us over for a drink and to look at their gifts. Pop had said he wanted to stay home, said he was sick and tired of singing "White Christmas," because people always asked him to sing *something,* and this year he didn't want to sing. When I opened the door, I saw him sitting in his chair. The paper was spread over his chest, his stockinged feet were stretched out in front of him on the hassock, and his hands were folded over his stomach, which was flat now and not the aggressive hard belly it used to be. His pipe lay in the ashtray on its side, and his glasses had slid down his nose a bit, making him look like a small-sized Santa after a hard night's work. A rush of tenderness engulfed me. When he was not talking, or gesturing, or scowling or laughing or snoring, his face in repose looked handsome and peaceful.

I tiptoed to the tree and moved a couple of packages until I found my brand-new Ansco flash camera. I inserted a flashbulb, having popped it into my mouth first to ensure the flash, and then I aimed the loaded camera at him. *"Popff!"* the flash exploded and I'd captured him at what might have been his best, I thought as I watched him stirring. His best.

He opened his eyes and determined that he had not, after all, been shot. "What are you up to, Half-pint?" he asked. Why had I expected him to be angry, shouting?

"Taking your picture," I said self-consciously. "You looked kind of cute there, so I thought I'd just take one of you."

He frowned. "Don't do that," he said gravely. "Don't ever take a picture of a sleeping person."

"Why not?" I said.

"I don't know," he said. "It just isn't good. It robs them of something, maybe."

"Okay, I won't," I said, subdued again. Suddenly I felt so

dreadfully, heavily sad that I got weary of standing, and I dropped down onto the floor and looked around at the small neat piles of presents, at the Christmas paper under the glass on our coffee table, at the pipe and the ashtray and the feet in their charcoal brown socks. *The last time,* something inside me said. *The last time.*

Pop yawned. "Did you have a nice time with Bernadette?"

"Sure. Lucy was there."

"Good. Nice girls. Both of them. Two nice girls."

"What did you do?"

"Ah, nothing much. Read the paper. Tried out my new pipe. I'm breaking it in now. Took a nap." He yawned again.

"Should I take another picture now that you're up?" I asked.

"Naa. Save the film for your ma and Teddy and your friends. They'll make better pictures than I will."

"You make a good picture, Pop. I hardly have any of you."

"Not today, okay?" he said.

"Okay," I said.

"Merry Christmas, Pint-size," he said, holding out his arms to me for the first time since . . . since . . .

I slid across the floor and knelt in front of his chair, letting the arms go around me in a hug. The sadness was smothering, overwhelming, a heaviness that was making me sink and drown. Neither of us spoke.

His hold on me loosened. "Merry Christmas, Poppy," I said, letting the old name slip off my tongue, letting my love for him roll off me, letting it exude and bubble up and brim over in one last wave.

And the sadness followed my father up the stairs as he went to his room to finish his long nap. Eventually, as the short day darkened, I got up and went into the kitchen, and scraped the carrots and peeled the potatoes for our gala Christmas dinner. Even the odor of the crisping capon could not fill my senses with delight. Not even the jellied cranberry, nor the red candles on the green tablecloth, nor the sauterne nor the sauerkraut nor the Tunnel of Love cake; nor Mario Lanza, Bing Crosby, nor *The Little Drummer Boy.* Not even Teddy's jokes and hugs, and not even his gift to me of an opal on a fine gold chain could lift that damp canvas tent of sadness from me.

We drank eggnog and watched a presentation of *The Nutcracker* on TV; and Pop talked a little bit about the spare, bare Christmases on the farm when he was a small boy; and my mother told of eating bread spread with lard all winter, and of receiving as a Christmas gift a single orange one year, and how thrilled she'd been; and Teddy confessed at last that he'd known for ages there was no Santa to leave cookies out for but had left them anyway, anyway, just in *case,* you know.

And Pop had laughed and had appreciated the sweetness of such a confession. I ached and longed to say something, to add to the gentle merriment of this evening, but I could not. I only sat and sponged it all up and could not speak my love as they could. Only I knew that this was *the last, the last,* and there was no way to say it, and no way to share it. So I sat and held it against my breast alone, and it was a beautiful night, a terrible night, and finally the eggnog lulled me, and I wandered off to bed and did not pray and did not dream.

Chapter 16

We had lost Rita Lee that fall of 1958, and it was not until the springtime that we were able to find her again. After our confrontation in the park when Pinky the cat bloodied Bernadette's face and Rita Lee said her two and a half cents' worth, she had glided out of our lives with a grace and elegance I did not know she possessed, this gawky girl with the washboard chest and the horsey face and the braids she still wore to be perverse when we were all curling and dyeing and snipping.

Bernadette and Lucy missed her only casually, but sometimes my heart clenched when I saw her walking, books primly carried in a plaid, buckled briefcase, all her papers in order, all her work having passed her mother's inspection. She walked high and proud, having become, it seemed, satisfied to have become at last a Tall Girl, disdaining the nicknames and the posings and the gigglings the rest of us affected. She was a loner, a thinker, and, although not brilliant or possessed of great insight, she was Deep. Everyone said so. Deep and quiet, like a dark pool that is only seldom moved by ripples.

I began to envy her, and to miss her terribly. My best thoughts and perceptions were going to waste on Bernadette and Lucy. Lucy was bright enough and had learned enough about books and movies to interest me, but she had become absolutely manic in her pursuit of boys. All our conversation revolved around the various devious and complicated schemes she was always devising to meet and talk to some hapless guy she'd set her cap for. Trouble was, she was wearing a different cap nearly every day—sometimes three or four in a single day!—and the whole thing left me breathless and embarrassed.

Bernadette was going the whole hog over at CYO now, working on being voted Best Dancer when we would finally graduate in 1962—getting an early start in building up her reputation as a Mover—and she'd dance with anybody who could keep up with her. God, she was good. The Bop, the Stroll, were only child's amusements for her. She was heavily into more complicated things, moving her hips and feet like a professional, letting her hair swing out behind her as she whizzed through turns that left me dizzy.

"Come on, Beeb!" she'd urge me when we'd practice after school. "Ya gotta keep up! Jeeze-ooh!"

She didn't sweat as much as I did, so she never looked as bedraggled and nauseated as I did when we finally collapsed. I have always suspected that therein lies the true secret of being thought of as Best Dancer—some innate sense of how to seem to dance without physical effort.

I paid a high price for my dancing. My hair hung like overcooked spaghetti over my flushed forehead; my deodorant consistently failed me, leaving wet rings under my armpits, forcing me to walk like a zombie with both arms clapped against my sides; my eyes got a little wild; my heart, surrounded already by too much fat, pummeled my chest and left me wheezy and gaspy. Bernadette just flitted around like an elf after a fast, hard dance, talking and joking with everyone. I was a wreck, and she was a daisy.

Bernadette and I talked, of course, but mostly it was about records and movies and teachers. Her sensibilities absorbed and recorded the most minute details about people's appearances, their mistakes, their jokes, their missteps. We laughed a lot. But about books, magazines, ideas—about these things, we did not talk, because we simply could not. She could not make herself go beyond the bare minimum when it came to schoolwork. We were all too straight to chuck our assignments, but Bernadette did as little as possible in order to squeak by. Her interests went elsewhere; her hopes and dreams were in her feet, in her body, in her hair and lips and nails. She saw herself only as others saw her. It was her goal, it seemed, to be the person They perceived her to be. When I said that to her, she looked at me as if I'd told her I enjoyed examining other people's feces at close range.

"What the hell are you talkin' about?" she demanded. "What's all this crapola, anyhow? Why can't you ever just leave a person alone without snooping around in their head? Cripes, girl. You're headed for the nuthouse. We're gonna have to call the men in the little white coats. God."

Gulp. I shouldn't have told her what I'd seen. She was as mad as Cara was the time I'd worn her falsies on my ears. She had that same violated, mortified look. What *was* that? Why did people get mad when you found out things about them? I did not discover until a college course in American Literature nearly five years later that Hawthorne had recognized this same thing in people, this terror of being known, learned, discovered and read like books, or looked at like illustrations for a manuscript. When I read of Hawthorne's insights, I saw again Bernadette's face when I told her about herself. "Leave me the hell alone," she'd cried that day, and I had, but I hadn't understood at all.

But Rita Lee was separate, apart from us by choice, and I could not seek her out, because it would have been a terrible intrusion, I sensed. If she wanted to talk to me, she would, I told myself. As it was, she was pleasant enough during class and was simply absent from our other activities. She spent her time in the library and at home with her animals.

Teddy, my real hero and my first choice for most conversations, was ridiculously busy being a senior in college, with all its attendant rights and responsibilities, such as getting smashed every weekend with the guys from K-A (Kappa Alpha, his fraternity, a bunch of handsome, nice guys whose major objective, it seemed, was to support the Great Old Southern Distilleries in a Gentlemanly Fashion); going out with a great number of different, pretty girls; and going to "flicks" with Garver, who was now the only companion he felt he could safely take with him. He just wasn't around.

Ma was never a talker. Her conversation centered around chores and duties and dirt and food and the neighbors and church and the laundry. It was hard to work your way into a conversation with her, because she was either busy or tired or watching TV.

That left Pop.

He went to work every day and came home with a brief-case of dark brown leather. With each passing year his responsibilities grew and his work load increased. He was looking thin but weighted. Gone forever were the bull-necked shirts, size XL, and the extra-long ties he wore so that they'd come down over his broad gut. When he was wearing sizes marked "portly," he had never looked heavy or moved ponderously, but now he was thick, sluggish. He was watching his diet, acting fussy for the first time that I could remember. Spices bothered him. Vinegar and acids bothered him. Fat meat was carefully trimmed. The portions decreased. He was not the same Pop. His glasses slid down his nose because his cheeks had thinned and could no longer provide support from underneath.

If he wanted to talk to me, he showed no signs.

Still, I stood at his elbow from time to time, asking questions about things I thought he might know. He would answer in his Sage of Dundalk way, as of old, but without the same old insistence that we be impressed with his declarations, and without the demand for close, adoring attention. Instead, he kept inserting phrases like, "Of course, not everybody thinks so," and "Don't take this as gospel, but . . ."

Cripes. What the hell kind of lecture was *that* on a given topic? I wanted—no, *needed*—some absolutes, some old Lincolnesque truths to ponder, some goods and bads, blacks and whites. But Pop could no longer produce them. He would sit and watch the news on TV and never utter a single damning expletive. He read of civil-rights activism and did not condemn or applaud. Gone were his compulsive commentaries on nearly everything.

True, he still protested weakly about my makeup and hairstyles and my jeans, which got tighter weekly as I gained weight, and he still examined his food for stray hairs. But the fire was gone, the flame just a flicker, and when he laughed, he did not hold his belly (it was not there) and roar with his lion's head thrown back. When he was mad, he said a single dispirited "shit" which might have been a little spit into a bucket. When he was moved, he said—and I shuddered to hear him say such a thing, such a *Baltimorean* thing from this German, this Wisconsin German—"Awww." Awww. That's what Baltimoreans said when they saw a puppy or a kitten in an advertisement, or saw a baby take its first steps in a high-grass park, or saw a little boy give his grannie a kiss on her withered cheek. Awww.

And Pop was saying it, too, as if he'd been born to say it, and not taught, not resigned to saying it. He did not even hear himself, but it was too late now to tell him, or to let on that I'd noticed. Too late.

I chided myself for succumbing to my absurd tendency toward the melodramatic. We were still soap opera fans, Ma and I, and I was given to saying things like "too late" to myself in a kind of an internalized emoting that made me want to snicker at me as if I were watching me in a movie.

Still, I kept saying it to myself, because it would have been too ridiculous to say it out loud. Too late.

In February Pop went into the hospital. I'd realized that he was going through what he called "tests," but I thought—

because he'd said as much—that they were routine and harmless and innocuous. Now he said he had to have an operation, that they were going to "explore." Teddy's face went blank for a moment, then white, then pink. He did not look up, did not look at Pop, or at any of us.

"Exploring for what? What are they looking for, Pop?"

"An obstruction in the bowel, I am told," Pop said, trying to smile. "Probably a fart caught crosswise." It was an old joke, one of our oldest, used for those times when Teddy and I did not want to go to school and went about clutching our tummies and moaning. "It's just a fart crosswise," Pop would laugh and send us on our way out the door to face whatever test we had. Now he was trying for that same look, that same cynical smile.

"Cripes." It was all Teddy said in response. Then, "When?"

"Tomorrow," Pop said, looking at his watch, as if he wondered if it were still today.

"So soon? What's the rush? Couldn't they wait till Monday?"

"The man said tomorrow," Pop said grimly. "I didn't argue."

"Who, Bisky the Brainless Wonder?"

"Naa. Some guy Bisky sent me to. Some guy named, ah, let's see, Burris. Adler Burris. Up on St. Paul Street."

"Nice office?" Teddy asked.

"Yeah. Big. Couple of secretaries. Knows what he's doing."

"Seems like it," Teddy said, satisfied now, knowing that at least we wouldn't have Bisky's incompetence to contend with.

"Sure. It's nothing to worry about," Pop said, putting out his hand to pat Ted on the arm. It was Grannie's gesture, my father's mother's gesture, that he was using. I had never seen him do such a thing.

"Okay, Chief," Teddy said, making his mouth go into a grin at last. "Right, Scut?" he asked me, encouraging me to participate in this good-cheer scene.

"Sure, right," I said too quickly.

"Anybody want pie?" Ma said then. "I made cherry and apple both," she announced with pride, so that we would all know how seriously she had taken this occasion.

"Yeah, great," we all said. I wolfed mine down eagerly and had two pieces, one of each, while Pop and Teddy each ate one conservative slice and Ma abstained.

After supper I practiced my heart out, going over those scales and arpeggios like a pro, and turning my Czerny exercises into bombastic arguments for vigor and vitamins. I played "Traumerei" because Pop liked it so much and then struggled through the first two pages of Chopin's "Fantasie-Impromptu," watching him flinch out of the corner of my eye each time the complicated rhythm and sequence got fouled up.

"I'll get it one of these days," I said guiltily. "It's not easy, you know."

"I know," he said. "Leave it go for now. Play 'Traumerei' again."

I played it for him, and he closed his eyes and sucked on his pipe and let the music fill him. I played it without haste, without strain, and it was quite beautiful. I had not known before that moment how beautiful, and now it was too late.

He would not let Teddy and me go up to the hospital with him. A guy from work drove him and Ma to the ancient, crumbling Saint Joseph Hospital, where the nuns strolled and the smells of the medicines mixed and mingled, invading nose and mouth with a metallic distaste. After supper, Teddy took us all up there in our own car, and we visited with Pop until he asked us to pull the curtains around his bed and let him get some sleep. They were coming for him on Saturday morning early, around six o'clock, and he wanted to be *ready*.

We left, promising to be there when he awoke from the

anesthetic on Saturday afternoon. He waved as Teddy pulled the curtain all the way shut.

The next morning we arrived early but could only get in a word or two and a squeeze of the hand, because Pop was already out of it, drifting away into some rarefied atmosphere. Ma put her hands together and rubbed them as if they itched, and she would not sit down. My stomach was growling, because I'd only had time to grab a handful of crackers on the way out of the house, so Teddy said to come on, we'd all go out somewhere and have breakfast. Ma said no, she'd stay, but why didn't we go if we wanted to. Teddy looked uncomfortable, not wanting to leave her alone and yet a little hungry himself, and eager to entertain me, to be the man, the father in this situation. We went, finally, and found a place to eat and hoovered down pancakes and sausage and coffee (it felt great to be swilling down coffee with Teddy like a tough old lady), and eventually we made our way back to the hospital where Ma was standing still, waiting for us.

Her face was a ruin, a bloodless revolution. "Pop's a dead man," she blurted. "Pop can't live."

No hello, no oh-my-God. Just that blunt, deadly pair of sentences. Ted stood stunned, and I swayed and leaned against him.

"I don't, I don't," Teddy began, faltering.

"I said he can't live," Ma said in a quiet screaming. "He's got to die. They opened him and sewed him right back up again. The cancer is the size of a football, Dr. Burris said. He said he didn't know how he'd managed to stay standing all this time. He said Pop should have been screaming in pain, out of his mind. But there's nothing he can do now. Nothing at all. It's all over."

"Oh, my God, my God," Teddy said, crying through his nose, the crying coming out of him in sour notes of raw agony. The tears burned as they fell, and he pulled at them as if he were trying to peel off the pain. Ma stood alone, Teddy alone, and I, I so alone, so frozen and alone, off to the side while

Teddy and Ma regarded one another in shared horror. Finally, each put out an arm to enfold me, but I stood still and would not come to them. So they came to me, and we three stood in a circle in the waiting room with its wooden-armed chairs and its hideous upholstery of Hawaiian passionflowers and its nosy occupants.

"Where's Bisky, that son of a bitch?" Teddy asked suddenly.

"He had nothing to do with this," Ma said.

"The hell he didn't," Ted said, his teeth grinding. "He should have known about this in time. He should have been up on Pop's case enough to know."

"Pop never went to him till January," Ma said. "Bisky couldn't do anything about a disease he didn't even know about."

"Ah, shit," Teddy keened, pulling Ma to him in a rough and awkward embrace. "Ah, Jesus Christ, Ma. Shit."

I pulled away from them, finding my own balance at last. No words tumbled out with my tears, no thoughts were forming to verbalize this grief, and no images conjured themselves up in order to help me deal with it. I just stood, and felt the hard floor beneath my feet and the chilly breeze that whipped through the room whenever somebody opened the main door to the hospital. I wanted to smoke a cigarette very badly, but to hurt Ma that way would have been unthinkable.

"God, let's get the hell out of here," Teddy said, gathering us up and pulling us out into the main hall and bundling us into our coats. He yanked open the door, stopped, shuddered, and said, "Ahh!" into the wet, windy air, then hurried to the car, unlocking all the doors so that we could pile in and just drive away.

When my father awoke that evening and opened his eyes, he saw his Chickie standing there with both feet firmly on the floor, dressed in his favorite dress, the red one of lightweight wool; and Teddy all spiffed up neatly; and me my usual lumpy, straightforward self. Our eyes were dry, and our palms were dry, and we talked of weather and comfort and that was all.

"Don't tell him," Burris had told my mother. "He'll give up hope. He's got to have hope. It's all he's got to go on now." Then the tall man had left abruptly, leaving our mother standing alone to wait for us.

"Don't tell anybody," Ma ordered us, as if our telling would make it true, would hurt Pop's chances for recovery. Nobody must know. Nobody. If we didn't tell, it would all go away. There would be no cancer if nobody spoke the word.

And for a few weeks, it was almost believable. In the hospital, Pop was willing to play cards a little, to get up and walk and gain strength, to drink water and eat Jell-O. (I hate Jell-O to this day, remembering his struggle to swallow it, chewing it like leather, gagging on it because nothing inside him wanted sustenance.)

There was nothing more to be done for him at the hospital, they said, and a week before Easter Sunday they sent him home to us, where they felt he would be more comfortable. We heaved his thinning body onto his bed, and he stared up at us in pale despair. "Ouch," he said then, smiling. "Damn thing still hurts."

"Yeah, well, it's gonna hurt for a while," Teddy said in mock frankness. "You know how it is. It's gonna be tender."

"Yeah, I know," Pop said, looking down to the place where the festering stitches had not healed, would never heal, watching them ooze. He covered himself with a blanket and sheet and bedspread.

"Mind if I take a little nap?" he asked, and we smiled down at him and left him to his dreams.

But when Teddy was not at home, Ma and I could not please him, could not lift him without hurting him. So we made the proper phone calls, and soon a hospital bed arrived, thanks to the Cancer Society; and then more calls were made, and soon there were LPNs to do the hands-on care, they called it, one for during the day so that Ma could do the regular duties, and one for during the night, so that we could sleep. It was expensive but worth it, we decided.

How thin he got lying there, manfully swallowing bits of custard and baby food. Twice his incision exploded and bombed putrid goo onto the walls and ceiling. When I came home from school Ma was busy mopping up, and the stench permeated all the house, and got into the furniture and the curtains and the wallpaper. Forevermore, it seemed to me, the smell of that rotting was in the house, even after I threw out the furniture and the drapes and the rugs and bought new, years later.

We did not speak of cancer. We never spoke of dying, or departing. He lay in his narrow bed, a high bed now so that he would be easier to tend, and looked at nothing or idly out the bedroom window if he wanted to, which was less and less often. His toenails turned yellow and grew long and hard, like ivory. His thick, wavy hair faded to pewter and straightened out. The stocky legs were straight sticks of white, veined and vaguely lumpy where muscles had once been. The barrel chest sank; the voice grew into a whisper that sounded like the rustling of brown leaves underfoot.

We did not speak, finally, of anything. To us and to his daytime nurse, an aging, sweet-faced, bustling woman named Mrs. Marner, he said nearly nothing. Feigning sleep, he would turn painfully to face the wall if one of us ventured too near.

But I would hear him in the nights. His nighttime nurse, a black woman named Lockerman, a single lady, she told us, was his confidante. His nights were so long, so endless. Eventually he would moan or speak, and Lockerman would go and stand close, putting her ear in front of his mouth. I saw her do this many times as I stole from my room to stand outside his doorway while Ma slept and did not hear. I believed that I would hear some shred or scrap of something that would make it all right. But he would not speak to me, and all I had was those whispers to Lockerman. It was she he pulled with him into the deep, black corners of his nights, and she to whom he confided his terrible pain, his hideous grief.

"Don't tell them," he implored her once in his creaky voice. "They'll lose their faith. They'll lose their hope."

"Darlin', you got to talk to them," Lockerman said, holding his hand, kissing it. I saw her. "You got to try."

"No," he said. "Listen." And she put her head closer to his mouth and nodded as he whispered, and said, yes, yes, Mr. Herman, of course, of course. . . .

And whatever it was, whatever his secret, she did not divulge it. Instead, she put her arm around my shoulders every evening when she came and squeezed and said, "Stand strong, baby girl. He need to know you standing strong for him." And puzzled, I'd nod wisely and bravely, not knowing the first thing about what she and he wanted from me.

They said he would die soon, and not to expect much. It was true that he was deteriorating rapidly, but something in me was restless for it to be over with, for him to be gone and away so that we could live again in that house; and I found myself tiptoeing around, peeking inside his room, waving at him, desperate to talk to him, desperate to be done with him, to put away the death and dying, to clean away the smells and stains of the death and the dying.

And all the while my mother prayed for his preservation and for the saving of his life, it did not occur to me to do so, because they had pronounced him dead once, and once was enough for me. No hope lingered in me, and nothing abided in me except a burning, bitter disgust and a fiery impatience for it to be over and done with.

Several weeks after the Easter bells had rung out with their sweet hope and their promise of victory over death and the grave, my father died on a hot Sunday May morning. Lockerman was there. Instead of going home at 7:00 A.M. as usual, she came to my room and sat down on my bed and roused me with a light touch.

"Baby doll," she said to me, close to my ear. "You want

to wake up now, darlin'. He say he want to see you now, so you go on in."

I went on in, but my father's eyes were not open.

"Poppy?" I said, my voice giving way in fear, in terror that he would be gone already.

He opened his eyes, looked briefly at me, moved his lips a tiny bit, then closed his eyes again and breathed a long, shuddering breath as if he were rowing away from shore in long pulls. Lockerman was beside me, behind me to my right, her hand under my elbow, holding me up.

My mother and Teddy were sitting on Ma's twin bed, holding each other, crying softly. My own eyes were dry, as were Lockerman's. She pulled me around to look into her long, smooth face.

"He going out easy now," she said calmly. "I called the doctor for you. You got nothing to do now but stay by him and stand tall like he wanted you to."

I nodded.

Bisky came, all dressed up for church, which he would miss now, but looking businesslike and dapper. "Got any coffee made?" he asked Ma, who nodded yes.

"Downstairs," Teddy said, not moving his eyes from the place where my father still lay breathing in slight, shallow little gasps. "Can you get it yourself, please?" he asked Bisky, and I thought with a little flip of my stomach how polite we all were, how proper and decorous, all arranged around the right side of Pop's high bed, watching him breathe, breathless ourselves waiting for the chest to rise a little bit again, to rise and fall just one more time.

I left the room and lay down on my own bed in my own room and looked at my Elvis Presley poster and did not cry. There was a song that spring, a sad, sad song that young girls cried over, a song called, of all things, "Tragedy," in which it seemed a young man mourned his dead love. "Blown by winds, kissed by snow," the young man sang, and young girls would let the tears slip and trickle onto their partners' Ivy

League plaid shirts and so what, because it was so beautiful, so tragically beautiful, and so terribly, terribly sad. But I did not cry because I was standing tall, just as Lockerman had said he wanted me to, and even lying down I was not vulnerable.

Suddenly I sat up stiff and stared and fought for a breath, and at that moment Lockerman came to my doorway, filling it up with her wonderful dark height, and said, "He gone now, darlin'. He gone to his Father and his rest just now. Praise God."

The soft slur of her words came to me in a trance, the same trance I fell into each time the world gave me too much —too much pain, too much fear, too much anger or happiness. I was able to get up and go to where Bisky was filling out official forms in his Sunday blue suit. My mother and Teddy were still crying and talking softly, and Lockerman was looking out the window for Pastor, whom she'd called to come and bear with us this terrible grief. I entered the room and looked at the way Lockerman had carefully, tenderly covered my father, preserving his dignity the best she could, tucking in the offensive toes; tucking the sheet and blanket up and under the thin shoulders; and turning the blanket at last to cover his gaunt and haunted face, covering up the miserable silence of that face so that I did not have to look upon the features of a stranger when I came to say good-bye.

Thank you, Lockerman, for covering him so. Thank you for folding back a corner of the blanket to look like a baby's hood, and nothing to fear, and nothing to hate.

Nobody our age had ever really been to a funeral. One kid said she'd been to her grandmother's, but nobody had let her see anything and she'd only gone to the cemetery, and not to the funeral home to look inside the casket.

Coffin. Casket. My father would have preferred a pine box, I knew, because it was the way he always spoke of death. "I'll be in a pine box before you finish," he'd say, to indicate his impatience with us bathroom dwellers whose private activities baffled him. A pine box. They didn't have anything like that at the funeral home. There were ornate, expensive caskets lined with velvet and satin. We finally picked one out, Teddy and I, because Ma had to shop for a black dress. She didn't own one. Pop wouldn't let her wear black, maintaining black was for old ladies. While Lena Rosling took Ma to Hutzler's and Hochschild's to look for a suitable dress, Teddy and I had to find a proper box in which to put our father.

At the funeral home, my friends crowded round and stood awkwardly, as if they were waiting to be chosen for a game of Farmer in the Dell. I was the cheese who stood alone. I walked over and placed myself in their midst, wanting their warmth around me, but they took a fast look inside the casket and gasped, and put their hands over their mouths. Some cried out loud—especially Bernadette, who came to me and flopped onto my shoulder and sobbed, "I loved him, Beeb. I really loved him." The boys went out onto the long porch of the funeral home and smoked and talked guy talk with the older men, people from my father's office, in stilted, polite words. The girls talked among themselves, trying to repeat the adults' phrases and sounding patently ridiculous. "He looks so nice," Lucy said to Bernadette. "He looks real natural."

He looked dead. He was a skinny, terrifying shell of a carcass that was already beginning to disintegrate. The mouth was sewn shut and plastered with pancake makeup. The hair, straight and dark gray, was slicked back and looked like faded patent leather. The cheeks were blushed a shocking magenta, and the eyelids sewn together. At my mother's insistence, he was holding his new pipe in his folded hands (no rosary? Bernadette wondered), and if I'd had my way, his *Sunpapers* would have been folded up across his narrow little hummingbird chest. He did not look "natural" without it, I wanted to yell into the crowd. He did not, in fact, look like a natural human being at all, I wanted to shout at them. He looked like a goddam skeleton with a fright wig on.

When they buried my father and I saw his coffin go thunk-clunk finally into the neat rectangle of a hole, something awful happened inside me. A cold dread overtook me, and my bowels turned to jelly. I was scared. The idea of his being down there, covered by a ton of dirt, and prey to rot and decay, nauseated me. I started to shake, and Teddy pulled me close beside him, and I shivered all the way home.

The neighbors had made enough food to feed Fort Holabird for a month, so there was no cooking to do. The trick was in storing all the various casseroles, pies, cakes, rolls, and breads they'd brought. Each dish was labeled so that we'd know whom to thank for what, and the guests would know whom to compliment. Also, I suspected, so that God would know whose crown to add the stars to.

My grandparents flew down to Baltimore, accompanied by Aunt Caroline, a first plane trip for all of them. "To think he went before we did," my father's mother moaned into her hankie all day long. "To think. Just think of it." And think of it I did. *It should have been you,* I wanted to say. *Trade with him; bring him back and go yourself,* I wanted to scream.

The funeral day was hot and bright, and I suffered from the heat, my legs rubbing together above the tops of the tight nylon stockings I'd convinced to cover my heavy legs. The garter belt kept slipping down and I had to tug at it from time to time, which upset my mother, who was embarrassed when I kept picking at myself and my clothing. My grandparents stood like statues—I had not yet seen the famous *American Gothic* painting, but once I did, it was these two familiar faces that stared out of the canvas at me. They were bib overalls, Oshkosh-b'-gosh people, and they were out of their element and too stunned with grief and pain to realize how out of place they looked among the businessmen and young people.

Aunt Caroline stayed close beside me, guiding me through the proper funeral-home etiquette, saying she was proud of me and in general making me feel competent and tall for my age.

My grandparents were distressed because I did not try to hurl myself into the open grave, or cry loudly and openly. "She doesn't seem to be affected," they said to Caroline, whose back stiffened and whose fists clenched in sudden anger. "She seems too cool."

"Just because a kid has a head on her shoulders doesn't mean she isn't concerned," Caroline snapped back at them. "Bebe's got her father's backbone, Ma. Can't you see that?"

My grandparents looked away, looked down at their shoes, looked down at their plates. I had decimated them with my nonchalance, had ruined their grief with my bursts of laughter when the men told jokes and the women traded gossip. It was unseemly that a child should let a thing like death roll off her like water from the duck's back. Up in my room, after it was mostly over, Caroline came to me.

"I don't know what it's like," she said, biting her dry lips, then wiping them with her lacy hankie. "I haven't lost a parent yet. Look at me—forty years older than you, and you've had a serious life experience that hasn't touched me yet."

"Gee, yeah," I said, impressed to think of myself so. I sat up straighter, mimicking her posture as she stood before the mirror pinning up loose strands of her long hair where they had stubbornly come undone from her schoolmarm's bun at the nape.

"So I can't put my arm around you and say that I understand," she went on, looking at my reflection in the mirror and not turning to confront me. It was easier to talk to her back. If she'd turned I'd have collapsed, and I was thankful that she did not come closer, did not touch me, or I would surely have dissolved, and I did not want to dissolve. I wanted to talk, and to listen to Caroline talk.

"But I do know about loss and about having people you love suddenly disappear," she said, her eyes going cloudy for a second, then clearing. "I know all about that."

"Yeah, I guess," I said, dreadfully embarrassed, knowing

full well that she referred to her abandonment by Oscar Welles.

She smiled. "I won't tell you," she said. "But I know how it feels inside the stomach and under the ribs and in the throat."

"Did you cry?"

"I don't remember," Caroline said. "I don't think it's important, the crying. What's important is how the person is remembered, whether it's with affection and generosity. If you can do that, the loss seems less severe, and the wound heals more easily." Silence for a few seconds, a deep breath, then, "But of course I speak strictly of my own experience and perceptions," she said briskly.

"Of course," I said. "I know that." I wished that I could have spoken my gratitude to her. I wanted so much to put my arms around her and to bury my face in her neck and to pull her long hair down around me to cover myself, but I sat tall and still and did not reach for her. She picked up a strand of my hair.

"If you let your hair grow long, don't tie it back into a bun like I did," she said. "All the natural wave will go out of it, and you'll regret it, Bebe. Let it fall free, or let it curl and blow around like a wild little halo. You'll like it better, and you won't always be jabbing at your scalp with these godforsaken pins." She pulled out one of her hairpins, a lethal-looking thing, and we both laughed over that.

A wild little halo. She had a way of using phrases that touched something in me. Her letters were like that, too—not newsy, really, but filled with little lilts and wordings that made them a delight. "Pa is beside himself," she'd written once, "knee-deep in manure and livid because Del had the gall to sprain his ankle and is lying around like a bum at the Mission House while Pa shovels out the cowbarn." She was a reporter and an illustrator of their lives, and her letters kept us close, kept us inside their world and their routines and their daily picture.

"You wear your grief like dove-gray silk," she said suddenly, and it so startled me, this observation, that I jerked away from her in alarm, as if she'd reached over and yanked off all my clothes in a single violent motion.

"I'm sorry," she said, her face stricken. "I shouldn't have said that. It just popped out. I meant that you are not used to it and that it fits you like a new, stiff dress that you feel you must not wrinkle or stain or wet or move inside. That's the way I see you today, like a girl inside her first ball gown, and not enjoying the ball a bit because she cannot move."

"How can you compare my father's death to a *dance*?" I said, half angry with her, confused now.

"I haven't done that," she said. "Forgive me. I'm not going to say another word about it. To explain it now would only make it seem worse to you. Just know in your heart that I understand, and that it's all right not to be perfect, not even in your grief."

"Okay," I said, not wanting, ever, to fight with her or to question her unreasonably.

She got up from my bed, pulled a handful of gray-brown hair out of her comb and brush, fashioned it into a little bird nest, and deposited it into my trashcan. She smelled faintly of lily of the valley, and the scent of her lingered in the room for long moments after she'd gone.

Caroline appeared again in my doorway. A strange thing, I thought. In my own version of this little movie the scene had ended, and it was now time for me to get up, go to the mirror, look for pieces of Caroline in my own face, sigh, and then let the tears come streaming down my young face.

I had seen enough movies to know how it should have been.

But it wasn't. Instead, Caroline came inside my room, her eyes wet with sorrow, and said to me, "Everybody thinks I'm strange, Bebe. People think that if you read poetry and go to museums and concerts and live alone with a dog you are creepy and eccentric. It isn't true, honey. I just wanted you to know. It isn't true. And the way I live my life satisfies me and is good, and don't let any of your small-minded relatives rob you of that truth. It's okay to be a little bit different and to do things the way you please. It is most certainly *okay*."

"Gee, I know that, Auntie Caroline," I said feebly.

"Good," she said. "Then that's the end of my speech. I'm sorry if I upset you. I just want you to have more courage than I did as a girl, that's all. I'd like to spoon-feed it into you so that you won't suffer the way I did."

"I won't suffer," I said nobly. "I won't. You'll see."

"Oh, my God, I hope not, sweetheart," she said, and came to me, and hugged my stiff, chunky body against hers, and kissed me on both cheeks like Frenchman meeting Frenchman.

And to make a long story short, when Rita Lee called me that night to find out how I was doing, I asked her to come over, and she said she would, and her mother wouldn't mind, not under the circumstances. It occurred to me that they were remarkably similar in shape, in posture, and in habits, my Auntie Caroline and Rita Lee Zimmerer. Great waves of affection and appreciation for them both poured over me, rocking me like a little boat in a warm, fragrant lake.

I was fifteen years old, and I knew every song ever written and could play the piano and do my homework in a half hour flat. I was mature for my age, well read, and possessed of a certain dignity and a knowledge of foreign movies that would carry me through this thing.

Grief could not really touch me. The pain, like all pain, would pass and be forgotten, and the wound would heal over. People live and people die. It's a fine and natural thing. The pain was simply a sign of mankind's weakness and inability to deal with the forces of nature and of nature's God. It was a sin to grieve. Pop was with God, right? Then I was dumb to be upset. We should be grateful and thankful, I thought. It's we who are in trouble, not him. We should be rejoicing because he is in heaven now, and no longer in pain. It was obvious, all of it.

I was fifteen years old, and impervious to the grief.

Blown by winds, kissed by snow . . .

It was just a song.

Chapter 17

Teddy graduated, he and Garver both, although not on the same day, because Garver had not gone to Hopkins but to Loyola. But there they both were, free at last and at loose ends, wondering what to do with themselves, neither much interested for the first few weeks in looking for a job but aware of their responsibilities and duties as Men of the World.

They decided to join the army.

Off they went to be soldiers, the two of them together under what was known as the "buddy system," whereby they would stay together through the proverbial thick and thin for four years, 1959 to 1963. They figured they could hack four years in army intelligence, which is what they were promised for their trouble, and we waved a gulping good-bye to them, The Touchdown Twins, at Penn Station one muggy, smelly day and then took a cab back to Dundalk because I was still only fifteen and not yet old enough to get a license.

Ma took driving lessons for a month but was not able to get her license. She could never quite seem to distinguish brake from accelerator, and when the instructor's hair stood on end and his foot came bashing through the floorboards and his piercing screams divided the evening air, Ma lost heart and gave him back his car keys and sold our car to some teenager for a couple hundred bucks.

Sure, there was insurance. Enough to pay off the worst of the big bills. But there wasn't enough to live on. Ma went to work in a bakery, and Teddy had money sent home each month for us, as if we were his wife and kids. Every single time a check arrived Ma was angry to think that Teddy was not spending the money on himself, or saving it.

It didn't worry me any, though. I knew Teddy wanted to do it, and I also knew it was his way of showing his love. He believed that he had not shown it sufficiently while our father was alive. He had told me so. "I have something to expiate," he told me somberly, and although the word was foreign to me, the concept certainly was not. Something to expiate. I let him expiate to his heart's content and did not argue with him.

An interesting thing happened to me during the months immediately following Pop's death. I became a minor celebrity among the kids we hung with and among their parents. Everyone felt sorry for me, or perhaps inquisitive. I think maybe they wanted to come close, to kind of rub elbows with a person who had walked with death and who had witnessed intimately its devastation. I think I became a temporary heroine, both for my stoicism and for my new status as half-orphan.

This gave me an excuse to mope through the last few weeks of school, barely talking to the teachers who sought to counsel and comfort me. When one of them came too close, I feigned interest in my classwork and asked a pertinent question before they had the chance to reach my pain. Eventually they became absorbed in their last-minute grading and report cards and the mounting minutiae of end-of-year crapola, and they forgot about me. They knew I would be going off to the brand-new Dundalk high school in the fall, and the counselors and teachers there could deal with me.

Good. I didn't want that particular kind of attention.

But I didn't mind the attention I got from the kids. Leonard Talarczyk started calling me a few weeks after the funeral, just to see how I was doing, he said, and to see if I was going to join Walther League at church in the fall. I said I was tired of all that hand clapping and hymn singing and hayriding and thought I must have outgrown most of that stuff. After a little pause he said maybe he had, too, and that most of those kids were sisses anyhow, right? First thing I knew, I had said that yes, he could come over if he felt like it, and he said he was going to get on his bike and shag on over. God, a *date*. Thoughts of Mancuso flooded my consciousness and I shivered.

It was okay, though. All we did was listen to some records and watch *The Untouchables* on TV. It was his favorite show. I personally preferred doctor shows, but who was I to argue?

Bernadette was surprised. "Talarczyk?" she said, her plucked eyebrows raised. "I didn't think he even liked girls. He's always making these *comments,* you know. I mean, I think he's got a *attitude* or something."

"Well, maybe," I said. "But he's all right. He brings stuff when he comes, like a bottle of Coke or a bag of chips."

"I think he's a nerd," Bernadette said. "He can't dance."

"Lots of people can't dance."

"Yeah, but he doesn't even *try.* Jeeze-ooh."

"So? Maybe he doesn't *want* to dance. Ever think of that?"

She evidently had not. Not wanting to dance was not in her mentality, not for anyone with the correct number of legs and feet. She shrugged.

"I hope you don't think I *care* if you want to fart around with Talarczyk," she said, flushing. "I mean, it's none a *my* business who you want to make out with."

"We don't make out," I said heatedly.

"Bullhockey," Bernadette said, grinning. "Don't kid me." She rolled her eyes ceilingward, shrugged again, and walked away down the hall to her home ec class, where a gaggle of girls were already boiling water and setting tables for another fiesta. Tuna casserole and biscuits. Budget cookery. I was not going today. I had an appointment with the official guidance counselor, who spent an hour trying to make me see that I ought to have signed up for the so-called enriched courses next year instead of the easier, more "general" courses Bernadette had opted for. I finally agreed. Bern wouldn't miss me anyhow. I didn't dance well enough.

Talarczyk wasn't so bad. We kissed and felt around each other a bit, but I was too embarrassed about how fat I'd gotten to let him explore too far. Eventually he lost interest and before long was hanging out at Bernadette's.

Then Paul Rosling asked me if I'd like to go to Methodist Youth Fellowship with him, and I said why not, because some other kids I knew went there every Sunday evening. It seemed a suitable way to get back at Talarczyk, Pastor, God, and the Walther League all in one fell swoop. MYF was fun. Popcorn, singing, bugging the advisers, quick kisses in the church parking lot.

I had always liked Paul Rosling. He was no genius, but he was solid, steady, and kind, not the kind of guy to go telling people you were fat or sweaty or easy or a pig. He was thick. Substantial. Real. When he kissed me, it was shy and innocent, like a picture taken through gauze, and if not intensely romantic, then at least not as hurried and gropy as Talarczyk's urgent, demanding style. I had the feeling, too, that Paul Rosling would have been as panicky if I'd gone exploring around his secret parts as I would have been if he'd invaded mine.

I did not get all As on my final report card. In fact, I dropped down to Cs in a couple of things. My mother did not even flinch. "I guess you couldn't help it," she said kindly. I was grateful.

The heat came that summer like a curtain of fire. And so it was down to the beach with Foote and Bisky. Not really to the beach, mind you, but to the Sparrows Point Country Club where I was sometimes a guest at the pool. The lifeguards were exactly the right age, build, and complexion for us all to fall in love with. One, a bronze godlet with white hair all over his body, head to toe, it seemed, had just graduated from Poly and was on his way to U. of M. in the fall. He was a reader, and I'd crane my neck up to where he was sitting absorbed in his books and check out the titles. Then I'd get the same books from the library and carry them conspicuously in my outstretched arms so that maybe he'd be encouraged to speak to me. He didn't.

Of course, his silent urging did get me to read such classics as *Auntie Mame,* some Robert Benchley collections, and most of what was then published by S. J. Perelman, so in his subtle way, he *was* important in my life. Teddy had introduced me to J. D. Salinger's *Nine Stories,* and I wallowed in them, reading and rereading them time and again, to taste again the flavor and rhythm of the dialogue, and to delight in the cleverness of the small details that made each character so special.

I read everything I could get my hands on that summer, Pop's old book-club books—from Frank Yerby to *Gentleman's Agreement.* I scarfed up everything in the library's small science-fiction collection and was so taken by the genre that I sat cross-legged out on the grass under the sycamores with an open notebook, writing story after story all with final sentences like, "And when he awoke, he prayed aloud in thanksgiving to discover his own familiar chair in his own familiar room," and, "When they discovered her in the morning, her once-raven hair streamed like silver down her bony back and her lips were drawn open in a stony grimace of horror." I thought that I would become the first (except for the smartypants Françoise Sagan, the little witch) teenage writer of substance, and I wrote in longhand in my notebooks and typed furiously on Teddy's left-at-home portable and then wondered what to do with it all.

Leonard Talarczyk and Bernadette were practically going steady that summer. Lucy Grabowski and Jack Price were a Thing. Rita Lee was taking modern dance and art, and went downtown (which we all called uptown) every day carrying either a wooden artist's case or a canvas bag full of dancing paraphernalia. Every time I thought of her in a dance class I snickered. Those long feet (flat, too) and gawky arms flying every which way, the single thick braid plopping up and down on her back, all that *sweat* . . .

As for me, it was good to sit under a tree and read and write, which was how I spent most of the muggy days and nights. At summer's end I stored it all away, in case I should ever begin to need to sort out all of the stories, the collected images, the bits and pieces of the chronicling I had begun.

Paul Rosling kissed me in earnest one hot-hot August night. Startled, I tried to pull away, but when I leaned back into the tree I was standing against, he pressed hard into me, his hands tangled into my hair, his breath all over my face. He was panting and crushing me, and I could barely get a breath. The bark was scratching into my back through my cotton blouse; his fingers were digging into my back, searching for the hook and eye that held my bra together.

When I tried to tell him no, no, his voice was harsh in my ear. *Yes, yes,* the voice said. As I arched my back to get away from the bark on the tree, his hands found the catch and unlocked my breasts, and his hands were all over them, sliding up and down, pinching and pulling and touching, first hard and then softly, wonderingly, and he was sighing, Ahh, Ahh. Suddenly it was good, and when he pulled up the blouse and put his lips to my skin, I sighed, too, and let him, although my heart was battering my chest. I looked around, in mortal terror that someone might be watching.

So I pulled Paul up by his fair, thick hair and said firmly, "Not now. Good Lord, Paul. We're right out in the middle of everything here. Jeeze. We've got to be sensible, right?"

"Yeah, right," he said, smiling into my face. That smile made me unaccountably happy, as if he'd said I looked like Marilyn Monroe or sang like Brenda Lee. That smile told me he loved me, even before he said it.

"I love you, Bebe," he said. "Beatrice Schmidt. Beattie.

Bea. B." I hadn't known Paul Rosling was capable of such playfulness, such charm.

Things were fluttering around inside me. My head buzzed. "I love you, too, Paul," I said. Just like in the movies. He pulled me tight against him and kissed me again, then held my face between his two hands.

"Thanks for—ah—letting me, you know . . ."

"Oh. Yeah," I said. "It's okay. But jeeze, Paul, not right out in the open. Anybody who came by could see us."

"I know," he said. "Next time I'll be more careful, I promise."

I couldn't say anything. I was afraid there would be a next time, and just as afraid there wouldn't.

"Paul," I said, whispering urgently. "Promise you won't tell anybody."

"Aw, Beeb," he said. "I ain't like them guys at school. You know that."

"I know," I said. Paul was quiet. A hard worker. Steady. Kind.

He took both my hands in his and squeezed them. "You want to go with me, or what?"

"Go where?"

"Jeeze, you make it so hard," he said. "*Steady,* dowad. You want to go steady with me, or what?"

"Sure," I said. Yes, yes, a thousand times, yes. Steady! Just like I'd always dreamed. A boy who'd be able to look past the weight and into the heart of a girl! All that stuff from the *American Girl* magazines came true! He really did see my finer qualities.

"Then let's go down to the courts tomorrow and play tennis, okay?"

"Yeah, good," I said.

I had a tennis racquet, shoes, and a can of balls that Teddy had left behind. Why not?

Bisky and Foote were there. They had both signed up to

take tennis lessons from Rec Council. Bisky was skinnier than ever, but her hair was long and golden, and her legs were tanned already, probably from going to the club every day and sticking them out in front of her so that the lifeguards would see. My own legs were white and stocky, and, to my mortification, there was one large blue vein showing on the right calf up near the knee, and I knew—I just *knew*—that I had the "very close veins" Rita Lee's mother was always bellyaching about.

Foote was there, too, but was not quite as threatening as the accursed Bisky. Barbara Foote was a nice, normal girl with a kind of a hard mouth. She didn't like much of anything when you came right down to it, but she knew how to make her dislikes seem funny. She was what my mother called a "live wire," always busy, always having something to say. She was okay.

Bisky waved to Paul and me as we sauntered over to the benches to wait for a court. She was volleying with Foote, and Foote did not wave her hand; she waved her foot. "Foot, get it?" she yelled to me. "Foot!"

"So?" I yelled back. I didn't get it.

"Foot! It's my name, dowad!"

"No shit, Sherlock," I called back, embarrassed not to have gotten her message.

"Hey!" Paul said sharply, grabbing my elbow. "Cut it out."

"Cut what out?"

"That trashmouth. I don't like it."

"Well jeeze, I'm *sorry,*" I said, tremendously offended and embarrassed even further. "She just makes me mad sometimes, that's all."

"Fine. Just cut out the dirty talk, okay?"

"God. Okay."

When we finally got a court, it was the one next to Bisky's. She and Foote kept hitting balls into our court which Paul had to return. Finally, it got silly, with Carla and Barbara deliberately trying to hit us with the balls, and we decided to play doubles. I figured we'd play them against us, but Carla said how about her and Paul against Foote and me.

With womanly wisdom, that ancient and accurate sense of impending loss, I knew without a doubt at that precise second that my days with Paul Rosling were numbered. Bisky kept tucking her white blouse inside her white shorts and pulling up her white socks so that his attention would be constantly drawn to her lithe body. She asked if anybody had a rubber band so that she could put up her long, heavy hair. He took another look at her hair and squinted into the sun to better see its color. He looked back at me and saw a chubby chunk, a thick-legged, perspiring stump whose fine hair could not withstand a half hour of heat and humidity. I looked greasy, sooty, exhausted, lumpy, and flabby. Bisky looked like an Olympic swimmer, broad of shoulder, long of neck, with the hard muscles of the born-thin.

Paul and I walked home slowly, his arm draped casually across my shoulders. I kept smiling up at him, trying to remind him how much I meant to him, trying to show I was game despite my handicaps, trying to convey my enthusiasm for our relationship, my need for him. But his eyes were not often meeting mine, and I knew that I had been right, that he was the quicksilver I would not be able to hold on to.

That night when the phone rang I was already depressed, and when I heard Bernadette's voice I didn't cheer up. She was doing a sort of nasal thing that she did when she was aggravated. "You're gonna kill me for tellin' you this," she said. "I guess I better not, huh? You'll just get broiled."

"Tell me," I said.

"Nuh-uh," she said. "It ain't right. I gotta go now, Beeb."

"Tell me!" I roared, already knowing, but wanting to hear it.

"I seen Paul over at Bisky's, right out on the front porch," she said reluctantly, but firmly, clearly. "They were sittin' on the glider big as life, and Bisky was practically sittin' on his lap. Cripes, you never saw anything like it."

265

"Okay," I said. "Thanks."

"You want to talk?" Bernadette said. She was a friend, blue and true.

"Naa," I said. "Hell with 'em both. Who needs 'em, right?"

"Yeah, right," she said, her voice picking up and brightening. "Ooh, that girl gets me, ya know? I can't believe her, stealing Paul right out from under your nose. What the hell kind of friend is that, huh? I mean, with her around, who needs enemies, right?"

It did not occur to Bernadette to castigate herself for stealing Leonard Talarczyk right out from under my nose, but then Talarczyk was not really all that much under my nose to start with. Whereas Paul—well, God, we'd practically gone all the way. I mean, it was *strange,* realizing that he'd had his way with me (well, part of his way) once and then had dropped me like the proverbial hot potato. The tears shot out of my eyes, and I called myself names in the summer darkness.

"Stupe," I said. "Tramp. Pig. That's what you get for letting him unhook your bra. Pig."

He did not call that night, nor the next day, nor the next.

Finally, I saw him coming home from the Acme on his bike with one small bag of groceries, and I waved to him, and he stopped his bike for me.

Small talk. I never knew how small it could be. He shuffled his feet around in the dirt; squeezed his hand brakes about four thousand times; ran his hand through his hair, which was adorable and windblown; yanked at his T-shirt; gave me a cigarette and lit it; fiddled with his brown paper bag; and finally, at last, came out with it.

"Ah, Bebe, I shouldn't have done what I did to you the other night. I mean, I was a real bastard, and I apologize."

"No, Paul. It was okay. Really. I didn't mind."

"No, no," he said. "It was wrong. You should save stuff like that for people you—I mean, you should only do it with people you, ah—"

266

"You said you loved me," I said. He looked away. "You said it."

"I know I said it," he admitted. "But I don't know why I said it. I just said it, you know, because it seemed like the right thing to say."

"I wish you hadn't now." My mouth had gone dry as bones.

"Me, too," he said. "But I swear, Bebe, I didn't mean to hurt you. My father said not to hurt you, no matter what, because you been hurt enough lately. He said to be kind, you know, and look what I did instead. I really messed up, Bebe. God, I'm sorry."

"Your father said what?"

Paul looked quickly at me.

"He said what about me?" I asked again.

"Oh. Well. He said you'd been through so much, I shouldn't hurt you. I should make an effort to bring you out a little, you know? He wanted me to be nice so that you'd start being with kids again. It was nothing bad, Bebe. Beeb—why the hell are you crying, now? What did I say wrong? We were only trying to be good to you, Beeb. Jesus, what's the trouble?"

But the rest of his babbling was lost on me. I was nobody's goddam charity case, not when it came to loving. The bloody hell with every single stinking one of them. Let them go find some other poor orphan to pretend to love—Paul and his moron of a father; and Bisky the Bitch and the Daughter of a Simpleton; and even Lucy, who had taken my Jack, my little Price, my first love.

The hell with everybody. They were snakes in the goddam grass. Screw 'em all.

I went to my room to finish crying. Bisky and Foote would never see me cry. Neither would Paul or his father. Or Lucy. Or even Bern. I didn't need anything they had to offer.

I just plain didn't need anything from anybody.

Screw 'em all.

Chapter 18

The first few days at the brand new Dundalk high school were fun, remeeting kids some of us hadn't seen since sixth grade. There was so much confusion (the teachers hardly knew the building any better than we did, and even the seniors couldn't lord it over us because they were at sea, too) that it was hard to meet Bernadette and Lucy for lunch, much less find each other after school or find seats close together on the bus. That's why I found Rita Lee again and was able to remake our friendship.

"I just want you to know I'm still sorry about your father," Rita Lee said one muggy September afternoon as we sat in the orange bus and waited at a traffic light while all the other kids yelled and swore and sang filthy songs out the windows.

"Thanks," I said. "Thanks a lot."

The guys in the back were singing at the tops of their lungs:

> Cats wear collars,
> Horses wear bits,
> Lulu wears a sweater, to cover up her—
> Bang-bang Lulu; bang-bang Lulu; bang-bang Lulu-
> uuuuuu;
> Ba da da da da daaaa!

My father had sung that tune to "Good Night, Ladies" with a barbershop group. I flinched when I thought of him now, listening to this parody of an old sweet song. Paul Rosling was among the singers, and I was surprised to see him there. He'd been such a quiet guy before Carla. Now he was in the Mr. Popularity contest every day, acting like Leon J. Cool and trying to impress everybody with new clothes.

Somebody in the back started singing a really nasty song to the tune of "Johnny Angel" in a silly falsetto. Even Rita Lee couldn't help giggling, and neither could I.

> Other fellas call me up for a date,
> But I just sit and wait—I'd rather masturbate—

We hooted with rowdy laughter, and it felt good—really *good*—to be among all the noise and movement. It had been a long, lonely summer.

"I shouldn't laugh, but I can't help it," Rita Lee said.

"Ah, don't always censor yourself," I said. "Laugh it up. Have a ball. Tomorrow we may die."

"Since when did you become so fatalistic?" Rita Lee asked. I turned to look at her. Fatalistic. Quite a term.

"I don't know," I said, warming to her suddenly. "Maybe when my father died. I can't tell."

"One person's death doesn't mean we should sit around waiting for our own, though, does it?" she asked me, her eyes behind the glasses concerned, sincere.

"I don't know. I don't know anything about it. All I do know is that it doesn't pay to put too much time and effort into loving people. They keep disappearing."

"Who? Who keeps disappearing?"

"Everybody. Like Teddy, even."

"He'll be back."

"You never know, though, do you?" I said, hinting at the kind of tragedy straight from the *Loretta Young Show* I'd watched throughout my childhood.

"That's true," Rita Lee said, biting her lip. "My father never came back from Germany. He was a soldier."

"Your father?" I asked, feeling blank. There had never been any such thing as Rita's father. It was only Rita and her mother. It had never occurred to me, not even once, to inquire about her father's whereabouts. I'd always just assumed he'd gone off somewhere, much like Oscar Welles or Price's father.

"Yeah, my father," she said, looking irritated now, embarrassed.

"I'm sorry," I said.

"Me, too," she said. Then she softened again. "But that's the thing, Beeb. You've got to understand that everybody is suffering about something. You're not alone."

"But nobody suffers like I do," I said baldly. It sounded so ridiculous that I could feel myself reddening.

"Bosh," Rita Lee said. What a strange word for a kid to use. But it came out of her like a gurgling spring, and I could tell it made her happy to say it, to feel the word on her tongue, to purse her lips for the "sh" at the end of it. It made her smile to say it.

"What do you mean—bosh?" I said. The word prickled.

"Balderdash!" she said, jubilant. I was fascinated.

"What else?" I prodded her.

"Hogwash. Bushwah. Horsefeathers!" she said, and we two burst out into gales of giggles.

"In a word, bullhockey!" I said, eager to join her, finding fun in the words, playing with them, tossing them like a salad or a hard ball.

"Enough, enough," she said, wiping her eyes with the back of her long hand. I saw with a little surprise that her nails had grown long and that they were polished a pale pearly pink, and that her hands no longer seemed too big for her body. Her long thin legs were crossed at the knee, and she sat casually but gracefully in the bus seat. She looked so *adult*. She didn't move the same klutzy way she used to. When she walked, her feet, still long but elegant-looking now, aristo-cratic-looking, pointed ever so slightly outward, as if she were wearing toe shoes with trailing pink ribbons.

"No, more," I said, egging her on, and she laughed again.

"It's fun, isn't it?" she said, sounding like a teacher, or like a college Big Sister should sound. "I started doing it about a year ago, but I'd just say the words to myself, inside my head, and kind of listen to them and get a kick out of it. They're just words most people don't use anymore, and to me it's like finding a bunch of neat old antiques up in the attic and bringing them all downstairs to admire."

"What a great idea," I murmured, impressed as hell. Here was another person who loved words and was not ashamed to say so. "What other ones do you know?"

"Well, I can trot out a list for you," she said, "but you might not think they're any good. I guess each person has to pick out their own favorite list, right?"

"Right," I said. "But tell me yours."

She rattled off a list of archaic words and phrases that amused, delighted, and perplexed me, as well as some modern words I wasn't familiar with. Wombat. Curmudgeon. Festoon and festoonery. Ods bodkins. Ye gods and little fishes.

Fascinating.

And so we were friends again, and better than ever, and better, no doubt, than we could have been if certain things hadn't happened. Certain things like fighting, death, problems, pain. She pointed it out to me.

"It's what art's all about," she said seriously one evening as we strolled home from the library. "Life and death, pain and sadness. Art is a reflection of life, they say."

I thought that sounded profound and said so. "That's a really deep thought, Rita Lee," I said, walking even more slowly.

"Well, maybe," she said, her tone a blushing acceptance of my compliment. "Maybe not. The thing is, the best art seems to come from people who know what suffering is. I mean, what kind of paintings do you think Bisky could paint? I mean, really?"

I snickered. "Herself in the center of a circle of adoring fans." It was unkind, and unworthy of me, but it felt so good to say it.

"Okay," Rita Lee said. "You get what I'm saying, right? She hasn't known any hardships in her life yet. She's still a green kid."

"We're only fifteen," I reminded her.

"I know," she said, "but we've seen life, and we've seen death, and we know things other kids don't."

She was right. It was true, and I started to believe that my pain and my face-to-face relationship with Death would make an artist of me. I could not paint and couldn't move gracefully enough to express it in dance, but cripes, could I sing, and boy, did I want to *write*.

"So write," Rita Lee said without fanfare. "Go ahead and do it. Who's gonna stop you?"

So I wrote. God, how I wrote. The pain, the isolation, the heartrending loneliness. I put it down on paper. Some of it I threw away, some I kept.

High school was awful. All that cheerleading crap, the constant vying for male attention, the emphasis on sports, the dress codes that kept us straight up and skirted, the rigidity, the catering to the mediocre in us—all seemed devised to insult and mortify. All those juvenile dances I never once got invited to—Sadie Hawkins dances, in which the girls invited the boys; the Shipwreck Dances, wherein everyone was supposed to look like a wreck; sock hops, proms, Sweetheart Dances, Homecoming Balls. Misery. Humiliation. You could come with a tittering clutch of nervous girls and stand in a group, girls dancing with girls to the fast dances, going off to the lav for the slow ones while the couples coupled out on the floor and the lights dimmed a little—or you could stay home reading and writing and twisting your wrists learning chords on the pity-guitar from Ma (a Christmas gift to ease the loneliness she was not supposed to be noticing) and sing sing sing in a soft voice to fill up the hollows and to level the craters and pits.

Folk music cheered and edified me, popular folk, that is —the Kingston Trio, the Brothers Four, the Irish Rovers. Ma bought me one album that knocked my socks off—"The Kingston Trio at the Hungry i"—and I discovered what I had suspected all along, that we "i's," we *intellectuals,* were probably the only people currently able to appreciate the perfection of this folk stuff. I thought I was in my element at last, among the "i's" who laughed at Mort Sahl and Shelley Berman and Lenny Bruce—jeeze—and listening to the people laughing on the record, laughing and clapping and appreciating the wit and charm of the singers and their material, also held me up and carried me through an otherwise empty, lonely landscape, and I was grateful. From then on, I bought every Kingston Trio album that came out and learned every word of every song. Rita Lee was proud of me, and she danced to what I sang, and for a while I think perhaps I may have fallen in love with her.

If not with her, then surely with her grace, her willowy ways; her intense face and her untouched body; her long hair, sometimes braided and thumping down her back, and sometimes loose and flying. She danced reels and jigs and African things, and danced to ballads with her long arms reaching for heaven, and to joking calypso songs with a black girls's laughing, graceful jerkings; and I was charmed, transformed, and as taken with her as she was with me. We never touched, or put our lips to each other's faces, or held hands or moved inside each other's personal, sexual spheres. We did not have to. We loved each other and were sometimes too intense and too enclosed, but we loved each other nevertheless, with a strange, strong, delicate defiance of all that we had ever known or learned about affection.

We got a reputation, the two of us, for being phony snobs who thought they were above the regular kids. It was true in part, but it was not because we chose to separate ourselves; it was simply that there seemed to be no place for us among the cheerleaders and the jocks around us.

Finally, we were released from our little island. Teddy came home on leave and bought me a car. He drove it up to the curb outside the house and jogged up the sidewalk, grinning ear to ear.

"What the hell is *that*?" I asked him in awe and wonder. It was white, a Chevy with the chrome of a 1955 model. Yet its fins branded it an unmistakable '57. "What the hell *is* it?" I demanded.

"It's a '56-and-a-half Chevy, lamebrain," he laughed, clapping the keys into my tingling palm, urging me outside and down the walk to where the car stood waiting, still smelling good from the dolling-up it had gotten at the dealer's that morning. "Nine hundred bills, kid. What do you think?"

"I love it," I said, the tears rolling down my cheeks. "I love it I love it I love it I love it to *death*." I looked inside. "Oh, shit," I said. "I don't know how to drive this thing. It's a stick shift."

"No problem," Teddy said. "Get in." As Ma watched with folded hands from the front window, Teddy settled me into the driver's seat; spoke to me gently of clutch and gas, pedals, and most emphatically about brakes; and off we went—ka-chunka-chunka, dok-dok-dok—bucking and backfiring all the way down the street while the neighbors shook their heads and frowned. It was bad enough a teenage girl got a car of her own, but, holy shit, look at her maniac driving. Paul Rosling was livid with envy. Bisky and Foote drooled. I got my license within weeks and was the envy of all who watched me whiz by, mainly up the road to Ameche's, the drive-in restaurant where everybody went who was Cool. I drove around and around in a circle, revving my little stick-six engine and letting girls—the six or eight of them who were all, suddenly, such good friends of mine—yell rotten things out the windows and sing rowdy songs.

We'd pull into a gas station, empty six purses for loose change, collect it, hand it out the window to the gas jockey, and say, "Ninety-two cents' regular, please, dear!" and he'd give us three gallons and a little bit more, and we were off again, singing and hooting and whistling at boys.

("Driver's license" in Balmer is, for some mysterious reason, given plural status. "Did you get 'em?" people would ask if they knew you'd gone uptown for your test. Well, kids, I got 'em, see, and let's *go!*)

Even Rita Lee went along. "I've been sheltered too darn long," she said, rolling her eyes and looking like Natalie Wood. "Lemme at 'em!" she hooted along with the rest, and while Bisky the Bitch tooled around in her father's aqua-with-white-interior '56 Thunderbird, the rest of us honked and squealed out and ripped around in my Chevy.

Rita Lee and I examined it from all angles, with the help of Bernadette and Lucy, friends rediscovered when I got 'em (my license) at last.

"The thing is, it's independence," Lucy said wisely. She had this thing about freedom and independence.

"Truer words were never spoken," Rita Lee said, doing a whirl right out of *West Side Story*. Since I'd gotten the car, Lucy and Bernadette were more willing to let Rita Lee do her little twirls and leaps without snickering. When you ride around with someone, there are certain things you just don't feel like pursuing anymore, like childish prejudices against art and literature.

To Bernadette the car meant the possibility of escape. "I mean, we can get out of here if we want to, ya know?"

"Yeah," we all agreed. But the thing was, Dundalk kids didn't go much of anywhere. I'd never driven uptown and had nightmares that someday I'd have to. We didn't dare go down to Pointer territory, and Parkville seemed an eternity away, Towson and Dulaney eons. No idea how to get there. No perspective on how our town was laid out or where the streets led. We were Dundalk Girls, not Baltimore Girls, and we were afraid of being accosted by City kids, or kids from unfamiliar parts of the county.

But we could if we felt like it, as Bernadette pointed out.

As for me, I sang lustily as we toured the area and always carried my guitar in the trunk in case I should get lonely for it. We were silly girls, all of us. We ate french fries and burgers at fifteen cents each, sang along to the songs on the radio (Golden Oldies, Moldy Oldies), and for all our hooting and screeching we picked up only the boys we'd known since the good old days at Dundalk Elementary; and then we threw them into the backseat, giggled with them, tickled them, threatened to depants them, kissed them all soundly, put the fear of God into them, and dropped them off at their homes, bewildered and all juiced up and vaguely disappointed, I imagine.

God, did we have fun.

But that was weeknights. Friday and Saturday nights left Rita Lee and me alone together, dateless, while the others all scurried off to movies and dances with boyfriends (everyone, it seemed, went *steady*), and on Sundays, we all stayed home to hurry up and do as much of our homework as we could bear to do. There was babysitting—forty or fifty cents an hour, and I cleaned up and did ironing, too—on Fridays and Saturdays, but I hated babysitting. Nights after the kids were in bed I'd sit and play my guitar and sing softly to myself in the half-light. And yes, dammit, I felt sorry for me, and I felt alone.

And then Bisky had a party, just near the last stretch of our junior year.

It started out okay, but then the thing we'd all been taught to fear and dread happened.

City Kids had come. They'd crashed. Girls wearing tight black slacks with the bottoms pegged, ankle bracelets, sweaters with deep V's, teased beehive hairdos, tons of thick, gooey makeup, especially around the eyes. Guys with pegged pants, Cuban-heeled shoes, leather jackets, black T-shirts with the sleeves rolled up over their Pall Malls, hard muscles like base-balls, pinched faces, "Chicago" haircuts—

Bisky's mother, who looked like an overdecorated cup-cake, was oblivious to these crashers. She accepted them as nice clean-cut kids from Carla's school and welcomed them inside unaware. Bernadette confided to me that Ma Bisky had been rather thoroughly smashed even before we'd arrived with our Dr. Pepper and Korn Kurls. Bernadette snorted into my ear and said that that was because she always *was* slightly "off kilter" from Old Granddad and Seven-Up. Unaccounta-bly, I felt bad. It wasn't funny.

Bernadette was dancing some hip-thrusting thing off in the corner with Foote's new boyfriend, Ray Hooper, and Foote was counting the ways she hated Bernadette because this date swapping simply was Not Done, even if Bernadette was the best dancer in school and Foote only mediocre. Dag-gers shot from her eyes to Bernadette's firmly packed little rear end. Rita Lee raised her thick eyebrows (she would not deign to pluck or shape them) and said, "Mercy!" which cracked me up and got me to giggling.

That was how I met Joe. He was sitting on the floor with a small set of bongo drums on his lap. He began to beat them softly while kids roamed around and sucked on little pony bottles (green) of Rolling Rock and pretended to be stagger-ing. When the music stopped blaring out of the stereo set Bisky had gotten for her birthday, I heard him break into a soft-voiced little tune, something about the "Zombie Jambo-ree" from one of my favorite Trio albums. In a flash, all caution hurled the hell with it to the winds, I was beside him, joining in, in soft, subtle harmony, rocking back and forth while his face broke into a grin and his hair moved up and down on his forehead as his hands beat out the jerky rhythm.

When the song was through, he clapped and threw his arms up into the air and whooped. He was a little snockered, I could see, but I didn't care. "Hey!" he shouted into my face.

"You like the Kingston Trio? Huh?" He barely gave me a chance to answer. "You know any more songs? Huh?"

"I know 'em all," I said happily.

"Then let's move on down the line," he said, crawling on hands and knees out of the club basement and up to the living room where, to my delight, I found Rita Lee talking to a serious-faced boy wearing clamdiggers and flip-flop sandals, his index finger stuck into the mouth of his Rolling Rock bottle, gesturing with it as if it were a pointer.

I sat down on the couch, and this guy sat down on the floor with the bongos and said, "Let's do 'Sloop John B,'" and I said, "Hurrah," and I fell in love with him as the first syllables rolled off his tongue. My voice blended perfectly with his, and in moments kids who had been lined up at the bathroom door came tiptoeing into the room to listen as we two sang all the verses and an extra chorus, taking cues from one another like seasoned pros, matching our phrasings perfectly, as if God himself had meant for us to meet and sing this way.

The applause, from six or seven kids, sounded thunderous to me. I was taken aback, appalled at my nerve and gall. Joe—he finally told me his name—was gracious, nodding and bowing as if he'd been performing all his life. Remembering the pitch, I started in on another, and before too long he was into it, leaving the bongos alone this time, just clapping a little, moving his body in rhythm with mine. Then somebody said, "Hey! Beeb! Gimme your car keys a minute. I'll go get the guitar out of the trunk." And when this guy said "guitar," Joe's eyes glistened, and he said, "You got your guitar? Cripes, I was afraid to bring mine." When the guitar came in and was pulled out of its case, he picked up the capo, fastened it to the neck, and began strumming in raucous chords a furious Trio tune, a favorite of mine; and we started to sing, and Rita Lee and Lucy joined in because they'd heard the record a hundred times at my house.

   . . . my dear Annie,
Oh, you New York girls, can't you dance the polka?

But the second time around, Joe signaled that he wanted
a solo, and on the chorus, he sang instead, "Oh, you Dundalk girls, can't you dance the polka?" to the delight of the
assembling crowd, all of them clapping and singing along
the best they could, all crammed now into Bisky's little living room, more like a parlor (poller, in Balmerese). Joe's
face was red with success, and I was feeling thirsty. When
somebody thrust a Rolling Rock into my hand, I held it naturally and gratefully, glad at last to be in the center of something again. I was in the middle of people who were doing
something that made, at last, *sense* to me. I was singing with
them—with Joe Steadman.

Oh, Joe. Glorious, dear, precious, marvelous, beautiful
Joe Steadman. Joe of the brown hair, of the brown eyes, of the
Goya guitar and the boots of leather and the long, strong
fingers and the baritone voice.

He was, he said, from Dulaney. Dulaney? My God, how
did he get all the way down here?

"With him," he said, gesturing vaguely at some skinny guy
who was arguing hotly with Bisky. He was Gerard somebody,
Bisky's cousin. He'd brought Joe for company, and in self-
defense. If the guys from the city, or even certain Dundalk
guys, were to find out he was from Dulaney, his ass was grass.
Joe was supposed to be his ally. Now Joe was making a spec-
tacle of himself, and Gerard and Carla were arguing as to why
he'd brought this jerk who was wrecking her party and about
how they were going to get rid of him.

"Show's over," Joe said breezily to the crowd. "Go on
downstairs and dance, everybody. Ladies' choice!" he added,
like an emcee. Bisky looked vastly relieved and grabbed Paul
Rosling by his arm and dragged him back downstairs. On his
way downstairs, Paul looked back over his shoulder at me and
—good God—winked.

"Beautiful, Bebe," he said wistfully, and my heart soared.

"Thank you, Paul," I said. He was good. Kind at heart.

"Sing some more," Rita Lee said. The guy she was with agreed and produced another Rolling Rock for Joe. There was still a smallish group of kids in the room, and it occurred to me that perhaps there were more kids than just Rita and I who were interested in things besides sports and dates.

Joe began to sing again, a Harry Belafonte thing from years earlier, about Kingston Town, Jamaica. As our voices blended, some memory came over me, and I saw my father's face as he sat singing, "Holy Holy Holy" next to me in our small, hot church on a spring morning. My throat tightened, and I heard, I thought, his strong tenor blending here with us now; and I closed my eyes and sang with an ache in my throat, missing him, but glad to be here next to Joe.

We sang the night away. The tough kids from Patterson High even drifted in to tell us we sounded really good, man, and we kept right on.

Bisky came up and said we ought to join the party downstairs, but by that time we'd all had a few more beers and weren't listening to her. Why couldn't she live and let live, and leave us alone? She was getting obnoxious, though, so Rita Lee, her eyes looking as if they'd been coated with oil and vinegar, grinned loosely and said why didn't we just trundle ourselves over to her house? She said her mother wouldn't mind, and even if she did, what the bloody hell?

When we arrived at Rita Lee's house, her mother blinked and pulled her cotton housecoat tight around her straight, thin body. She did have varicose veins, I noticed, seeing her white, bare legs sticking out of the bottom of the housecoat like broomsticks. They did look painful. I was immediately sorry for the times I'd snickered about them. She was reluctantly gracious and pretended not to notice how loud we were, and how flushed. "Go on out to the backyard," she said. "I'll get some chips and soda for you all."

Rita Lee hugged her mother and said she loved her. "I

love you too, baby doll," her mother said. The six or eight of us went out to the little yard and sat on lawn chairs in a circle. That didn't last long, though. In moments, we were sitting on the damp grass, laughing and singing, and it turned out that the guys had brought a couple of pony bottles each in their pockets and inside their shirts, and there we were, singing oh, you Dundalk girls, can't you dance the polka? over and over again.

Joe lay flat on his back and looked up at the sky. He howled to the half-moon above him mournfully. "Oh, jeeze, oh, jeeze," he cried. "Just look at me, look at me. I'm a disgrace to the goddam Naval Academy."

"Ah, c'mon, Joe," his friend, Carla's cousin, said in a bored voice. "You don't even go to the Naval Academy."

"You know nothing about it," Joe said with his last shred of dignity before he burst into tears. "You know nothing." Then the tears came, and his friend, Carla's cousin, laughed again.

"This guy's a nut. Don't listen to him. He's never been near the Naval Academy since we went there on a field trip in the sixth goddam grade. He's fulla shit."

"Leave him alone," I said. "He feels bad enough as it is."

Tenderly, I put the back of my hand against his cheek, and Joe pulled me down next to him on the grass. My heart raced and my knees shook. I remembered the time Paul had put his hands on me; it had been hot then, too, and we had been out in the late night damp like this, and something in the smell of the crushed grass beneath Joe and me reminded me of that night with Paul. Joe put his hand on my back and pressed me closer to him. I lay half on top of him, and he sighed a long, shuddering sigh.

"You're a big girl," he said, his eyes closed. I stiffened and tried to sit up, tried to get away from him, but his long arm held me tight against him.

"I like big girls," he said. Then, "Are you gold, Bebe? Are you made of gold, Miss Beatrice Schmidt?"

"What?" I said, half laughing, not knowing what to make of him.

"My father is a learned and valuable source of information," Joe said, opening one eye and focusing on my questioning face. "My father knows all, tells all. My father says that you can look all you want, all over the world, east to west, north to south, but you'll never find a girl to beat a Dundalk girl. They're pure gold, he says."

I laughed. "So what are you and your father doing in Dulaney?"

"My father was not wise enough to take his own advice," Joe said sadly. "My father married a very rich girl from Dulaney Valley, and look where it's got him."

"Where?" I asked.

"Nowhere. Nowhere except miserable," Joe said, and I thought how much his line sounded like something from a soap opera. I wanted to laugh, because it made about as much sense as his Naval Academy speech, and he was starting to worry me. I finally find a guy who likes big girls and singing and has a brain and a way with words that amuses me, and who is he, really? He's a nut, that's what.

"You're not nowhere. You're here," I said.

"Yeah, I know," Joe said, and pulled me even closer. He wiggled and writhed around in the grass and slid himself down so that his face was directly in front of mine. "Kiss me?" he said shyly, and I felt suddenly womanly, suddenly in charge and adult.

"Never ask," I said in my woman's voice, husky and full of promise. "You must never, ever *ask* for a kiss. You must take what you know belongs to you." Oh, God, did I say that? I would use it in my book someday.

He kissed me. I kissed him. Beer breath and the shivers. His hands moved all over me, and it was not as I had remembered. It was not evil, not like Mancuso's slithery touch, not sneaky and intrusive, and not pushy and rough like Talarczyk's. . . .

This was Joe's touch, Joe's hand, the hand that played the guitar so beautifully. He let his hand rest lightly on my hip, then laid it down and kneaded my rump for a moment. "Ahhh," he sighed into my ear as he took a little nibble. "Perfect. Like a pillow."

He kissed me again, and I was in heaven. I was loved at last. I put both my hands on either side of his face and shook his head a little. "Are you real?" I asked him softly, and he nodded, but something was wrong. He lunged for me again, more aggressively this time, and his mouth went for the side of my neck. Hickey! He wanted to put a hickey on me, to brand me with a big red suckmark. I hated those things. The girls at Dundalk wore them like red badges of victory on Monday mornings, and they made me sick. I pushed at Joe, whispering for him not to do that to me.

His hands slid up and under my wraparound skirt and found the elastic top of my underwear. "Let me, let me," he said, and everything in me screamed no! but before I knew it, I was making it easier for him, letting myself go loose and easy, welcoming him.

But he turned his head and said directly into the long green grass to the left of his cheek, "I'm a goddam disgrace," and then he got quietly sick. There was nothing for it but to wait and let him get it all out of his system, all that beer and junk. The excitement seemed to have been too much for him.

A miserable soggy feeling came crawling up into my consciousness. He would never have done this to me if he hadn't been drunk. He really didn't give a damn about me. I was just the only body at the party he thought he could get away with mauling. Christ almighty, when would I learn? I would not let him see me cry. I crept away from him, crawled over to where Rita Lee and her guy were discussing something kind of esoteric, and told her I was leaving and going home alone. She was instructed to see to it that Joe Steadman and Bisky's beanpole cousin got back to her house safely.

"Veddy good, madam," Rita Lee said, and laughed.

I drove home crying.

It was too much, I thought all that night and the next day. It was unfair and hideously cruel to be led on that way. These guys didn't know what it meant to a girl like me to believe, no matter how hopelessly, that there was for us a measure of love and romance in this tough old world as well as for the cute girls, the petite and sassy and tricky little girls. It was terrible of them to mock us this way. We had feelings, too. Precious, tender feelings that deserved to be tended like private gardens of lovely flowers. Joe Steadman had kindled something in me I'd prayed was dead and gone—my hope. My passion and my sense of promise. Now it was bothering me again, the loneliness, the isolation, the terrible separation of being both nonstandard in the looks department and irregular in the brains and sensibilities area. I was so *alone.* God, even Rita Lee had found somebody to lean on. Why did it always have to be this way? Would I have to go through life single?

> I never will marry; I'll be no man's wife;
> I expect to sleep single all the days of my life.

The old song curdled my spirit, and I lay on my bed most of the next morning, a Saturday, while Ma bustled around like a hired girl doing her work and mine. Later on she would bullwhip me with her accusing looks while she sat and soaked her aching feet and rubbed lotion into her reddened hands.

The telephone rang. Rita Lee.

"You'll never guess!" she said, as breathless as Bernadette or Lucy would have been. "Guess who just called me!"

"Your new boyfriend," I said, pretty sure I'd guessed right.

"No. Better. Yours."

"Mine?"

"Yeah, yours. Joe called me. Joe Steadman, from last night, remember?"

"Yeah, I remember. What about him?"

"He called me. Bisky's cousin called her, and she called me, and I called him and told him all about you so he could tell Joe."

"Why didn't Joe call me himself?"

"He didn't know how to reach you. Besides, he wanted to check out if you were mad at him for upchucking all over the place."

"Yeah, well, so what?"

"So," she said, drawing it out to make it Cooler, "he's nuts about you. Drooling over you. He can't stop thinking about you. He wants to come down today to see you."

"Oh, yeah?" I said. If I'd been any more unconcerned, my legs would have given way beneath me.

"Yeah, he's trying to call you right now."

Silence for a second.

"Holy shit," Rita Lee shrieked. "Hang the hell up, girl!" I had never known her to use such language. I hung up.

He called.

It was true. He was taken with me. He wanted to come down. All the way from Dulaney. Good grief.

"Okay," I said. "And bring your guitar, huh?"

"Damn straight," he said. Oh, he swore just *right.* Just like the Marlboro Man. Joe. Joseph.

Ma was beside herself when she met him. "He's *nice,*" she said on Sunday morning. "He's really nice. And he plays so nice. And he's got such a nice face."

Nice, huh?

Oh, I thought so.

And the funny thing was, never after that first fumbling night did he or I try to go to indecent lengths with each other. We even talked about it.

"It isn't that I don't want to, Beeb," he said earnestly, looking deep inside me, searching. I looked straight into him, too. "Because believe me, I *want* to," he said, laughing a little.

"Me, too, Joseph," I said, laughing a little.

"But the thing is, I'm just not *ready,* you know?"

"Oh, I know, Joe," I said. "I really do know what you mean."

And then we hugged and kissed. We did that a lot. And somehow a great big millstone undid itself from around my neck, and the next time I kissed him I felt like something out of *State Fair,* and it was sunny and cloudless.

Bisky just couldn't understand it. In the lavatory one day just before school ended for the summer, she said to somebody standing beside her at the sink, "I don't get it. What's a guy like Joe Steadman coming all the way down from Dulaney to *get,* you know?"

"Ah, shove it up your ass, Bisky," somebody said back to her.

It was Rita Lee.

"That's tellin' her," another voice chimed in.

It was Barbara Foote.

Bisky shut her mouth.

It was my seventeenth summer.

Chapter 19

We were really strapped for money, but it was okay. Ma was only allowed to work part-time or she'd lose her social security benefits, and I babysat for peanuts with the neighborhood moppets, and there was the money Teddy, bless him, sent each month. But it was hard. Ma brought home about forty dollars a week, and I made maybe five . . . but hamburger was then thirty-nine cents a pound.

I got cards and letters in the mail from Joe Steadman, addressed to "Beatrish Mitt." He said that's the way my name sounded to him, and why would people name a kid something that you couldn't pronounce? I said that's why people should call me Bebe, or Beeb, or B., but Joe liked to use people's full names; he even encouraged me to call him Joseph when we were kissing and hugging.

Everybody was busy applying to colleges or nosing around for jobs after graduation. I didn't know what to do. The only school I could afford was the little local community college, which lots of people called "grade thirteen and fourteen" in a miserably snide manner.

Teddy wanted me to go to someplace that would encourage what he called my natural talents in music and theater and stuff, but when we looked at the Northwestern and Iowa catalogues, we shut them again in despair. No school in its right mind would give me a scholarship, either. My grades were so shabby and my attitude and attendance records so poor that I'd be lucky if the community college would take me.

Rita Lee wanted me to go with her to New York where she would study dance and art. I would go to Columbia and study journalism, and we could both work as waitresses or maids or something that we could do part-time.

Lucy wanted me to go to the University of Maryland with her. We'd be close to home, she said, and yet far enough to get away with murder. She was reading *Sex and the Single Girl* and getting ideas.

Bernadette was going to business school for a year, because her best grades were in typing and shorthand, and that's where all the jobs were. Why didn't I just chuck the whole dippy college idea? After all, I hated school anyhow, right? Cripes, why let myself in for four more years of sitting with my eyes closed behind big sunglasses, sleeping through expensive courses?

Bisky was going to Penn State. Foote was going straight to work in her uncle's cleaning store and would go to school at night if she felt like it. She didn't like school any better than I did.

Ma just kept wringing her red hands and saying over and over, "You and Teddy just decide what's best, and somehow we'll make it through. You've got to do what you want, Beatrice. Otherwise it's all a waste of time and money anyhow."

In the end I applied to and was accepted at the community college. About twenty kids from Dundalk would be going. Joe had been accepted at U. of M., though, and the thought of being separated from him depressed me. I'd never find anybody to replace him, and it was a foregone conclusion that separation meant breakup. I could not face it, and one May night just before graduation I laid my head on his shoulder and cried my eyes out.

"My God, Beatrice," he said, panicky. "What is it?"

"I can't stand the idea of losing you next year," I said. I could not control the hiccuping and snuffling.

"Aw, baby, don't cry," Joe said, pulling the hair away from my face, kissing my cheek. "It won't be so bad. You get lots of holidays in college. We'll see each other in October, and then again on Thanksgiving, and at Christmas, and then there's that long vacation in February. It'll be cool."

"No, it won't," I said. "It'll be awful. I can't stand it now, and it hasn't even happened yet."

Joe didn't say anything else. He just hugged me close to him and told me not to cry, it would be okay, it would be fine. Like a child, I let his words comfort me.

"Come on," he said. "Let's sing."

Music was his solution to everything. We were being asked to sing now—weddings, parties, even the Dundalk High School senior banquet, although Santino put up a hell of a fuss, insisting that it was degrading for us to invite somebody from—ugh!—rich, snotty *Dulaney* to sing for our banquet. Nobody listened to him, though. It didn't matter if Joe had money and a big house and all kinds of financial advantages; he was a good guy, and everybody liked him.

Graduation day was imminent, and we Dundalk girls sat outside on the cool grass signing each other's yearbooks and telling each other how much we'd liked each other and how well we'd known each other, and to never forget Phys. Ed. 10, and to stay as sweet as we were, and that we deserved the very best futures the Lord could provide. We were so *old* then, so mature and adult, and we pondered the term "Commencement" and said that we could not really feel as if we were *beginning* anything; we could only feel as if we'd come to the end of a road. Something of this sharing there took the edge off my bitterness and isolation. We really had been through a lot together, and it had not really been so terribly bad. As I sat among the Dundalk girls and talked and laughed and even cried a tiny bit, I felt, finally, comfortable.

We graduated. Bisky's mother leaned hard on Doc

Bisky's arm and grinned like the Cheshire cat throughout. Ma and Pa Erdman clapped thunderously when Bernadette minced across the stage in her high white heels, and Cara cried real tears and Pa Erdman gave a loud, long whistle and everybody laughed. Lucy's mother reeked of Lily of the Valley by Pegeen, and Rita Lee's mother shed tears when Rita floated across the stage with her dark hair full and loose around her shoulders. Both the Erdmans wore their teeth for the occasion, and Ma E. was dolled up with every single Pegeen product she owned, including false eyelashes, one of which hung at half-mast and caused her to blink perhaps four times as much as usual. Cara tried to induce her to remove them, but she would not. It was her Big Day, by Gawd, and she was damned if she was going to spend it in some ladies' room farting around with her makeup. Pa Erdman gave me a hug and invited Ma and me to be in their pictures. Cara must have taken a hundred, and her boyfriend fifty more.

Teddy was not there, but we sent him pictures. He wrote to me and sent a check. "Take yourself to the movies, Scutbrat. Or buy yourself some books for school next year."

I was in one of those moods where I loved everyone and could not bear to let anyone go. On graduation day, I hugged Carla Bisky and told her I loved her and would miss her. She backed away, startled, then melted and came back inside my hug and said, in tears, that she'd miss me, too. "You're okay, Beeb," she said in a little sobbing voice. "You were always smarter, ya know? But it's okay. Right?"

"Right," I said, and then Foote, old tough, smartmouth Foote, was inside our hug and we tripled it, and then along came some guys—Lucy and Price and Ray and Paul, and I longed for Joseph to be there, too, but he was at his own graduation and could not come till later. It was glorious, all of us crying, even the guys with their Peter Gunn haircuts and their pants worn short at the ankle, and we were, at last, brothers and sisters. If I longed for my father, it was fleeting, because the circle was tight and the tears and the pain felt wonderful.

That evening, we Dundalk girls rode around in cars and honked and yelled our jubilation, our Celebration and Rite of Passage. There were twenty parties for the class of '62 to drop in and out of, and some people were driving down to the ocean. For a while I was tempted, but no, no—it was also scary and dangerous, and I was never one to savor adventure.

Price yelled to me from the car he and Lucy were flying away in, "There's not a hair on your ass, Schmidt!"

I could hear Lucy's high, rippling giggle as the '54 Mercury roared off into the night.

Rita Lee and her friend (she always called him that and would not consent to go steady with him, no matter what), Les, who was still a junior, and Joe and I and Erdman and Talarczyk (they no longer went steady but were still friends) took a leisurely tour of Dundalk. I showed Joe the library, the post office, the park, all of our houses.

We stopped the car at the elementary school and pointed out our classrooms to each other, where we'd sat in fourth grade and in which hallways we'd squatted and "ducked and covered" in the weekly air-raid drills all through the years. Joe had the grace not to get bored, and he did not make supercilious comments about how corny it all was.

Later we went back to Bernadette's. Joe and I sauntered out into the eight-by-eight backyard, carefully protected with chain-link fencing. Standing in the reflected light from the kitchen, he put his arms around me and kissed me and said, "It's time I gave you your graduation gift, right?"

"Sure," I said. I *had* been wondering about it. From my babysitting money I had saved enough to buy him a Photo-Ident bracelet engraved with his name, and he had gone ape over it. But he hadn't given me anything. Now he pulled from his pocket an envelope and handed it to me. Inside was a beautiful card, full of flowers and silvery lettering, and inside that was a neatly folded letter.

"Open it," he said. But I felt afraid and didn't want to. "Come on, Beatrice," he urged me. "It doesn't bite."

I opened it. I read it, and read it again. It was a letter of acceptance to Essex Community college—my own junior college—and it had his name on it.

"Joseph!" I screamed. "What did you do? Whatever got into you?"

"I couldn't do it, Beatrice," he said. "I couldn't go off without you. It wouldn't have been any good. Who would be there to sing with me?"

I cried for the fortieth time that day. I cried all over his shirtfront, and he laughed deep and rich, and I do not recall ever in my life, before or since, feeling quite so complete, so full, so blessed. For that precious hour there was no sadness, and no memory of sadness. I felt as if he'd asked me to marry him and to share his entire life, heart, and soul.

The evening passed in a haze, and eventually it was later than it had ever been. Then we were in my living room, and somehow as we stood entwined for the night's last kiss, it seemed appropriate that we lie down somewhere and take our time and do all the things for each other that people in love did.

But we did not. Joe pulled away and looked at his watch and said, "Holy Moses. Look what time it is. My mother'll kill me."

The next morning I would have slept until noon, but the telephone rang and my mother was not there to answer it. So I stumbled out of my bed. Bernadette's voice gasped and shrieked and I could not understand her, and was able to distinguish only her panic and terror. I could not make sense of her words, and then her mother got on the phone. I could hear Bernadette keening in the background, and Ma Erdman said in her gentlest voice, "Hon, you got to sit down now, babe, you hear me? Can you do that for me, hon? Now we got to tell you, so you got to listen, darlin'. . . ."

And I said, "No. Don't tell me. Don't tell me anything."

But Mrs. Erdman was insistent, and she talked over my words and would not stop. "You got to be quiet, now, girl," she commanded softly. "You got to listen to me. Hush, Bernadette. Hush a minute because Mommy can't talk with you yelling like that, baby doll."

"I don't want to know," I said weakly. "Please—"

"It's Lucy," Ma Erdman said, louder now. "Lucy and her boyfriend, that little Price boy."

"Oh, my God, Lucy!" I said. "What about Lucy?"

"She's gone, baby," Ma Erdman said. "Her and Jackie Price. They drowned in the ocean sometime during the night."

"Ahh, Jesus," I cried. Bernadette's voice broke out into fresh shrieking, and we mourned, we three, and I separate and not able to touch them.

"See, Jackie was drinking too much beer and he decided to go swimming. He went in the water before anybody could stop him, and Lucy, she wouldn't let him go out alone. She took off her shoes and went in after him. But he got lost from her, and she was calling and calling for him, but she couldn't find him. Then the other kids kept yelling for them to come back, but, hon, they never come back. Then the kids went for the shore patrol and the police, but it was too late."

"How do you know they're dead?" I asked, trying to hang on.

"They found the bodies," she said. "Lucy's mother, she's got herself in such a state I don't know what we're gonna do with her. You want to come over here, hon?"

"I'll be over," I said. How could my mouth form words? "But first I want to call Joe and my mother."

"Okay, hon," Ma Erdman said. "But come on over as soon as you can. Bernadette, shiz takin' this awful hard."

"Tell her to hang on. You call Rita Lee, too. She'll want to be with us."

Joe came. My mother came home from work early. We clung together in a hot, humid circle across the street from the place where Lucy Grabowski had lived.

Another minus. I could not bear it. And Price. My God, little Price. My heart broke and mended and rebroke a thousand times that week.

I walked down to Price's house. Inside, I could hear sobbing. When I knocked on the door, Mrs. Price opened it and let me in without a word of greeting.

"I'm sorry, hon," she said. "I just can't talk to you."

"I know," I said. "I just wanted to come down and tell you —tell you—"

"What, hon?"

"How much Jack loved you," I blurted. "He was so proud of you."

"Is that the truth?" she said, looking away from her grief for a moment, interested now.

"Yes, it's the truth," I said, my hands shaking badly. I did not know if it was the truth or not, but I wanted to do something for Jack, wanted to give him a gift, something lasting.

"In fact, in the seventh grade, we were all supposed to write a little composition in class about the person we admired most, and Jack wrote his on you. I remember it. I sat right next to him." He had written it, I recalled, on "Mickey Mantle: Star of the Yanks," but this didn't seem to me like a lie. I knew without a doubt that if he were to sit down right now to write such a composition, he would entitle it, "My Mother."

"Bless his heart," she sobbed into her wadded tissues. "And bless you, too, Beatrice, for coming down to tell me. God, nobody's here but me. I'm all alone here."

It was terrible. I left so sodden with pity that I felt heavy and old and bloated with it. Jack's street. Price's house. Here we had talked and laughed and tossed the football. The tears came again. I had never known that the human body could produce so many tears.

I went home, waiting for Joe to come back. Each time I cried, he cried, too. That surprised me.

We buried Lucy and Price from the same funeral home and laid them both in the same cemetery, one service right after the other. I do not recall a single word the ministers spoke concerning Lucy and Jack. There were no words. I watched Rita Lee as the tears slid from beneath her puffy eyelids. I half expected her to break into some strange dance, but she stood still and tall in the sunlight. Bernadette, true to form, had snapped out of the worst of her grief and, along with her mother, had organized a buffet for after the funerals.

Lucy's parents bore up well, but Pa Erdman was crushed. "It's too close to home, ya know?" he kept saying. "It could have been one of mine." He kept hugging Cara and Bernadette and me all day, and clapping Mr. Grabowski on the back where the man's thin shoulderblades protruded through his summer suit. "Great God almighty, how could a person stand it, to lose a kid that way?" and fresh grief would come pouring over him, and he would cry and cry.

I went home and wrote poems for Lucy and Price. I wrote them for Pop, and for the lost love of Caroline and Oscar Welles, and for my mother who was bereft, and for Teddy who was alone and separate from us who loved him best. They were awful, but they helped.

I wrote them for me. Lots of them. And stories, too. Stories about people losing things, parables of loss and grief. I was sinking deeper into the quicksand of it. I did not ride around in my car and sing dirty songs. Everything reminded me of Lucy. "Sister." I did not listen to old songs on the radio, the Buddy Holly songs, the oldies but goodies, because she and I had sat so often on my bed and had sung along, and the singing brought such a lump to my throat that I could not breathe. I looked at her picture in the yearbook, read her letter to me on one of the back blank pages. I cried every day.

Joseph was firm with me. "You're overdoing it," he said

one night a week later. "That's enough now. You've going too far. It's got to stop, Beatrice."

I stopped.

"It coulda been worse, ya know?" Bernadette said over the phone, trying to comfort me.

"How?" I said. How could it have been worse?

"We coulda been there, ya know? We coulda been standing there on the shore, not knowing what to do, not knowing how to help them, Beeb. It coulda been worse than it was."

She was right. That would have been worse.

For her, for Joseph, for us all, I laid away my grieving and put it underground with my father and Lucy and Price, where it could lie quiet and untouched, sacred.

Silent.

Chapter 20

All my days I had fantasized about living rich. I had seen enough Cadillac ads to know what rich people looked like, and had seen enough movies to know about white rugs and bars that had built-in seltzer squirters and walnut paneling. But Joseph's house was the first actual Rich Person's House I'd ever been in, and I was disappointed.

Everything is relative, I'd heard. I guess that, relatively speaking, the Steadmans just weren't quite as rich as the white-rug crowd. They had a Lincoln, but it didn't have that gorgeous wheel on its trunk proclaiming Wealth and Power. I mean, it was nice, but . . .

And I think I expected rich people to be Cool. That is, I didn't expect Joseph's father to be in stocking feet, sitting in an old leather chair that was badly worn and halfheartedly looking at the newspaper. When we met, he was sucking on a cigarette whose smoke made it nearly impossible to see him.

Joe's mother came striding in from the kitchen. She stopped short, looked me over as if she was going to buy me, then said, "So—so this is what you gave up your education for."

I wanted to crawl under the couch and never reappear.

"Joey's First Girlfriend," she said, as if she were reading the title of a book she'd found in the gutter.

"You might as well sit down," she said then, and Joe and I sat down on the couch across from Dad.

"Call me Dad," Dad said, smiling through the haze.

"Thanks, Dad," I said miserably. I didn't want to call him Dad.

"You may call me Mrs. Steadman," Mrs. Steadman said evenly.

"Okay," I said. If my I.Q. had seemed more like my weight than my age I would have been more comfortable, but as it was, I writhed under her scrutiny, growing lumpier and more unwieldy by the second.

"You don't smoke, do you?" she asked pointedly, pushing the ashtray toward me.

"No," I said.

"Yes," Joe said simultaneously.

I took out my Salems and lit one with a match, my fingers shaking. I choked and coughed.

"Been smoking long?" she asked, and I gasped in reply.

It was horrible. She talked around, in front of, in back of, and through—but not *to* me. I had the feeling that she'd throw out my cup and plate and tableware when I left. Joe was mortified and got me out of there as fast as he could.

"My father liked you," he said when we got into Joe's new car, a graduation present, a neat little Ford with no frills.

"How could you tell?" The man had spoken only to his wife, and had winked at me once, and had shaken my hand when we left.

"He shook your hand," Joe said, smiling. "That's his signal for, 'I like you. Come back.'"

I wondered why he didn't just say so.

"Your mother didn't like me."

"That's an understatement," Joe said, looking dark and tense. "She detests you. But don't feel special. She hates everybody. That's the way she's acted about every friend I ever brought home. Like they had leprosy and had just spent the day rolling in pigshit."

I giggled. "So it's not just because I'm—ah—a little heavy?"

"Are you kidding? One guy I brought home—a kid who used to work in the photography club with me—she insulted for fifteen minutes because he was too thin to suit her. She's a case."

"Why is she so hateful?"

"I don't know. It has something to do with the fact that she married out of her class or her element, or something. She thinks that being married to Dad has cut her off from her old friends with real money and all."

"So why did she marry him?" I asked, all innocence.

"She had to," Joe said, and his smile was crumbly. "She was pregnant with me."

I was shocked. Nobody I knew had ever admitted a thing like that to me. It didn't seem right.

"I can't believe it," I said.

"It's true," he answered. "I'm a bastard."

I strove to make him feel better about it. "Yeah," I said, "but now that she's got you, I know she's glad she had you, after all."

"Get off your cloud, Beatrice," Joe said harshly. "She can't stand me, either. She hates me."

"She does not," I said hotly. It was ridiculous for him to say a thing like that.

"She does," he said. "She's never had a good word to say for me for as long as I can remember. She's a witch. Someday she's going to leave, and then Dad and I are going to have a ball."

I was confused. "How do you know she hates you?"

"I don't want to tell you."

"Tell me."

The words came out of him slowly at first, haltingly, like a parade with soldiers out of step, tripping each other up. At times I wanted to stop him, to put my hand over his mouth and say, "Enough," but I did not. He had said he didn't want to tell me, but he did. He had to, or burn out his insides with the gall of it.

Locked into closets. Locked outdoors in the bitter cold. Days on end with no meals, for punishment, because he had insulted her cooking. Tied to his bed and beaten with a broom handle. Worse.

It was impossible. It was a nightmare, something he'd exaggerated and blown up out of all proportion. It was James. James and his gramma, but that was different. She was an old drunken witch, but this was a house where rich people lived, and two parents. Such things did not happen inside houses like this.

He had made it up.

"Why didn't your father help you?"

"He was never home. He didn't know. He was a salesman then. He traveled all week long."

"Why didn't you tell him?"

"She said she'd kill me. I believed her."

"I never want to see her again," I said.

"Okay," he said. That settled it. I put my hand on his leg as he drove and did not comment upon the tears that kept rolling down his cheeks. He did not sob or moan the way I did when I cried. His crying was silent and dignified, and new to him. It had started with Lucy and Price, and now this personal grief seemed at last worth crying over, too.

"I love you, Joseph," I said. "Someday we'll have a little boy, and we'll correct him without ever spanking him. I promise you."

"Thanks," Joe whispered, and stopped crying. I felt like Mother Nature herself, and I would enfold them all, all the bruised and beaten and battered children of the world and would nurture and comfort them in my loving arms. While I lived, no child would suffer.

Chapter 21

I was eighteen years old.

College was wonderful. One hundred day students. A family. I met kids from all over town—our side of town, that is. Edgemere, The Point, Kenwood, Overleigh, Parkville, Towson, Dulaney. It was the best. I could not believe what I was seeing. Apparently each of the schools had been harboring fugitives from apple pie and saving us up to present en masse to the hapless administrators at old ECC—ECC Tech, we called it. Jeans, fringed boots, rawhide jackets, girls in black tights and jumpers (five years ago they would have been called "beatniks") with their hair pulled back into long horsetails or parted in the center and falling straight down and loose. Rita Lee would have liked it.

She was in New York. She left her mother and went as she'd planned to, and then had written to tell me she'd gotten a job at a small girls' high school, doing clerical work there half the day. The other half she spent at a dance workshop. In the evenings she went to art school. It was hard and demanding, all of it, but she liked it and would be looking for a roommate if she couldn't make me change my mind.

Joseph and I dove into community college life, organizing hootenannies, finding people with instruments, giving impromptu concerts, playing touch football in the grass next to the little parking lot (big enough for about forty cars). We challenged other community colleges to kite-flying contests, wrote for the newspaper, partied, played pinochle, and got what I liked to think of as an "academic foothold" in preparation for the four-year school we'd have to pick someday.

In the lounge people played records by Woody Guthrie and some new weird guy named Dylan, which we pronounced Dye-lan until one of the English instructors pointed out that he was named after Dylan Thomas, and then we acted as if we'd known that all along. I'd gotten deeply into Joan Baez. She was my idol, my favorite, that clear, true soprano of hers cutting through all the pap they'd been feeding us over the radio for ten years. Then the radio started playing something else, something so wild and different and wonderful that we turned it up when we drove around and sang along with gusto. The Beatles.

Long after we should have been on our way home, we sat for hours in the lounge, talking about the Peace Corps and Vista, and all the faith, hope, and charity we had to share with the Great Family of Man. I would teach English in Africa, and Joseph would teach them our music, and learn theirs. We listened to the songs of Miriam Makeba and thrilled to their exotic sound, rich with joy. We philosophized about God and man, and came to the conclusion that if He were really there —and He probably was not—then surely he was ho-hum about our little trials and errors, and was not the personal God the pastors had claimed He was. It was up to us, we believed, to save the world God had made. He had probably washed his hands of it.

We learned political science and sociology and the rudiments of psychology and some English and some of the elements of speechmaking. Our football games with other schools were played in gym shorts, with faculty rounding out the teams because there weren't enough players. We rattled our Pepsi machine for change with which to play poker. We laughed. God, how we laughed.

Rita Lee's letters dwindled, but remained positive and upbeat.

"Come on up and visit," she said in her before-Christmas letter. "I thought I'd be coming home for the holidays, but it turns out I can't. I lost my job at the school—late too many times, I guess—and now I'm working as a waitress, and they won't give me time off during the holiday week, so here I am. I could quit, I guess, and look for something when I came back, but it's harder than you might think getting work when you can't work full-time. Well, enough complaining. I'm thinking about studying at Balanchine's studio, but I don't know anything definite yet. Ta-ta, me loovley sweetling. Happy Christmas. Haul in a Yule log and have wassail in my memory. God, I'll miss you all. Love to Bernadette and everybody. R.L."

She came home for Easter, but she looked so pale and thin that we tried talking her into staying, but she was adamant.

"I'm supposed to be thin," she said wanly. "This is a good weight for me. Dancers are lean, don't you know that?"

"Don't look at me," I laughed. "I'm no authority."

She hugged me. "Stay like you are," she said, smiling. "It's the only way I can feel superior to you. You're such a gem I don't like to put myself next to you for comparison."

"Oh, Rita, don't compare yourself with me. Let's don't ever do that again, okay? I don't want to stand next to your thin body, and you don't want to challenge me to a spelling contest, right? Good. Then let's just be sisters and forget about it."

We laughed and hugged each other again.

She was going to come home for the summer, but didn't. She needed to work, she said, to save up money for the fall, when her costs for tuition would be higher. Besides, she wrote, she loved Manhattan and was learning to make it in the Big World, and signed her letter Ritalee, explaining that the name looked "stagier." Since she was going to class with people named things like Tanya and Sophie and Renata and

Daria, she felt too Dundalky calling herself Rita Lee.

Bernadette was happy at business college, making all A's, and Foote had kind of dropped out of sight and was dating someone she'd met at the cleaning store. She was thinking of going down to Fort Meade or over to Social Security to get a job. She was considering getting married and would need more money to pull it off.

Married. I looked longingly at Joseph and wondered what it would be like. . . .

Still, I could not conceive of living intimately with someone, not even Joe. I used to lie awake worrying how on earth I would ever be able to manage being married without ever appearing naked in front of my husband. Naked was a concept I couldn't deal with. I couldn't even bring myself to think of looking at *him*.

Bisky got pregnant her first semester at Penn State and came home at Christmas sick as a dog. Her father wouldn't let her go back and wouldn't let her marry the boy, who was, she said, kind of cute but no hero. Paul Rosling said he'd marry her, but her father again said no, and this time she cried and lamented and felt really rotten. Paul was working as an apprentice mechanic at a garage in town and was making enough money to support them, but still her father said no. He said it would be a goddam American tragedy if she let this boy marry her. He said they'd never get over it, not really, and that Carla did not have the sense to get married, much less raise a child. The next time I saw Carla in February, she told me she had lost her baby, and her eyes were deep and hollow.

"Well, my God, what happened?" I asked clumsily.

Her eyes filled up, but no tears fell. "I don't know," she said. "I just lost it. Never mind."

"You going back to school?" I asked.

"Naa," she said, looking over my shoulder. "I don't feel like it. And my father doesn't feel like sending me. I'll just stick around here and do something. I don't know."

She married Paul the following winter. I never saw her again.

My new friends at ECC Tech were growing closer, warmer. We did projects together, helped people study, were not particularly competitive, and loved our school. It was a second home, with a more congenial family than most people had. We stayed late at night and got there early in the morning.

We put on plays. Wonderful, wild things that lots of people came to see. Molière. Clifford Odets. The Russians. The Absurd. And we were full of Vision. We were above politics, above money, above greed. We were free. Ready to meet the world's challenges. We had survived the Cuban missile crisis and were ready for anything now.

And then they shot him, our President, our Jack, the man who inspired our dreams. We listened, standing at stunned attention, students and faculty alike, as people came running off the parking lot shouting, "The President's been shot! He's dying!" There was a long afternoon of silent crying, of strangled disbelief, of frustration and fury as young men put their fists into walls and young women put their knuckles to their teeth. Blood, quarts of it, it seemed, on Jackie's classically simple suit, and she held his head and cradled it, and she glared into the sightless eyes and said, it seemed, "Live— damn you, *LIVE*!"

But he did not. The grief was a thing you could read and touch in faces everywhere. For months, years afterwards, we would stop suddenly and turn, and remember in a vivid flash where we were and what we were doing and what was said when we heard the news. I saw the killing of the man they called Lee Harvey Oswald as it happened. I heard the crack-crack-crack of shots, like a child's cap gun, and I watched the man they said had murdered Jack go down.

Joe sat in our living room and watched in black and white as the newscasters commented on the scenes unfolding before us. It was the first grief I had ever witnessed on TV, and the cortege passed slowly, and we wept aloud, all of us, unashamed.

And that night, Joseph and I lay on the rough rug and kissed and comforted each other, and suddenly made silent love to each other. Neither of us exulted or made comment, or smiled or exchanged small words of reassurance. Tomorrow we would give more time to thinking of it, but for that long and empty night, we simply lay without blame.

The next evening we sat on the couch and watched more TV coverage. We had seen JohnJohn saluting, had seen the wide-eyed baby Caroline standing like Shirley Temple, straight-legged and uncomplaining. Jackie, the newspapers said, was valiant.

I, for one, had had enough of grief and grieving. I opened a letter from Rita Lee that had been left lying unread on the coffee table. I had simply forgotten about it.

"I'm not coming home for Christmas," it said. "I might as well tell you—I'm living with a guy. He's beautiful, B. Really beautiful. He has the beauty of the universe in his eyes, and the power of victory over oppression. I'm not going to the dance workshop anymore. And the art school was too much. There simply isn't time anymore. We've got to get our government out of Vietnam, you see, and Jacob and I are working practically night and day with the Movement. It's a terrific group, Bebe. You'd love and admire these people. Our work is vitally important to the survival of mankind, and to the preservation of peace on earth. I couldn't come home to listen to Mother droning on about plum puddings and Christmas wrappings while half the world lies suffocating under the blanket of oppression. You do see, don't you, Bebe? Say you'll miss me and come up here and meet these people. You won't believe what we're capable of, and how the world will bless us for our love. Ta-ta, Sweet Bea, RL."

It made no sense to me. Who was this Jacob? Didn't these people have last names? I showed the letter to Joseph, who looked at it casually and then put it down.

306

"It's nothing to worry about," he said, rubbing his eyes. "Come here, okay?"

I slid over next to him, and he put his hand on my breast as if it were a part of his own body. "Come closer," he said thickly, and one glance showed me that he had not forgotten what we'd done, that the experience had indeed been real and would doubtless be real again and again.

We went to the floor in an easy motion, but there was no smiling, no anticipation as we undressed each other. Something stabbed me, but I let it go. I endured the guilt because the act of love seemed to be a thing prescribed, like a soothing herb or a folk remedy, and it occurred to me that it was easy, after all, being naked in front of Joseph, and not the awful thing it had seemed. He moved so easily, so naturally, and was not given to calisthenics or to feats of prowess such as I'd read about in the books Lucy Grabowski had smuggled to me centuries ago from the deep pockets of her car coat on the school bus. Rather, Joseph made love in a dreamlike way, so gently and thoroughly that I was tempted to ask once, "Is it over?"

Christmas came and went. After Christmas, more from the Beatles, a new, harder, driving kind of sound, and a movie we adored. Bob Dylan sang of violence and the evils of War, and of the Masters of War, and Rita Lee's letters, less and less frequent, echoed the rebellion of the music. Joan Baez and Bob Dylan sang together about how God's on Our Side. I stopped going to church and upbraided myself for my sheep-like years of following meaningless traditions. I ran from God in all different directions, seeking his replacement in litera-ture, in art, in poetry, in film, in drama, in my own talents, in lovemaking, in nature.

Joseph sang less and less of love and dove for a while into a woody barrel of old-time drinking songs and, as long as he was at it, began drinking to keep up with himself. When we sang duets, we no longer phrased our lyrics by eye contact. The singing eventually became flat and colorless, until one afternoon at school I just looked down at the table where my books were laid out and said, "I don't feel like singing today, Joe." He put down his guitar case and leaned up against the wall and put one foot on top of the other and said, "Me, either." He kissed me on the cheek and put his guitar back inside the car, and that was the end of it. We didn't sing anymore.

We went to some movies, we studied together, and we made love regularly and tried to be careful. (He kept his Trojans in the snakebite kit in the first-aid box in his car.) We told ourselves and each other that we were really free. We were modern. We were well within our rights and privileges.

By March we were making love with a passionless, grim kind of dedication to some principle or other, and one chilly night I just turned to him and put my hand on his chest and said, "It's over, isn't it, Joseph?"

"Over?" he said, cocking his head like a puzzled dog might.

"It's just over, honey," I said. "I don't know why we keep doing this. We aren't even enjoying it."

He rolled over, and I put my arm around his naked body and hugged him to me as we lay like two spoons on the floor. We usually did not lie like that, because it seemed too ludicrous, two large naked bodies on a chilly rug in the early night. We usually dressed hurriedly in order not to get "caught." Now I did not want to let him feel naked and exposed. I moved even closer to him, warming him with myself.

"I guess you're right," he said quietly. "It's no good, is it?"

"Not really," I said.

We did not talk much about it. We just both kind of let go as we might have released a tired helium balloon when we'd had our share of fun with it. I did not cry, and Joseph did not bemoan our loss.

"I want to tell you something, though," he said as he tied his shoelaces and looked for his gloves. "I want you to know something."

"Okay," I said, wanting to shield myself, but I needn't have worried. Joseph's goodness was intact, part and parcel of himself.

"My father was right. You're gold. Pure gold."

"Aw, Joseph," I said, coming to him, bending into his body for a long last embrace. "If I'm gold, you're diamonds, honey. I'll always love you, I mean it."

"And I'll always love you, you Dundalk girl," he said, smiling down into my face like a kindly uncle.

"You're so good," I said, the lump starting in my throat.

"You made me good," he murmured. "Now I gotta do it all on my own."

He went home and took nothing with him. All the things he'd brought stayed behind with me, the records and paperbacks and knickknacks and remembrances. When we met in school for the next two months we spoke civilly to each other, even warmly, but never intimately, never, ever again.

Rita Lee sent a note, unsigned, explaining that she and Jacob had been forced to leave their apartment because the FBI had it bugged, and that I was to destroy her notes, all of them, and not to write to her or try to find her. She would find me, she said, and she would do everything in her power to try to keep in touch.

I touched the edges of her scribbled note, wondering if she still twirled and leaped when she was hard put to express herself in words. I wondered if she still did those lovely, soft, pencil-shaded drawings of young girls and tennis shoes and Jello-O packages, those playful, romantic drawings that made the commonplace so enchanting.

I missed Rita Lee passionately, profoundly. When Teddy came home I told him all about it, about her note, and he shook his head and said, "Leave her alone, Bebe. Let it all be. The girl is in trouble. Big trouble. All she can bring home now is problems. She can't come home again."

"You're just being literary," I accused him. "You're just making phrases."

"I'm not," he said, and his eyes were as kind as Joseph's, as kind as Pa Erdman's behind his crabby mask.

"I know," I said, sighing. "But why did she have to leave and get all screwed up with these people? Why the hell couldn't she have stayed *here* and learned to dance and to draw? I don't get it."

"Some people just can't stay put," he said, in the same voice he'd used forever to comfort me. "Some people are too big for their little nests, and they have to fly."

To argue with him would have been pointless. He was, as always, right.

Rita Lee was gone. Bernadette commiserated, and we drank wine in the moonlight in August and talked about old things and times remembered.

"Remember how I used to think she was a sis?" Bernadette said wistfully.

"Yeah," I laughed. "I know."

"We're the ones, you and me. We're the ones who're the sisses."

"Oh, yeah?"

"Sure. We're the ones sittin' on our back porches two years after high school wondering where everything's gone to. Right?"

"God, yes. Right."

"And you're going no farther than good old Towson State in the fall, right?"

"Yeah, right. So?"

"So we never got out to see the world, did we, Beeb?"

"Not yet. But we will, Bern. We can do it whenever we want to."

"You think so?" she asked, looking at me. "You really think so?"

"Sure," I said.

"You got a hat?" she asked me suddenly.

"Yeah," I said, laughing, knowing what was coming next.

"Well, go talk through it," she said. " 'Cause that's all you're doin' here."

I snorted. We looked at each other and laughed.

"God," Bernadette said, squeezing my hand and leaning into me. "Remember that day you put Cara's falsies on your head?"

"God, yes," I said. "Wasn't that the all-time *best*?"

"We were something, weren't we?"

"We still are," I said.

"Hell, yes," she said.

The moon was too bright to waste. We picked ourselves up and strolled around the "ship" streets in the still, quiet night. The little kids were in their damp beds; the bigger kids were glued to the floor in front of their TV screens; the grown-ups were sitting out, some of them, and some waved and some ignored us. We walked up to Dundalk past the Strand Theater, past the Strand Five-and-Dime, past the bakery, closed and dark, past the police station and Read's and the Arundel and all the other good old familiar places. Then we made our circle and came back to my front steps, and my mother stuck her head out the door and said, "Come on in. I got iced tea made and there's the best movie on TV. Come in and see it with me."

"Cripes, let's live it up," Bernadette said, grinning at me and my mother.

"Jeeze, I wonder what the poor people are doing for fun," I said.

We went inside and shut out the night behind us.